THE MOBSTER'S LAMENT

RAY CELESTIN

THE
MOBSTER'S
LAMENT

MANTLE

First published 2019 by Mantle
an imprint of Pan Macmillan
20 New Wharf Road, London N1 9RR
Associated companies throughout the world
www.panmacmillan.com

ISBN 978-1-5098-3893-6

Typeset in 13/15pt Fournier MT by Jouve (UK), Milton Keynes
Printed and bound by CPI Group (UK) Ltd, Croydon, CR0 4YY

Visit www.panmacmillan.com to read more about all our books
and to buy them. You will also find features, author interviews and
news of any author events, and you can sign up for e-newsletters
so that you're always first to hear about our new releases.

*To my aunties – Georgia, Maria, Marina,
Panayiota, Sofia, Voula and Marie*

CHARACTERS

Ida Young (née Davis), *private investigator*
Michael Talbot, *private investigator (retired)*

THE LUCIANO FAMILY
'Lucky' Luciano, *boss, deported to Italy*
Frank Costello, *acting boss*
Vito Genovese, *acting underboss*
Joe Adonis, *Costello's lieutenant*
Gabriel Leveson, *Costello's fixer*
John Bova, *a mole in Costello's clique*
Nick Tomasulo, *a mole in Genovese's clique*

NYPD
Lieu. Det. David Carrasco, *assigned to the D.A.'s Homicide Bureau, Michael's contact*
Lieu. Det. John Salzman, *Narcotics Division, Gabriel's contact*

OTHERS
Benjamin Siegel (deceased), *the New York mob's West Coast representative*
Albert Anastasia, *underboss of the Mangano crime family*
Bumpy Johnson, *Harlem racketeer*

'Would you like to have an image that will give you an idea of my life? There is a person at the wheel of a car on a road unknown to him. He is unable to stop the car. The things passing through are unexpected, new, different from the trip that he wanted to make. It is terrible for the man who is at the wheel of his own life to realize that the brake doesn't work.'

FRANK COSTELLO, MOBSTER

SUNDAY NEWS

NEW YORK'S PICTURE NEWSPAPER

City Edition Final   Sunday, August 3rd 1947

LOCAL NEWS

HARLEM HOUSE OF HORRORS

———

FOUR FOUND SLAIN IN UPTOWN FLOPHOUSE

———

NEGRO VETERAN ARRESTED AT SCENE

———

VOODOO LINK TO SAVAGE KILLINGS

———

Leonard Sears – Chief Crime Correspondent

Manhattan, Aug 2nd. – Thomas James Talbot, 35, an NYC hospital worker was arraigned this morning on four charges of first-degree murder following a killing spree late Friday night at a hotel on W. 141st Street. Police were called to the Palmer Hotel after reports of a disturbance and found a scene of carnage, with bodies littered throughout the hotel. In a room at the rear of the building they discovered a blood-soaked Talbot, still clutching money and narcotics he had stolen from his victims. Talbot, a hotel resident, fled the scene but was apprehended after a short chase.

———

'The most gruesome crime scene I've ever encountered'

———

All four victims were stabbed to death, with some slashed across the throat, and others partially dismembered and disemboweled. Bodies were discovered in the reception area, a passageway, and two

I

guest rooms. Police Captain John Rouse described the crime scene as 'the most gruesome I've encountered in over thirty years as a police officer. All the victims were savagely attacked, and killed in cold blood'. The murder weapon, most likely a long-bladed knife like a machete, is yet to be found.

VOODOO PARAPHERNALIA

Talbot, a WWII veteran who served in the Pacific campaign, had rented a room for some weeks on the hotel's top story. When a search of his room was undertaken numerous items with links to voodoo rituals were discovered among his belongings – charms, amulets, bone-casting sets, skulls and robes. Bottles containing unidentified liquids were also found, and religious items from the Pacific Islands. Similar items were present in a room on the second floor where two of the bodies were found, along with literature relating to the Temple of Tranquility – a Harlem voodoo cult. It is yet to be ascertained whether the killings were undertaken as part of a voodoo sacrifice ritual, or whether Talbot and his fellow devotees, who also lived in the flophouse, fell out with tragic consequences. By the end of the night, Talbot was the only resident of the hotel left alive.

MISSING HAULAGE WORKER FOUND AT SCENE

Among the dead was Arno Bucek, 25, the only white victim. Bucek was reported missing by his parents in Queens six weeks previously. It was in the room where Bucek's body was discovered that Talbot was initially discovered by police. It is believed that Talbot was attempting to steal narcotics and money from Bucek's room when the police arrived. It is unclear what Bucek, a heroin addict, was doing in a Negro flophouse, and where he had been for the six weeks between his disappearance and death. The police have not ruled out the theory that he was being imprisoned for purposes of ritual torture.

COURT APPEARANCE

Talbot appeared emotionless and bedraggled at the arraignment hearing in the Manhattan Criminal Court. First-degree murder charges were filed by Assistant District Attorney Russell Patterson, and a date of August 11th was set for a preliminary hearing on the charges. Talbot did not enter a plea. He was remanded and sent to be held in custody at Rikers Island.

LIST OF VICTIMS

Below is a list of the victims discovered at the scene:

—Arno Bucek, 25, discovered on the first floor. Killed by multiple cuts to the torso

—Lucius Powell, 29, discovered on the second-floor corridor, believed to be a member of the Temple of Tranquility, killed by multiple cuts to the torso

—Alfonso Powell, 32, discovered on the second floor, brother of Lucius, believed to be a fellow member of The Temple, killed by a single cut to the throat

—Diana Hollis, 45, discovered in the hotel's reception area. Miss Hollis was a hotel employee, found with injuries described as 'particularly savage' by Captain Rouse

---

For more on this crime, and further photographs of the ghastly scene, turn to page 4.

PART ONE

NOVEMBER 1947

'As a clue to the operational problems confronting the office, one has only to consider the complexity of life on the island of Manhattan. Here, 2,000,000 residents of heterogeneous lineage, race, religion and color, and 3,000,000 commuters and transients are jammed into the most congested twenty-two square miles in the world. Nowhere is crime found in such astonishing volume; nowhere does it assume so many imaginative and diverse forms; and nowhere may a criminal so readily lose himself in a crowd.'

REPORT OF THE DISTRICT ATTORNEY,
COUNTY OF NEW YORK, 1946–1948

1

Come, see the vampires. Watch them lope across Times Square. Watch them jostle and throng as the stars wheel through the night. The hookers and pimps and junkies, the dealers and hustlers and chiselers, the elbow sneaks, the blade-men, the braggarts, the dead pickers, the lush-rollers, the runaways, the stay-outs and layabouts and down-and-outs, the wastrels and the bottom dogs, lured to the heart of the world's greatest city by its neon blaze, its quicksilver jazz, the promise of a score. From flophouses on the Bowery, from dope-pads uptown, from the fruit bars strung like fairy lights along the docksides of Chelsea and Brooklyn, from sucker-joints, from bebop clubs, from hack ranks, from laundromats, from stage doors and artists' lofts, from cold-water tenements and penthouses in the clouds, from bridges and freeways, from the blackness under the 3rd Avenue El, from tunnels, from alleys, from basements, from gutters, from shadows, out of the city's very cement, the darkness had come and formed itself into something dangerous and alive: the empire of night had arisen.

Among its hordes walked a tall, dark-haired man in his thirties, with his trench-coat collar turned up and his Stetson slouched low. He hid a haunted smile; a face which bore the marks of a life spent hustling on the streets of New York. His long-dead parents had named him after the archangel Gabriel, and all his life he had walked a little wearily, as if the weight of a pair of wings pressed down upon his back.

He passed jazz clubs which emitted a swirl of bebop into the night, sex shows daubed in illuminated signs – *GIRLS, GIRLS, GIRLS* – lighting up the sidewalks like fairgrounds. He caught his reflection in the plate glass of all-night cafeterias, a reflection that distorted as he moved. He skirted advertising boards outside dubious movie-houses, ignored the shouts of the rope-callers leaning in the shadows and arrived at his destination: 1557 Broadway, Horn and Hardart's Automat. He gazed up at the building, at its giant stained-glass windows, its red neon sign perched two stories high.

He paused before he stepped inside, looked around. If anyone spotted him, it might mean his death, or worse, the death of the girl. And it was the girl he was risking it all for. Get in, get the passports, get out. Leave before any stray glances sent six years of plans unspooling.

He entered and saw the place was jam-packed, roaring with people, customers standing two deep in front of the vending boxes. Gabriel peered through the crowd and the thick pall of cigarette smoke and spotted the forger at a table near the wash-rooms, sitting alone. He fought his way over and slid into the chair opposite him, saw immediately how close to death he looked; haggard and yellow-skinned and dull-eyed. Gabriel wondered again why the forger had chosen to make the hand-off in Times Square in the middle of the night. Maybe he wanted to get laid one last time in one of the brothels sprinkled around the neighborhood like confetti. But the man had explained he'd booked himself in on the overnight from Penn Station, and was so ill these days he didn't sleep anyway.

The forger's voice was ragged and soft and Gabriel had to strain to hear him over the din of coffee spigots, coin slots and waitresses clattering plates into piles. It was one of those places that amplified noise, that turned all sound into a rattle and sent it careening around the walls.

The forger took a sip of the coffee in front of him and winced. Gabriel handed him an envelope. It contained enough money to see the man to Toronto, into the clinic, enough pain-killers to make his last few weeks on earth bearable. The forger's death would ensure his silence, which was why Gabriel picked him. Getting the passports was the last piece of his escape plan, and when he heard through a friend of a friend that the forger was on his way out, he went to meet him over in Jersey and made him an offer.

The old man hoisted his suitcase onto the chair next to him, opened it and rummaged around. Gabriel looked over to see what he was taking on his death trip – neatly folded clothes, a Pan Am washbag, a Reader's Digest copy of *Spinoza*. The man had folded over the corners of a dozen or so pages, making Gabriel wonder what wisdom they contained. It also made him think of the Doc, who peppered his speech with quotes from *Ethics*.

'*To understand is to be free*,' Gabriel said.

The forger paused and looked up at him, a frown unfurling across his brow. Gabriel gestured to the book. The forger nodded, then got back to his search, rustled a paper packet from the suitcase and handed it over.

Gabriel opened it and took out the passports. They were of the highest quality. The old man had put all his decades of experience and craftsmanship into them; they were, after all, the last documents he would ever forge, the last time he would practice his art.

Gabriel pocketed the passports and complimented the forger on a job well done. As the man was about to reply, however, he descended instead into a coughing fit. He pulled a handkerchief from his sleeve and Gabriel saw that it was stained bloody brown.

As he waited for the old man to recuperate, Gabriel looked about, checking to see if anyone he knew was in the place. His eye landed on the food dispensers, each one made of glass, the size of a shoebox, placed one on top of the other all the way up the walls. People dropped nickels into slots, turned handles, took food from the dispensers – a plate of macaroni and cheese, a tomato soup, a fishcake, a Key lime pie.

On a table further down, college kids were scoring tea from a

Puerto Rican teenager in a leather jacket. At other tables sat bleary-eyed cab drivers and telegram messengers, dancing girls, junkies and johns, the outcasts and oddballs who filled Times Square each evening, and evaporated each dawn. Gabriel would miss them when he was gone, even though he knew them for what they were, as cynical and opportunistic as the city they called home. And he would miss New York too, its roar, its energy, its restlessness, the way it slammed against you. Like no other place on earth. The cities of Europe and Asia had been decimated in the war and now New York stood alone. In the dark skies of Upper Bay, the torch in Liberty's hand burned brighter.

The automat's front doors fluttered open and a party of tourists from the Corn Belt wandered in. They looked about as if they'd stepped into some modern-day Babylon, and after a few awkward moments, turned and exited. The door swung shut, and through the condensation on its window the lights and sights of Times Square were transformed into a prism of multicolored streaks, making Gabriel think of constellations, hallucinations, the drip painting back in his apartment.

He turned to the old man, who took a last sip of his coffee and nodded.

'Happy to be leaving?' Gabriel asked, wondering if the forger shared his own mixed feelings about moving away.

The forger mulled over the question. 'Happy, sad – same thing,' he said.

Gabriel wondered if the insight had been gleaned from Spinoza.

He helped the man up, offered to escort him to Penn Station.

'It's a lot of money you've got there,' Gabriel said, hoping the forger wouldn't feel patronized. 'These streets are rough.'

The forger shook his head.

They stepped out onto the sidewalk, into a drizzle that had started while they were inside. The forger turned up the collar of his coat, flipped a flat-cap onto his head. He gave Gabriel a look and Gabriel guessed at the man's frosty manner – he had asked for forged passports for himself and a thirteen-year-old girl. No option to explain the girl was his niece, that the pair of them were running away for the girl's own good. Gabriel had to let the man think the worst of him. But he was used to it. In his past Gabriel had been a night undertaker, a petty crook, a skip-tracer, a gambler. All of which had schooled him in disapproval. These days he ran a nightclub on behalf of the Mob, and acted as a fixer when needed. He was good at it. He had a breezy manner other mobsters lacked, the charm and calm to handle delicate situations. But for the past few years, Gabriel had been stealing money, and in ten days' time, on Thursday the 13th, the Mob would find out.

As he watched the forger disappear down Broadway, heading for Penn Station and Toronto and a morphine-slicked slide into the great unknown, another Spinoza quote came to mind: *a free man thinks of death least of all things*. He wondered if it was on one of the pages the man had folded over.

He lit a cigarette and scurried through the crowds to the nearest taxi rank. As far as he could tell, he had done the deal unseen. Mission accomplished, but his anxiety only dimmed a touch. He'd been living in a cloud of it for weeks now. If Gabriel and his niece hadn't made it to Mexico by the time his skim was discovered, they were both as good as dead. A beach in Acapulco, or shallow graves in a forest upstate.

He reached the taxi rank and got in line behind a gaggle of wealthy revelers, the men in shiny suits, the women pearled and minked. Further on, groups of merry-makers stumbled about. It was the first weekend of the month and the streets were full of payday drunks. Gabriel looked around at the carnage, spotted a noticeboard affixed to the wall of the building opposite. A couple of years ago it had been covered in posters for war bonds, now a plumage of paper scraps was pinned to it that fluttered in the wind, turned mushy in the drizzle. Police bulletins, lost and found, missing persons.

Gabriel stared at the last. There were dozens of them. Mostly girls, mostly young, from all over America, last seen boarding buses or trains in towns he'd never heard of. Last seen wearing this or that. Some of the notices had photos pinned to them. Some of the girls didn't look that much older than Gabriel's niece. He thought about the hustlers who prowled Penn Station and the bus terminals looking for runaways, easy marks, fresh meat, *GIRLS, GIRLS, GIRLS*.

He heard a car horn honk and turned to see he was at the front of the queue. He hopped into the waiting cab.

'Where to, pal?' the cabbie asked.

'The Copa.'

The cabbie nodded and pulled into traffic, and Gabriel looked again at the posters, thought about all the world's missing people, the disappeared. In ten days' time, one way or the other, he and his niece would be among their number.

2

They hauled north through Midtown, leaving behind Times Square and its midnight rainbow. They cut onto 7th, then 52nd. They passed the jazz clubs on Swing Street, which were still pulsing with neon, music and movement. They turned up Madison, which was quieter, more respectful of the hour. The classical facades of its offices and apartment blocks were daubed in stillness and shadows, making them look tomb-like, as if the street was lined either side with crypts. Gabriel imagined the whole city a necropolis, skeletons behind every door.

The cab turned onto 61st Street and signs of life: the Copacabana, located on an otherwise fusty residential street in the upper-crust Upper East Side. There was still a queue of people snaking up the sidewalk, waiting to get in. There were bouncers and cabbies and revelers heading home. That nightclub buzz. The dull thud of music shook the air.

They stopped behind the broadcast van parked up by the entrance to the Copa Lounge next door. Gabriel hopped out, paid the fare and looked up at the sign: *Never a cover or a minimum.* He walked past it, to the entrance of the Copa itself. The bouncers opened the rope, let him in. He nodded his thanks.

He stepped into the foyer and went down the stairs and the sound of the band upped a notch, then the doors to the dancehall opened and the music hit him like a blast wave. The two a.m. floorshow was reaching its climax; Carmen Miranda on stage, shimmying away in a tight satin dress, headscarf packing half a bowl of fruit. Behind her a bevy of Samba Sirens broke hearts with their hips, matching Miranda's movements with unnerving precision.

The club was nearing its capacity – seven hundred people, spread out across the various floors, mezzanines and terraces. On the stairs and ramps that connected them all, captains and waiters rushed around. The Copa had started out as a modest attempt to bring the glamorous hotel nightlife of Rio De Janeiro to the cold north, but had become so popular they'd had to constantly expand the space. They opened a cocktail lounge upstairs and WINS started broadcasting a radio show from it – *the famous stay-outs drop in with their pin-ups. And you're invited!* Then someone decided to turn it into a movie; *Copacabana*, starring Groucho Marx and Carmen Miranda. Since the movie required a sound-track, the Copa became a song as well: 'Let's Do the Copacabana'. It was this song that Miranda was dancing to now. The Brazilian singer-dancer-actress had been booked into the club for five weeks as part of the film's publicity tour, and the song was the climax of the floorshow. As her hips shimmied to the atomic rumble of the conga drums, Gabriel cast his eye over the crowd.

At the bar Frank Sinatra and Rocky Graziano were involved in some kind of limbo competition with a pair of girls Gabriel thought he recognized from the theatre posters on 42nd Street. He could see the effect of Benzedrine in their eyes. One of the girls fell onto the carpet and they all burst out laughing. Frank slapped Rocky on the back, like they'd achieved something of note, and maybe they had.

Behind them were a few second-rate film stars and half the Yankees outfield, who'd been in the club every night since their World Series win a month back. Men from the Bonanno crime family mooched about with some women who might have been their wives or girlfriends or mistresses. Members of New York's four other Mafia families were scattered about. On one of the far terraces, high up, in the darkness behind some fake palm trees and mirrored columns, Gabriel spotted Mayor O'Dwyer seated at a table with a crowd of suits, stirring a swizzle stick round a joyless mai tai.

The mayor looked up, and through the roar of dancers his eyes met Gabriel's. They nodded at each other. O'Dwyer was elected with the support of Frank Costello, the head of the Luciano crime family, the not-so-secret owner of the Copacabana, the man on whose behalf Gabriel managed the club. Gabriel tried to make out the other men at the mayor's table, but it was too shadowy. One of them picked a pill from a cigarette case and tossed it into his mouth.

As the band reached a crescendo, Gabriel took one last look around the room, and felt crushed once again by what he saw, the thought that this was where they had come to, this decadence was what peace had brought, the end result of the world tearing itself apart, of millions slaughtered and shadows burnt onto walls. He wondered, as he often did, if maybe the world hadn't died in the conflagration, and they were all carrying on their existence in limbo, a necropolis, and he was the only one who'd noticed.

The band reached the end of the song in an avalanche of conga rolls and horns. A roar went up from the crowd and people hugged each other, and some kissed. Eyes glistened.

Miranda bowed.

The emcee took the mic and announced the band would be taking a break and now here's Martin and Lewis to keep you all entertained.

Dean Martin came onto the stage holding a whiskey, Jerry Lewis with his hands in his pockets. Martin thanked the emcee, and held up a finger to him as he exited the stage.

'Behind every successful man,' he said, 'there's a surprised mother-in-law.'

The drummer flung off a roll. The crowd burst out laughing.

Gabriel turned his back on it all, headed to a door marked *Staff Only* and pushed through it into a dank, gray corridor. The door shuttered behind him and killed much of the sound. After a few corners he reached his office, unlocked the door and stepped inside. It was a windowless space, as gray as the corridor, with a year-round smell of damp. It was dominated by a green baize table at which three men counted stacks of money. They put the money into piles, wrapped the bills in bands, added them to trays, licked pencils, scribbled on lists. The accounting was complicated, a list of what they actually made, a list of what the tax authorities would hear about, a list of what went to the official owners, a list of the skim Costello and the Mob would take. Gabriel was probably the only person in the operation who could keep track of it all.

He locked the door and slumped into his chair, and the two passports felt like they were burning a hole in his jacket. Six years of planning, ten days to go, and he was succumbing ever more to the jitters.

He lit a cigarette, noticed he was being eyed by Havemeyer, the oldest of the men sitting around the table counting stacks.

'What?' Gabriel asked.

'Costello wants to see you,' Havemeyer said without breaking his count.

Panic thumped through Gabriel's chest, coursed through his torso.

'He was here?' he asked.

Havemeyer shook his head. He finished counting off the stack, wrapped a band round it, laid it on a tray, made a tick on a list. Only then did he turn to look at Gabriel. The lime-colored cellophane of his visor caught the beam of the overhead and sent a shaft of lurid green across his face, making him look like a character from one of the comic books Sarah left scattered about the apartment.

'He called,' said Havemeyer. 'Left a message with Augie.'

'He say what he wanted?' Gabriel asked. Then realized it was a stupid question. The city bugged Costello's phones, and even though Costello hired a telephony expert to scan for them, he still only ever discussed business in person.

'What do you think?' said Havemeyer.

Gabriel tried to calm himself. Maybe Costello had a job for him and it was all OK. Or maybe Costello had found out and Gabriel's grave was already being dug.

'You sweating?' Havemeyer asked.

Gabriel shook his head. 'It's raining out.'

It looked like the old man bought it, because he nodded and got back to his count.

One of the men heaved a tray of money stacks over to the safe in the corner, a squat piece of cast iron, whose lumpen shape had always reminded Gabriel of a bomb. Another of the men opened the safe door, and the dollar bills were consumed by the darkness at its heart. If everything was an illusion, if they had indeed descended into the underworld, this bomb was the furnace that powered the dream.

Six years of planning, ten days to go, and he'd been called in by the boss of all bosses.

3

Four hours later, Gabriel, Havemeyer and two security goons stepped out of the Copa's stage door into an ash-colored dawn. The goons sent the roll-shutters that covered the entrance crashing to earth and the noise roared down the alleyway and made Havemeyer jump. He looked around him with red, rheumy eyes and Gabriel thought how a man Havemeyer's age shouldn't be working nights in a club anymore.

The goons padlocked the shutters and handed Gabriel the keys and then they went their separate ways; the goons for a workout in Bova's gym in Williamsburg; Havemeyer back to his sofa in the Heights, because his wife liked to sleep late; and Gabriel for a meeting with Frank Costello, the 'prime minister of the underworld'.

He walked to 5th, where the sidewalk was busy with suits and secretaries, shop girls, Negro maids, kids hawking papers. The night rain had left a sheen across the city, made the pavements slippery, the air clammy and close, despite the chill. Gabriel hailed a cab to take him to the other side of the park. He could use the drive to prepare for the meeting. He needed to come across relaxed, normal, steady. Like he wasn't about to vanish with a giant wedge of stolen Mob money.

He lit a cigarette and remembered the beaches in Mexico as he'd seen them during the war. He felt the scorching heat of the sun on his skin, the pure white light bouncing off the sand, the calming shush of the waves. For a moment he was no longer on the bleak streets of New York in November.

And then he was again.

Cold and tired and anxious in the hard gray dawn.

They passed the subway station and people were streaming out of its exit. Every work day half a million commuters flooded into Manhattan via its tunnels and bridges, which made Gabriel wonder if the island's rarely seen soil compressed under their weight, sank a little, if the river lapped ever so slightly higher against the piers?

The cab approached Columbus Circle and came to a stop at a red light. Gabriel smelled the warm, sweet fragrance of freshly baked bread, saw a bakery truck pulled up outside a grocery. The bakers were unloading trays of bread covered in wax paper. Gabriel felt a pang of envy. The bakers had food to show for their night's work. What did Gabriel have? He and the fifty people he employed had spent the night conjuring up an illusion of exotic Rio in a basement on East 60th Street. A lavish phantasm that vanished every dawn. Nothing left of it but a few hundred hang-overs being slept off across town, and the last traces of the congas echoing in his head.

The lights turned green and the cab headed north. He counted off the streets as they ticked by on his left, 60th up to 71st. On his right, the park was poised on the tipping point between fall and winter. There was frost on the ground, and the trees had lost their leaves, revealing their black, spindly armatures, a smattering of birds' nests, a long-deflated balloon some child must have cried over in the dog days of summer.

The rain picked up again, pattering hard against the cab's windows, fragmenting the world into translucent beads. They pulled up outside the Majestic Apartments, a twin-towered Art Deco building at 115 Central Park West. At one time or another, most of the city's Mob bosses had owned apartments there. Now only Costello was left. Gabriel paid the cabbie and got out into the

drizzle and wind, then through the entrance, nodding to the door-
man, into the reception area, where he was hit by a burst of warm,
dry air.

'Here for Mr Costello,' he said to the concierge, who nodded
and waved Gabriel up. At this time of day there was always a
steady stream of people arriving to see Costello.

The elevator took him up eighteen stories, opening onto a
red-carpet corridor at the end of which was the door to apartment
18F. Any other Mob boss would have security guards at this point,
if not in the reception area downstairs, or out on the street. Not
Costello.

His openness was something Gabriel always liked about his
boss. Costello didn't carry a gun, didn't employ bodyguards,
didn't have a chauffeur drive him around. When Costello had an
appointment, he caught a cab, alone, unarmed. Like any other
New Yorker. This as much as anything made the city feel that
Frank Costello wasn't half so bad, that although he was the boss
of all bosses, head of the commission, leader of the five families,
chief of all organized crime, in charge of an army of over two
thousand men, he was more than anything a local boy done good.
Manhattan's gangster.

Under his leadership the Mob had earned more money,
grabbed more influence, come into more power than at any time
in its history. All this under a man who'd never even wanted to be
the head and had only taken the job reluctantly.

Gabriel knocked on the door and after a few seconds, Costello's wife Bobbie opened up.

'Morning, Gabby. How's tricks?' she asked, leaning in to
kiss him.

She had a high-pitched, little girl's voice that had stayed with
her through the decades.

'You know,' Gabriel replied. 'Getting ready for winter.'

'Here to see Frank?'

'Sure.'

She turned and led him down the corridor.

Bobbie was a petite woman, pretty, brunette, quick-witted. Like many Italian gangsters, Costello had married an outsider, a Jewish girl from 7th Avenue, just around the corner from the East Harlem slum in which he'd been raised. It was another part of the Frank Costello fairytale – marrying the rich girl from the right side of the tracks. He'd been twenty-three at the time of the marriage, Bobbie fifteen.

'How's the Copa?' she asked.

'Same old.' He smiled. 'Latin music, Chinese food, American sleaze-balls.'

She laughed.

Two dogs came yapping up the corridor, a miniature Dobermann and a toy poodle, barking and scowling. Bobbie kneeled down to shush them.

'Would you shut the fuck up?' she said, grabbing them by their collars. 'I don't know what's wrong with them.'

The dogs continued to yap at Gabriel and he wondered if they could sense a traitor in their midst. If, like cancer and fear, dogs could also smell betrayal.

'How's Sarah?' Bobbie asked, ushering the dogs down the corridor.

She always asked after Gabriel's niece, and when she did, Gabriel felt a tinge of something in her voice. Bobbie and Costello were childless, maybe the reason why they doted on the two dogs.

'At the moment, crazy about comic books,' he replied.

'Yeah,' she said. 'Every kid in the city's got their nose in a comic book.'

'I wouldn't know.'

'You need to get out more in daylight hours,' she said, giving him a sly grin.

They reached the lounge and went straight in. The scene inside had always reminded Gabriel of a hotel restaurant at breakfast time. Along the far wall tables had been set up, laden with serving trays of bacon and eggs, pastries and breads, toast top-pings, coffee pots, a samovar of tea. Two bored-looking maids stood next to the tables, waiting for people's orders, and all across the rest of the space, on sofas and chaises-longues, by the win-dows, by the piano, next to the fireplace and the slot machines, were the luminaries, standing or sitting or leaning, drinking, eating, talking, planning, scheming. Gabriel spotted suits from City Hall, Wall Street, trade unions, all but one of New York's crime families.

Every week Costello hosted breakfasts here, and so the day began for many of the city's political players. It was all part of Costello's grand plan – to ingratiate himself with the upper crust, do them favors, lend them money, blur the lines between legit-imacy and racketeering, make so many friends, it was impossible to be weeded out.

And the plan had worked, so far. Costello not only organized the nation's crime, but much of its commerce, too. New York was home to the most powerful economy the world had ever known. Half the country's imports and exports flowed through its port, a port that was controlled by the Mob, making this the heart within the heart of the world's greatest city, the nightmare within the dream.

'I'll see if he's free,' said Bobbie. 'Help yourself to food and coffee.'

She headed through the din and Gabriel lit a cigarette and checked to see if his hands were shaking. Then he headed over to the buffet tables and grabbed a coffee, scanned the room. The decor was gilded, vintage, luxurious, overdone. Furniture had been bought in bulk to fill the apartment's vastness and make it look homely. A wood fire crackled in the hearth, above it hung a How-ard Chandler Christy in a gilt frame. There was a gold piano, and in each corner, a slot-machine from Costello's New Orleans oper-ation, all of them rigged to pay out. Costello's idea of hospitality.

Despite all the finery and furniture, the room was dominated by its windows; unhindered views of Manhattan in all its pale glory, shimmering in the morning drizzle. The Dakota was next door, the park opposite, beyond it the lofty, old-money towers of the Upper East Side and Gabriel's own apartment. To the south, the skyscrapers of Midtown rose row after row into the rain-clouds like so many knives.

Gabriel looked down into the park. The rain had melted most of the frost that had covered the ground earlier.

'Gabby,' someone said.

Gabriel turned to see John Bova standing next to him. A low-level pimp in the Luciano crime family, owner of the Brooklyn gym Gabriel's security goons trained in. Bova had the physique of a boxer gone to seed, and a red, splotchy face made grotesque by a thick scar that ran down its right side.

'Bova,' said Gabriel. 'You're up early.'

Bova paused, not sure if he was being needled. 'Here to see the boss?' he asked, fishing for information.

'Nah,' said Gabriel. 'I'm here for the snacks.'

Again Bova eyed him. Again Gabriel enjoyed the man's confusion.

There were two factions in the Luciano family, the one Costello and Gabriel belonged to, and the other one, headed up by Vito Genovese, the family's underboss out in New Jersey, power-hungry and itching to usurp the throne. Bova was supposed to be in Costello's clique, but was actually a mole for Genovese. Costello and Gabriel both knew it, but kept Bova around anyways, in case of emergency.

'What about you?' Gabriel asked.

Bova shrugged, though Gabriel could see him puff out at being the topic of conversation. The man was everything Gabriel hated about mobsters: violent, self-satisfied, egotistical, nowhere near as sharp as he thought he was.

'Here making contacts,' said Bova. 'You know how they say,

poor men get up and go to work; rich men get up and make contacts.'

Gabriel wondered if Bova had been studying self-help business manuals. The man ran a stable of over-the-hill prostitutes from a collection of rat-infested apartments scattered around Columbus Circle. He strung them out on dope, sent them onto the streets in the coldest weather, beat them when profits dropped. Meanwhile, almost everyone else in the room was a civic leader. Gabriel wondered exactly what contacts Bova was hoping to make.

'Any idea who the kike with the leather face is?' Bova asked, gesturing to a sun-tanned, gray-haired man standing next to the samovar. Bova liked to use Jewish slurs whenever Gabriel was around.

Gabriel gave him a look. Bova caught it.

'No offense,' said Bova. He shrugged, then a mean little smile twisted his lips.

'That's Jack Warner,' Gabriel said. 'The movie producer.'

'Warner as in Warner Brothers?'

Gabriel nodded. Costello and Warner were old friends. Gabriel looked at the man and realized that something was going on. The last couple of nights he'd noticed a few other Los Angeles-based movie producers in the Copa. He made a mental note to ask Costello about it.

The door on the far side of the room opened up and Bobbie smiled at Gabriel and gestured him over. Gabriel felt a wave of relief to be getting away from the overweight pimp.

'So you are here to see the boss,' said Bova. 'What's cooking?'

'I wish I knew,' said Gabriel, heading across the room to Costello's study.

PART TWO

'In short, the County of New York, island of greatest concentration, greatest wealth, greatest culture, and greatest splendor, in keeping with its superlatives, presents a law enforcement problem of greatest magnitude.'

REPORT OF THE DISTRICT ATTORNEY,
COUNTY OF NEW YORK, 1946–1948

4

The sun rose on the state of New York, and picked out a line of silver glinting south through the Hudson River Valley – *The 20th Century Limited*, the overnight express train from Chicago – threading itself like a needle through the landscape, past mountains and shimmering lakes and forests ablaze with autumn colors, drawn inexorably to the magnet heart of New York City. The railroad track turned a wide arc on the approach to the Bronx, affording the passengers a view of Manhattan's skyscrapers, their pinnacles bathed in the fresh, cold light of dawn.

Then the train completed its turn and roared into the city, snaking between tenement roofs and pigeon lofts and giant billboards bolted onto scaffolds. It soared over the Harlem River, dipped down onto Manhattan, the buildings either side rattling past like marching soldiers. It reached 97th Street and plunged into the Park Avenue tunnel and all turned black for the final approach to Grand Central Terminus, where the train pulled into platform thirteen, came to a stop, and the great hustle of people shouldered its way out into the station.

Ida alone remained in her seat. She watched the others leave as if witnessing some unfathomable migration of beasts – the businessmen, the families, the tourists – bedraggled and bleary-eyed, many of them regretting their choice of an overnight train which disgorged its passengers so unceremoniously into New York's unforgiving rush hour.

When the passageways were empty, she rose, plucked her

27

suitcase from the overhead compartment, and found her way through the debris to the restroom. It was cramped and unheated, so the cold bit at her skin, but there was a sink with a mirror above it, which was all she needed. From outside she could hear the porters unloading the train, the bustle of the station, the dull roar of thousands of hard soles against marble, and in the distance, the rumble of the world's greatest city, eight million people rising to make another day.

She brushed her teeth, washed her face, fixed her hair, re-applied makeup, washed her hands. She stared at herself, checking to see if recent traumas had left their mark. A little gray at the temples, a few wrinkles at the eyes, a softness to her features. She looked younger than her forty-seven years, and what she'd lost in youth, she'd gained in self-assurance and poise. Or so she liked to tell herself.

Ida stepped off the train, reached the end of the platform and caught her first glimpse of Grand Central in full flow. Torrents of black suits cascaded through the station's honeycomb of passages, up and down its marble stairs, out of exits, onto platforms, across the giant expanse of the main concourse, a cavernous space split by razor-sharp sunbeams that burst in from the skylights above.

The rush and noise contained something of the buzz Ida had always associated with New York; the itchy, excited energy of people on the move, tackling overstuffed schedules at breakneck speed. Just as Manhattan's skyscrapers allowed ever more real estate onto the island, so too did the city condense people's days, concentrating time, intensifying, thickening, compacting it. Ida wondered if it wouldn't fray her nerves, if she wouldn't break down through sheer claustrophobia.

She slipped through the torrents as the tannoy system boomed, reached the benches where she was supposed to meet Michael. She looked up at the brass clock above the information booth. The hands atop its milk-glass face told her she was still a little early. She waited, looked around, at the rush, at the sunbeams, at the fug, at the station's ceiling miles above her, the paintings that covered it obscured by years of grime and cigarette tar.

Eventually, she could make out what the paintings depicted – the constellations, in gold lines on a deep-blue background, both the stars themselves, and, superimposed on the universe, the ancient Greek mythical figures that represented them. Amidst the golden dust of the Milky Way, she made out Orion, Taurus, Aries, Pisces. Her eye settled on Gemini for some reason, the twins clinging to each other as they careened through the sky, one holding a sickle, the other a lyre. Something about the figures' movement, the way it echoed the rush on the concourse beneath them, made her uneasy.

As she deliberated on why that could be, she noticed someone approaching through the crowds. Michael, a hand raised, waving. He stepped through one of the sunbeams streaming in from the skylights, and his figure flashed and glowed, dust swirled. Then, just as quickly, he exited the beam, and the flash evaporated, and Ida's eyes adjusted.

He reached her and they hugged and clung onto each other as tightly as the Gemini twins tumbling through the Milky Way above.

'Michael,' she said.

'Ida. Welcome to New York.'

They disengaged from the hug and Ida looked at her friend. Michael was in his early seventies, although it was hard to tell because of the smallpox scars that covered his face, obscuring wrinkles and softness. Despite his age, he still had a straight back, still retained his tall, gaunt appearance. But he had changed in the months since Ida had last seen him. He looked weary, shaken by the disaster that had smashed into his life, trailing upheaval and trauma in its wake. She should have been happy to see him, a familiar face in an unfamiliar city. Instead she was concerned. She tried to think what she could say that wouldn't sound trite, wondered if her voice would betray how concerned she was.

'How are you?' she asked.

'Battling on. You?'

'Itching to get started.'

He nodded, acknowledging the sentiment. 'Thanks for coming,' he said flatly.

'You think I'd stay home?'

She smiled, and a second later he echoed it, and they stood there awkwardly, and the question that had been bugging Ida the last few weeks nagged at her again – why hadn't he called her earlier? In the twenty years she'd been running her agency, she'd become an expert in miscarriages of justice. She was the first person he should have called.

'You want to go by your hotel?' he asked. 'Drop your things off? We've got the crime scene to go to and then the island.'

She shook her head. 'I've only got that,' she said, gesturing to the thin suitcase at her feet. 'Let's get started. I'll check in later on.'

They turned and headed for the subway entrance, and she looked again at her downtrodden friend.

'We'll get through this, Michael,' she said. 'We'll see him set free.'

And even as she spoke, she realized she'd already failed at not saying anything trite.

'Sure we will,' Michael replied.

But she could sense his disquiet, an uncertainty echoed in her own emotions. She realized the same misgiving was gnawing away at them both, a fear that this, the most important case they'd ever had, might just be the one they couldn't win.

5

Monday 3rd, 7.25 a.m.

When they emerged from the subway station Ida saw that the sunny spell had come to an end, the skies had marbled and a freezing wind was blowing in from the river.

'Welcome to Harlem,' said Michael.

Ida smiled and pulled her collar tight and they headed south down Lennox Avenue, a wide tree-lined thoroughfare of brownstones and apartment blocks dotted with restaurants, bars and stores. On the sidewalks people were bustling towards the subway station and the bus stops; Negro women on their way downtown to white people's houses, clutching brown paper packages that contained their maid's dresses, folded up tight; men dressed in peacoats and flat-caps heading to warehouses and factories; gangs of children dragged down by school books.

Ida caught the voices of these people as they passed – many of them spoke like she did, with Southern accents. In New York, as in Chicago, the city's Negroes were mostly from the Cotton Belt, refugees from its race hate and grinding poverty.

As they walked, Ida noticed the people staring at Michael – a tall, thin, white man so far uptown. He didn't seem to be bothered by it. He'd married a colored woman back in New Orleans, raised two colored children, moved to Chicago, lived for years on the Southside. He was used to society at large casting him looks. Now one of those children had moved to New York and had been accused of a multiple homicide. Hostile locals was the last thing he was worried about.

A drizzle picked up, floated down from the sky onto the sidewalks and curbs, where Halloween decorations from the previous weekend had been left out for the garbage vans – cut-paper skulls and skeletons and witches, pumpkin heads in piles, rotting, half-collapsed, their jagged smiles sinister.

Ida pulled her collar tighter against the rain, Michael pushed his hat down low. They cut onto 141st Street, over Seventh Avenue, and here, in the smaller streets, things were more run-down, and Ida saw again that Harlem was much like Chicago's Southside – pawn shops, dope pads, shuttered-up gin mills. Once-grand houses were crumbling now, tarnished by broken cornices, rusted railings, boarded-up windows. The streets were smattered with discarded furniture, overflowing trash cans, other universal signs of decay. Different cities, same slum.

They arrived at a row of dilapidated brownstones. Michael pointed to a building opposite a root doctor's shop.

'That's it,' he said. 'The scene of the crime.'

They crossed the street and approached the building, a corner brownstone with a long sign running up its brickwork – *The Palmer Hotel* – umber letters on a background which at some point had probably been yellow ochre, but years of smog had turned to a shade somewhere between jaundice and bile. The building was broad and foreboding, seemed to loom down at them from the sky, as if its masonry might rear up and crash onto them at any moment. It wasn't the kind of place you moved to, it was the kind of place you ended up. What the hell was Michael's son doing there? The boy had graduated from Northwestern, medical school, had practiced as a hospital doctor before the war.

Ida looked at Michael. 'What's the plan?' she asked.

'Remember Dave Carrasco?'

'From West Town?'

Michael nodded. 'He moved out here about ten years ago. He's a detective now with the DA's Homicide Bureau. Technically he's working for the prosecution, but he owes me a favor, so he's been helping me out. He let me have a look at the case jacket, come by the crime scene. He'll be here soon. Come on, let's get out of the rain.'

They walked over to the doorway of the root doctor's shop, stepped under the awning. Ida looked at its windows. They were covered by white net curtains and above them hung a sign – *Prince Moses – Authentic New Orleans Root Doctor. Offers Voodoo Spell-casting, Love Potions, Curse Removal & Exorcisms, Magic Candles & Oils.* On the windowsill was a row of brown jars, a label pasted on each – *Follow Me, Boy – Evil Be Gone – Protection – Wealth.*

Ida stared at the curlicues of the letters.

'Smoke?'

She looked up to see Michael had gotten a pack of cigarettes from his pocket. She took one. They lit up and watched the hotel through the rain, Ida wondering again how Tom had ended up there. She remembered reading the news report back in her office in Chicago – *The Harlem House of Horrors Slayings.* She remembered the shock at seeing Tom's name. She'd called up Michael's house and Annette, Michael's wife, had picked up the phone, told her Michael was already on his way to New York.

The shock had faded over the intervening weeks, but the confusion hadn't. Ida had known the boy since he was a child, had seen him grow up, felt he was something like a nephew to her. Tom had always had a gentle manner to him, had wanted to be a doctor so he could help people. The idea that he could hurt anyone made no sense to her. It was completely against his nature, against everything he stood for.

She turned to look at Michael. She wanted to talk to him about the situation, how he felt. He'd stopped working ten years ago, then out of the blue, a call from Rikers Island, and now instead of enjoying his retirement, he was standing on a street corner in Harlem in the rain. The strain of it was clear in his demeanor, how sullen he was, how withdrawn.

'Who's your lawyer?' she asked.

33

'Len Rutherford. He was probably our sixth choice. The first five wouldn't take the case unless Tom pleaded guilty, and now Rutherford's seen the evidence he's pressuring us to do the same. The consensus is Tom should admit it, go for a plea deal, then maybe he'll get out when he's my age.'

Michael took a toke on his cigarette, didn't look at Ida, didn't take his eyes off the crumbling facade of the Palmer Hotel.

'I didn't think I'd ever have to do this kind of work again,' he said bitterly. 'What was the last case we worked together? I can't even remember.'

She thought quickly, running through their adventures in her mind, trying to place the most recent one. They'd worked together at the Pinkertons' Chicago Bureau for nearly a decade, but even after that – when Ida had set up her own agency and Michael had gotten a job at the Treasury Department – they still teamed up for the occasional case, when Ida needed Michael's help, or he needed hers.

'That Chinese bookie who went missing,' Ida said. 'Back around the time of the Steel Mill riot.'

Michael remembered, nodded. The rain pattered on.

A Plymouth pulled up outside the hotel, and Michael gestured to it, and they crossed the road. A man got out of the driver's side. He was middle-aged, chubby, sported a bushy moustache and a Chesterfield coat in a houndstooth weave.

'Detective Carrasco,' said Michael. 'You remember Ida?'

'Sure, sure,' said Carrasco, holding out his hand. 'How are you doing, Miss Davis?'

'Good, Carrasco,' Ida said. 'Although it's Mrs Young these days.'

Even two years after he'd died it felt strange using Nathan's surname, as if his death meant she no longer had a right to it.

'Apologies,' Carrasco said. 'Here.'

He had a thick paper binder in his hand, which he passed over to Michael.

'It's the case jacket,' he said. 'You can keep that one. Got a secretary who's sweet on me to make a duplicate.'

'Thanks, buddy,' said Michael, taking the binder.

'Shall we?' Carrasco said, gesturing to the hotel.

They walked up the front steps and into the building. The reception area was dingy and close. On one side was the reception desk, separated from the rest of the room by a partition inset with a wire-mesh window. Beyond it there was a staircase leading to the upper floors, a corridor going into the depths of the building.

They approached the reception desk, and through the wire mesh, Ida saw a tall, gangly Negro man leaning back in a chair, reading the sports section of the *New York Mirror*. On the counter behind him was a grid of pigeon holes, and a Bakelite radio, set to a station playing blues.

The man eyed them over the top of his paper but offered no greeting.

Carrasco flashed his badge. 'NYPD,' he said. 'I called. We need to go over the crime scenes again and the suspect's room.'

The man looked at Carrasco with a blank-slate expression. Then he languidly turned to the pigeon holes behind him and grabbed three sets of keys, laid them out on the counter. Carrasco picked them up, handed them to Michael.

'I'll stay here,' said Carrasco, guessing correctly that Michael and Ida wanted to go through the crime scenes on their own. 'You got any questions, just shout.'

Michael nodded. 'Thanks,' he said. He turned to look at Ida. 'Where d'you want to start?'

She thought, remembered the details from the newspaper articles she'd pored over in the intervening weeks.

'Tom had a room on the fifth floor?' she asked.

Michael nodded.

'Let's start there.'

*

Room 502 was cramped and dreary, with an empty bed-frame in one corner, a wardrobe in another, and a table and chair underneath the window. A depressing room, made more so by the knowledge that this was where Tom had spent his last days before being arrested.

Michael opened the case jacket, flicked through the paperwork inside, passed Ida a sheaf of crime scene snaps. The photos showed the room as the cops had found it on the night of the murders: a mattress and sheets on the bed, clothes on the chair, books on the floor, but most notably, voodoo-style trinkets, strewn all across the room. Strange things – straw dolls with screaming black faces, ornate crucifixes, an icon depicting the Virgin Mary surrounded by snakes, a miniature coffin filled with straw and mud.

'This voodoo angle's an attention-grabber,' Ida said.

Michael nodded, catching what she was getting at.

'Tom says he never saw those things before in his life,' he said. 'Not till they showed him the crime scene snaps. I believe him on that. The boy hasn't stepped foot in a church since he was fourteen years old. He's not even religious, much less superstitious.'

Ida nodded. Looked at the photos once more. In the silence, the sound of the radio in the reception area floated up into the room, the twanging chords of Guitar Slim's 'South Carolina Blues', far off and ghostly.

'You got Tom's witness statement?' she asked.

Michael nodded, fished it out of the binder and passed it over.

Ida scanned it. In his statement Tom claimed he was in bed asleep when he was awoken by the sound of a disturbance downstairs. He went to investigate. Saw the two dead bodies on the second floor, and the other two bodies on the first floor. Went into the room where one of the bodies lay and that's when the cops burst in and arrested him.

Ida looked up at Michael. 'He's saying he slept through four people being murdered?'

'It don't make much sense to me neither.'

'And this is the story he's sticking with?'

'Yup.'

She looked at him, sensing anger for the first time. The fact that there was still a spark of it in him allayed her concerns about his wellbeing. A little. She walked around the room, passed the window and peered out of it. On the street below someone had arrived at the root doctor's shop, had turned on the lights. A neon sign she hadn't seen before flashed, sharp against the pale autumn light – in lines of blue it depicted a skull in a top hat, and below it in green, the words *Louisiana Voodoo*. It made her think of New Orleans, of her parents, of everything she'd lost in the thirty or so years since she'd left home.

Ida looked around the mean apology for a room once more and a dispiriting sensation quivered through her.

'Let's check downstairs,' she said.

On the way down, she inspected the walls and floorboards and risers for any stains or scratches or other clues that might by some miracle still be there after so many weeks.

Nothing.

'This is where the first two bodies were found,' Michael said when they'd reached the second floor. 'The Powell brothers.'

He unlocked the door to room 202, the first door off the stairs, and they stepped inside.

This room was larger than Tom's, nicer too. There were two single beds, two wardrobes, a sink, a one-burner gas stove. Like Tom's, the room was on the side of the building facing the street out front.

Michael extracted more photos from the binder, passed them over. The first body lay in a puddle of blood out in the hall, multiple stabs wounds across the chest and stomach. One of the arms was tossed backwards, fingers touching the staircase's bannister.

The second body was in the room, lying belly down near the window. Blood splatter and streaks covered the wall. In a close-up from later on, the body had been turned right side up, revealing a deep gash across the neck, the white gleam of spinal column.

'These were the two brothers who were in the voodoo cult?' Ida asked.

Michael nodded and took out more photos. Voodoo trinkets like the ones in Tom's room. Also pamphlets from the Temple of Tranquility, the cult of which the Powell brothers were supposedly members. Ida studied the photos of the pamphlets. The Temple looked like a back-to-Africa church. She'd seen dozens of similar organizations in Chicago and had never understood their appeal.

'What did the brothers do for a living?' she asked.

'No one seems to know.'

She studied the room as it was now, compared it to the nightmare in the photos.

'There's something else,' Michael said wearily.

He handed her a photo of a wristwatch dusted with aluminum powder, revealing a fingerprint.

'It's Alfonso Powell's watch,' said Michael. They found it on his wrist. They matched the print to Tom's left index finger.'

Ida looked up from the photo to Michael, noted how ashen he looked, despite the red scars across his face. 'What did Tom say?' she asked.

'Said he never came in this room, much less touched the bodies.' He said it so flatly, it was almost like he was challenging her.

Ida nodded, not rising to it. 'Let's carry on,' she said.

They locked up the room and descended to the reception area. Carrasco was leaning against the wall, smoking a cigarette. He nodded when he saw them come down. The receptionist was still sitting in his chair behind the desk, reading the sports pages.

They turned down the corridor which led to the rear of the building, passing a payphone affixed to the wall. In the shadows at the back they reached the door for room 103. Michael opened it up. It was even gloomier than the others, with the same layout and furniture as Tom's room. There was a sprawling, dark brown blotch on the floorboards which Ida guessed was dried blood, long-since stained into the wood. The place reeked of death, even after all this time, despite the fact that lemon-scented detergent had been doused about the room and the window had been cranked open.

The rain was coming in through the window, pattering onto the sill, dripping down the wall. The window had iron bars over it and beyond them Ida could see the alleyway to the side of the building. Next to the window was another door, heading, she guessed, into the yard at the rear of the building.

Michael sifted papers and handed her more crime scene snaps. They showed the room drenched in blood, the body of a young, white male, blond-haired, lying by odd coincidence near where Ida was standing. His torso had been slashed repeatedly, exposed intestines making his mid-section look like it had exploded. He'd almost been hacked in two.

'This is where the cops found Tom?' she asked.

Michael nodded. 'Red-handed, supposedly.'

Ida thought of Tom as a child, Tom as a doctor. She tried to make him the architect of the slaughter. Couldn't. She looked again at the photos, at the images of the victim, Arno Bucek, the white boy who'd gone missing weeks before the murders then inexplicably had turned up in a Harlem flophouse. In amongst the photos were evidence shots, of the heroin and money that a blood-soaked Tom was apparently trying to steal from the room when the cops discovered him.

'None of this makes sense,' she said. 'What's Bucek doing in Harlem with two hundred and thirty-eight dollars in cash and twenty grams of low-grade dope?'

'The cops say he was a pusher.'

'A skinny Polish kid in the middle of black Harlem?'

Michael smiled a bleak, knowing smile.

39

Ida looked again at the photos, played spot the difference between them and the room as it stood before her now. The bed had been tossed, the mattress leaned up against the wall, covered in blood spray. Around the window frame were bloody hand-prints. She noted blood splatter, body positioning. She noted the distance markers the cops had set up. She noted scratches and grooves on the floorboards around the body, splintering patterns. She noted where the forensics had dusted for latent prints, their choice of touch-and-grab surfaces. She made a mental image of the room as it was on that night in August, looked up, meshed it with what she could see now, let the two form a single entity.

But something wasn't right. Something didn't mesh. Didn't add up.

'You spotted what's missing yet?' Michael asked her.

She looked up at him, saw a slight smile playing on his lips.

'I've seen something's missing, but not what.'

'There're no photos of the door,' he said.

She flicked through the photos. That was it.

'All these close-ups,' he continued. 'And no one thought to take a photo of the door.'

She walked over to the door and kneeled in front of it. She ran her finger down the edge of its frame. No scratch marks, no cracks. She examined its outside edge. That too showed no signs of having been forced, or having been recently repaired.

'It's quite the oversight,' she said.

They shared a look, acknowledging what it all meant. Then she rose and they went back into the reception, where the receptionist and Carrasco were as they'd left them.

More photos. Diana Hollis, last of the four victims, the night receptionist. Not the quick kills afforded the Powell brothers. The scene looked more like what had happened to Bucek, except here the wounds were concentrated around the woman's crotch. Hollis lay in the passageway leading out from the desk area. Close-ups of the partition and blood streaks across the floor suggested the killer went back there and dragged her out before killing her.

'Hollis worked the nightshift here?' Ida asked Michael.

Michael shook his head. 'She was filling in. I don't think women work nightshifts much in hotels in Harlem. Not in these kinds of hotels anyway.'

'Where was the regular guy?'

'Night off.'

Ida gestured towards the man behind the mesh. Michael nodded, indicating he was the one who should have been working that night.

'He's also the hotel owner,' Michael said.

Ida looked at the man through the mesh. His eyes didn't leave his newspaper.

She scanned the rest of the room. She noted the cheap linoleum on the floor, bubbling up in spots. She noted the stamped-tin ceiling, painted a muddy beige. She noted the payphone next to the stairs.

'Any photos of the payphone?' she asked.

Michael sifted paperwork and shook his head.

'How were the police alerted?' she asked.

'Anonymous phone call reporting a disturbance.'

'Did anyone request the call records from Bell for that phone?'

'I don't know,' said Michael. 'We'll have to ask Carrasco.'

'It's worth a try.'

They nodded at each other. Michael returned the keys to the receptionist, and together with Carrasco they stepped back out onto the street, stood on the sidewalk in the drizzle.

'Well?' Carrasco asked.

'It's a start,' said Michael. 'Thanks, buddy.'

'No problem,' he said. 'Anything you want me to do, let me know. You want a ride anywhere?'

Michael shook his head. 'No, thanks,' he said. 'But there is something else.'

He asked him about the phone records, and Carrasco said he'd look into it. Then he hopped into his Plymouth and drove off and they watched the car disappear up the street.

'He gets caught helping us out, it's not just his job he'll lose,' Ida said. 'He's going to prison.'

'Yeah,' said Michael, lighting a cigarette.

'Must be some favor he owes you. What did you do?'

'Saved his life. And his family's.'

Ida smiled. Michael smoked.

'C'mon,' he said, 'we can catch the subway to the ferry port.'

They crossed the street, passed the root doctor's shop, and through the gray sheets of drizzle, Ida saw the icy green neon of *Louisiana Voodoo* flashing in the gloom once more, the skull in the top hat.

'So what's your take on it all?' Michael asked.

Ida turned her gaze from the shop. 'Same as yours, probably. It's got police conspiracy written all over it.'

'Yup,' said Michael.

'There's the photos of the door to Bucek's room going missing,' Ida said. 'Or never being photographed at all. Then there's the anonymous tip-off and the timing. How the hell did they respond so quick? To reports of a disturbance in the middle of Harlem on a Friday night in the height of summer. Then there's the hotel owner mysteriously taking the night off. Like he was tipped off. And then there's all that voodoo junk. I mean, if I ever saw a police plant it's right there. Me and you both know Tom isn't superstitious. He's a doctor, a man of science. The voodoo angle's pure diversion. Racial bias, black magic stereotypes, zeitgeist hysteria. It's all set up to send a jury off in the wrong direction. And the only people who could have put it there were the cops.'

Michael nodded. 'You see the root doctor's shop over the road?' he said. 'I'm wondering if the responding officers didn't go in there, boost the merchandise and dump it in their rooms.'

'I wouldn't put it past them,' she said. 'And then there's the

42

most important thing of all – the murder weapon. If the cops really did chase Tom out of Bucek's room and catch him in the alleyway, where the hell's the machete? He'd have to have thrown it away either in the hotel or in the alley, but the cops say they never found it. It's good, Michael. We've got enough to go on. Enough to get started.'

She looked at him to see if her words had provided him with any reassurance, but she couldn't detect any emotion on his face. He took a drag on his cigarette.

'Going up against the police isn't good, Ida,' he said. 'Cops, conspiracies. Someone powerful was behind this. We've got to send a colored man into a court-room and try and convince a jury he's telling the truth, and the good, white police of New York are guilty of framing him. And if the police are covering things up, it means Tom's in danger. Every day he's in prison they can arrange a jailhouse hit to keep him quiet. And if they hear we're making any progress, that's exactly what they'll do. If they decide to attack, he's as good as dead. My boy. Who I raised from a baby.'

She stared at him, and realized that mixed in with his bewilderment, anxiety and anger there was another emotion too – guilt. It was irrational, but if anything similar happened to her son, she knew she'd feel the same. Somehow she'd find a way to take the blame off the boy's shoulders and ladle it all onto herself.

'So we're working against the clock,' she said. 'Against the authorities, in a city that isn't home turf, and we can't let anyone find out what we're up to?'

'That's about the size of it.'

'Good,' she said. 'I like a challenge.'

She smiled at him and waited, and eventually, against his will, something broke inside him, and he smiled back.

PART THREE

PART THREE

'Costello has succeeded in becoming as mysterious a figure as the American underworld ever produced.'

HERBERT ASBURY, *COLLIERS*, 1947

6

Gabriel entered Costello's study and crossed its wide expanse. The room was larger than most people's apartments, and decked out much like the lounge, with expensive furniture under a high, molded ceiling. Costello was sitting at a giant mahogany desk on the room's far side, silhouetted by the giant windows behind him. Across the acres of green-baize desktop from Costello sat Joe Adonis, Costello's lieutenant.

The two men eyed Gabriel as he walked towards them and took a seat. He put his hands in his lap to hide the shakes, covered them with his hat for good measure. He felt the moisture all over his head and wasn't sure anymore if it was rain or sweat. He told himself again it was nothing; that they couldn't possibly know about the racetrack accounts, not yet, not till the audit came back on the 13th.

'And how is our favorite night undertaker?' Adonis asked Gabriel with a smirk.

Gabriel ignored the jibe.

Adonis's smirk morphed into a grin, and the grin turned his face into that of a child. Adonis was forty-five years old, but a perennial adolescent. And possibly the vainest man in New York. He was born Giuseppe Doto, but changed his name to Adonis after he read a magazine article about the Greek god of beauty.

Costello frowned at Adonis. Adonis shrugged.

'How's the Copa?' Costello asked in his low growl. Numerous bouts of throat cancer had left him with a ragged rumble of a voice. Despite this he still smoked a few packs of English Ovals a day.

'Fine,' said Gabriel. 'Mayor O'Dwyer was in last night. I couldn't make out his dinner companions. They left at about four in high spirits.'

Costello nodded, took a sip from the espresso cup in front of him. Part of Gabriel's role as manager of the Copa was to keep his boss appraised on the comings and goings of the city's elite. Nightspots were often where powerful men slipped up.

'I saw Jack Warner outside,' Gabriel said. 'And there've been a few movie-men from LA in the Copa the last few days. Any idea what's going on?'

Costello shrugged in that way of his. 'These government hearings into the commies,' he said. 'There's a meeting next week at the Waldorf to figure out what the plan is. I guess a few of them are trickling in early. You know how movie folks are.'

Gabriel nodded and looked over at his boss. Costello was a swarthy man in his fifties, with a generous nose, a lined face, and olive-black hair combed straight back. He wore an impeccably cut drape suit, its navy-blue fabric making his sunlamp tan look all the more unnatural.

'So what did you call me in for?' Gabriel asked, drumming his fingers on the brim of his hat to the incessant conga rhythm in his head. He wanted to get things over with as soon as possible. Discover his fate. A ditch upstate or the beach in Acapulco.

Adonis and Costello shared a look. Gabriel tensed, waited for the inevitable. He swallowed panic, pushed it down into the bottom of his stomach, where a whole rhythm section had struck up.

'Vernon Hintz,' said Costello, finally. 'We caught him on the take.'

Gabriel nodded. Relief flooded through him but he tried not to show it. It wasn't about the race track. It was something to do with Hintz, a money launderer who cleaned cash for all New York's five crime families.

'And?' Gabriel asked.

'And he isn't on the take anymore,' said Adonis.

Meaning Hintz was now in a ditch somewhere.

'Poor Vern,' Gabriel said. 'I liked the guy.'

'Sure,' said Adonis. 'He was nice. Apart from being a thief.'

'What's the world coming to when your money launderer cooks his books,' Gabriel quipped.

Adonis glared at him. Costello suppressed a smile.

'Anyway,' said Costello, 'before Hintz departed our presence he told us a few things to ingratiate himself, stave off the inevitable.'

Gabriel nodded, wondering, as he had done for months now, where Costello was getting his vocabulary from.

'Hintz told us a story,' said Adonis. 'About this Benny Siegel business.'

'Which business?' Gabriel asked, for Benny Siegel left a lot of business in his wake.

Costello leaned forward. 'Hintz told us that when Benny was in New York last summer, he approached Hintz and asked him to launder two million dollars for him. Cash.'

'Cash?' Gabriel repeated.

Adonis and Costello both nodded wearily and things started to make sense.

Benjamin Siegel was the New York Mob's representative out in Los Angeles. A few years previously, Siegel had had a hare-brained scheme to build a luxury hotel and casino in Las Vegas, a backwater town in the middle of the Nevada Desert. He drummed up three million in financing from his mobster friends back in New York. Spent it all before he'd even started construction. Put the bite on for another three million. Spent that. Then came to New York looking to borrow yet more money. Ended up borrowing another two million, much of it from Costello. Eventually the casino – named The Flamingo, after Siegel's long-legged girlfriend – opened its doors, way behind schedule, and way over

49

budget. It was a flop. It hemorrhaged yet more money. Someone got fed up and gunned Siegel down with a 30-30 military carbine while he sat drinking coffee on the girlfriend's sofa in Beverly Hills.

Now Costello, via the dearly departed Hintz, was suggesting Siegel had never planned to put the last two million of borrowed money into his Las Vegas pipe-dream.

'So Benny borrowed money from everyone in town for the casino,' said Gabriel. 'And then tried to steal it?'

Costello leaned back in his seat. 'That's about the size of it,' he said.

'It's an OK scam,' Gabriel said. 'Benny knows the casino's going bust, so he asks everyone for money, pretends he's putting it into the casino, then when the place closes down he tells them all the money got lost in the bankruptcy. Except it didn't.'

From the lounge, a round of laughter rose up. Gabriel thought he could hear Bova's cackle rising up above the fray.

Costello let the laughter subside. Gabriel looked through the window at the washed-out image of Central Park.

'Benny arranged to deliver the money to Hintz, in cash, but he never did,' said Costello. 'We had Joe Katz fly out to the Flamingo a few weeks ago. Look the books over. Can you guess what he found?'

'Accounting irregularities?' said Gabriel.

Costello nodded. 'The two million never entered the corporation bank accounts, or any of Benny's personal accounts. It wasn't in the safe at the Flamingo, or at his house, or at that whore of a girlfriend's house. It wasn't in any of her accounts either. Not even the Swiss ones Lansky set up.'

'He didn't have the money when he got off the plane from New York,' Adonis interjected.

'How'd you know?' Gabriel asked.

'We spoke to his driver, and that Polak accountant him and Dragna use, and a customs agent at the airport who runs frisks for us,' said Adonis. 'Unless he threw the money out the plane half-way between here and California, it's still in New York.'

'Our two million bucks is out there somewhere,' said Costello, waving a hand in the air, gesturing to the window, to Central Park, to New York, to the ether.

This was why Gabriel had been asked here. He and Benny were old friends, fellow yids. Gabriel knew Benny's pals, possibly knew his stash spots. Plus Gabriel had money-laundering experience, had done jobs like this in the past. In Gabriel's head, the congas beat their panic rhythm once more.

'So Benny left two million dollars of your stolen money in New York,' said Gabriel, 'and you want me to find it?'

Costello nodded. Took a last sip of his espresso. 'That's about the size of it.'

There was no way Gabriel could get it done in the ten days he had before leaving town. If at all. And he had to get it done before he left or he'd never escape. And he couldn't refuse because that would look just as suspicious. He was trapped. He wanted to light a cigarette but didn't have enough confidence in his hands just yet, so kept them tapping away that conga rhythm on the felt of his Stetson.

'There's something else,' said Costello.

He turned to look at Adonis, gestured for him to take up the thread.

'When Benny came to see Hintz asking to launder the money, Hintz started telling him about all the fake companies he'd have to set up, all the accounts, giving him a breakdown of how much it would all cost. Benny told him he didn't have to set up any accounts, he could move the money through some companies Hintz had already set up for one of the other families.'

Adonis raised his eyebrows, let Gabriel do the sums on what that meant. All the city's crime families used Hintz. If what Hintz had said was true, Benny had conspired with one of the other four families to steal the money.

'Did Hintz say which family?' Gabriel asked.

Adonis shook his head grimly.

'Hintz said Benny never mentioned the other family,' Adonis explained. 'He was supposed to come back to New York to arrange all the details but he ended up splattered all over Virginia Hill's sofa before he could.'

Gabriel looked at them both. 'What about Genovese?' he said. 'He must have an account with Hintz.'

Costello's face soured at the mention of his traitorous under-boss.

'Benny and Genovese got sore with each other last year some-time,' Costello said. 'They hated each other. There's no way they'd work together on this.'

'You sure?' Gabriel asked.

'Sure, I'm sure. Don't even think about it,' said Costello.

Gabriel eyed his boss, wondering why he was so quick to brush aside the Genovese angle.

'You see Benny when he was out here?' Costello asked.

'Sure,' said Gabriel. 'He popped by the Copa to say hello.'

Gabriel thought back to the previous summer, to Benny's last trip to New York, making the rounds of the city's Mafia families trying to scrape together the ill-fated two million. Benny had come by the Copa with his usual entourage of movie stars and ingénues and mobsters. They'd talked, in private, and Gabriel got the sense there was something on Benny's mind, something beyond his money problems and the hole he'd dug for himself in the Nevada desert. Gabriel had got the sense that Benny wanted to tell him something, but didn't have the heart. At the time Gabriel had dwelled on it, but as the days passed he'd forgotten all about it.

'Did he seem himself to you?' Costello asked.

Gabriel frowned, wondered if there was more to all this than Costello was letting on.

'Sure,' said Gabriel, lying. 'Why wouldn't he?'

Costello shrugged. Adonis cleared his throat. Gabriel got the feeling it might be a good idea to change the subject.

'He might've banked it somewhere,' Gabriel said. 'With another launderer. If he did, it's going to be hard to trace.'

'Hintz said he was bringing it in cash,' said Adonis. 'Why would he risk banking it for the week he was back in California? And if he was stupid enough to bank it, then we want to know the name of the bank.'

'So I'm gonna be looking for what?' said Gabriel. 'An attaché case stuffed with dollar bills stashed somewhere or other in the greater New York city area? He could have stashed it with one of his girls and she's spent it all. Or dumped it in a locker in a train station. He could've taken a long-lease on an apartment and stuffed the money under the mattress. This is needle-in-a-haystack stuff.'

He looked at Costello, who met his gaze with an inscrutable expression.

'Not an attaché case, Gabby,' Adonis said. 'Too small for a couple of mill. You'd be looking for a knapsack. Maybe a pair of 'em. Those big military ones.'

Adonis grinned, all teeth, no warmth. Costello glared at him. Gabriel sweated.

'You're good at this kind of thing,' said Costello, turning to Gabriel. He took a linen napkin from the desktop, wrapped it round his forefinger and commenced massaging his gums and teeth. 'Ask around,' he said. 'See what you can find. I need this money, Gabby.'

There was a hint of desperation in Costello's voice. The man had urged all the other families to invest in Benny's Las Vegas pipe-dream, and when Benny had lost all their money, Costello was made liable for their losses. Frank Costello, prime minister of the underworld, boss of all bosses, was in hock to the tune of millions to all the city's other crime families. And now it turned out one of those families had helped steal the borrowed money.

If the investigation wasn't handled sensibly, it could lead to New York's first Mafia war in nearly two decades.

'No one else knows that the money's still on the loose?' asked Gabriel.

'Just us,' said Costello. 'And it needs to stay that way.'

Gabriel nodded. If any of the other families found out, they'd go searching for the money themselves, find it, pretend they hadn't, and still press Costello on the debts.

'Find the money,' said Costello.

'And find out which of the families was involved,' said Adonis.

Gabriel thought about his slim chances of success, the fact that he was supposed to be skipping town the next week, the fact that he had to find the money before he left or he'd never be free of them, about all his years of careful planning unraveled at the eleventh hour. 'Sure thing,' he said, steadily, over the sound of the congas pounding away in his head.

7

Gabriel caught a cab back to his flat on East 64th, a classic seven
on the tenth floor of a Gilded Age apartment block. He floated up
in the elevator, unlocked his door and stepped through the hallway into the lounge. He'd rented the place fully furnished –
flocked wallpaper, fusty old paintings, a smattering of ancient
sofas and chaise-longues – and could only guess at the identity of
its previous tenant.

He could hear the shower going in the bathroom, and Mrs
Hirsch pottering about in the kitchen. He headed over to the
drinks trolley to pour himself a 'nightcap', and nearly slipped on
the carpet of comic books strewn across the parquet. He sighed
and leaned down to pick them up. *Adventure Comics, Marvel Mystery Comics, All-Star Comics*. In amongst them he found Sarah's
sketchbook and a few loose pencils. He laid the lot next to the
decanters on the drinks trolley, poured himself a Glenlivet,
downed it, poured another, and stared out of the window into the
streets below, the corner of 64th and 4th. A trio of Negro nannies
were pushing prams towards Central Park, a white woman in a
neck fur was hailing a cab, a delivery van idled at the lights.

Gabriel looked at all this and then at the rooftops stretching
north. He lost himself in the view, and as he always did when he
was standing at a height, he day-dreamed of jumping off. For
some reason he always imagined it to be an elegant act, a graceful
swoop into nothingness, the wings on his back unfurling to save

him. Though he knew from bitter experience that a death from a height was anything but serene.

So he thought instead about Benny's missing millions and how the hell he was supposed to find the money in the next ten days. He thought about Benny coming to the Copa the previous summer, leaning against the bar, something he wanted to say, that haunted look in his eyes.

On the other side of the building, a train rumbled down the Third Avenue El tracks, sending a dull clattering into the air. Gabriel put the tumbler down, lit a cigarette and his gaze landed on Sarah's sketchbook. He picked it up, flicked through it. Batman, Superman, The Shadow, Dick Tracy, a female figure Gabriel didn't recognize with a cleavage that strained both the top of her dress and the laws of biology. Villains in an assortment of get-ups. All of them flying, punching, kicking, jumping. Sarah was talented; the figures rippled with life, even though most of them were only half-finished, trailing off at the edges into shading blocks, armatures, perspective lines, and then disappearing altogether into the misty white of the sketch pad.

He carried on flicking through the pad and came to other images that made him stop – Mexican images. Day of the Dead. Skeletons holding guitars and trumpets, wearing garlands and sombreros. Gangster skeletons dressed in suits, smoking cigars, holding tommy-guns hosing fire, which Sarah had colored in zigzagging orange and red.

'Little early, isn't it?' said a nasal voice behind him.

He turned to see Mrs Hirsch standing in the doorway of the kitchen, hand on hip, an apron over a brushed-wool sweater.

'You seen these?' he asked, holding up Sarah's Mexican sketches.

Mrs Hirsch frowned and limped over, her house slippers slapping on the parquet. She was past sixty and heavy in the hips. She took the sketches in hand, held them close to her eyes, squinted, focused.

Only three people knew about Gabriel's plan. Gabriel, Sarah, and Mrs Hirsch, who, along with Gabriel, had raised Sarah since she was a baby, when Gabriel's sister had been murdered.

'This is not good,' said Mrs Hirsch, looking up at him. 'This is anxiety.'

'You think?' said Gabriel sarcastically.

Mrs Hirsch gave him a look. 'Talk to her,' she said. 'You want a coffee to go with that whisky?'

Gabriel nodded. She turned around and limped back across the lounge.

'You spend any longer perched in front of that window, you'll turn into a gargoyle,' she said as she disappeared into the kitchen.

It was a favorite saying of hers, maybe because Gabriel did spend so much time at the window. He turned, rubbed his temples and looked around the room. He'd made a few additions to the apartment – the police radio scanner, the strongbox, the pigeon coop on the roof, the drip painting, which sat propped up against the wall next to the windows, unhung. He'd won it months ago from an art collector in a poker game. The man assured him it would be the next big thing, painted by a drunk from Wyoming who was set to be the new Picasso.

It depicted nothing but spots and splashes, made by the painter dripping paint directly onto it. The splashes looped around each other, through each other, all different colors and thicknesses. When Gabriel was drunk or tired or had taken a few Bennies, the thing came to life, moved, shifted, danced. Gabriel could see the painter throwing the paint down, could see the movement the man's arm had made all those months ago, the energy of it, the performance, recorded forever in the shape of the thing.

'A man throws paint on a canvas and calls it art,' said Mrs Hirsch, who was standing next to Gabriel holding out a cup of coffee. 'I mean, actually *throws* paint. You got all these lovely paintings here and you stick that monstrosity up. Sarah could do better.'

Gabriel took the coffee, took a sip, felt sick. They both stared at the painting. He should hang it up, it would add more credence to the story he was going to ask the world to buy, that he and Sarah were happily settled in the apartment when intruders broke in and killed them.

Gabriel and Mrs Hirsch both turned to see Sarah standing behind them, staring at them as they stared at the painting.

'I'll get your food,' Mrs Hirsch said to Sarah. She threw a knowing look Gabriel's way then headed off into the kitchen.

Gabriel turned to look at his niece. She was dressed in a plaid skirt and a baggy brown sweater which set off her red hair. She had her mother's face, the freckles, the milky skin, the rosy cheeks, as if newly scrubbed, an air of Alpine freshness. She was almost fourteen and the older she got, the more Gabriel saw his long-dead sister whenever he looked at her.

'What?' she asked.

He had to confront her over the sketches, but he didn't have the heart. He was tired enough. He'd talk to her after he'd had some sleep, whenever that might be.

'Nothing,' he said.

They met like this twice a day — when he was returning home from work, she was leaving for school. In the evenings they passed each other coming the other way, their lives revolving in opposite orbits.

'You look tired,' she said.

'Long night,' he said.

'Aren't they all?'

They smiled at each other and he suppressed the urge to ruffle her hair. Beautiful girl. Talented, warm, hesitant, modest. He'd led her into danger with his way of life, and now he had to do everything he could to lead her back out. This was who he was doing it all for, his last living relative, the one person in the world he'd happily die for.

She turned and headed off to the kitchen to get her breakfast.

Gabriel poured his whisky into his coffee, walked over to the police scanner, kneeled, turned it on, sat on the sofa. He closed his eyes and lights roared around his head. He zoned in on the shrill chatter coming out of the scanner. God knew why, but it soothed him.

'Hit-and-run on 96th and 3rd. One down. Brown '44 Plymouth. Front-left damage—'

In knots of static and chirping came the sound of New York waking up, the morning fruit of the night before's crimes – a hodgepodged stream of traffic accidents, muggings, burglaries, rapes, dead bodies fished out of the river, out of paper-strewn alleys, off benches in the park, the aftermath and residue of drinking sessions and fights, of dreams fulfilled and nightmares come true, the whole morning clean-up after the empire of night had receded once more.

'Mugger fleeing East 73rd into Central Park. Back-up requested—'

Gabriel had been looking for a way out of the life for years. Over time a feeling had taken root in him that things were closing in. That, like every other mobster, the longer he stayed in the life, the closer he got to a prison cell or a shallow grave. Every day the feeling grew stronger, the cage grew smaller, till it got so he couldn't even remember a time when he had peace of mind.

And then, six years ago, during a poker game, he'd won a fifty-percent stake in the Saratoga Racetrack in upstate New York. The other fifty percent was owned by Albert Anastasia, the underboss of the Mangano crime family, unofficial head of the Brooklyn docks, founder member of Murder Inc, a torturer and prolific killer, the embodiment of the Mob's violence machine.

When Anastasia heard he was partnered up with Gabriel, he asked Gabriel over for an informal chat, explained how if there were any irregularities, or Gabriel got in the way of the race-track's smooth operation, Anastasia would have him disappeared. And Anastasia was probably good for it. Rumor was, his personal body count was in triple-digits. Gabriel sat there and nodded, secretly happy, because in Anastasia's threat, Gabriel had figured a way to get himself and Sarah out of the trap.

'Canal Street and Allen. Probable Burglary. Chinese interpreter requested—'

On the following Thursday afternoon, Gabriel would go to the auditor's office downtown and pick up the books for that summer's season of the racetrack. In previous years, Gabriel concealed his skim well, but this year he'd done it sloppily, so the auditor would pick up on it. He'd return to the apartment, where it'd just be him and Sarah – Mrs Hirsch had Thursday nights off, spent them with her sister over in Queens. Gabriel had arranged for Anastasia to come over in person to pick up the books around nine p.m.

Anastasia would take the books and leave.

Gabriel would turn over furniture, pull up rugs, cut his arm and leave the place drenched in blood. At ten p.m., the concierge would go up to the rooftop to smoke a joint like he always did, at five past ten, Gabriel and Sarah would slip out of the building, walk down to Lexington, catch the subway to Penn Station, from there a bus to Florida, from there to Texas, and from there the fake passports would get them from San Antonio to Monterrey, to Mexico City, to freedom.

'Pier 88. Body found. Officers on scene. Request attendance of Homicide Bureau Detectives—'

On Friday morning, Mrs Hirsch would return to work, find Gabriel and the girl missing, the apartment ruined, would call the police and scream murder, giving them a half-day's head start. Cops would investigate, Costello would investigate, a single conclusion would be reached – Anastasia came over to collect the books on Thursday night, saw that Gabriel had been stealing from him, an argument ensued, Anastasia killed Gabriel and Sarah and hid their bodies. Anastasia had done such things in the past. Anastasia flew into blind rages. He'd probably deny it, but everyone would know he was lying; he had a triple-digit body count after all.

Gabriel and Sarah would get away clean. Gabriel would finally have done right by the girl.

'Spectators at corner of Amsterdam and 134th. Possible knife fight. Officers in the vicinity for crowd control make yourselves known—'

'Bye, Uncle Gabby.'

He opened his eyes to see Sarah heading out of the door, on her way to school. The door slammed shut, shook his skull. He rubbed his temples and looked around the apartment, imagined the shadow fight with Anastasia once more. He calculated again which pieces of furniture to turn over, where to splatter the blood, he drew parallels with the drip painting on the wall behind him – a performance recorded.

'Multiple shots. Suspect heading north on 5th. All units clear the air—'

He'd planned it for years, and for every mis-step and hiccup, he'd come up with contingencies, had mapped all the branches of cause and effect. The only thing he hadn't prepared for was to be asked to find Benny Siegel's stolen millions ten days before it was all supposed to go down.

Six years of planning, ten days to save it all.

'I don't know what I hate more, that painting or that police radio. Why can't you put nice things in this house?'

Gabriel turned to see Mrs Hirsch in the hallway, putting her coat on.

'You want anything from the store?' she asked.

He shook his head.

'Thursday,' he said. 'You need to cancel your night off.'

Mrs Hirsch paused, frowned.

'You been given a job?' she asked warily.

Gabriel nodded.

'Costello?'

Gabriel nodded again. She straightened the collar of her coat and shuffled over, perched on the sofa as Gabriel told her about Benny's missing millions and the task of finding them.

'And if you don't find the money by the time you're supposed to leave?' she asked.

'Then I can't leave,' he said. 'If I leave without finding the money first, everyone'll think I found the money and ran away. They'll chase me forever. Till my dying day. So much for a clean break. For all the years I planned it.'

He looked at her and she nodded, pondering his predicament, taking in its ramifications.

'But if you don't leave, you'll have Anastasia to deal with,' she said. 'It'll all have been for nothing.'

'Exactly.'

Gabriel thought about that triple-digit body count again. The danger of having Anastasia come after him. The madness.

Mrs Hirsch considered. 'Better get searching, then,' she said, rising, heading for the door.

He smiled. She left.

Mrs Hirsch was one of the only people in New York he'd actually miss when he was gone. He closed his eyes and the darkness relaxed him, but he knew he couldn't sleep – the passports were burning a hole in his pocket. He had to stash them and get to work.

8

Gabriel stepped out onto the rooftop and walked over to the pigeon coop. He shivered in the cold, but he was glad to be up there. He'd always loved being on rooftops, ever since he was a kid. They had a special kind of serenity, were a wilderness all of their own, in a city where wilderness was hard to come by. This was probably why so many New Yorkers owned coops – as an excuse to get out onto the rooftops, into the stillness, the calming embrace of the sky.

After his parents had died, when it was just Gabriel and his sister scratching a living on the streets, sometimes in winter they'd climb the fire escapes of apartment buildings like this one, buildings with central heating. They'd sleep in the spaces between the heating vents to save themselves from freezing. Sometimes they'd wake up covered in soot, with coughs that wouldn't leave them for weeks, so his sister would have to steal pastilles from pharmacies.

Sometimes, in the mayfly days of summer, they'd sleep on the roofs just to be under the night sky, to watch the stars wend their way through the darkness. When fall came round and they returned indoors, the rooms always felt like prison cells.

Gabriel thought of the sister he'd shared so much with. The sister so violently taken from him. He thought of Sarah who looked so much like her and how he couldn't let the same thing happen to his niece.

He reached the coop and the pigeons rose up and swirled

about behind the wire-mesh. He unlocked the door and stepped inside and everything rattled with their movement.

He hauled some of the cages from the storage bench that ran the length of the coop. He unlocked the padlock on the bench, swung open its top to reveal the stash space within. He took out the strongbox, unlocked it, placed the passports inside, nestled them next to the cash and the guns. Took one of the guns out – a Smith & Wesson .38 Special – and cast his eye over it, slipped in some rounds, pocketed it. He locked everything up, returned the coop to how it was, took one last look around and left.

As he finished locking the door, he looked up at the building across 64th Street which towered over his own building. In one of the windows an ancient woman was scowling at him. Their eyes met. She turned and disappeared. He carried on staring at the empty window, then at the others that surrounded it, like so many boxes piled on top of each other, like the automat the previous night, the glass dispensers with their food going cold, congealing.

His thoughts were broken by a roaring noise below him – a train passing along the steel ribbon of the Third Avenue El tracks, belching soot, producing an unholy thunder, shaking every joist and strut in the scaffolds that held the tracks fixed three stories above the earth. The locals had been campaigning for years to have it scrapped, thereby allowing the Upper East Side to detach itself even further from the rest of New York. Sooner or later, the campaign would succeed.

Gabriel watched the old train lurch uptown towards Harlem and the Bronx, a great iron slugger who didn't know he was beaten yet, as unpopular and out-of-place amongst the grand apartment blocks as Gabriel and his pigeon coop. The neighbors had made countless complaints about his pigeons – rooftop coops were for tenements and slums, for Brooklyn and Queens and other immigrant quarters of the city, not for the Upper East Side, home of the city's merchant princes and robber-barons.

Gabriel had only moved to the neighborhood because it was

close to the Copa. But he'd found as soon as he'd relocated that he couldn't walk two yards without encountering a well-cultivated sneer. Maybe he should have stuck to the Upper West Side, with Costello and all the other gangsters.

He lit a cigarette and stared beyond the El tracks, over the rooftops to the river shimmering in the distance, to Welfare Island, and beyond that, the haze of Queens.

Mrs Hirsch's words floated into his head, her warning about the dangers of spending too long staring out over the city, the risk of becoming a gargoyle.

He turned and trudged back towards the stairwell. He was about halfway there when the door to it opened and the concierge stepped out. He was young, and from Brooklyn too, which made the pair of them feel like they were allies in this building of antique wealth. This was the concierge whose ten o'clock smoke break would unwittingly help Gabriel in his plan to escape.

The concierge saw him, nodded, held the door open for him, yawned as Gabriel approached. The two men also had in common the fact they worked nights.

'You not clocked off yet?' asked Gabriel, stopping.

'Pauly's late,' said the concierge. 'Came up to check the heating vents. Mrs Ollson in apartment five's complaining again.'

Gabriel smiled.

'What's so funny?'

'Nothing.'

He thought of rich Mrs Ollson in apartment five, indignant over a blocked heating vent. He thought of himself and his sister all those winters ago, covered in soot, chased down the street by pharmacy clerks, hopping onto street-cars, getting away.

Just then another elevated train roared past, heading downtown this time. They both turned to watch it as it waddled down the tracks, disappeared behind the roof of Bloomingdale's, where the passing trains made the crockery in the homeware section rattle.

'I know they ain't no good,' said the concierge, nodding after it, 'but I'll be damned if I won't miss 'em.'

Gabriel took a toke on his cigarette. 'Amen,' he said.

He nodded at the concierge, popped his cigarette back in his mouth, headed down the stairs. He'd come up with a plan for finding Benny's money. He needed to be on the street to execute it. Ten days to go. Becoming a gargoyle wasn't the only metamorphosis he had to worry about.

PART FOUR

'There is a feeling throughout the land that the returned veterans have been engaging in crimes to such an extent as to endanger the very foundation of civil life and safety. Indeed, some people have spread before the public a canvas on which the ex-service man is shown bludgeoning all passers-by and after maiming them, robbing them of their possessions.'

HARRY WILLBACH,
JOURNAL OF CRIMINAL LAW AND CRIMINOLOGY, 1948

9

The ferry ploughed its way through the gray water towards Rikers Island, a stretch of land shaped like a teardrop that lay in the middle of the East River, halfway between Queens and the Bronx. Ida sat near the boat's prow, reading the case jacket, looking up occasionally at the shoreline in the distance, pale and misty in the morning light, rising out of the water indistinctly. Around them the river was a floating traffic jam – ferries, freighters, carfloats, barges, even fishing boats – their green and red lights glittering like jewels in the otherwise gloomy landscape, funnels emitting sooty black smoke which was lifted by the wind into the gunmetal sky.

Michael leaned on the railing next to her, staring instead across the boat at the other passengers sitting on the benches that lined the deck – wives and children of inmates paying visits, lawyers, prison workers. All of them were wrapped up in heavy winter coats to shield them against the bitter winds that swept across the river. Many of the wives seemed to know each other and sat in groups chatting. Their children sullenly watched the boats, or raced around the slippery deck chasing seagulls, shrieking as much as the birds they were pursuing.

As the ferry approached the island, Ida closed the case jacket and inspected their destination, watched as its features became steadily more distinct – treeless scrubland, a rocky shoreline, low, red-brick buildings, all of them surrounded by razor-wire and security walls. The island had a strange, lumpy quality to it, grassy mounds rose up out of the scrub, whole sections were at an angle to the water.

When they reached the island, the ferry bumped against the jetty, was tied up, and they all descended. They made their way over a rickety wooden walkway above the marshy ground. At the end of the walkway were a pair of metal gates set in a long, brick wall, behind which was the sprawling complex of Victorian buildings that made up the prison. The visitors formed a line at the gates and as they waited for the guards to open them up, Ida surveyed the landscape they had just crossed. Frost lay all across the marsh, making the foliage and black earth sparkle like some Arctic tundra, as if the boat had come ashore in Iceland or Greenland, rather than New York.

Then she spotted something odd in the distance; smoke rising up from the black soil, and here and there, in amongst the reeds, the frost seemed to be glowing, and deep underneath it, orange lights bloomed and faded, like jellyfish coming to surface and diving once more. Ida was reminded of the eerie blue lights of the will-o'-the-wisps that darted across the swamps back home in Louisiana.

'This whole island used to be a dump,' said Michael, following her gaze. 'The garbage is still there under the ground and it catches fire sometimes, comes up through the soil. It's on account of all this being built on garbage mounds that the buildings are crumbling.'

He nodded to the building in front of them; the imposing facade was riven with cracks that darted down the mortar between its bricks. A whole wing seemed to have settled below the rest of the building, subsiding into the marsh. This was the cause of the island's slanting, uneven quality that Ida had noticed on their approach. She thought of the city using the place to discard its unwanted refuse, then its unwanted humans, and the place seemed even more mournful.

The guards opened the gates. The line moved forward and

they were instructed to head inside. They stepped through into a muddy courtyard, entered a barn-like reception hall that was subdivided by ropes and poles. They were directed to a desk where their IDs were checked and noted down, then they were told to wait once more.

'How long's visiting time?' Ida asked Michael.

'Half an hour,' he replied.

'Barely enough time to get started.'

'Yeah,' he said. 'I think that's the point.'

After fifteen minutes, guards entered and shouted out names, and they were led in groups through a door into a hall filled with rows of numbered tables. Behind each one sat a prisoner in chains. The hall was gloomy and windowless apart from a row of thin skylights high up in the ceiling which were covered in a thick layer of grime that made the anemic morning light even more so.

Michael and Ida were led to table eighteen, where Thomas James Talbot waited.

Ida struggled not to show her shock. She hadn't seen him since before the war and he had changed dramatically. He was chubbier than she remembered, though he still had his father's physique in there somewhere. His hair was going gray and receding. Even more alarmingly, he had a great bruise on his left cheek, lumpy and topped with a scab. But beyond even that, it was his eyes that startled her. They had lost their shine, their joy, there was something haunted to them, traumatized. The same deterioration she'd seen on Michael was apparent on his son, but writ greater, stronger, more heart-wrenching.

They sat and he gave them both a cheerless smile.

'Ida. It's good to see you,' he said.

'It's good to see you too.'

'Pop,' said Tom, turning to look at Michael.

Michael nodded and Ida picked up on some frostiness between them.

'What happened to your face?' Michael asked.

'Fight in the food hall,' said Tom. 'I wasn't involved, but I caught a stray elbow. It's nothing.'

Michael eyed him like he wasn't entirely convinced. And neither was Ida.

She glanced at the other prisoners sitting at the tables around them. Most of them looked accustomed to this world. Hard-edged men, bruisers, thugs, killers. And there was Tom, bookish, mild-mannered, caring and gentle, trapped in the same jail as them. If it came to a fight, to an assault, to an attack, the boy was as good as dead. How easy it would be for the cops to arrange a jailhouse hit to keep him quiet. She wondered if Michael had told Tom exactly how much danger he was in.

'Thanks for coming,' Tom said to Ida. 'I need all the help I can get. I didn't do this, Ida. I swear to God. I'm a doctor. All I've done my whole life is try and help people.'

'I know, Tom,' she said. 'We're gonna find out the truth and we're gonna get you out of here.'

At this he smiled and his downtrodden expression brightened ever so slightly.

'Visiting time's only half an hour,' she said. 'So we need to be quick. I'm going to ask you a lot of questions. A lot of questions that you've probably already answered a hundred times over, but I need to hear them from you. I had a look at the case details on the ferry over, and there's a lot of inconsistencies, Tom. A lot of things in your account that don't make sense. I'm going to ask you about those and you have to be honest. OK?'

'Yeah, sure,' he said. 'Whatever it takes. Like I said, I didn't do this.'

'OK,' she said. 'Let's start at the very beginning – why were you living there, Tom? The Palmer Hotel? Why a dive like that?'

At this he paused, the question touching a nerve. 'Rent was cheap,' he said. 'I was down on my luck.'

Ida picked up straight away that he was hiding something.

'You weren't working?' she asked.

He shook his head. 'I quit the hospital a few months earlier.'
'Why?'

Again he paused, pained by the question. He shot a look at his father, then shrugged. 'I was getting sick of it,' he said.

Another lie. Ida looked at Michael, could see the pain on his face. He knew Tom was lying too. If the boy stuck with this story, he didn't stand a chance.

'How long had you been living at the hotel?' Ida asked.
'A few weeks.'

'And in your statement you said in all those weeks you never saw Bucek, the white victim, even once. Not till the night of the murders.'

'That's the truth. I would've remembered seeing a white boy in there.'

'See, that's the first inconsistency. He was signed into the guest register six weeks before the murders.'

'I swear I never saw that kid in my life. That room they say he was staying in was closed up the whole time I was there. He didn't live there. I never saw him, and the Powell brothers never did neither. They would have told me about it if they had.'

'You knew the Powell brothers?'

'A little. I got friendly with them after I'd moved in. We'd share a drink in our rooms some nights. I wasn't part of the Temple they belonged to. The newspapers said I was, but they got that wrong.'

'The Temple of Tranquility?'

'Yeah. They take in dope addicts, try to wean them off it, preach all this Black Star Line stuff at them, you know, Marcus Garvey, back-to-Africa. They tried to get me to go down there a few times, but it wasn't my thing. All that hokey voodoo stuff they found in our rooms? I never saw it before in my life. Not in my room, not in their room.'

'So if you didn't go to the Temple of Tranquility and you didn't go to your job, what did you do all day?'

'What do you mean?'

'What did you do all day? With your time? How did you spend it?'

Tom shifted in his seat. 'Walk,' he said, sheepishly.

'All day?'

'Sometimes. I'd walk all the way down to Battery Park and back again. Catch the train out to Brooklyn or Queens and walk back.'

'Why?'

'So maybe when I got home I was so tired I'd pass straight out. Some days I'd drink.'

He looked embarrassed. Ida felt a pang of sympathy and she knew from her own bitter experience what he was trying to hide, and that this story about walking the streets was the truth.

'Some days when it was raining I'd go to the library,' he said. 'There's a soup kitchen in the neighborhood for veterans, I used to help out there sometimes, too.'

'Is that what you did the day of the murders?' she asked. 'Go walking?'

He nodded. 'I woke up, washed, left the hotel. Caught the subway down to Coney Island, walked up the coast to Sunset Park. Bought a sandwich. Caught a bus to Brooklyn Heights. Walked the rest of the way home. I got back about nine.'

'And when you got home,' said Ida, recalling what she'd read in Tom's police statement, 'you went to sleep and woke up to the sound of screams?'

'Yeah,' said Tom. 'I went downstairs and saw the Powells were dead, went into the reception area. I saw the money and the dope in Bucek's room, stepped inside to take it, and that's when the police arrived.'

Ida stared at him. 'Tom, I'm gonna level with you,' she said. 'This doesn't look good.'

'You don't think I know that?'

'This whole account doesn't make sense. No one's going to buy it. You need to tell us a plausible story.'

'I'm telling the truth.'

'You're saying four people were butchered in the same building as you and you slept through it. All those people died and they only screamed once? It doesn't add up. Plus, you walked into Bucek's room because you saw his stash and money there?'

'I was broke.'

'Tom, if you want a jury to believe it was someone else who killed those people you're going to have to explain why the killer left Bucek's money and drugs out in the open, where you could see them from the corridor.'

Tom looked at her flatly, with an inscrutable gesture that reminded her of his father.

'And your fingerprint on Powell's watch,' Michael added quietly. 'How are you going to explain that?'

'I don't know how any print got there,' said Tom. As soon as he said it, he lowered his head, and Ida wondered if he was crying. She shared a look with Michael. Tom raised his head, and she saw his eyes were dry, stony.

'I want you to tell me in detail what happened that night,' Ida said.

'OK,' he said. 'I got home about nine and I went and took a shower. I was sweaty from the walk. I came back to my room, poured myself a few drinks and passed out. I had the radio on. I woke up at some point, heard something, screaming maybe. Heard a car outside. It was hard to tell 'cos the radio was on, and 'cos of the nightcaps I'd had, and how damn tired I was. I went back to sleep. Few minutes later I heard another scream. I woke up. I didn't know what to do. I waited. Didn't hear nothing else. Then I went down to see what was going on. Saw Lucius's body on the second-floor corridor, Alfonso's in their room. Suddenly I was back in the field hospital in Saipan. My head was spinning, I wasn't thinking straight. I snapped out of it eventually, realized

I'd better go check on Miss Hollis. Walked into reception, saw her all cut up, blood everywhere.

'Then I saw the light on in the back room, at the end of the corridor, the door was open. That door had never been open in all the weeks I'd lived there. I walked over, looked in. I saw Bucek's body, saw how cut up he was, and the first thing I thought was what the hell's a white boy doing here? Then I saw the money and the dope. I should have got out of there and called the cops. But I didn't. I went in to take the money 'cos I sure could have used it. Next thing I know there's police rushing into the room.'

Tom looked at her, and across to Michael. Then something seemed to break in Tom, some wall whose debris tumbled out of him in a long, pained sigh.

'That's the God's honest truth,' he said. 'I never killed any of those poor people. And whoever it was that did it, sometimes I wish they'd killed me too, so I wouldn't have to be sitting here in this hellhole facing the electric chair.'

He paused, his lip trembling, tears forming in his eyes. Ida could see he was telling the truth. As surely as he was lying about what he was doing in the hotel and why he'd quit his job at the hospital, she knew he was being honest when he protested his innocence. When he spoke again it was in a shaky voice, filled to the brim with emotion.

'I don't know what happened that night,' he said. 'I don't know how that stuff got in our rooms. I don't know why I didn't wake up earlier. I'd been drinking, maybe that's why. I had the radio on. My room's five flights up from Bucek's. Three flights up from the Powell brothers'. Here's what I do know. Someone dumped all that voodoo stuff in our rooms. Someone put my fingerprint on Powell's watch. Someone tipped off the cops 'cos they turned up there faster than any cop's ever responded to anything in the whole history of Harlem. And none of us had ever seen Bucek before his body turned up in that room that night.'

He lowered his head and sobbed.

Michael reached out a hand and clasped Tom's across the table. Ida looked around the room, at the other inmates, bruisers, thugs, killers. She thought again how easy it would be for the cops to arrange a jailhouse hit to keep him quiet. How if it came to an attack, he was as good as dead.

10

As the ferry departed the island, Michael leaned against the railing and looked south across Ward Island to Manhattan, its monoliths silver and pale. In the distance coal barges and lighters blew their horns, seagulls squawked to one another in their jangling language, one noise more melancholy than the next.

On the deck the same families who had been on the journey over sat in their places once more. The nervous excitement they'd displayed on the way there had evaporated. Even the children sat slumped in their seats, allowing the gulls to circle the boat unmolested. What had been an appealing river cruise on the way over, was nothing but a commute on the way back, an obstacle to the warmth of home. Michael had undertaken the journey countless times since Tom's incarceration and he knew the feeling well, the depression of spirits, the grayness, the way the prison seemed to suck all the energy out of limbs and minds. It was on these rides back from Rikers, on the freezing waters of the river, that he missed his home the most, missed his wife all those miles away, was gnawed by sadness and guilt.

He tried to imagine what a prosecutor and a jury would make of Tom's statement, his feeble explanations, the fingerprint on the victim's watch. It inevitably led Michael to nightmares of the chair, wood and leather and metal, crackling with electricity in the darkness.

This was why he'd asked Ida over from Chicago. The best detective he'd ever worked with. His protégée, his colleague, his friend. If there was anyone who could help him find a glimmer of hope in the situation, it was Ida.

'Smoke?' she asked.

He turned to see her standing next to him, holding out the silver cigarette case he'd passed on to her when he'd retired. Michael had received the case himself from his own mentor and he wondered what had happened to the man all those years ago in New Orleans. He plucked a cigarette from the case and they lit up.

'You never told me what happened with the job offer,' he said.

She turned to look at him with an awkwardness that made him think of the nineteen-year-old girl he'd first met in Chicago almost thirty years ago, fresh off the train from New Orleans, shivering in the northern snow. He was proud of the woman his protégée had become, the way she'd dealt with all the traumas that had come her way, the death of her son's father before the boy was even born, having to raise him alone, and then the death of the man she'd married afterwards, killed in the war. *Sick at heart and lonely to her bones*, Michael's wife had said about Ida after a Christmas party a couple of years back. But she'd battled through it. Although, with her son going off to college, Michael guessed the loneliness had returned. For the first time in years Ida had that look she'd had when she was young; that lost look, that vulnerability, that sense that she was easily bruised.

'The job offer,' she repeated, almost wincing.

A few months earlier she'd approached Michael and asked his advice about a job proposal that had come her way – an investigator from the Treasury Department whom Ida had collaborated with on a few cases had offered her a role in a new agency being set up in Washington. President Truman had signed the National Security Act back in July, formed the Central Intelligence Agency, for which Ida's acquaintance was recruiting. The job would mean Ida leaving her own agency, taking up a post in California. She'd been debating whether or not to take the job ever since, and as far as Michael could tell, she hadn't yet reached a decision.

'It's still on the table,' she said eventually. 'There's security checks I need to pass. People need to vouch for me. I'm not exactly the regular type of person they hire.'

'No, I don't suppose you are.'

They smiled, fell silent. Michael stared at the choppy waters ahead, felt Ida looking at him, thinking of a way to broach the subject.

'It's not so bad,' she said eventually.

'Don't sugar-coat it, Ida,' he said. 'If it was anyone else but my son we'd both be sitting here talking about how guilty he was.'

'But he *is* your son. We both know him. We know he could never do something like that.'

He paused, took a toke on his cigarette, nodded.

'I used to be so proud of him. I gave him a chunk of the reward money from the Van Haren case and he used it to pay his way through medical school, became a doctor. How many colored doctors are there in the country? Then he volunteers to work as a medic in the war. And then he comes back, and what? He quits his job, moves to a flophouse, spends his days walking the streets, getting drunk with a pair of down-and-outs. I don't know who that person is, Ida. I don't know why he's lying to us.'

He met Ida's gaze then turned to stare ahead again. In the waters near North Brother Island a tug-boat blew its whistle, long and plaintive.

'Plenty of men came back from that war damaged,' Ida said. 'They don't all turn into knife-wielding maniacs. I know your son told us some lies, but he was telling the truth when he said he didn't kill those people.'

'I know he was,' said Michael.

'So if Tom didn't kill them, someone else did,' Ida said. 'That's where we start. Someone else went in there, killed those people and left. Then Tom woke up in a drunken stupor, went down there, stupidly tried to steal the money out of Bucek's room and got caught.'

'Why would someone break in and kill them all?' Michael asked. 'Why them? Why that particular hotel on that particular night?'

He'd been down these avenues of logic countless times over the last few weeks, and his suppositions all ended in dead ends, creating just as many questions as answers.

He watched Ida take a drag on her cigarette, stare across the waves. They were approaching Manhattan now, could see the bows of the ships birthed along the docks.

'Let's put aside the crazed lunatic theory,' Michael said. 'Let's say it wasn't a random attack. Let's say someone went in there to deliberately kill those people and then the cops went in afterwards to cover it up. Why did they do it? Why does someone walk into a hotel and slaughter its residents like that? And why do the cops collude in it?'

'Maybe someone broke in to steal Bucek's stash and money and it all went wrong,' Ida said.

'I don't know,' he replied. 'All these people killed with a machete. You don't take a blade to a smash-and-grab, you take a gun. And you don't hang around cutting up bodies, and you sure as hell don't leave the money and drugs there.'

Ida looked at him and nodded. 'You're right,' she sighed. 'But whatever's going on here, my money's on it being connected to Bucek. He's the piece of the puzzle that makes the least sense of all. He's a white kid from Queens. He gets back from the war. He returns to his old job, living with his parents. Then one day he disappears, and turns up six weeks later dead in the Palmer Hotel with a pusher-sized pile of dope and money.'

'And toxicology reports saying he had large amounts of heroin in his system,' Michael added.

'You don't go from salaried employee to dope-addict-pusher in six weeks,' said Ida. 'And the whole time he was there, Tom never saw him?'

'And neither did the Powell brothers.'

Crime scene photos flickered through Michael's mind. Bucek on a slab in the morgue. Pale, skinny. His torso slashed to pieces.

'There is something I've been thinking about,' Michael said. 'But so far, it's a dead end.'

'Go on,' said Ida.

'Maybe Bucek was in there hiding out,' Michael said, voicing the one conclusion he'd come to in all those weeks that seemed to make sense. 'Hiding out from something or someone. He'd gone on the lam. And whatever it was he was running from caught up with him that night.'

Ida mulled it over.

'That works,' she said. 'Except for one thing. If you're a white kid looking to hide out in New York City, why in the hell would you go to black Harlem? It's the area you'll stick out the most.'

Michael nodded. 'And there's the dead end,' he said.

They fell silent, watched the traffic ploughing across the water, the gulls.

'I buy the police conspiracy angle,' said Michael. 'I buy them dumping the voodoo stuff, turning up so soon. I even buy them getting the hotel owner to doctor the guest book. But what about the fingerprint? Tom's fingerprint on the Powell brother's watch? That's the most damning piece of evidence in the whole case. And I just can't see a way out of that.'

Ida looked at him, frowned.

'Any forensic can move a fingerprint,' she said. 'Find a touch plane in Tom's room. Spray a print with ninhydrin, impress it onto clear tape, lift it, deposit it wherever you want. Flat surfaces work best, like the glass of a wristwatch. I know a professor in Chicago, an expert witness; he'll testify to say all that fingerprint proves is someone in the NYPD was involved. Add it together with everything else. It all works in our favor.'

Michael processed what she was saying, felt a tide of both relief and embarrassment rising up, tried to swallow it down.

'What is it?' Ida asked.

He shook his head. 'I didn't know that about transferring a print,' he said quietly.

As much as it provided hope, it made him feel out of touch, rusty, useless, old. She must have seen she'd knocked his confidence, bruised his pride, because her expression softened.

'Why would you know about it?' she replied, in a gentler tone. 'It's new technology. You've not been working for how many years? It's why you asked me to come.'

She looked at him and smiled, and it reassured him, warmed him, stirred some long-dead optimism inside him. This was exactly why he'd asked her to come, to feel that distant glimmer of hope.

The ferry reached its slip and they disembarked with the other passengers, headed along 134th Street to the subway station at Cypress Avenue.

'Have you told Tom about the police angle?' Ida asked. 'About what it means? The danger he's in?'

Michael shook his head.

'I just told him to be careful,' he said. 'Explained what to do to keep himself safe.'

They reached Cypress Avenue just as the last of the morning's Sanitation Department trucks were rattling past, heading for the dumps to the north of the city. The grinding machines in the rears of the trucks were still churning, sending a grating noise into the air, trailing a stench down the street.

They watched the convoy as it roared past, then Ida turned to Michael.

'I'm going to go to my hotel and check in,' she said. 'Let me have the case jacket. I'll go over it this afternoon and we'll talk in the evening.'

He nodded, passed over the binder. Then he took a spare set of keys for the apartment he'd rented in Midtown and passed them over, too.

'So you've got the run of the place,' he said.

He'd offered to let her stay at the apartment, but she'd turned him down, choosing instead to book a room uptown. She took the keys, slipped them into her pocket.

'I'm glad you're here,' he said. 'I couldn't do this on my own.'

'Sure you could.'

'I'm old,' he said. 'Old and rusty. I thought I'd retired and then Tom ends up embroiled in this. Last ten years I've been reading the paper and going fishing. Most I've ever done to challenge myself is the crossword. I should have kept my hand in.'

'You didn't know this was going to happen,' she said.

He shrugged.

'It was bad luck we had to get involved in this, Michael,' she said. 'But not for us, for *them*. They framed the son of the best detective Chicago ever saw. They're not going to know what hit them.'

She smiled at him and the sentiment of her words began to have an effect. He smiled back and they hugged, and the wind blew down the street, icy and sharp, and Michael felt that glimmer of hope once more.

11

Ida sat on the subway train as it rattled towards 125th Street station, staring at the map of the transit system on the opposite wall. Colored lines drooped across the city like spaghetti, black blobs marked the intersections, arrows the directions of travel. Just like the asterisms on the ceiling of Grand Central that morning, the map seemed to suggest everything had its path laid out, a pre-defined passage through the world. This was the reassuring fiction of maps.

She thought of Tom roaming the streets of New York without direction or purpose, his life gone astray. Whatever he'd seen over in the Pacific kept him up at night, made him quit his hospital job, sent him stumbling through New York trying to make sense of it all. She thought how Michael's life, too, had been shunted off course because of it, re-routed to a distant city. And so it was with Ida's husband, who'd been wrenched away from her to fight overseas, leaving Ida behind to navigate his absence.

The train pulled into 125th. She walked crosstown to Black Harlem, through streets that were quieter than they had been that morning. She arrived at her hotel, the Hotel Theresa, a towering building on 7th Avenue that took up a whole block between 124th and 125th. Ida wondered again why she'd chosen to stay in Black Harlem. She was a Negro, light-skinned enough to pass for white, so she had her pick of New York, but she'd settled for Harlem. Maybe the choice showed a lack of imagination, of the independence she liked to pride herself on. As she walked up its front steps, she looked up at the building's white bricks and terracotta, its bay windows, delicate stonework, and thought on the differences with the Palmer Hotel, just a handful of blocks away.

She stepped inside the lobby and crossed to the reception desk. 'Hello. I'm here to check in, please.'

'Name?'

'Ida Young.'

Again that imposter feeling from using Nathan's family name.

'Where you from?' asked the receptionist.

'New Orleans,' said Ida. 'By way of Chicago.'

'I'm from Lafayette.'

The girl smiled and passed over Ida's keys.

The room was small, but it was clean, and, best of all – it was warm. Beyond the bed was the entrance to a tiny bathroom, next to it was a dresser with a radio on it, and next to that a window that looked out onto Seventh Avenue. Ida took off her shoes and hose, washed her feet in the tub, ran warm water over them, felt it soothe her skin.

She returned to the bedroom and shoved the bed into a corner, lay all the documents from the binder out on the carpet in tiles – the witness statements, police statements, crime scene snaps, fingerprint blow-ups, timelines, blood and fiber sample inventories, room layouts, floor-plans. She sat cross-legged in front of it all.

She sifted evidence.

She read everything once, read it again. So much of the evidence didn't make sense or contradicted itself. So much didn't add up. And on top of all that, she had a lingering feeling that she was missing something else, something important. She'd realized long ago that the things which nagged at her mind came in two forms – things that were present but shouldn't be, and things that were absent but shouldn't be. The things that were present created a feeling of confusion – the voodoo dolls, the fingerprint, the money and the dope. The things that were absent were more unnerving –

the missing machete, the missing crime scene photos, the missing motive, the missing killer.

But there was something beyond all that, and because she didn't know what it was, it was all the harder to grasp. How did you clutch at an absence? How did you define the void that would solve it all? The only way was to construct the shape around the hole, its outline, and see what fitted into it. This was what she lost herself in.

Time passed. Thoughts twirled, ideas spiraled. Certain points kept coming to the fore of her consciousness, making themselves known. Miss Hollis savaged in the reception. The Powell brothers sliced up. She put them aside. She thought about Bucek. White boy in Harlem. On the run six weeks. What had he been running from?

She flicked through the morgue shots of Bucek. She looked at the wounds. She compared them to the wounds on Miss Hollis. She stopped on the photos of Miss Hollis's midsection, the groin deformed by the machete, upward thrusts, a steel-bladed simulation of the act of love.

She went back to the Bucek morgue shots, compared them to the crime scene photos. She looked at the mess the killer had made of the boy's torso, noticing how his arms and legs had been left untouched. She looked at the flawless skin of his limbs and compared it to the skin on his stomach and chest, which had been ripped and slashed, lacerated so as to get to the life inside.

As she stared at the wounds she got the feeling again that something was wrong. Ida was clinically detailed when it came to images. Get the imagery right and all the emotions and theories fell into place. What was missing from these images? The question bumped against her mind. She stared and tried to calm herself, waited for the answer to appear in the spotlight of her thoughts.

Nothing came. Her thoughts broke off.

She sighed and looked up at the window. Gray clouds spitting rain. She checked her watch. Hours had passed and she'd not made the breakthrough she needed. But equally in those hours, she hadn't thought of Nathan, of loneliness, of fear. She decided to take a walk to clear her head while it was still light.

She left the hotel and headed west through the afternoon gloom. She stumbled upon a park and decided to walk through it. The rain had melted most of that morning's frost but some of it remained, in patches under bushes and trees, like ghostly white shadows. She sat on a bench, looked up at the branches dissecting the sky, the yellow globes at the top of the lampposts.

She heard a noise behind her – a snake of children on their way home from a school trip. She watched as they disappeared northwards, taking with them their joyful, careless racket. The park became quiet once more, just the wind, the rattle of a newspaper delivery van on St Nicholas Avenue.

A sense of loneliness crept up on her, of detachment. Everyone else's lives in this unfamiliar place were continuing on as normal, moving forward as if she wasn't even there, just as they'd always done. The city hadn't pulled her in, hadn't made a place for her, and so she was outside of it, looking in, contemplating her own absence from the world. That was the loneliness of walking through a strange city – the sense that this was what life looked like without you. This was how ghosts walked the earth. Would this be how she spent her days if she took the job in Los Angeles? Wandering around like a ghost?

It was another reason she had come to New York, to see if she could hack it in a new city, to see if she had it in her to make the break she desperately needed if she had any chance of moving on from Nathan's death, the break she was too scared to put into motion. In the shivering cold of the park, she imagined the Pacific laid out before her, the shush of the waves, glittering sunrise, endless sparkling blue.

She rose and continued walking. She thought of Tom roaming these same streets. She'd known he was telling the truth in the jail about his endless walking because his behavior mirrored hers after she'd learned Nathan had died. She'd taken to working, Tom had taken to wandering the streets, walking all day so when he got home he passed straight out, rather than lie in bed reliving his traumas, wrestling with the bouts of nightmarish introspection Ida knew all too well.

When Nathan had first been sent overseas, she'd faced the situation head on. She'd stayed glued to the radio and newspapers, absorbing the news like clockwork. She let it order her day, made it a routine and a ritual. She couldn't pass a news-stand without scanning the headlines, checking for mentions of Nathan's army fighting in Europe. When the radio was on in a shop or a bar she strained her ears. At the cinema her heart raced as the newsreels came on, raced again when she collected her mail each morning.

And then at some point, fear took hold completely and she became too scared to look. She avoided it all, clung to the mantra that no news was good news. When she walked past a man on the street reading a paper, she no longer arched her neck.

She learned to fear what lay in wait. It was the future that churned up people's lives, that stood like a great blackness in front of the world, a void out of which were thrown wars and epidemics, hurricanes, earthquakes, a farrago of catastrophes. There really was no limit to the horror tomorrow could bring. And all that anyone could do was stay rooted in front of the blackness and be battered by it.

So Ida turned and looked the other way, fell into memories of the past, because the past had one great advantage; you knew how it turned out. Even if it was terrible, at least it had certainty, and so provided comfort in unstable times, balm for the bewildered.

Only late at night, in cold-sweat bouts of introspection, did she view this forced indifference as a betrayal of Nathan. And that was how it continued for over two years, until one day, a telegram came. It didn't say much, except that he'd been killed on the field of battle in Normandy many days earlier. That his sacrifice was heroic.

Ida spent months in a daze, her grief a barrier which made the world go silent. The days slipped by like distant traffic. Only when she was with Jacob did things seem real. He kept her tethered to the world, kept her from retreating completely into dreams of her life as it should have been, if only it had stayed on course. But even her relationship with Jacob was affected. She needed to make sure the bereavement didn't damage him, so every interaction was muffled by that concern, was tainted by it.

When Jacob was at school she immersed herself in work. When he went to sleep, she worked again, worked all the empty hours to stop herself from thinking, from falling down that pit in her mind that her thoughts dragged her to during any moment of stillness.

Then in October of 1945, there was a knock at the door. A chubby young man in an army uniform squeezing his green beret in his hands. He told Ida he had served with Nathan. She invited him in, made him coffee. He had come from New York and was on his way back home to Ohio. He talked to her about Nathan and the years they'd spent together. As he spoke she realized how much of Nathan's life in those final years had been lost to her and the chasm yawned once more. He told her he was with Nathan when he died, and asked her if she would like to know what happened.

What to say? She wanted to know, but at the same time knew that the details of his death would make his ending definite, complete. Vague as things were, they were unfinished. Did the coffin need more nails?

They came to a compromise. He stayed there and wrote it all down instead, filled pages. She made him food and more coffee. In the morning she took him to Union Station. They waved goodbye and never spoke again. She put the pages in an envelope, sealed it, left it in the sideboard and never opened it. And there it stayed, sometimes reassuring, sometimes sulfurous.

Time passed. Jacob finished school and she lost him to a law degree in Berkeley that August and the apartment became ever quieter, and she was alone, really alone, for the first time in nearly two decades. It brought the bereavement into starker relief, concentrated it. What started as a mere sense of loneliness, became loneliness itself, grew, took hold. These last few months she'd realized loneliness had an undertow which could capsize her if she wasn't careful. Then Michael called her about Tom, and she'd come. What better place to be lonely than New York?

She returned to her hotel. Caught the elevator to her floor and as it rattled upwards she felt a pang of longing for her empty apartment in Chicago, the bed so often left unmade, its sheets so often rumpled with insomnia. She returned to her room and it was only then she noticed the hunger gnawing at her stomach. She called down to reception and ordered food. She ate and worked, the work pushing away bad thoughts, as always.

She thought of the money. Of the heroin. Of the white boy. Another lost soul. She imagined Bucek dealing out of a Harlem flophouse. Couldn't make sense of it. But the heroin stash was dealer-sized. The Medical Examiner's report. Toxicology. Dope in Bucek's bloodstream at overdose levels, suggesting Bucek was on the needle, a heavy user, had mainlined just before the attack. He must have been completely out of his mind when whoever burst in and killed him.

She went back to the crime scene photos – to the gashes and slashes, the blood. Again it nagged at her; something was missing from the photos.

What was it?

She put the photos down. She sighed. She looked out of the window, at the dark clouds scudding past in the night sky. Grand Central Terminal came to mind. The constellations on the ceiling. The gods in their robes being pushed along by invisible lines of forces, slaves to their predefined path through the world. Maybe this was why she'd felt unsettled when she'd looked at them.

What she thought was a problem just for humans, also went for stars and gods. Maybe the whole of existence was an exercise in powerlessness, endurance, clockwork.

She thought of the stars and fate, of divination, of entrails, slashes, the flawless skin on Bucek's arms.

She paused. Her thoughts grew still. Then realization rushed through her mind.

That was it.

The missing piece.

She grabbed the morgue shots to make sure she was right. She was. Bucek was a habitual user. So why weren't there needle marks on his arms? No astral map of puncture wounds or comet trails? How easy not to notice they were missing amongst all the cuts and gore. The toxicology reports were a lie. Maybe the killer juiced him up, or maybe the doc in the morgue. Bucek wasn't a junkie, was just made to look like one in a clumsy cover-up.

And just like that, tumblers fell into place, one after the other, unlocking a whole segment of the mystery. The void at the center of things took shape.

Ida jumped up and scrambled for her bag, found the number for Michael's apartment, called him from the phone on her bedside table.

'Hello?' he said.

'It's me,' she said. 'Bucek wasn't a junkie. He doesn't have any marks on his arms. I'm looking at the morgue shots right now.'

Silence on the line as Michael processed what she was saying.

'So if he wasn't a junkie, and he wasn't a dealer, how comes he had a stash of money and drugs in his room?'

'Because they weren't his,' said Ida. 'They were someone else's. Someone else was in that room with Bucek. Someone who owned a stash of money and drugs.'

'A dope pusher was in there with him,' said Michael, realizing. 'And when the attack happened, he either ran off and escaped, or the attackers took him away.'

'Exactly,' said Ida.

That was what was missing, the shape of the emptiness that tied it all together – the hotel had another resident, a mystery guest.

'So maybe Bucek wasn't running *away* from someone,' said Michael. 'He was running *to* someone. Bucek went to hide out with the pusher who lived at the hotel.'

Ida remembered Tom saying no one ever saw Bucek in the hotel, and something else clicked into place. The floor-plan.

'Bucek's room was on the first floor,' she said. 'The only one with direct access to the alleyway on the side. Whoever rented that room could get in and out of the hotel without any of the other residents seeing. A perfect spot for hiding out.'

'And to sell dope from,' said Michael. 'Maybe the hotel owner rented that room out to people he knew were on the run or dealing. Which means the Palmer Hotel isn't just a flophouse, it's a dope-pad.'

'And dope-pads are attacked all the time,' said Ida, grinning. 'That's it. That's the reason for the attack. Bucek wasn't the intended victim, the other man was, the pusher.'

They both fell silent and Ida felt the warmth of a break-through buzzing through her; she wondered if Michael was feeling it, too.

'If all this is right,' he said, 'it means the hotel owner is in on it. He knew there was a dealer there and was probably getting kickbacks, kept his name off the guestbook.'

'But he added Bucek's name to it after the murders.'

'And he took the night of the murders off.'

'That's our lead,' said Ida.

'Yup,' said Michael. 'We need to press the hotel owner.'

PART FIVE

'Bugsy Siegel, who has beaten a great variety of raps ranging from rape to murder, used to be co-captain of the Bug and Meyer Mob of gunmen and blackjack artists. Now he's got things pretty well sewed up in Los Angeles and along the Pacific Coast and is said to be moving into Nevada where gambling is legal. With Eastern and California money, he seems to be trying to build up Las Vegas as a rival to Reno.'

HERBERT ASBURY, *COLLIERS*, 1947

12

Gabriel spent the hours after getting the job from Costello careening through New York in his sky-blue Delahaye, the sports car he had – like so many things in his life – won in a card game. He stopped by the Savoy-Plaza Hotel, where Benny had stayed. He spoke to Orville Hayes, the hotel detective, a man Gabriel had worked with in the past. Gabriel asked him if Benny had taken his usual suite – he had. If he'd left anything in the hotel's safety deposit boxes – he hadn't. If Benny had used the hotel's car service – he hadn't. Strange, because Benny normally did.

Gabriel offered Orville a Frank Costello-sized kickback if he fixed up Gabriel with the phone records from Benny's room. Orville said he'd work on it.

After that Gabriel drove the length of Manhattan, Brooklyn and the Bronx. Looked up Benny's acquaintances – friends, old flames, business partners, mistresses, enemies. He asked them all the same questions, about the money without ever mentioning the money, without letting the secret get out. People gave him the names of more people to speak to. But no one had anything useful to say.

Day turned to night. He went home to catch a few hours' sleep then stopped by the Copa, told Havemeyer he was on a job for Costello. Told him to hold the fort.

Then he visited the nightspots Benny had visited. El Morocco, 21, La Martinique, The Hurricane. When the nightclubs closed Benny and his entourage had headed to the after-hour spots – The

97

Stage Delicatessen, Lindy's, Reubens. The man had even found time to visit 52nd Street jazz spots and Midtown theater-crowd dives. Gabriel's dip into the last days of Benjamin Siegel morphed into a swirl of nightclubs, restaurants, hotels and bars that left him feeling both dizzy and empty, despairing of his old friend's vacuous way of life.

Everyone who'd met Benny on that trip said the same thing – Benny looked good, Benny looked happy, Benny was the life of the party, Benny picked up the tab.

The man was in town begging for money to save his casino and his life, but he spent the trip like he was researching a New York City travel guide. Something didn't add up. Especially when Gabriel thought of Benny at the Copa, looking haunted, holding back.

The only tip Gabriel got came from the manager at Hanson's. Benny had strolled in there one night with fifteen close personal friends. The manager had to rearrange tables. Then he went outside for a smoke and ended up chatting with the driver of Benny's car, a young yid whose name the manager didn't catch.

Other witnesses confirmed the existence of the car and the driver, though not much by way of his identity. If Gabriel could find the driver, he could get a complete list of everywhere Benny had visited, including any banks or stash spots. But how to find the identity of the driver?

Night turned to day and still nothing.

More than twenty-four hours after being given the job, Gabriel was no closer to finding the money. And as his list of people to speak to got shorter and shorter, a realization dawned – he would have to visit the one person in New York he really didn't want to see before he left town. As he became reconciled to the fact, he figured he'd better make an appointment with the Doc, because he was starting to flag, because he needed something to keep him going, because he didn't want to see her sober and sleepless. He needed fortification.

He called the Mackley Hotel, where the Doc worked, and they agreed to meet, appropriately enough, in the drugstore deli on 34th, right in the shadow of the Empire State Building. Gabriel knew the spot. When people threw themselves off the viewing platform twelve hundred and fifty feet above, they tended to land on the sidewalk opposite the drugstore, making it a destination for New York's more macabre people-watchers.

Gabriel got to the deli early. It was small, bright, white-tiled and airy. The pharmacist's counter took up one side of the space; opposite was the deli counter and the tables and chairs. A radio somewhere was tuned to NBC, the volume low. There were customers at the drug counter – a middle-aged woman in a bolero-length fur, and a boy wrapped up in a peacoat – but the deli counter was empty, the old-timer who manned it sitting instead at a table next to the meat-slicer, hunched over a pack of cards.

Gabriel smoked a ciggie, drank a coffee. He looked over at the old man, saw he was playing solitaire and he instantly thought of Costello. His boss was an accomplished player of poker, pinochle, bridge, *sette-e-mezzo*, a Hungarian game called *klobiosch*, but when he wanted to think, he'd break out the cards and play solitaire.

'It's a bum's game,' Adonis had said to him once. 'There ain't no skill to it. You're just sorting whatever comes out of the deck.'

Costello had smiled. 'That's exactly why I play it,' he'd said. 'All it needs is one more suit and it's exactly like the five families.'

And he'd turned his head down and got back to it. Adonis shot a confused look at Gabriel, but Gabriel had understood. Costello was practicing how to deal with whatever was tossed his way out of the pack, by the hand of fate, studying how happenstance cascaded through the world, caused the shifting of alliances, the sundering and recombination of bonds.

The front door opened and the Doc stepped in, stooped against the cold, wrapped up in a fedora and a camel-hair coat. He spotted Gabriel and headed over to his table. They nodded at each other. The Doc was in his sixties, jowly, with splotchy skin and winter in his hair. He took off his coat, draped it over the back of a chair, slid into his seat, wheezing as he did so.

The waiter came over.

'A celery tonic,' said the Doc. Then he turned to Gabriel. 'You eaten? You don't look like you've eaten.'

Gabriel shook his head.

'Bring us some pickles, some bread, whatever the soup of the day is,' said the Doc.

The waiter nodded and headed off. The Doc turned to Gabriel and looked him up and down.

'How's life, Gabriel?' he asked. 'This goddamn cold getting you down?'

Gabriel shrugged. 'Could be worse.'

The Doc gave him a shrug in return, pulled out a paper packet from his coat pocket, and handed it to Gabriel. Gabriel took a peek inside: Benzedrine and Dexedrine to wake him up, Seconal and Nembutal to put him to sleep.

'Better living through chemistry,' said the Doc, pouring a glass of water from the carafe on the table and raising a mock toast.

Gabriel slipped the packet into his coat, slid a large denomination bill across the table. The Doc took the bill, folded it, hid it inside his sports jacket.

The Doc had been an MD at Beth Israel until his junkie nephew was caught hawking stolen prescription blanks on 105th Street and they were traced back to the Doc. He resigned in exchange for the hospital not referring the matter to the medical authorities, got a job in the Mackley Hotel, across the street from where they were. Ostensibly he was employed to look after any guests who fell ill. In reality, he used the consulting room to distribute pills and prescriptions, with the hotel management receiving kickbacks at thirty percent gross.

'You're looking tired, Gabby. How comes?'

'Running errands for Frank Costello.'

'What errands? You're already running his nightclub.'

The waiter returned with a glass and a bottle of Dr Brown's Celery Tonic, popped the cap, poured the drink, put it down on the table. When he'd gone, Gabriel told the Doc about having to look into Benny's last days, without mentioning the missing money. He told him how he'd been at it all this time and had come up blank, and now there was only one person left to see.

The Doc frowned, trying to figure out who it could be.

'Beatrice?' he asked.

Gabriel nodded. The Doc grinned.

'Is that why you needed chemical Dutch courage?' he said.

Gabriel said nothing. The Doc laughed.

The waiter returned once more, this time with a tray bearing a plate of pickles, a basket of rye bread, and two bowls of chicken noodle soup. The Doc broke a slice of bread and picked up a spoon. Gabriel eyed the pickles wearily, unnerved by the brilliant formaldehyde green of their skins.

'Hitler killed how many millions of us over in Europe,' said the Doc. 'And here you are doing the same to yourself.'

'You're the one selling me the pills.'

'I don't mean the pills. I mean you being a lapdog for Costello. You need to move on, Gabriel. Before you wind up as dead as Benny.'

Gabriel knew it, but couldn't say so. He thought instead of Mexico, of Cancun, of flocks of flamingos swooping over the mud flats of Yucatan, the sunset glittering on their wings.

'Mobsterism was a one-generation deal for the Jews,' said the Doc. Gabriel had heard the lecture before, countless times. 'We arrived here, we did what we had to do to survive. Then we moved into the middle-classes and washed our hands of it. You stick around too long doing that kind of thing, you end up dead. The Jews learned it, the Irish learned it. The Italians and the Negroes haven't. What about you, Gabby?'

'I haven't learned it,' he said.

He wasn't sure why he let the Doc hector him thus. They'd known each other since Gabriel was a child, since Gabriel's sister had died. The Doc was on duty at the hospital the night she was thrown out of that window, fell fourteen stories. Gabriel wondered if he put up with the Doc because he'd never really known his own parents, barely remembered them. Maybe that explained Mrs Hirsch, too. Gabriel took his family where he could find them.

'Eastman dead, Rothstein dead, Reles dead,' said the Doc, reeling off a list of Jewish gangsters – the kosher nostra – who'd bit the bullet. 'Schultz dead, your pal, Benny Siegel, dead. You and Lansky won't be far behind unless you change your ways. Adaptability, Gabriel. That's the key to survival.'

Gabriel thought about the Doc's fall from grace, from Beth Israel to hawking pills out of the Mackley Hotel's consulting room. He wondered if this is what he meant by adaptability. He gave the Doc a look which said as much, and the Doc caught it.

'Ah, I know what you're thinking. I'm lecturing you to stay alive and selling you a packet full of death,' he said, jabbing the spoon in the direction of Gabriel's coat. 'But this is part of my own adaptability. I'm saving up to move out of New York.'

'Move where?' Gabriel asked, half expecting to hear the man say Mexico.

'Eretz Yisrael.'

Gabriel laughed. The Doc looked offended.

'Israel's a pipe dream,' said Gabriel, trying to explain himself.

'We'll see,' said the Doc, eyeing Gabriel carefully. 'One thing I know. New York's no place to grow old. You not eating your soup?'

Gabriel looked down at his food. Steam was rising from the bowl. The surface of the broth was broken here and there by gleaming white noodles, carrot, tarragon, strips of chicken. He wasn't in the mood to eat, but he knew he should before he took the pills. He lifted up the spoon and it felt like lead. But the food sent a warmth down his throat and into his stomach that spread throughout his body. He suddenly felt nourished, and tired.

'The Italians were lucky,' said the Doc.

Gabriel looked up at him, but the Doc was busy with his food, somehow contriving to both lecture and fill his face all at the same time.

'Mussolini goes on an anti-Mafia campaign so half Italy's mobsters leave for America. The Jewish and Irish gangsters are moving into the middle-classes, so the Italians fill the vacuum. Luck. Within a few years gangsterism's given the biggest boost it ever saw by Prohibition and they're the ones in place to profit. Luck. Then there's the Great Depression and the whole labor force unionizes and the Italians are there to get involved. Luck. Then there's the war and Mussolini's the enemy so Italian-Americans get trusted advisor status. Luck. Then it turns out J. Edgar Hoover doesn't believe in the Mafia, sends the FBI off chasing communists instead. Luck. These Italians have ridden a wave of luck like nothing I've ever seen. Been riding it for decades. They're as lucky as the Jews are unlucky.'

All the talk of luck made Gabriel think of Costello and his obsessive solitaire-playing.

'What's your point, Doc?'

'My point is their luck's going to run out some day. Soon. And when it does, you don't want to be around, Gabby, believe me. You need to change. Or you'll end up dead.'

Gabriel thought on this. Took another spoonful of soup.

'*A free man thinks of death least of all things*,' he said, quoting a Spinoza line back at the Doc he'd heard the old man reel off a thousand times.

The Doc's spoon stopped moving. He looked up at Gabriel, started laughing.

'Very good,' he said. 'At least I've taught you something.'

The Doc ripped a piece of bread in two and threw it into his bowl to mop up the last of the soup.

Gabriel was still smiling when the death of his sister popped into his head.

'Say, Doc,' he said. 'Spinoza ever say anything about revenge?'

The Doc thought. 'He must have,' he replied. 'Everything you need to know you can find in Spinoza. I'll root around.'

They finished their soup and paid and stepped out onto the cold street. They buttoned up their coats. The Doc looked Gabriel over, sizing him up, like he was in the consulting room, diagnosing.

'There's two ways to be in this world, Gabby,' said the Doc. 'You can have a heart that's made of clay. That can change, be molded by the world, that can leave you vulnerable, damaged, hurt.'

'Or?'

'Or you can have a heart that's made of stone. And that's even worse.'

The Doc patted him on the shoulder and ambled off across the sidewalk, heading for the intersection that led back to his dingy consulting room.

Gabriel watched him go, lit a ciggie, walked over to his car, got in.

He didn't start the engine. He opened up the Doc's packet, dry-swallowed two Benzedrine tablets. Looked up at the Empire State Building. He was feeling gloomy and it wasn't just the job, his imminent departure, the dip into Benny's last days. It had something to do with what the Doc had told him. Something about Israel, or maybe Gabriel's response to it.

That was it.

He'd laughed at the Doc's plan to escape, but how could he not draw a parallel with his own plan to flee to Mexico? Maybe his own dreamed-of escape was just as ludicrous as the Doc's. His heart sank. He wondered if everyone in New York didn't carry around some promised land inside of them, some mirage that would evaporate if they ever actually approached it. Benny had tried to build his dream out in the desert and look where it got him. For the first time Gabriel felt that maybe, despite all his planning, he might never reach Mexico. The feeling transmuted into dread.

He looked up at the cliff-face of the Empire State Building and thought of his dead sister falling to earth. Maybe a body would streak through the sky at twelve hundred and fifty feet of accumulated velocity and explode onto the sidewalk in front of him.

13

Magic hour and the sky was thickening gold. Gabriel parked up on the south side of Union Square and waited for the giant clock on the tower of the Consolidated Edison Building to tick down. He chain-smoked Luckies and thought about things in the rat-a-tat way he did when the Benzedrine was kicking its way through his nervous system. Benny, Costello, the missing two mill, the Doc, the forger, the Savoy-Plaza, Mexico City, Beatrice Iverson, all of them swirling around the wasteland of his head.

He watched the square, its oblong of grass and trees, the ring of roads that ran round its edges, the fringe of skyscrapers beyond. Up near 15th Street was an empty lot where hydraulic cranes were spinning the skeleton of a new building into being. Gabriel thought about the Doc and adaptability. Stone or clay. Gargoyle or man. He thought about New York, changing daily, always shifting, rearranging, adapting itself to fit its own needs, buildings torn down, roads ripped up, bridges raised, land reclaimed, tunnels dug. To leave New York was to miss out on its great tango of destruction and regeneration, danced with steel girders and granite slabs and cranes that pierced the sky. The Doc was right – metamorphosis was the only thing on which you could rely. Adaptability was key.

Night descended. The lights above Orhbach's and S. Klein were switched on, the giant Coca-Cola sign above the building on the corner of 16th Street commenced flashing a bright electric red. The light flooded the sidewalks and the greenery of the square for the few seconds it was on, before returning them to blackness once more. The on-off flashing seemed to make the world vibrate.

Gabriel got out of the Delahaye, popped on his hat, pulled his trench-coat collar up against the wind and dodged traffic to get to the square, cut across it, then crossed traffic once more to get to the building with the giant Coca-Cola sign bolted to its roof. He reached the door and scanned the buzzer labels, found the one for the Beatrice Iverson Dance School and pressed the buzzer. Waited.

It buzzed back and he caught an elevator up nine flights, came out in a cramped corridor and followed signs till he reached the dance studio. The top of the wall between it and the corridor was made of glass, so he could see inside. It was a larger space than he was expecting, a rectangle with a parquet floor, mirrors and ballet rails framing the edges.

A dozen or so girls dressed in leotards were running through a routine while an old fruit in the corner rolled through a polka on a battered, upright piano. At the head of the class stood Beatrice, looking poised and graceful, even though she was only dressed in dancer's leggings and a loose blue shirt. Her hair was pulled up in a bun, and still blonde as hell.

He watched her as she watched the girls, eagle-eyed, gave instructions to the ones that weren't quite doing it right. Even in the slightest movements she exuded athleticism, litheness, that mix of strength and elegance all the best dancers possessed.

She turned and their eyes met through the glass. She recognized him. She frowned. She smiled. And he could see she was swallowing sadness with it. Gabriel's heart raced with equal parts excitement and dread. And the girls continued to polka.

He turned to watch them from the corridor, and Beatrice got back to giving instruction. The pianist finished the song dead on six o'clock and Beatrice wound up the class, and the girls relaxed. Some did stretches, some went straight for their bags and the exit. Beatrice waved him in.

He squeezed through the door as the girls were going the other way, stepped into the studio. The pianist looked at him, then at Beatrice.

She gave him an *it's OK* look and he started gathering up his sheet music.

Beatrice crossed the room towards Gabriel and he saw she was barefoot. They met in the middle and he looked into her eyes, was glad to see they hadn't changed in the chasm of years, still gray flecked with gold, still incomparable.

They stared at each other some more. Gabriel lost.

'How's it going?' he asked.

'It's going,' she said.

Around them, the dancing girls continued to depart, skittering past while throwing on thick winter coats, chatting, lighting cigarettes.

'You should thank me,' Beatrice said, nodding at the last of them. 'If I'd told them you were the manager of the Copa, there would have been a stampede.'

Gabriel smiled. 'We're well-stocked for dancing girls,' he said.

'Try telling them that.'

'Bea,' shouted the pianist. 'I'll be in Dillon's till eight if you need me.'

'Sure thing, Herb,' she said, shooting him a smile, before turning back to Gabriel.

'C'mon,' she said. 'I need a cigarette.'

She turned and crossed the parquet and Gabriel followed. As she walked, she reached back and pulled a bobby pin from her hair, then another, then again, then her hair came loose in a blonde cascade that swept down her back, swayed this way and that, glittered, glowed, left Gabriel mesmerized. She'd done it when he was just behind her. A signature move. Showing him what he'd lost. The fool.

She reached a door at the end of the studio, opened it and they stepped into darkness. He heard a switch being flicked and a weak orange light appeared from a reading lamp on top of a sideboard. He saw they were in a corner office, messy and cramped, strewn with folders and paperwork. There was a desk and a chair and a few filing cabinets and a window that looked out onto the darkness of the square below.

She headed for the desk, sat in the leather chair behind it and stared at him.

Everything flashed red for three seconds. The Coca-Cola sign outside. Gabriel realized they must be right below it.

'You get used to it,' she said.

Gabriel looked around, saw stacks of photos – head shots and publicity shots of dancing girls – scraps of yellow paper clipped to them with contact details. Beatrice was a dancer, with brains enough to realize as thirty was approaching that she didn't have much of a career left, so opted to open a dance school come talent agency. Gabriel had heard she'd been doing pretty well for herself. She'd always had business sense.

She picked up a pack of cigarettes from the desktop, took one.

'Still smoke Luckies?' she asked, tossing him the pack.

Gabriel nodded, took one. Wondered if he was still under the effects of the Benzedrine, and if she could tell.

'I heard the business is going good,' he said.

'Sure. If the talent agency keeps going like it is, I can quit taking classes altogether.'

'You don't like teaching?'

'I like teaching,' she said. 'I don't like the hours. The night-classes. I got another one tonight – eight till ten-thirty. Do that five nights a week plus the day job and pretty soon something feels like it's got to give.'

'Yeah, I know the feeling,' Gabriel said.

They looked at each other again, acknowledging their mutual weariness.

'How's Sarah?' Beatrice asked finally.

'Good,' he said. 'She'll be fourteen next year.'

Beatrice nodded, coming over all sullen, maybe at being made aware of time lost.

'Send her my love,' she said.

Beatrice and Sarah had got on like sisters. The hardest part of calling off the engagement had been telling Sarah it was over. She'd cried for days. This was what he'd been dreading. Going over the past. Beatrice and Sarah was the family he should have had, the life he could have led. He could see the loss of it pained Beatrice just as much as it did him.

'So,' she asked. 'You here for rhumba lessons?'

Gabriel smiled, lit up, leaned against a sideboard opposite the desk. 'I'm looking into Benny's affairs,' he said.

'Little late for that, Gabby.'

'So everyone's telling me.'

'Well, you must be getting desperate coming here,' she said, hitting the nail on the head, as always.

'You see him when he was here in the summer?' he asked.

She frowned. 'What's this all about?' she asked.

Gabriel shrugged, communicating it was a question he couldn't answer. She understood, but carried on giving him that look.

'Humor me,' he said.

'All right,' she said eventually. 'I saw him. He called me up. Said he was in town. We met up. Went out for drinks.'

'He seem himself?'

She paused. 'He was whining a fair bit,' she said. 'So, no.'

'What was he whining about?'

'The Flamingo, what else? How the whole thing was going wrong, how he was in hock to everyone, how he was in town putting the bite on, how he'd had to beg Costello to ask the other families for money. But you know Benny, we had a few drinks, got stoned, and he was back to being happy as a lamb.'

Gabriel nodded. So Beatrice was the only one Benny dropped the happy-go-lucky act for. If only temporarily.

'Where'd you meet him?' he asked.

Again she gave him that look. 'If you tell me what you want to know, I might be able to help,' she said.

Gabriel thought about telling her the truth. He thought about their shared past, the days of youthful fun. Of the eight million souls in the city, she was one of the few he might consider trusting. Despite what he'd done to her.

He shrugged. She sighed.

'Jesus, Gabriel,' she said. 'It was six months ago.'

She paused again, sifted through her memories. Her eyes narrowed.

'We met at mine,' she said. 'He picked me up. We drove to the Astor Hotel. We stayed there drinking. Then we went to Casa Mañana, La Cona, maybe. We stopped off at Kellogg's Cafeteria. Didn't make it to the Copa that night. Sorry.'

She said the last with a wry grin.

'You two see anyone that night?' he asked.

'We were out on the town. We saw most of New York, and much of New Jersey.'

'You talk to his driver?' he asked.

'No.'

'See what he looked like?'

'Just some kid. Gawky. Jewish maybe. Not the usual kind of driver he hired.'

'Benny do anything strange that night?' Gabriel asked.

'Like what?'

'Like say anything strange? Talk to anyone he wouldn't normally. Anything.'

'No,' she said, shaking her head.

But the look in her eyes made a liar of her.

'You sure?' he asked.

'Do me a favor, will you?' she said, 'and sit down. You're giving me the jitters perched up there.'

Gabriel smiled. He pushed off the sideboard he'd been leaning against and sat at the desk opposite her. The red lights outside flashed on and off once more, as if he needed any more warning of the danger.

'What is it, Bea?'

'It's nothing,' she said.

'Tell me. Maybe I can use it.'

'Remember Jasper?'

'Sure.'

'He's opened a bar down in the Village. A fruit place. We made a detour there on the way to La Cona. Benny went in, left me in the car. Five minutes later he came out, told me not to tell anyone we'd been down there. You know, real serious like.'

Gabriel thought. Benny at a fruit bar in the Village. Benny trying to keep it secret. It didn't add up. Even if it was Jasper running the bar.

'Thanks, Bea,' he said. 'You tell anyone about it?'

'Who would I tell?' she said.

Then she smiled and they fell silent. She took a drag on her cigarette, the smoke curling languidly through the red beam coming in from the window.

'Remember Mexico?' she said.

The mention of Mexico startled him, but then he got it. The trip they'd all taken to Mexico back in '42. The war had cut off the Mob's dope-supply routes from Asia. Someone had the idea to get dope from Mexico instead. Mexican poppies weren't as strong, but they'd do till the war was over, plus Benny could oversee the imports from Los Angeles.

Gabriel, Beatrice and Benny headed down there. Gabriel and Beatrice were still engaged back then. Beatrice brought along her brother. They cruised towns along the border, contacted names they'd been given, set up deals. Gabriel heard about some growers further in. Beatrice and her brother headed back to New York, Benny to LA. Gabriel headed down to Mexico City on his own. Met the growers, arranged a deal. Then he heard about the

Yucatan. Headed to Cancun. It was there he'd seen the flamingos, the mud flats, the beaches, the sunsets. It was there he dreamed about when he returned to New York, the waves lapping in his head ever since. It was there the escape plan really hatched.

'Sure, I remember Mexico,' he said.

They both smiled and he realized here was another New Yorker he'd miss when he was gone, even though he hadn't seen her in years. The closer he got to leaving, the more he realized how much there was to lament.

'How's your brother?' he asked.

At the question, Beatrice squirmed, looked uncomfortable for the first time since they'd stood in the dance studio gawking at each other like a pair of teenagers.

Beatrice's brother was a low-level dope runner for the Gaglianos, hence why they asked him to come along on the trip. At some point he'd started getting high on his own supply. Ended up in hock to the Gaglianos and had gone on the lam. Last Gabriel had heard, the Gaglianos had put a hit out on him.

'I don't know,' she said. 'He disappeared months ago, haven't heard from him since. And even before that, the only time I'd see him was when he'd turn up here or at my apartment, dressed in rags, begging for money. I heard he was robbing grannies in East Harlem before he skipped town.'

She looked up at him through the gloom. They stayed silent a while.

'Benny tell you much about the Flamingo?' Gabriel asked.

Beatrice shrugged. 'Just that the whole thing had been a disaster. That he'd borrowed money and was pissing it away. He had real flamingos out there, you know that? On the forecourt. They're not desert birds. Every morning they were scooping up the dead ones and trucking in replacements.'

She paused. 'He named it after her,' she said softly.

'I know,' said Gabriel. Virginia Hill, who Benny called Flamingo on account of her pins.

'I guess Benny was a legs man,' said Beatrice.

'Word is she was stealing money from him,' said Gabriel. 'She had a Swiss bank account set up.'

Beatrice nodded.

'I was there for opening night,' she said. 'I was in LA, had a meeting with a booking agency. Benny heard I was in town, called me up and invited me along. I turned up a few days early, that's how I managed to make it. You ever been to Vegas?'

Gabriel shook his head.

'It's a hole,' she said. 'There's an airport and a strip of highway connecting it to the city and it's all lined with saloons and whorehouses like it's still the wild west. And that's it. I mean, that's really it. An airport and bunch of shitty bars. But you get to the end of it and there's Benny's hotel. It looks like someone ripped a building out of Monte Carlo and dumped it into the middle of the set for *Stagecoach*.'

Gabriel grinned. Beatrice continued.

'On the way back from the airport, he stops and puts his hand on my shoulder and points at all these rundown bars and says, "Imagine this the entertainment capital of America".'

She stubbed out her cigarette in the overflowing ashtray on her desk. 'Then on the opening night the hotel's still not ready, and he's saying we'll have to keep everyone in the casino all night. And then comes the kicker – all his celebrity friends from Hollywood he's paid to come up, all the "fine people" he's been cultivating all these years, they all get stuck in LA at the airport 'cos of a fog. It was the worst opening night in history. You could have cut the atmosphere with a spoon. I've never seen Benny looking so depressed, like he wanted to slit his wrists.

'As soon as the weather cleared up I went back to LA and caught the plane back here. Then he pops up a few months later telling me he's begging for change to keep the place going.'

Gabriel nodded, thought of the missing two million dollars.

'I saw Benny at the Copa,' he said. 'When he was over that

last time. There was something up with him. Something he wanted to tell me. Something he was holding back.'

Beatrice couldn't meet his gaze. She turned to look at the blackness the other side of the window. The blackness turned red. Her eyes glinted in the gloom. And maybe Gabriel's did too.

'There's something you're not telling me,' he said.

She didn't turn to look at him, just carried on staring at the blackness.

'Benny was holding back on me when he came to the Copa,' he said. 'Now you are, too.'

She paused. Then something seemed to shift. She turned to look at him. Her eyes darkened.

'How many years has it been, Gabby?' she said.

He shrugged, even though he knew the number of years and months.

'You sure you want to know?' she said.

He nodded.

She sighed.

'Benny said he'd heard about someone,' she said. 'Someone from the past was back in town. He wasn't sure if he should tell you or not. He asked me what I thought. I told him not to say anything.'

'Who'd he see?' Gabriel asked, a sickness rising up in him. A woozy dread.

'Faron,' she said.

The feeling was like being stabbed. His breath caught, the room seemed to lurch around him, right itself, lurch once more. An aftershock of Benzedrine sent an atomic rumble through his chest. He wasn't sure what to say. A million questions and none of them would come out.

Bea filled the silence.

'He wanted to tell you, Gabby,' she said. 'I begged him not to. I knew what it'd do to you.'

Gabriel tried to think but his thoughts were spinning and he couldn't catch hold of them. He suddenly felt hot, sweaty, faint. He suddenly wanted to get out of there, into the refreshing cold of the street, but he didn't know if he had the energy, it was like the wooziness had exploded inside of him and incinerated all his strength.

'I've got a right to know,' he managed to say.

She paused, softened, nodded.

'You do,' she said. 'But your friends have got a duty to keep you from pain.'

'Where did Benny say he saw him?' he asked. 'In New York?'

She shook her head. 'All he said was he'd heard Faron was back in town,' she said. 'That he'd come back.'

'But he hadn't actually seen him?'

Bea shook her head. 'Just said he'd heard.'

'How'd he hear?'

'I don't know, Gabby.'

'Was he back working for someone?'

'I said I don't know. Jesus.'

He saw she was crying. Teardrops nestled in her lashes, catching the light of the city from the window, holding it tight.

'I'm sorry, Gabby,' she said.

'Don't be,' he said. 'I'm glad you told me. It's more than Benny did.'

'We didn't tell you 'cos we didn't want you doing anything stupid,' she said.

He glared at her. Shook his head. Stared at the floor, felt the past churn up his insides, felt long-dead demons resurrecting.

'I'm sorry about what happened,' he said.

She looked at him and shrugged.

'I guess it's time I split,' he said.

She nodded.

He rose, and was surprised to find the room only swayed a little. They headed out of the bloodshot office, through the studio, to the corridor.

They stopped at the door, looked at each other.

'I'm sorry, Gabby,' she said.

'Don't be,' he said.

He saw the teardrops still caught in her lashes.

'Come by the Copa sometime,' he said.

'Sure,' she said, although in the years since they'd split up, she'd studiously avoided the place.

'And if you ever want to come back here for a dance lesson,' she said, 'let me know. I could improve your footwork.'

'You already have.'

He turned and headed down to the street.

Nine days to go, and the man who killed his sister was back in town.

PART SIX

DAILY NEWS

NEW YORK'S PICTURE NEWSPAPER

City Edition Final   Tuesday, November 4th 1947

NATIONAL NEWS

'SCARFACE' AL CAPONE DEAD AT 48

UNDERWORLD KINGPIN OF A VANISHED ERA PASSES AWAY AT FLORIDA HOME

Leonard Sears – Chief Crime Correspondent

Miami Beach, FL, 3rd Nov. – Al Capone, ex-Chicago gangster and Prohibition Era crime leader, died in his home here tonight. 'Death came very suddenly,' said Dr. Kenneth S. Phillips, who has been attending Capone since he was stricken with apoplexy on Tuesday. Dr. Phillips said death was caused by heart failure, which in turn was caused by the social disease Capone had suffered from for years.

For more on this story, and a full obituary, turn to page 4.

14

Tuesday 4th, 5.30 a.m.

Winter hadn't even started and already Frank Costello had a cold. He went to bed fine, woke up at four in the morning gasping, like he couldn't breathe, like he was drowning in mucus. He spent the next few hours lying in the twilight, hocking up emeralds, summoning the strength to get down to the pharmacy. Every time he inhaled it was like the lining of his nostrils was on fire. There was an acrid lump of something at the top of his throat that no amount of coughing or blowing would dislodge. He tried till his ears popped, till his eyes watered, till Bobbie kicked him out of bed.

He needed lozenges, tissues, cough syrup, eucalyptus oil, the works.

On top of the movie producers, and the missing money, and Gabriel acting shaky, and the war with Genovese that was brewing, and the fact that he was in debt to every other mobster in town – and that they would have killed him earlier that year if Luciano hadn't intervened from his exile overseas. On top of all that, a goddamn cold.

And what made it worse was it meant he couldn't smoke.

So he got up at half five like he normally did, but instead of taking the dogs for a walk through Central Park, he threw on a coat, a silk scarf and a Stetson and headed down to the pharmacy on 70th. Saw it didn't open till eight. Felt like an idiot. Went back to the apartment.

He made himself a black coffee and ate a piece of buttered toast – his regular breakfast – even though the toast stuck to the thing in the back of his throat and sent him off into a coughing fit again. He read the paper. Saw the article about Capone dying. Felt a pang of sadness, more at the passing of an era than for the man himself. Capone had been dying for years. Costello had caught wind of it on the prison grapevine back in the thirties. Capone had lost his mind in Alcatraz from the syphilis. People who'd gone down to see him in Florida after he'd been released said he acted like a child, a goofball, wheelchair-bound, dribbling, couldn't remember his own name. And so had died the last ghost of the twenties.

Costello made a note to send a wreath to the funeral.

As he read, the sun rose, sending gold across the lofty spears of Manhattan. He watched the effect, watched the smog coming in from the factories across the river in Jersey.

At seven-fifty-five, he left the apartment and went down to the pharmacy again. Eight o'clock rolled around and still the place wasn't open and Costello was standing on the street like a bum. Goddamn he wanted a cigarette. He'd smoked through colds before. He'd even smoked through cancer a couple of times. But he knew it didn't help. Lay off the smokes and the cold would go away a whole lot quicker.

Five past eight and he was inside the pharmacy, told the man behind the counter to give him everything he had. Left five minutes later with a paper bag stuffed full.

He returned to the apartment and loaded up his pockets, left again. He waited on the street while the concierge strode out into the road and flagged him a taxi. Costello palmed the concierge a twenty. Everywhere he went, he did so in a cloud of tips.

'Where to?' said the cabbie, flipping the flag on the meter down.

'Mulberry,' said Costello.

The cabbie merged into traffic. Costello made plans. Another day of keeping the empire intact, keeping himself from being killed or arrested, thinking three steps ahead. He had to drop off money for a widow, then go on to a meeting with Cheesebox Callahan about the movie producers, lunch with Adonis, then he had to go to Duke's for the weekly strategy meeting, and finally an appointment with Dr Hoffman.

He stared out of the window and watched the city waking up, kids selling papers on street corners, men loitering by their shoeshine stands, shivering in the cold. He watched the shops flickering past, the clots of traffic at every intersection. As they travelled south, the numbers of the cross-streets ticked down, 60th Street, 59th, 58th, riding Manhattan like an elevator.

They got snared up in Midtown where the tracks of the street-car that ran crosstown to the 42nd Street ferry were being ripped up. The cabbie had to drive all the way over to 5th before he could get around the roadworks, got stuck behind a double-decker bus.

'I hate these jams,' said the cabbie. 'But I ain't sad to see the street-cars go.'

Costello nodded, even though he disagreed with the sentiment.

Everything in the city was changing. The street-cars were being lost, the elevated tracks, the tenements, too, were being pulled down, the slaughter yards of Turtle Bay were being cleared to make way for the United Nations; in Jamaica Bay, Idlewild was being turned into an airport. Old New York had survived the war and now it was being ripped up by reformers.

When Costello was growing up, men from his slum left their houses each morning to travel to Queens and the Bronx to help lay down bricks for all the tenements that were springing up. Italians were given the worst jobs back then, digging tunnels, sewer work, hauling garbage. It was why so many mobsters still claimed to work in the garbage industry. Now those same tenements built by the vanished men from Costello's childhood were being pulled down, to be replaced by the solution to New York's housing shortage – the projects – low in rent, low in crime, high in stories and dreams.

When Costello was young he loved how New York was always shifting, making room for itself; now he was getting older, he just wished it would stop. The faster things changed, the more the past jostled against the present, the more the friction of the future was felt.

He watched out of the window as they passed the roadworks, travelled down 5th. Midtown turned into Greenwich Village turned into Lower Manhattan.

The cab pulled up at the corner of Mulberry and Grand.

Costello paid and hopped out, crossed to the building where the old woman lived and ascended two flights to her apartment. Her husband was serving ninety years up at Dannemora, a prison so far north, so remote and cold, it had been nicknamed Siberia. Costello knew it well. It was where Luciano had been imprisoned, the head of Costello's crime family who had since been deported to Italy. It was in the prison when Costello went to meet with Luciano that he found out he had been made acting boss. At the time Costello was already a millionaire, semi-legit, could have made a go of going straight maybe. But out of nowhere, he was put in charge of American organized crime, in charge of a family of nearly five hundred criminals, sucked into the power vacuum against his will.

The old woman opened the door. Costello stepped inside. Like most cold-water tenements the front door opened into the kitchen. It was a dim and dreary place, the only light coming in from a tiny window that was obscured by a fire escape. Costello handed her the monthly packet.

Her husband could have squealed, could have landed Costello and Luciano and Adonis with electric-chair convictions. But he hadn't. He chose to spend the rest of his life in Siberia, and this was why, so his family could eat. There was enough money in the packet to see the woman into a much nicer apartment; Costello couldn't fathom why she stayed where she was.

She took the packet with a bowed head and moans of thanks,

like she'd received a benediction. He didn't have to deliver the packets personally, but he did. He liked doing it. Liked staying in touch. And it wasn't all altruism. Word got around. Others in the family knew that if they kept their mouths shut, their people would be looked after like this.

When she heard Costello had a cold, she dragged him to the kitchen table for some chicken soup she happened to have made the day before. He tried his best to get out of it – he was supposed to be having lunch at the Astoria, like he always did, where the best chefs in New York prepared his food. He didn't want to eat here, with this old crone, in this hovel, but she assured him her soup would make him feel a million bucks.

So he sat in her cramped kitchen for politeness's sake and they chatted while she heated up the soup in an ancient pot on a two-ring gas burner. As they batted the breeze he noticed a crucifix in the gloom, high up on the wall. A cheap plastic thing dipped in phosphorescent paint to make the savior's body glow a sickly green. Costello thought of the garish billboards that floated over Times Square in the night.

The woman laid the bowl on the oil-cloth-covered table in front of him.

Within a few spoonfuls his sinuses cleared, he could actually taste the soup, he could smell again. The aroma coming off the bowl, the faint scent of mold in the room, the wax she'd used on the linoleum floor. The woman was right; he actually felt OK.

Before he left she handed him a brown paper bag of oranges, from a grocer who got them from Italy, just like they were back home. She assured him they too would help the cold.

He thanked her and left.

Next.

He had to walk all the way to Broadway to find a cab.

'Where to, pal?'

'The Astoria.'

He broke open one of the oranges on the way back uptown, and it did taste good, just like the ones he'd eaten on his only visit to Italy.

When he got out of the cab he walked past the Astoria, crossed the street, kept going, to a nondescript office building just opposite. He spoke to the receptionist and caught the elevator up four floors. He knocked on a door and was let in to a shady, stuffy room with a window that looked out onto the hotel opposite. The room was filled with telephony equipment, wires everywhere, magnetic tapes, recorders. There were four kids in there, sitting at a table with headphones on, listening, writing down notes. And in the middle of it all sat Gerard 'Cheesebox' Callahan, Costello's telephony expert, a New York Telephone Company employee who'd gone rogue. Costello had met him in the thirties when Cheesebox used to gaff his slot machines for him. Since then, Costello had been using the Irishman to sweep his own phones for government bugs, to put bugs in other people's phones, to inter-fere with race-wires so Costello and his pals could bet their lungs out on races they already knew the results of.

Like the kids in the room, Cheesebox had headphones on, was listening to something. When he saw Costello he held up a finger – signaling for him to wait. Costello nodded, walked over to the window, stared down into the street below. He could see the Astoria opposite, its granite walls with their art deco gold trim and grid of windows.

Somewhere inside the hotel, over two days the following week, representatives of all the studios in Hollywood would meet, forty of them in total, to decide the fate of the Hollywood Ten, the movie-men who'd refused to testify to HUAC, The House Un-American Activities Committee. The Hollywood Ten had been cited for contempt of Congress and the movie industry needed to formulate a response. Some of the studios wanted to blacklist the men, kick them out of the industry, side with the government in its anti-communist crusade. Others wanted to defend the men, stand by their rights, were spoiling for a fight with the authorities. Their final decision would affect the Mob, so their business was Costello's business, and with the meeting in New York, he could influence the decision. Costello had no clue why they had chosen New York as the venue for the hastily convened conference, a city right on the other side of the country from Los Angeles.

It was a rare stroke of good luck. Movie-men would be pouring into the city over the next few days, hence all the equipment in the room, the feverish activity.

'Been grocery shopping?' said Cheesebox, taking his headphones off, pointing at the paper bag of oranges in Costello's hand.

Costello tossed him one.

Cheesebox was named after a gadget he'd invented; a wooden cream-cheese crate filled with telephonic equipment that could be connected to New York Telephone Company phone lines. The box was an exchange in miniature, relaying incoming calls to a different address. Bookies would give their customers a number to call – the number of the address where the cheese box was installed, and it pinged their calls on to an address in a whole other part of town. Government agents tracking illegal bookmaking operations would spend months tracing a bookie's line, then bust the number's address, only to find an empty room with a cheese box in it. Since then, Costello had bankrolled him to expand his operations.

'Been a few marks coming in early,' Cheesebox said. 'We've already been listening in on them.'

He put the orange on the table, handed Costello a bunch of spiral-bound pads filled with pencil scrawls – the notes the kids had made from the wires they were sitting on.

'Good work,' said Costello. He slipped the pads into his pocket, nestling them against his pharmacy supplies.

'Over the weekend we're going to get bugs into the function room they're holding the meeting in,' said Cheesebox. 'The restrooms next to it, too. In the meanwhile, we'll work on the remaining rooms.'

It was Costello's pal Jack Warner who'd tipped him off about the meeting, had told him which producers were likely to vote for blacklisting, which wouldn't, which he wasn't sure about. Of the dozen or so who definitely weren't, Costello had already arranged female company for six of them, would have photos taken, just in case. He didn't like the blackmail angle, it was a last resort. Always best to talk to people first.

It left another six producers. Cheesebox had bugged the hotel rooms they'd be staying in. Costello had experience of swinging elections. He'd done it countless times with City Hall and New York's judges. He and Luciano had even swung the presidential candidate for the Democrats back in '32 at the convention in Chicago, swung it Roosevelt's way.

'There's, uh, something else I need to tell you about,' said Cheesebox.

'Go on.'

'These two producers who turned up early. Rosberg and Jackson. They had a lunch date with someone you might be interested in.'

'Who?'

'Your old pal Vito Genovese.'

Costello felt his spirits sink at the mention of the name. What was Genovese doing interfering in the Waldorf meeting? Genovese's interests lay on the East Coast and in Europe. In the transcontinental dope line he'd set up, moving heroin from Asia to Europe to New York, where it was distributed around the country. Genovese wasn't involved with the movie-men out in LA. Or at least, he shouldn't be.

'You catch it on the wires?' Costello asked.

Cheesebox shook his head.

'The two of them went out for lunch,' he said. 'When they came back, we caught them talking about the meeting they just had with Vito. Apparently, he made them some kind of offer. They were mulling over whether to accept it or not. It's all in there.'

He pointed to the notebooks poking out of Costello's coat pocket.

'Thanks, pal,' said Costello. 'Keep listening in on them, they might let something slip. Anything else big comes down the wire, you let me know straight away.'

'Will do,' said Cheesebox.

They nodded at each other. Costello popped his hat on and headed out the door.

Next.

The Astoria's Starlight Roof for lunch with Adonis. The top floor of the same hotel Cheesebox was bugging. A short walk back through the mid-day bustle of 49th Street, the cabs gleaming yellow in the wintry sun.

Adonis was waiting for him in their usual booth.

'You brought your groceries to lunch?' he asked on seeing Costello's bag of oranges.

Costello ignored him, sat. 'You hear about Capone?' he asked.

'Yeah, poor bastard. Who're we sending to the funeral?'

'Who can we spare?'

Adonis thought. 'Petrelli?'

'OK,' Costello said. 'Petrelli and the biggest fucking wreath you ever saw.'

Adonis nodded. 'Poor bastard,' he said again.

Costello tossed him the notepads. Told him what Cheesebox had to say about the movie producers meeting with Genovese.

'Maybe he wants to star in a movie,' said Adonis.

'I don't like it,' said Costello. 'What the hell's he up to?'

As long as all the families kept working together and avoided another war, nothing could interrupt their winning streak. And all the bosses wanted to carry on working together. All of them except Genovese. The one man who could bring an end to the golden age. Who didn't get it. That was the thing about golden ages, you never knew when you were living in one. They only ever existed in retrospect. But Costello knew. Because he'd helped usher it in.

And Genovese was threatening it.

The waiter came over and Costello ordered another soup, Adonis a steak.

'Speaking of our friend in New Jersey,' said Adonis, 'I had a call from my boy over in the tenth.'

The tenth was the tenth police precinct, Chelsea. Where Adonis had a cousin who sent information their way.

'Last night they arrested some kid in a sweep on one of them cafeterias off Washington Square Park,' Adonis said. 'Selling dope. When the cops searched his pad they found enough of it to have him sent away for fifteen to twenty. Back at the precinct he offered to rat out his whole supply line, including where his supplier got the dope from.'

'Vito Genovese?' said Costello.

Adonis nodded. 'Said he had evidence,' he continued. 'Offered Genovese up right there in the room, to my cousin.'

This was why Costello told his men never to deal drugs. Not for some moral reason, but because the prison sentences were so harsh, people cut deals, ratted out their bosses to escape them. Drugs were a crowbar into a man's soul.

'What did your cousin do?' Costello asked.

'Said he'd think about it. He called me up this morning. Maybe we could turn him.'

Costello nodded, thought about it. Adonis was suggesting they coerce the kid, make him one of their own informants, someone in the Genovese camp who could feed them information. Costello already had a mole over there in New Jersey – Nick Tomasulo – but Costello had a feeling Genovese was onto him. Genovese wasn't inviting Tomasulo to important meetings anymore, wasn't letting him hear anything that Costello might find useful. He was being treated in much the same way Costello treated Bova, the gym-owner-come-pimp in Costello's camp who was a rat for Genovese.

'What do you think?' Costello asked Adonis.

'Tomasulo's compromised.' Adonis shrugged. 'We need a new mole. It'll take a while for this kid to work his way up, but it'll be worth it.'

It would take a good few years for the kid to rise up the ranks and be useful. Way too late for him to supply anything worthwhile in regards to Genovese's meeting with the movie-men.

'Where is he now?' Costello asked.

'The kid? Still locked up in the basement of the tenth. My cousin's waiting on our word.'

Costello drummed his fingers on the table. Thought about Genovese and the movie-men.

'OK,' he said. 'Let's turn the kid. Tell your cousin to set him loose and we'll pick him up in a couple of days. I'll speak to Anastasia about helping.'

Adonis nodded.

When they needed to turn someone, they got Anastasia to do it.

Their food arrived.

Costello's soup tasted terrible compared to the one he had in Little Italy, but he sucked it up anyway. As they ate they went through Cheesebox's notebooks. A lot of movie-man talk. Which films were coming out, which ones looked like turkeys, which actors were causing problems on set, which ones were sleeping with each other. Adonis drew Costello's attention to an anecdote about the actress Barbara Stanwyck.

'Barbara Stanwyck,' said Adonis. 'Who'd have thought. Good-looking girl like her.'

'What's that got to do with it?'

'Just, you wouldn't think she's the type.'

When they finished eating Costello took an orange from

the bag, peeled it and ate. Adonis eyed him. Costello craved a cigarette.

They rode the elevator down to the ground floor.

'You coming to Duke's?' Costello asked.

Adonis shook his head. 'I'll go and speak to my cousin, get things set up.'

Costello nodded. 'I'll talk to Anastasia. He should be there today.'

They went outside and got the concierge to hail them cabs.

'Barbara Stanwyck, hunh?' said Adonis.

Next.

'Where to, mac?' said the cabbie.

'Cliffside,' said Costello.

'Cliffside, New Jersey?' said the cabbie, in a tone like Costello was an idiot.

'Yeah, Cliffside, New Jersey. You know another Cliffside you wanna tell me about?'

'You're crazy, pal,' said the cabbie.

He turned to look at Costello, to tell him to get out of the cab. It took a moment before his jaw dropped.

'I mean. Yes, sir. Straight away.'

He turned back around, flipped the flag back up so the fare wouldn't be reported and they merged into traffic.

Costello sneezed, blew his nose. He poured eucalyptus oil onto a handkerchief, held it up to his blocked sinuses. The cabbie flicked looks his way through the rearview as they headed down-town, towards the Lincoln Tunnel. Costello knew the man wanted to ask him questions, but didn't know where to start. Costello stared out of the window. He craved a cigarette. He craved another batch of the old woman's chicken soup.

He turned to look behind him and in the trail of traffic saw two black sedans. He always picked up tails at the Astoria, the agents who followed him knew he was a creature of habit. He turned back around. He'd long ago given up trying to figure out exactly which parts of the government were stalking him – the Federal Bureau of Narcotics, the Intelligence Divisions of the NYPD and the IRS. The only agency not interested in him was the FBI, Costello was certain of that. J. Edgar Hoover was too busy looking for communists to bother with organized crime, and Costello wanted to keep it that way. Hence his interest in the Waldorf meeting.

Costello had met Hoover a few times in nightclubs around New York; they had a mutual friend in the gossip columnist Walter Winchell. Costello had found Hoover pleasant company. Hoover being in charge of the FBI was the best bit of luck the Mob had ever had. The one government agency with the reach and resources to take on the Mob, and it was headed by a man who had gone on record saying he didn't believe there was such a thing as organized crime. No one was sure why Hoover thought it, or said it, at least. What mattered, though, was keeping it that way, and part of that was getting the FBI off the movie industry's back.

Around a decade earlier the film studio bosses had looked around their industry and seen most of the workers they relied on had been unionized, a consequence of the Great Depression and the New Deal. Many of the unions were radical, were demanding things, many leaned hard to the left. To get rid of what they saw as communists holding the industry hostage, the studio bosses had done what no sensible person should ever do in those situations – they called in the Mob. The Mob further infiltrated the unions it already had its tentacles in, infiltrated others, then started breaking them up, blackmailing, cracking skulls. Within a few years they'd taken control. It was only then that the studio bosses realized what they'd done – replaced unions backed by communists, with unions backed by the Mob.

Now they were in charge, the Mob put the bite on way worse than the communists ever did. What did the studio bosses expect?

Then came Senator McCarthy and HUAC and the anti-communist probe into Hollywood, a whole decade too late. If the movie industry didn't distance itself from the communists, the FBI would come sniffing around. The best way to stop it all before it became a problem was for the industry to make a big statement that it was with the government, and the best way to do that was to throw the Hollywood Ten under a bus. That way everything stayed as it was – feds vs reds – and the Mob could carry on doing as it pleased. The golden times would roll ever on.

Hence Costello trying to swing the vote at the Waldorf meeting in favor of blacklisting. Hence Cheesebox bugging the hotel.

But in the middle of all this, Genovese was talking to film producers. Why? Costello needed to get to the bottom of it. Genovese ousting him wouldn't just be a disaster for Costello. If Genovese took over the Mob, the golden days were over, because Genovese would run the organization into the ground through violence and bad choices and a basic lack of understanding, because Genovese was everything Costello wasn't – he used violence liberally, smuggled drugs, refused to work with non-Italians, believed power came from shows of force. Costello never understood this logic – to him, the greatest sign of weakness was needing to display your strength.

The cab hit the Lincoln Tunnel and everything went dark. In the blackness Costello thought about the meeting at Duke's, about the appointment with Dr Hoffman in the late afternoon. Dr Hoffman had told Costello the cause of his insomnia was depression of spirits, the cause of his depression of spirits was a lack of self-worth, and the cause of that was his inferiority complex. Or something like that. The solution was to better himself, the doctor had told him, and one way to do that was to consort with better types. It was shrink talk for stop hanging around with mobsters and you'll feel better.

And here he was on his way to Duke's.

If Costello could have stopped consorting with the Mob, he

would have done it. He never wanted to be a mobster, and some-how he'd ended up boss of the whole goddamn thing.

The cab came out of the tunnel and sunlight flashed, bleaching Costello's vision. He closed his eyes, waited for the burn to fade. They spun round the Weehawken helix and headed north towards Cliffside. Costello took in Jersey. All around he saw smoke-stacks, a hinterland of factories and warehouses. To his right were the docks, some burned and rotting in the mud, others alive with traffic – cargo ships, freighters, tugs, lighters, towboats carrying railroad carriages across the sparkling river to the fuzz of Manhat-tan in the distance.

They headed up Palisade Avenue and the cabbie pulled up outside the drab exterior of Duke's Bar and Grill. Since the thir-ties New York's gangsters had been moving to Jersey to escape New York State's zealous prosecutors. So Duke's had become a hang-out. There was good food, soundproof rooms, a suite up-stairs. Some of the Jersey-based bosses were there every day. Costello made a weekly visit on Tuesdays.

Costello got out of the cab. He looked down the street and saw the two black sedans that had been tailing them had pulled up a block further back. He sifted through his bankrolls; he had one in each trouser pocket, right side for spending, left side for loans. He peeled off a hundred and passed it to the cabbie.

'Jeez, thanks, Mr Costello, sir.'

'No problem,' said Costello.

'Sir,' said the cabbie, having finally summoned up some cour-age. 'Can I ask you a question?'

'Sure,' said Costello. 'But quit with the *sir*, would ya?'

'Got any tips for getting rich?'

Don't drive a cab, Costello thought.

'Sure, bub,' he said. 'Steal a dollar a million times.'

The cabbie frowned at him. Costello grinned.

'You steal a million dollars,' he said. 'They'll be after you all your life. But steal a dollar a million times, no one bats an eyelid.'

The cabbie thought about it and grinned. Laid out in those words was the definition of the rackets, of the skim. Take the thinnest of slices enough times, and you'd end up a millionaire and no one would be all that bothered.

Costello turned. The cab drove off. The cold air made Costello cough. He hunched over, felt like he might puke, had to wait a few moments for it all to subside. He rummaged around his pockets for the glass bottle of cough syrup he'd bought in the pharmacy, opened it, downed half of it right there on the street. As he wiped his mouth he looked about him. Noticed more Fed sedans parked on the other side of the street, outside the Palisades Amusement Park.

He turned and walked to the back of the restaurant, to the entrance the mobsters used, went up the stairs, stepped inside a close, smoky room. The blinds were drawn, giving everything contours. A dozen men were in there, arranged around a table that was strewn with money, wires, telephony equipment, tools, racing forms, newspapers, tumblers of whiskey, beers, plates of food.

There they all were in the murk, the lords of the underworld. The racketeers. The vampires. Costello made out Albert Anastasia, Joe Profaci, Tommy Lucchese, Willy Moretti, his brother Solly, Vinnie Mangano. Assorted capos. The five families were all represented, the Jersey families, too. Here were many of the men Costello had convinced to invest in Benjamin Siegel's Las Vegas delusion. The men Costello owed millions to. And maybe one of these men had conspired with Benny to steal the two million bucks Gabriel was currently looking for.

Costello ran his eye over them, one by one. He thought again of Dr Hoffman's advice on consorting with a better class of person.

'Frank,' said a few of the men who'd spotted him.

'You been grocery shopping?' said Willy Moretti on seeing Costello's paper bag.

Costello settled down at an empty spot near the middle of the table, peeled an orange.

'You hear about Capone?' someone shouted at him from the depths of the room.

'Sure,' said Costello.

'Poor bastard,' said Moretti.

'Last time Joe was down in Florida he went by the compound,' said Vinnie Mangano. 'Al was sitting at the edge of the pool with a fishing rod. "Watcha doing?" Joe asked him. "Trying to catch a fish," he said. Trying to catch a fish in a swimming pool.'

There was a pause as they all considered this.

'Poor bastard,' said a voice somewhere Costello couldn't make out.

The chit-chat resumed.

He turned to look at the television perched on the sideboard. It was tuned to a broadcast of the HUAC hearings, showing a flickering image of a furtive, bookish man, sitting on the other side of the table from the committee, reading a statement into a microphone. The glow of the television screen in the otherwise murky room made Costello think of the old woman's apartment that morning, and the phosphorescent Jesus, sickly green, floated in the darkness of his mind's eye.

Next to the television was a radio, with a wire coming out of it that led to a telephone receiver. Cheesebox had connected the race wire to the radio for them, so they could hear the race commentary coming out of the radio, instead of having someone listen in on the telephone and relay them the details second-hand.

Costello made eye contact with Anastasia, the Mob's murderer and torturer in chief. Anastasia was in the rival Mangano family, but he and Costello were close, much to the annoyance of Anastasia's boss. Costello nodded at Anastasia, signifying something was up. Anastasia nodded back. He was a pudgy man with a bulbous nose, and he exuded a sharp, penetrating menace. He'd been a founder member of Murder Inc, the gang of hitmen for hire who killed over four hundred people all through the tail-end of Prohibition, the Depression, and into the forties. Anastasia's personal tally was rumored to be in triple-digits. These days he passed himself off as a businessman.

Costello thought about those triple-digits, about consorting with better types. He got the handkerchief with the eucalyptus oil on it and put it to his nose. The stench of cigarettes in the place was simultaneously making his cold worse, and making him want a smoke.

'Hurry the fuck up,' said a voice. 'The race is about to start.'

Costello checked his watch. It was the Champagne Stakes at Belmont. The men in the room would all be gambling. Every one of them was an inveterate horseplayer. Under other circumstances Costello would have put a few grand on that morning with his bookies in Detroit and Cincinnati. But he couldn't be seen to be gambling while he owed the other men in the room so many millions; it just wouldn't seem right. Even if one of the men might well have stolen two of those millions back.

Solly walked up to the sideboard where the radio was. He turned up the volume on the radio and the race commentary boomed out of the speaker. It drowned out the sound of the HUAC hearing coming from the TV. Costello looked at the black-and-white flickering screen again. It had cut from the HUAC hearings to the face of someone he recognized. Senator McCarthy, talking into a microphone. He was different to when Costello had met him; his face a little fatter, his eyes a little narrower.

'Who's got what?' Costello asked, turning to the room.

'A grand on Vulcan's Forge,' said Willie.

'Vulcan's Forge, too,' said Lucchese. 'Five grand.'

'Two gees on Vulcan's Forge,' said Anastasia.

Everyone else chimed in. All in all, they'd staked close to fifty thousand on the race. All on Vulcan's Forge.

'Jesus,' said Costello. 'What d'you all know?'

The men sniggered.

'What's the odds?' he asked.

'Seven to one.'

The race started. The commentator's voice boomed out of the radio speaker. Vulcan's Forge was nowhere. The men's faces dropped. They started cursing the horse and the trainer and the jockey and the punk who cut the grass. Then, at the halfway call, Vulcan's Forge was in third, then, with two furlongs to go, he was in second. And everybody was up and screaming in Italian. Then, with a hundred yards to go, he was in first.

He brought it home.

Everyone was up, cheering, dancing, someone starting throwing the stacks of cash on the table into the air, a rain of twenties, fifties, hundreds. Someone started singing *Funiculì, Funiculà* like they were all at a wedding and then everyone else joined in, dancing round the table, through the rain of dollar bills.

This was the weekly strategy meeting.

This was the golden age.

PART SEVEN

'A group of industrialists finance a group of mobsters to break trade unionism, to check the threat of Socialism, the menace of Communism, or the possibility of democracy . . . When the gangsters succeed at what they were paid to do, they turn on the men who paid them. The puppet masters find their creatures taking on a terrible life of their own.'

ORSON WELLES, FILMMAKER, 1944

15

First thing that morning Michael had called Carrasco and told him about Ida's theory, that the hotel was probably a dope-pad, that the owner might have secretly harbored a dealer, the real target of the attack. Carrasco said he'd do some digging.

Michael put the phone down and left his apartment, a cramped one-bedroom affair on West 58th and 7th. He walked a few blocks to a gunsmith's. He bought a Belgian .22, a carton of rounds, a holster, a cleaning kit in a faux-leather pouch. He'd returned to the apartment and laid out his purchases on the bed, sat in the chair and stared at them. At first he'd told himself he'd bought it all just to be on the safe side, but the truth was he needed the gun, would be reliant on it, and that rankled Michael, reminded him of all he'd lost, of what he'd become – an old man who was out of touch with the world, who didn't have the confidence in his arms to punch or in his legs to run.

He rose and strapped on the holster, inspected the gun, loaded rounds into its chamber, laid it flat on his palm, felt its weight, gleaming black. Then he slotted it into the holster. Death encased in metal and leather. Echoes of the electric chair.

Michael had been haunted by visions of the chair for weeks. It lurked in the recesses of his mind, crackling with deadly force. If it was the last thing he did, Michael would save his son from it, and that started with getting what he needed to know from the hotel owner. One way or the other.

He waited for Carrasco to call back. Three hours later he did.

His digging had unearthed a possible motive for why the hotel owner had become entangled in it all. Which meant Michael had leverage against the man, leverage that meant he might not have to resort to the gun after all.

Michael caught the subway up to 125th Street. Crossed blocks to the hotel. White man in the ghetto, trailing stares in his wake. But years of living on the Southside had made him immune to it.

He reached the hotel, walked up its front steps once more. The man was behind the reception desk, reading the *New York Mirror*. He lowered it a little, saw who it was, narrowed his eyes. The radio was on again, playing jazz this time. Michael approached the wire mesh, leaned down, felt the weight of the gun nestled by his heart, the pull of the holster's leather. He saw the hotel owner's eyes were red raw from sleeplessness.

'You want to look at the rooms again?' the man asked, a trace of annoyance in his voice.

Michael paused. The man hadn't asked for ID. After Michael's appearance with Carrasco the day before, he assumed Michael was a cop.

'No, I wanted to talk to you,' said Michael. Speaking through the mesh like he was at a confessional.

The man swallowed. 'I ain't got nothing to say to you.'

'You sure?'

They stared at each other, the blur of the mesh shadowing both their views.

'We've done some investigating,' said Michael. 'Looks like maybe you didn't tell the whole truth in your statement.'

'Oh, yeah?' said the man. He let the newspaper drop into his lap. 'How you figure on that?'

'You said you didn't know why the hotel was attacked.'

'I didn't and I still don't. I wasn't here that night. I've told you all this already.'

'It's just a coincidence you happened to take the night off?'

'I take a night off every week. Maybe they knew I wouldn't be around and that's why they attacked.'

'Or maybe someone tipped you off beforehand,' Michael said, laying it out there to gauge the man's reaction.

The man failed to stifle a twitch.

'Looking back it would have been better maybe if you'd stuck around,' said Michael. 'Wouldn't look so suspicious. In retrospect, I mean. Wouldn't look like someone had told you it was going to happen before it did.'

The man did a good job of keeping the glare fixed to his face, but the paper in his hand trembled ever so slightly. The man's reaction went some way to proving the hunch they had about him.

Michael decided to take a chance.

'It's all right,' he said. 'I know you're not the bad guy here. I know you did it for a good reason. Because of your son, right?'

At this the man folded his arms across his chest. Maybe as a display of anger, maybe to smother tell-tale emotions.

'Your son's up in Dannemora, right? Doing a ten-stretch for armed robbery? Up before the parole board in what? Six months?'

The man's lip trembled, he frowned at Michael, acting offended. Which was good.

'Is that what the cops used to twist your arm?' Michael asked. 'Told you if you didn't play along they'd pull strings with the parole board? Keep him locked up? But here's the thing. Thomas James Talbot's in prison, too. But he isn't facing a prejudiced parole board. He's facing the electric chair.'

Something changed in the man's demeanor. His eyes narrowed, his face closed tight.

'You don't know nothing about it all,' he said, leaning back in his chair, playing it hard-boiled.

But Michael could hear emotion in his voice. He was making inroads.

'I know there was a dope pusher in that room with Bucek. And you were getting kickbacks, and a hit was arranged and the cops told you it'd all go smoothly, but the next day you woke up to four people dead.'

'You don't know nothing about it all,' he hissed.

'I know the guilt's tearing you up 'cos you swapped shifts with Diana Hollis and now she's dead. But there's a kid up in Rikers looking at a jolt. And if you don't tell me what you know and you let him die, that's another man's blood on your hands.'

Michael could feel himself getting angry, breaking the first rule he had for working any case. He needed to calm down, check himself, especially with the gun strapped to his chest. But this wasn't an ordinary case.

The hotel owner stared at him through the mesh. Michael could see water in his eyes, emotions swirling across his face. Confusion, pity, guilt, defiance. The man wanted to talk, Michael could see it. He wanted to be unburdened of his sins. But he was scared, too. Michael had offered him absolution, but first he needed to offer him reassurance.

He kneeled down so he was level with the man, looking at him straight through the mesh.

'Tell me what happened,' said Michael, more softly. 'And it won't go any further. I'm not with those other cops. I'm the good guy. I'm the guy who'll make sure no one finds out you said anything. I'm the guy who'll help you save an innocent man's life.'

The water that had been pooling in the man's eyes began to stream down his face.

'You want to save a life, don't you? Make amends?' Michael paused. 'That's gotta mean something to you after all those people died.'

'You don't get it,' the man said. 'I wanna help that boy up in Rikers. But I can't. They didn't say my boy wouldn't get parole. They said they'd have him killed.'

Michael's heart sank. The two of them were in exactly the same bind.

'They're not gonna touch your son,' Michael said. 'One way

or the other. If they think you've talked, it's you they're going to kill. And deep down, you know it. The only way out of this for you, for your son, for everybody, is catch these men and have them locked up. Tell me the names of the cops you were paying protection to. Tell me the name of the dope pusher. Tell me something so I can get started fixing this mess. Don't let them get away with what they're doing.'

The man looked down. 'She was my girl,' he mumbled. He looked up, his face soaked. 'Diana Hollis. You saw what they did to her.'

Michael nodded.

The man wiped tears from his face.

'I didn't know the cops. They weren't the usual bagmen. They just came in that day, stated asking questions, about the guests, what rooms were occupied, where everyone was at night. Then they told me I had to keep it secret that they'd come. Then they started talking about my boy up in Dannemora. But I didn't take the night off on purpose. I always take Fridays off. They must have known that.'

'Who was the target? Gimme a name.'

'Gene Cleveland. He rented the room back there.'

'He sold dope?'

The man nodded. 'He paid me double rent to keep quiet.'

'You know why they were after him?'

'No.'

'Where is he now?'

'I don't know,' the man said. 'He disappeared the night it happened.'

'What about the cops, you get their names?'

The man glared at Michael. 'What do you think?'

'What did they look like?' Michael asked.

'Like cops,' said the man. 'White, middle-aged, red faces, beer guts.'

'Were they in uniform?'

The man shook his head.

'Could you spot them if you saw them again?'

'I ain't doing no line-ups. I thought you said this wouldn't go any further.'

'It won't.'

'Bullshit.' The man's expression hardened, like he'd realized he'd spoken too much. 'You need to go now,' he said. 'I've told you enough.'

'Please, I need to ask you about Cleveland.'

'I've told you enough.'

'I need to know where I can find him.'

'You ain't gonna find him,' said the man. 'After what happened that night, he's long gone.'

'You know anyone who knows him?'

'No!'

The man slammed his fist onto the desktop, hard enough to break bones, trembled as he stared at Michael, mucus pooled on his upper lip.

'I wish I never let that sorry motherfucker in this place. I hope he's dead. Then maybe they'll leave me alone. Now get out of here.'

Michael paused. He'd let the interview run away from him. He could have got more if he'd played it better. But he knew from bitter experience there was no reeling the man back from this.

He rose unsteadily, his hand on the counter, ruing how rusty he'd gotten, how bad his technique, wondered if he'd ever get it back.

'You've done a good thing,' he said. 'But you need to take care. These men might come after you. Not because of what you told me, but just because you're involved.'

'You don't think I know that,' the man said, defeated.

The sun was bright on the street. Michael had a name. From the name he could trace a line back to the attackers. He'd got what he'd come for and the gun had stayed nestled in its holster the whole time. But he didn't feel any sense of achievement. He felt used up somehow, powerless, low.

Two school kids walked past, stared at him. Maybe because he was white, maybe because of all the smallpox scars across his face, the scars that in the past had helped make him look fear-some. Maybe they stared because he looked as much of a wreck as he felt.

He eyed the kids back, watched them as they crossed the road in front of the root doctor's shop with the neon sign. Something nagged. Michael considered, imagined the police arriving on the night of the murders, seeing the carnage, thinking they needed to obfuscate, muddy the waters, seeing the root doctor's opposite, going in there and gathering up the voodoo junk, strewing it across Tom's and the Powell brothers' rooms.

He followed the children's path, approached the shop. Under-neath the flashing green *Louisiana Voodoo* sign was a placard declaring the shop sold *Authentic Mary Laveau Love Potions*. Michael shook his head and stepped inside.

It was a small store, looking something like a down-at-heel pharmacy. There were tiny red lights dotted about, icons of the Madonna on the walls, there was a section at the back partitioned off by an ancient net curtain whose fabric had curdled yellow. The curtain swirled to the side and a man stepped out of the back – middle-aged, dark-skinned, unshaved and unkempt, dressed in a gray wool suit and mustard-yellow sweater.

'Afternoon,' said the man, surprised maybe that his visitor was white.

'Afternoon,' said Michael, browsing the wares on the counter. The hokey, inauthentic aura established by the window display continued inside. There were dream books and spell books and lucky-number books for sale. Rabbits' feet and monkey paws. Crocodile teeth. There were jars full of strange-looking roots in murky liquid, soil, bark-like substances which the labels informed him were snake-skins.

Michael had been involved in busting similar places back in Chicago. The owners were soaking the herbs supposed to help with colds and other ailments in antihistamines. The potions designed to fight off melancholy were laced with morphine. If the customers had known what they'd become addicted to, they could have bought the same drugs on the street for a third of the price.

And there in amongst the herbs and the potions were the same objects found in Tom's room and the Powell brothers' room. The straw dolls, the crucifixes, the icons. The cops had boosted them from here and dumped them in the hotel and probably hadn't even paid the man. A huge risk for the cops to take. Why had they felt the need?

'Anything I can help you with?' the man asked, and this time Michael caught his accent. Louisiana by way of New York.

'Maybe,' said Michael. 'What time do you close at night?'

'Oh, about eight o'clock,' said the man, frowning.

'What about weekends?'

'A little later, depending.'

'What about one Saturday night last summer? When there was the incident in the hotel over the road? You open late that night?'

The man paused. 'I was closed the night those murders happened,' he said, the accent veering from Louisiana all the way to New York.

'Anyone break in?'

'No.'

The man was lying. Lying and scared of the police. It was all the confirmation Michael needed. He headed for the door and opened it and the cold from outside swept through the store. He turned back to look at the man.

'That sign in the window,' Michael said. 'Your authentic Marie

Laveau potions might seem a bit more authentic if you spelled her name right.'

He smiled, stepped out on the street, headed back up the block. He had what he'd come for. He had a name. But who was Gene Cleveland? And why the hell did the attackers want him so bad they murdered four people to get to him?

16

The Temple of Tranquility was located in a brownstone on 133rd Street between a radio repair shop and a dime-a-dance nightspot. When Ida got there she saw the place was closed, but there was a noticeboard outside which she stopped to read, a piece of paper pinned above the other notices: *Soup Kitchen Tonight. 8.00 p.m. Come eat and learn about the Aquarian Gospel of Jesus Christ. All welcome.*

Other scraps of paper gave notice of previous events, lectures on the Kings of Africa, the Black Star Line, Freemasonry and the Establishment. There were details of programs designed to wean people off narcotics. She thought about the last, wondered if it provided a link between the dope pusher in the hotel, and the Powell brothers and the temple.

She stepped back and looked up at the brownstone, decided to go back that evening and see what the Aquarian Gospel of Jesus Christ had to say.

She returned to her hotel, picking up food along the way, and sat in her room going over the evidence once more, waiting for Michael to call. She phoned Tom's lawyer – the third time she'd done so – and for a third time she was palmed off by the man's secretary.

She thought about calling Jacob out in California, but when she checked her watch she saw it was still too early. Just as she was starting to feel antsy and the evidence was beginning to blur, the phone rang: Michael.

'You get anything at the hotel?' she asked.

'Oh, sure.'

He told her the hotel owner had spilled. There had been a mystery guest – a man called Gene Cleveland who'd disappeared on the night of the killings. He told her how two plainclothes cops had coerced the hotel owner. He told her that he'd failed to get a description.

'I'm gonna call Carrasco,' Michael said. 'Get him to run a check. What are you planning?'

'I've got time to kill before going back to the Temple,' she said. 'I might canvas the local junkies, see if I can find one of Gene Cleveland's customers.'

There was silence over the line.

'You got a gun?' Michael asked.

'Sure, I got a gun.'

'Take it with you. Call me when you're done.'

They ended the conversation. She took her .38 out of her suitcase, inspected it, loaded it, inspected it once more, slipped it into her holster, left the hotel.

She made a beeline for the Palmer. She walked the blocks adjacent to it, talked to junkies and drunks and vagrants with sidewalk eyes, wrapped up in blankets, huddled around trash-can fires. The conversations all ran similarly – *I'm not a cop, I'm looking for Gene Cleveland. Used to sling dope out of the back of the Palmer Hotel. You know him? There's money in it. I'm not a cop.*

Blank stares, shakes of the head, one man said he'd stab her, one man spat at her, another just hissed at her, narrowed his eyes and hissed. Some were kind, gentle, told her they were sorry they couldn't help her in voices that belied deep mental disturbance. With most of them she had to fight the urge to cover her nose.

Amongst the junkies she spotted a pattern – they were all male, between twenty and forty, Negro. Many seemed to congregate around the derelict, burnt-out buildings that littered the neighborhood, the empty lots that collected weeds and refuse. Many wore giveaways from the Salvation Army mixed in with military items – combat jackets, brogans, suntans ripped at the knees – making Ida wonder how many of them had fought in the war.

She walked till she was footsore, down to the wastelands by the riverfront, into its vast web of backstreets and thin gloomy alleys, rotting piers, glowering, tumbledown factories, nameless diners. Here, too, were armies of the dispossessed. There were a couple of promising leads that turned out to be men stringing her along for the money.

She stopped at a hash house for a coffee and a sandwich, and it was there, as she sat perched on a counter stool, that the loneliness hit her. The ghostly sense that the stories in this city were not her own. She compared herself to the men she'd been talking to all day, noted how their isolation and detachment mirrored hers.

She finished her food and left. The afternoon waned and magic hour came. The sky was filled with a million tons of golden light that seemed to press down on the city with malice and glee.

Night descended.

Ida wondered how many more junkies there could be on the streets, if she'd already run dry. But more came out as the night lengthened, and she realized what she was witnessing was an epidemic. Just like in Chicago. Addiction rates had dropped during the war, but once peace returned, the smugglers had re-established their routes, and the slums had been flooded with dope.

No one provided her with a lead. None of the scores of people she stopped to speak to. Meaning either she wasn't as good at canvassing as she used to be, or that Cleveland's clientele were located elsewhere.

She checked her watch and saw it was almost eight o'clock.

She got to the Temple late. Saw when she did arrive that the door was open and the windows were spilling yellow light onto the street. There were people on the steps outside, Negro men nattily dressed in suits and red caps, the kind Ida had seen Arabs wearing back in Chicago.

She walked in and signs led her to a large echoing lecture hall filled with rows of chairs. At its front was a short dais, on which stood a man behind a lectern, giving a speech. Along the walls were a few more of the men in suits and red hats. In the seats were a mix of regular folk and down-and-outs. Ida twigged what was going on. Before the hungry were allowed any of the food from the soup kitchen, they'd have to sit through a lecture.

The man giving it was dressed in the same black suit and red hat garb. He was dark-skinned, portly, had a bushy beard that didn't sit well with his otherwise sharp attire. Ida took a seat near the back. Glad to be in the warm, felt her skin bristle from the change in temperature.

'There's a river, my brothers and sisters,' said the man. 'A river of dope. It starts in the jungles of Asia, it flows to the sea, across the oceans, through the port of New York, into syringes, through needles, into bloodstreams. Negro bloodstreams. It's a powerful river, and it can only flow with the collusion of governments.'

At this many of the audience murmured their approval.

'Governments paid off by the blight of the Italian Mafia, the guardians of this river, the men who make money out of our community's destruction. The Mafia and their friends in government and their friends in our own community, because, let us not forget, they couldn't ply their trade if it wasn't for their colored lackeys. Men such as Bumpy Johnson and his like.'

At the mention of the name a shocked hush ran through the crowd. Johnson was the Negro mobster who controlled Harlem, who'd gotten rich filling the neighborhood with Italian dope.

'I'm not afraid to say it,' said the man, waving a finger through the air. 'We should all know the devil in our midst. Does not Corinthians tell us that bad company corrupts good character?'

Ida looked around at the audience, noted again what a strange mix it was, the haggard men hunched over in their seats, filling the hall with an overwhelming smell, and as far away from them as possible, the well-dressed men and women who'd come to hear the lecture, looking as prim as churchgoers. Beyond them were the men in the strange hats, standing in the aisles either side of the hall.

On the walls behind them were banners charting the history of the Pan-African movement, posters salvaged from the Black Star Line, photos of Booker T. Washington, W. E. B. Du Bois, other men Ida didn't recognize. In amongst them was a photo of a woman, a light-skinned woman in what looked like Victorian clothes. Ida squinted to make out the label beneath the photo. Couldn't. There were paintings of the Virgin Mary and Jesus. The imagery was all confused – Arabic head-dress, African banners, Christian icons.

Ida noticed an open door further up, through which she could see another room, smaller – the soup kitchen. At the far end of it was a row of folded-out tables, two women in aprons setting out bowls of soup.

'God bless the junkies,' said the lecturer. 'For they are the human oil that makes the machine roll. The Mafia make money selling them drugs. The police make money arresting them. The lawyers and courts make money convicting them. And the prisons make money locking them up. Politicians use them to get votes. Doctors and nurses use them to experiment. A whole, great wedge of our economy is propped up by the junkie. So God bless the junkie. Oil is not the black gold, brothers and sisters. Junkies are the true black gold.'

The lecturer finished up to a round of polite, if weary, applause. People rose. The well-dressed types stood about chatting. The vagrants shuffled through the door into the soup kitchen and huddled around the food.

'Hello, sister,' said a voice. 'May I be of assistance?'

Ida turned to see one of the men in red hats standing next to her. A man in his thirties, good-looking, dark-skinned, with short hair and a thin moustache.

'I, uh, saw the sign and thought I'd come in.'

'You enjoyed the lecture? Brother Paul's a good speaker.'

Ida followed the man's gaze to the lecturer, who was milling about the seats at the front, talking to a group of audience members.

'I came in late,' said Ida. 'But I didn't catch anything much about the Aquarian Gospel of Jesus Christ.'

The man laughed. 'Oh, that's for the second half of the lecture, after the poor brothers have had their soup.'

He gestured towards the doorway and smiled at her again, but there was something stiff in it, formal. Ida noticed that the well-dressed people were filing out of the hall. She wondered if the gospel was to be preached only to the men in the soup kitchen. With a detective's cynical mind, she wondered if somehow the Temple was profiting from the men it was feeding, what the percentage in it could be. She'd encountered plenty of similar operations in Chicago. One way or the other, someone ended up getting fleeced.

'I'm going to be honest with you,' she said. 'I'm a private detective.'

She opened her purse and took out her detective's license, passed it over to the man.

He frowned, took it, studied it.

'State of Illinois,' he muttered. 'You're a long way from home.'

He said the last in a cold tone, handed her back her license.

'I know,' said Ida. 'I was hired by the parents of Thomas Talbot. He's the man accused of killing the Powell brothers. They were members here.'

The man's jaw tightened.

'We've had enough of answering questions,' he said. He turned and nodded to a group of red hats near the exit, gestured for them to come over. The lecturer saw what was happening and approached, too.

'What's going on?' he asked, looking from Ida to the young man.

'This sister here is a detective, looking into the Powell brothers.'

'A *private* detective,' said Ida. 'I'm working on behalf of the parents of the boy who was wrongly accused.'

'Wrongly accused?' the lecturer repeated.

He turned to the group of young men who had by now surrounded Ida and waved them away. They dispersed, slunk back to the edges of the room. Ida relaxed a little.

'Brother William here's a little sensitive on the subject of detectives,' said the lecturer, nodding at the young man Ida had been speaking to. 'Since the murders we've had the police coming here, the press, even some men from the government we had reason to believe were working for the FBI. You can see how we might have had enough of investigations?'

His manner was soft and gentle. The cynicism and self-righteousness he'd displayed whilst giving the lecture were no longer in evidence.

'Those stories in the paper were lies,' he said. 'The Temple's not a cult. We try and help people, clean them up, wean them off drugs. The establishment tries to shut us down because we're messing up their plans for profit and a subservient underclass. But all we do is feed our brothers, dry them out, show them the right way to live their lives.'

'The right way being what exactly?' Ida asked, thinking about the Temple's mix of iconography. 'Christianity?'

'We're a synthesis of Christianity and African religion,' he explained. 'We're not a voodoo cult.'

Ida nodded, unsure how a synthesis of Christianity and African religion was any different to voodoo.

'And the Aquarian Gospel?'

'A book by the preacher Levi H. Dowling. It contains many truths. Mystical truths. Much of it derived from the akashic records.'

Ida studied the man, wondered if he was being sincere, realized the conversation had wandered far from the murders.

'Do you know anything about the Powell brothers, or their murders, that the authorities don't?' she asked. 'Something that might see an innocent Negro man set free. I'm here privately, anything you say is in confidence.'

The lecturer paused and Ida could see he was formulating a lie, that he knew something but was hiding it.

'The Powell brothers were good people,' he said. 'It's a shame what happened to them, and a symptom of the wider evil afflicting Harlem. Beyond that, I know nothing. I'm sorry, sister. Now if you don't mind, I need to prepare for the second half of the lecture. Let me show you out.'

He smiled at her icily and raised his hand to the exit. It was only then she realized the hall was empty except for the two of them. She looked around at the stately portraits on the walls, then at the vagrants eating their soup in the adjoining room, and was filled with an unsettling sense of misfortune.

The lecturer accompanied her to the steps outside. She buttoned up her coat and the whole while he stood there smiling at her.

'Thank you for your time,' she said.

The man nodded, gave her an Arctic stare that belied the smile that was fixed to his lips.

She headed down the street, turned a corner onto a narrow, quiet avenue lined with brownstones. She'd walked a couple of blocks when she got the feeling someone was following her. She checked reflections in the windscreens of the cars parked at the curb, varied the length of her steps, confirmed the feeling – someone was stalking her down the otherwise empty avenue.

She saw an alleyway up ahead, narrow, dark, perfect. She

upped her pace, turned down it, took her .38 from her holster and waited.

A few seconds passed.

A chubby Negro man in a gray Chesterfield coat turned the corner to be greeted by the sight of Ida pointing her gun straight at him.

He jumped back, raised his hands. Ida looked him up and down, saw the corner of a red hat poking out of his pocket.

'You followed me from the Temple,' she said. 'Why?'

He paused before speaking. 'You wanted to know about the Powell brothers,' he said.

Ida noticed he was shaking, his eyes were glassy, spittle was drying at the corners of his mouth.

'What have you got to tell me?' she said.

He paused again. 'Could we do this somewhere warmer,' he said. 'Without the gun.'

Ten minutes later they were round the corner, sitting at a table at the rear of a diner. Ida ordered a coffee and told him to get whatever he wanted. He craned his neck to look around the diner for the fifth time since they'd entered, scared that someone in there might recognize him, might spot them together. Then he ordered eggs and steak, fried bread and an orange juice.

'You don't eat at the Temple?' Ida asked.

The man turned to look at her, grimaced, making Ida wonder what was wrong with the food they were serving up, if maybe they were lacing it with something.

'What did you want to tell me about the Powell brothers?' she asked.

'Well,' said the man, 'it's real generous of you to buy me dinner, but, uh, food ain't the only thing I'm struggling with at the moment. If you catch my drift.'

'How much?' she asked.

'Twenty'll be plenty,' he said in a sing-song voice, a grin on his face.

Ida took a twenty from her purse and handed it over, wondering on the odd way the man's nervous energy was manifesting itself.

He put the money in his pocket, nodded his thanks.

The waiter arrived with their drinks.

'So?' said Ida, when he'd left.

'I was friends with the Powells,' the man said. 'Alfonso mainly. Met them in the old days. They were big-time dealers before they fixed up and went on the square. Used to work direct for Bumpy Johnson.'

'OK,' said Ida.

'Anyway, a few days before they got killed, they came by the temple, said they'd seen something – a white man coming out of the apartments opposite the hotel they lived in. They were all shook up about it.'

'Why?'

'It wasn't just any white man, it was some mobster they knew from their dealing days. Some myth from back in the thirties called Faron.'

'Faron?'

The man nodded.

'Like I said,' he continued, 'they were all shook up about it. Got it into their heads he was staking the place out.'

'Staking out the Palmer? Why'd they think that?'

The man shrugged. 'Damned if I know,' he said. 'But they was sure as hell shook up about it. And in light of what happened afterwards, I mean, I guess they were right to be, no?'

The man turned to scan the diner once more. Ida studied him. There was something about the way he was talking, the speed of his voice, the glassy look in his eyes, the nervous twitches. She cursed herself for not seeing it earlier. The man was on the sleeve. A former junkie who'd fallen off the wagon, but he didn't want anyone at the Temple to know, so here he was, telling Ida the Powell brothers' story in exchange for much-needed junk money. She'd spent all day talking to junkies but hadn't realized this man was one, too.

'What else did they say about it?' she asked.

'Nothing.'

'They say anything about Gene Cleveland?'

'Who's that?'

'Pusher worked out of the backroom of the Palmer?'

He shook his head.

'How about Arno Bucek? The white boy they found there?'

'The dead kid? I don't know nothing about that. Like I said, it was just that one conversation, the day after they saw the man. That's the story.'

Ida nodded.

'You tell the cops about this?' she asked.

'You think I'm stupid?'

Before she could answer the waiter slid a plate of food onto the table in front of the man. The man grabbed a knife and fork and started shoveling egg and fried bread into his mouth.

Ida rose and put on her coat, dropped money onto the table for the man to settle the bill, resisted the urge to ask him once more what was wrong with the food in the Temple.

17

Michael exited the subway at Canal and headed into the down-town rush of stop-start traffic and overflowing sidewalks and steam rising in plumes from ventilation grills in the road. At the shoeshine shacks outside a Woolworth's store, businessmen sat in a line, reading the papers or chatting while their shoes were cleaned.

Michael passed by them. He trudged down Centre Street and the Criminal Courts building loomed into view, a behemoth covering three whole blocks. It towered over the roadway, rising skywards in a surge of masonry. It was newly built, grand, impos-ing, monolithic, one of those giant government edifices designed to display strength, solidity and permanence, designed to make anyone who looked at it feel powerless and small.

This was where the District Attorney's Office was located, where Carrasco worked, one of the dozens of NYPD officers attached to the DA's Office Squad and its various investigation bureaus. This was where Michael couldn't be seen with Carrasco lest someone spot them and Carrasco was sacked, or arrested. This was where the faceless state machinery was working to have Michael's son electrocuted, the same machinery Michael had spent so much of his life serving.

When he'd first heard of Tom's arrest, he had rushed to New York on the train, convinced there'd been some mistake, that soon enough it would be corrected. The machinery worked; Tom would be released. But days went by and Michael realized something was wrong. So he got the evidence file from Carrasco, read it, and immediately saw they were up against a conspiracy.

All those years he worked for the police, the Pinkertons, the government, he dealt with corruption every day, swam in it; he should have known not to trust the system. But he wanted to believe that it would work for his son. If it didn't, then what did it say for all his years of toil? When eventually he realized it wasn't going to happen, he felt like a fool. How had he managed to become *more* naive as he'd gotten older? He realized he needed to take matters into his own hands so he'd called Ida, the best detective he knew. Maybe he'd let too much time pass, maybe his misplaced faith would see his son executed.

He carried on down Centre Street, turned left, crossed Columbus Park, heading towards the church Carrasco had told him about. A good place to meet, his friend had said, no one goes to church downtown.

As he walked he noticed more and more Chinese people in the park, sitting on the benches despite the cold, reading, chatting, smoking. He exited the park and came upon a street whose shop signs were almost exclusively written in Chinese, their colors so bright they almost seemed to glow against the pale, autumn light.

Soon enough he came upon the church. It was a squat building of gray stone with a giant copper tower above it which years of oxidation had turned pale green.

Michael entered. Carrasco was right, the place was deserted except for someone unseen putting the church's organ through its paces. The sound filled the nave, bounced off its stone walls and high ceiling. Michael sat in a pew near the back and waited, thinking, watching the steam of his breath in the cold air, the candles flickering in their holders, the light streaming in through the Gothic stained-glass windows. Despite the boom of the organ, the place felt peaceful, especially after Michael had navigated the torrents of people out on the streets.

He heard a noise behind him, turned to see Carrasco enter holding a briefcase. He looked around, saw they were alone and sat next to Michael.

'Goddamn, it's cold,' Carrasco said.

'Language, Carrasco,' said Michael, smiling. 'You're in a church.'

Carrasco put his briefcase between them on the pew, opened it up. Took out a folder and passed it over.

'Gene Cleveland's rap sheet,' he said. 'It's pretty thin. Your mystery hotel guest only has one offense. He was rousted in a bebop club in Midtown at the start of the year, selling dope to the patrons there.'

'What the hell's *bebop*?'

'Language, Michael. Apparently, it's a type of jazz.'

Michael took the folder and opened it up, two mostly blank sheets of paper and a photo of Cleveland affixed to the top. The photo showed a Negro man in his early thirties with short hair and the dazed expression you often saw on people whose mugshots had been taken in the middle of the night.

He had a soft face, puffy cheeks, small eyes. He looked unassuming, unremarkable. Michael scanned the sheets; the date of birth made him thirty-two, the place of birth made him Missourian, no registered address. Michael flipped to the arrest details; January of that year, picked up in a sweep of a nightclub on 52nd Street.

'I spoke to the arresting officers,' said Carrasco. 'They picked him up after some of his customers fingered him. He's small fish. Part-time musician, part-time pusher. He plays in a band and sells horse to people out of the clubs they gig at.'

Michael nodded and looked through the rest of the record.

'There's no address, or known associates,' he said. 'You get any leads on that?'

Carrasco shook his head.

Michael thought. Narcotics officers must have been involved

in having Cleveland set up, and Carrasco had been sniffing around the Narcotics Division for information, a division that only had a handful of officers.

'Who'd you speak to in the Division?'

'Lieutenant called Wilson.'

'You trust him?'

'As much as I do any other cop.'

'What cover story'd you use?'

'I told him we had a murder suspect we caught in possession who'd fingered Cleveland as his dealer and I wanted to know if the man existed. He bought it.'

'Thanks, Carrasco,' said Michael. 'This is great.'

'I got you a précis.' Carrasco passed him over a sheet of paper.

In the depths of the church, the organist reached the end of the sonata he was playing, launched into a fugue. Michael remembered what Ida had told him about the man at the temple, how he mentioned the Powell brothers had been spooked by a mobster they'd seen casing the hotel.

'You get anything on this Faron character?' he asked.

'There's no file on Faron.'

'He's clean?'

'Not exactly,' said Carrasco. 'I asked around. The guy's pretty much a myth, a street legend. You ever hear about the Pike Slip Diner massacre?'

Michael shook his head.

'Back in '33, a guy walked into a diner on Pike Slip at gone two in the morning, hosed everyone in there with bullets and disappeared. Turned out two of the victims were off-duty cops. Crooked ones. People figured it as a Mob hit but none of the families ever looked like they were involved. Rumor was the shooter was called Faron. A gun for hire from out of town. That's basically it. The guy, if he is a guy and not just a name, is more of a myth than anything else. You sure you got the name right? Faron?'

'That's what Ida said,' Michael replied.

He thought about Faron going into the diner and killing everyone, drew parallels with the massacre in the Palmer Hotel.

'Anything else from back in '33?' he asked.

Carrasco shrugged. 'There was a rumor he jumped on a ship to Italy. No one ever heard from him again.'

'No rumors about where he was from?' Michael asked.

Carrasco shook his head. 'It was the thirties,' he said. 'The Depression. The homicide rate was through the roof, Murder Inc was killing people every week. Guns for hire were moving city to city. The only description for him I got was that he was big and had a funny way of talking, like an accent.'

'What kind of accent?'

'The kind that's hard to place.'

Michael nodded. 'Thanks, pal,' he said. 'Not just for this. For everything. I know what you're risking. I appreciate it.'

'If it wasn't for you, I wouldn't be here today,' Carrasco said. 'I'm not a man who forgets. Plus I'm getting to work a case with the two best detectives Chicago ever saw.'

'Please', said Michael, 'just be careful, OK? You know what they say, you play it both sides of the fence, you end up with your pants split.'

Carrasco smiled. 'Sure, pal. I'll take care. Listen, I need to get back to the office before this music drives me crazy.'

Michael grinned. They rose and headed for the door.

'Say, how'd you figure out there was an extra guest in the hotel?' Carrasco asked.

'I didn't,' said Michael. 'Ida did.'

'Sharp lady.'

Michael nodded.

They stepped out of the church and squinted in the sunlight, looked around. People were streaming down the sidewalks. The autumn sun was still gilding everything with freezing light.

'Shame there ain't really any leads to go on in that file,' Carrasco said.

'The jazz club's a lead,' said Michael.

'How's that?'

'Ida's got a pal who's a jazz musician.'

PART EIGHT

TIME

Monday, November 3rd 1947

ARTS & ENTERTAINMENT

THE END OF THE BIG BAND ERA

The era of swing music, that mainstay of the radio-waves for more than a decade, is coming to an end, if reports from the music industry are to be believed. In the past eight weeks, Benny Goodman, Tommy Dorsey, Harry James, Les Brown and Jack Teagarden have decided to disband. Gene Krupa and Jimmy Dorsey have cut salaries. This week Woody Herman gave up, too. The 'Herman herd' came to a stop just one year after it won the band-of-the-year poll run by the jazz magazine *Metronome*. The large staff of musicians required by the big band orchestras means they are expensive to run, but perhaps the main reason for the downturn is that people are simply not enjoying the music anymore. In empty ballrooms up and down the country, bands are playing mainly for the waiters. Our music correspondent, Giles Boardman spoke to Tommy Dorsey last week at the Biltmore Hotel on Madison Avenue . . .

18

A battered old tour bus, mud-caked and rickety, drove into the 38th Street bus station on the West Side of Manhattan and came to a stop in the middle of its vast, empty forecourt. The driver killed the engine and its death rattle ceased, but he made no move to open the doors. The passengers did it themselves, and shuffled out single-file, seventeen Negro jazz musicians in rumpled, slept-in tuxedos, among them the band's leader, Louis Armstrong.

Louis descended the steps, rubbed his face, wished he had some water to drink, to get rid of the sour taste in his mouth. He'd been asleep for much of the night. The band had smoked some joints in the back of the bus and while the others played yet another of their endless card games, Louis had passed out, somewhere East of Harrisburg. A lifetime of being on the road had taught him the trick of falling asleep anywhere, buses, airplanes, ferry decks, freezing cold dressing rooms, colored-only waiting rooms, benches at the ends of platforms in deadly Jim Crow railroad stations.

He yawned and lit a cigarette while he waited for the luggage to be unloaded. There was no one at the bus station to meet him. He'd told Lucille he didn't want her driving crosstown so late at night. He'd catch a cab home to Queens, displaying a faith in the goodness of humanity that was far-fetched enough to believe a colored man in Hell's Kitchen at gone three in the morning could get a cab driver to stop for him. More likely he'd be catching the subway and wouldn't be home any time soon.

He yawned again, leaned against the side of the bus and smoked with his eyes closed. The tour had been a disaster. A bigger disaster than the tour before that – which, in turn, had been a bigger disaster, too. And so on, back into the mists of time, to when Louis was an actual star. He was forty-seven years old, and if this latest debacle of a tour had proved anything to him, it was exactly how washed up he was. Somehow he had slid from poster-boy of jazz to has-been.

Angry voices made him open his eyes. He looked about him to see, a few yards away, some of the band members arguing with the driver. He wasn't surprised. The driver was a white man from South Carolina, gray-haired and unshaven, with a nose that drinking had taken through the spectrum from red to purple to blue. He'd stayed just sober enough not to crash the bus, and drunk or not, had referred to them all as niggers throughout the six-week tour.

The band's bassist and one of the trombonists were at the heart of the dispute. It looked like the prelude to a ruckus. The trombonist groaned, turned and walked over to Louis. He was a young, light-skinned twenty-four-year-old from the Bronx called Shelton. Louis liked him, even though he knew that the kid would rather be playing at bebop jams over in Harlem than touring with a fusty old outfit like Louis Armstrong's Big Band, that he had only taken the gig for the money. But then most of the band were only there for the money, Louis included.

'What's going on?' Louis asked.

'Motherfucking redneck won't give us our luggage,' Shelton said.

'Why not?'

'He just went into the depot and they told him the company's not been paid,' Shelton explained. 'He's not releasing our things till he's got payment.'

Louis saw how riled up Shelton was. He knew the kid carried a knife, a pearl-handled, stiletto-bladed switch, even took it on stage with him. Many of the band members brought along weapons when they toured the South.

'Shit,' said Louis. He flicked his cigarette onto the ground and walked over to the driver.

'Now what's the problem, sir?' Louis asked.

'We ain't got our money is the problem,' said the driver, turning his beetroot of a head in Louis' direction. Louis got the impression the man was enjoying the fact that his passengers had come up short, proving correct his prejudices about black incompetence, untrustworthiness.

'We were supposed to receive fifty percent up front, and fifty percent before the end of the tour. Well, guess what? Tour's ended and we ain't seen the second fifty percent. This is the last time I ever take a booking from a bunch of niggers.'

'Sir—' Louis said, but was interrupted by Shelton.

'The fuck you calling him "sir" for, Louis?' he said.

'Learn some manners, boy,' the driver said.

'Don't call me boy,' Shelton said, coiling up.

Louis raised his hands, gesturing for everyone to calm down, thinking about the knife in Shelton's pocket and the angry streak in his character.

Why *had* Louis called the driver sir? Because he'd grown up in New Orleans, forty years back, and that was just how you talked to white people, even lowdown trash.

'Now,' said Louis. 'My management company were supposed to pay you by check; you sure it's not in the office in there, maybe it's been mislaid?'

'Nothing's been mislaid, boy,' said the driver. 'You get us our money. In cash. You'll get your things back.'

Groans of anger rose up from the band. Louis noticed white people were congregating to watch the exchange, in the shadows of the barns where other buses were parked up, in the kiosk-like offices that littered the yard, along the entrance to the depot, where it gave out onto the street. These men were Hell's Kitchen whites. Rough Irish. Mechanics, night-birds, drunks, fighters. Louis didn't like where this was going.

'OK, sir,' he said, using the word once more without thinking, knowing how this was making him look to his much younger, much less accommodating band-mates. 'How much are you missing?'

'One hundred twenty-five dollars.'

Louis didn't have that kind of money on him. The banks wouldn't be open for hours. He could call Lucille, drag her out of bed, tell her to go to the safe and see what money was in there. If there was enough, get her to drive it out from Queens to Manhattan for them.

'All right,' said Louis. 'Lemme call my manager. There's been some misunderstanding. That's all. I'll call him up, you'll get your money. Now, you got a phone I can use?'

'There's a payphone over there,' said the driver, grinning. He nodded to the other end of the depot, across the cement wasteland of the forecourt, to a spot where there were a few gas pumps and a razor-blade-and-condom concession.

Louis turned to his band-mates. 'I'll get the money,' he said.

'You do that,' came back the voice of the bassist. 'We been stiffed enough on our pay checks this damn tour.'

Noises of agreement rose up from the band.

Louis turned and made the long walk of shame to the payphone.

He fished through his pockets for some change. Lifted up the receiver and dropped a coin into the slot. He gave the operator Joe's number and waited to be connected. He'd get Joe out of bed, get him down here with the money. He was fed up of this shit.

He looked across the depot to the tour bus in the distance with the sign on its side – Louis Armstrong's Big Band. It embarrassed him. The beached whale of the tour bus that ferried his dying band across the country. The young men standing in front of the bus embarrassed him, too. Their tuxedos rumpled, bowties loose, their eyes red from sleeplessness and tea.

Maybe they treated it all like a joke because they sensed things were coming to an end. They were working for a has-been, a one-time great who was on the skids. That was why they didn't practice, turned up late, with stains on their suits, stoned or drunk, why they missed their cues, played bum notes.

Crazy thing was, Louis didn't blame them. He wasn't a band leader. He didn't have the cut for it. He was a trumpet virtuoso, a gifted singer, arranger and composer. But he didn't have that ruthless streak you needed to be in charge of a score of unruly jazz musicians, to take all those egos and conflicting interests and hone them into something better than the sum of their parts.

Somehow, without him even noticing, Louis had ended up in charge of one of the worst jazz bands in the country and the paying public knew it and they'd stopped turning up to his shows. The one-nighters and long hops wouldn't be so bad if the gigs they played weren't half empty. Some nights it felt there were more people on stage than in the audience.

'Hello?' said a groggy voice coming through the receiver.

'Mr Glaser, sir,' he said. 'It's Louis.'

'What time is it?'

Louis checked his watch. 'It's coming up to four a.m., sir.'

'Is everything all right?'

Louis explained the situation and Joe said he'd have the cash couriered over within forty minutes. He seemed genuinely embarrassed. Joe was normally meticulous with the band's itinerary, schedule, roster, with all the paperwork. Louis wondered if this hiccup – that was what Joe had called it – was the sign of some change at the management company, of Louis becoming less of a priority, slipping down the rankings.

Louis thanked Joe and replaced the receiver. He stared across the forecourt to the band in the distance, to the clapped-out bus, to the bloated, dying whale of his career. He walked back towards them.

'My manager's going to have the money couriered over. Said it'll be here in forty minutes,' Louis said to the driver.

The driver glared at him.

'I guess you'll have to wait, then,' said the driver.

He turned and headed for the office.

'Can you at least open up the bus so we can sit down while we wait?' the trombonist called after him.

'Nope,' shouted the driver without looking back.

'It's goddamn freezing out!' the bassist pleaded.

The driver acted like he hadn't heard, disappeared into the shadows.

The bassist turned to look at Louis. He had sixteen pissed-off faces staring at him, not to mention the fighting Irish dotted about.

'This is bullshit,' shouted the bassist.

'I know,' said Louis.

He walked round the end of the bus, slumped down onto the cold macadam, leaned his back against one of the bus's wheels, and closed his eyes. Not for the first time in the last few years, he asked himself how the hell he'd ended up like this. He needed to change something before things got worse. Half the jazzmen he'd grown up with in New Orleans had ended up destitute. Men who'd had a hand in inventing the music, who'd been rich and famous at one point. The precariousness of life as a jazz musician was enough to drive you mad, if the drink and drugs and race hate, long hours and unending travel didn't take you first.

'Mind if I join you?' said a voice.

Louis opened his eyes. Shelton.

'Sure.'

Shelton sat down next to him. Pulled a joint from his tuxedo pocket, lit it, took a toke, shared it with Louis.

'Ain't this a bitch,' said Shelton. 'Dig the shit on that white trash motherfucker.'

Louis could dig it. But by the standards of his youth back in New Orleans, the driver was positively pleasant.

They smoked the joint and froze in the night-time cold. It got so bad Shelton's teeth got to chattering and probably because of the joint they both found it hilarious and couldn't stop laughing.

Half an hour later a courier arrived in a taxi cab with an envelope. Fifteen minutes after that, their luggage had been released and they were all heading home.

Louis didn't even bother trying to look for a cab, he walked to the subway with the rest of them, jumped on the first train that came along, changed at Times Square and caught the Seven for the long ride out to Corona. He sat alone in the smoking car, watched his ghostly reflection in the window, rushing through the blackness. He thought back to the tour, and all the tours before it, all merging into one grueling slog, so many tours he never spent more than a couple of months at home in Queens each year.

Savannah, Georgia, a decade back. Their bus pulled into the dusty old town, and they'd walked past a little stall at the side of the road, a homeless man selling a miserable selection of vegetables. A voice called out. Louis turned to look at the homeless man. It took a good few seconds to recognize him.

Joe 'King' Oliver. Louis's mentor. The man who had brought Louis from New Orleans to Chicago. A man as big as Duke Ellington in his day. A man who was mobbed by fans when he walked through the Southside.

Dressed now in rags, unrecognizable, selling vegetables in the dust. When Louis saw him, he cried. And so too did the man he called 'Papa' Joe. He gave him the hundred and fifty dollars in his pocket, told him to head back to New Orleans and start recording again.

But a year later he was dead.

Other jazz greats fared as bad – Bunk Johnson was driving a sugar wagon in the backwaters of Louisiana, had sent Louis a begging letter, asking for money to have his teeth fixed, so he could start playing his horn again.

These stories could be Louis' story if he didn't fix up.

But in the midst of all this, there was hope. A concert next week. In New York. Something radical. Its promoter assured Louis it could be the fix his career so desperately needed. Louis wondered on the man's youthful optimism, wondered if hope was by its nature fragile, if it always came thinly, in glimmers. It was hard for Louis to believe things could turn around.

He'd noticed for a while now that wrapped up in his decline was a peculiar sort of lucklessness. It wasn't just the band and dwindling audiences and pay checks not arriving when they should. There was a cloud of ill-fortune shadowing him – if a rain shower came, he'd get caught in it, if there was a train to catch, he'd miss it, if there was a loose paving stone, he'd trip up on it, and when he rose and dusted himself off, a black cat would cross his path.

And now a concert, a way out, an escape route. But would his bad mojo mess that up, too?

The train came out of the Steinway tunnel and was flooded with pale blue light. The sky was quivering, shaking off night. Louis watched the sun rise as he travelled east across Queens. Electric lamps floated past. On platforms clots of people waited, huddled up in winter coats.

He got off at 103rd Street, lugged his suitcase and trumpet case down the platform, stared at the train disappearing north and thought of his childhood. His mother taking him to the railroad tracks outside New Orleans to forage for dandelions and peppergrass to use as laxatives.

On the corner of 104th Street the traffic lights hung in the air like red lanterns. Around him the neighborhood was coming to life. A few Pullman porters were heading home, having finished overnight runs from Chicago, Boston, Baltimore. They recognized

Louis, nodded hello. World-famous jazz musician in a rumpled tuxedo, dragging his luggage through Queens.

A horse-drawn coal cart rattled past, the coal merchant at the reins, two kids who must have been his sons sitting alongside him, looking half-asleep and annoyed at having to help on their father's rounds before school. Louis grinned, imagined what it would be like to have a child. He'd had three wives and countless girlfriends and he had not a single son or daughter to show for it, had slowly realized over the years that there must be something wrong with him.

Despite the sun rising, the cold didn't let up, and Louis' hands were freezing by the time he reached his home on 107th. It was a modest house, blocky and red brick, located on a quiet street in the otherwise noisome neighborhood of Corona. Lucille had picked out the house, it was near where'd she'd grown up, in a mixed, middle-class area, one of the few places in New York outside of Harlem that black people could actually buy houses.

He climbed the steps, yanking his cases up after him, unlocked the door, and stepped inside. The hallway was murky in that way houses are just after dawn. He left his luggage by the door, didn't turn on the lights, went into the kitchen to make himself a coffee, did so quietly so as not to wake Lucille.

As the water heated, he looked around the kitchen – the cupboards, the crockery, the photos and pictures on the wall. It was homely, pleasant, tidy and clean. It was a good place to live, to be part of a family. He thought how two days earlier he was in the segregated South, playing a concert in a town that could explode at any minute. He stared at the fruit in the bowl on the counter and thought of King Oliver, dressed in rags, crying.

He looked again at his surroundings with a dull fear that all this was on the verge of being lost. That something needed to change.

He saw there was a note on the pad by the phone. He stopped to read it and smiled. It was in Lucille's perfectly looping hand – *Welcome back, baby. Wake me when you get in. P.S. Ida called, said she's in town, staying at the Theresa, wants to talk.*

PART NINE

'By devious means, among which were the terrorizing of witnesses, kidnapping them, yes, even murdering those who could give evidence against you, you have thwarted justice time and again.'

JUDGE SAMUEL LEIBOWITZ, AT THE COLLAPSE OF
VITO GENOVESE'S MURDER TRIAL, 1946

19

Gabriel had spent all day chasing down the last few leads he had for Benny and had come up short. One after the other the leads had sputtered, dimmed, extinguished, till there was only one left. And all the while he'd been plagued by thoughts of Faron, distracted by visions of his sister's killer stalking the city, hunting for yet more victims. He wondered how Benny had found out the man was back in town, if Faron was somehow mixed up with the missing money.

Late in the afternoon Gabriel returned home, popped a couple of Seconals and caught a few hours' sleep. In the moments before he passed out, he saw his sister's body in the blackness, lying in a pool of blood on a sidewalk, crumpled, twisted, hospital gown fluttering in the breeze.

When he woke he gave in to the urge he'd been resisting all day to go chasing after Faron. He called a friend in the NYPD and arranged a meeting for that evening. Then he sat down for dinner with Sarah and Mrs Hirsch, even though he was too sick to eat, and spent most of the meal staring at his food.

'You OK?' asked Mrs Hirsch, when they were clearing up the dishes.

He nodded. How to tell her the man who'd killed Sarah's mother was back in New York, just a few days before Gabriel and Sarah were supposed to be skipping town.

'Remember you need to talk to her,' Mrs Hirsch said, gesturing to Sarah, who was sitting in the lounge.

Gabriel nodded. Mrs Hirsch turned and went into the kitchen. Gabriel knew she would take an age over the washing-up. There was a dishwashing machine in there but Mrs Hirsch never deigned to use it, considered its presence an affront to her housekeeping skills.

Gabriel walked through into the lounge, looked at Sarah, wrapped up in a raveled and shapeless sweater, listening to a detective serial on the radio. He reminded himself it was for her he was doing it all. He went to the drinks stand and poured himself a whisky, went to the coffee table and picked up Sarah's sketchbook.

'I nearly tripped on this the other day,' he said, holding it up. 'I saw the Mexican stuff.'

Something changed in her look, her expression frosting over with teenaged defiance.

'OK ...' she said, batting the ball back to his side of the court.

'You trying to get us killed?' he asked.

She shrugged, stayed silent, pretended to turn her attention back to the radio.

He told himself this was the wrong time to go through it, that he was still all churned up from hearing the news about Faron. But he ignored his own good advice.

'Sarah?' he said, sounding more annoyed than he'd meant.

'No one's going to see,' she moaned, petulance pouring out like a dam had burst. 'And even if they did, so what? I drew a few Mexican skeletons, doesn't mean we've run away there.'

Gabriel wasn't sure how to go with it; angry or disappointed.

'The minute we're gone, there'll be cops and gangsters crawling all over this place,' Gabriel said. 'I want you to burn these. OK?'

'*Sí, Tío.*'

'And cut that out, too.'

'I've got to practice. It's not like you can speak the language.'

'I'll learn it.'

They stared at each other, stranded in an icy silence. Gabriel heard Mrs Hirsch in the kitchen, washing dishes, listening in.

'If we stayed in New York,' said Sarah, 'we wouldn't have to worry about all this stuff.'

There was exasperation in her voice, anger.

The atmosphere curdled further.

Gabriel wondered, as he often did, if he'd done the right thing telling her about the plan. If he'd done the right thing all along, being honest with her about how he made his money, the danger they were in. He'd tried to prepare her for the worst, explained what to do if he disappeared one day, or if they were separated, told her where the stash spots were, the meeting points, the bank accounts she should use. He'd even taught her how to use a gun.

'We've been over this a million times,' he said.

'*You've* been over this a million times. You're dragging me away from my friends and everyone I love and I can't even say goodbye. I could stay with Mrs Hirsch,' she continued. 'And you can go off to Mexico on your own.'

Sarah looked at the open door to the kitchen. Gabriel knew both Sarah and Mrs Hirsch would favor such an arrangement, making him the bad guy, the destroyer of lives and relationships.

'That wouldn't work,' he said.

'Why not?'

'Because they'll come after you to get to me,' he said flatly.

'And whose fault is that?'

Gabriel had no answer, and Sarah knew it, and here was the unavoidable injustice of their situation – by going to Mexico she was being punished for his mistakes. Point made, victory complete, she rose and stomped out of the lounge.

A few seconds later her bedroom door slammed shut, shaking floors across a couple of city blocks.

The noise brought Mrs Hirsch hobbling out of the kitchen.

She looked at Gabriel's face, figured how things had gone.

'She'll come round, Gabby,' she said. 'Give her time.'

Gabriel nodded, took a sip on his whisky. Mrs Hirsch returned to the dishes. Gabriel was left alone.

Falling man.

Half an hour later he was in Italian Harlem. He parked the Delahaye on 106th Street. Waited. Anxious and bleary-eyed, still thinking about Faron's return and the argument with Sarah. The petulance she'd displayed wasn't her. They'd never argued in the past. This was all the result of what he was doing to her.

He regretted not playing it better. The moments he spent with her were precious because they were so brief; their routines intersected only momentarily each day. How had he managed to fumble the baton? Maybe there was something in Mrs Hirsch's admonishment. Maybe he was becoming a gargoyle, turning to stone, aloof, watching the world from a distance.

After a few minutes, an unmarked cruiser pulled up behind Gabriel and a large man in a brown suit got out, Lieutenant Detective John Salzman. He crossed to the Delahaye and opened the door, looked at the passenger seat, the tight space, the low-down floor of the sports car.

'How the hell d'you get in this thing?' he asked in a gruff voice.

'Ass first,' said Gabriel, 'like most things in life.'

Salzman grunted, squeezed himself in, settled, looked around. He nodded his approval at the plush interior.

'So how much you pay for something like this?' he asked, gesturing at the car.

'I wouldn't know,' said Gabriel. 'I won it in a card game.'

Salzman chuckled.

'How's things in the division?' Gabriel asked.

Salzman was Gabriel's man in the Narcotics Division, probably the most corrupt part of the outstandingly corrupt NYPD. Dealers paid the division two thousand a month to distribute unhindered between 110th and 125th. Harlem. They also caught a piece of the dope shipments that moved through the Port of New York, brought into the country by the Gagliano crime family and Vito Genovese, shipments that were distributed all across the East Coast. Before working Narcotics, Salzman had been in the much less lucrative Homicide Division.

'Pushers push,' he said. 'Junkies junk, jigs get sent to Rikers. What's on your mind?'

'I need you to run a search.'

'Shoot.'

'Guy named Faron,' said Gabriel. 'A hired gun.'

'Faron?' said Salzman, trying to place the name. 'The diner slaughter perp from back in the thirties? He's a myth.'

Gabriel shook his head.

'I heard he's back in town,' he said. 'I need to find him. Fast. Can you ask around?'

'Sure.'

'And something else,' said Gabriel. 'Faron likes cutting up girls. Can you speak to your guys in homicide, get me details of any dead women, prostitutes mainly, who've been found mutilated, in the last six months. Picked up in red-light zones. Dumped in industrial areas.'

Salzman frowned. 'Six months is a pretty big frame,' he said.

'I'll pay.'

'How much?'

Gabriel gave him a number, a large chunk of the Mexico money.

Salzman whistled through his teeth. 'For that kinda money, I'll do your laundry.'

He grinned till he saw the look on Gabriel's face. 'Leave it with me,' he said.

Salzman got out of the car. Gabriel watched his cruiser drive off.

He wondered once more what he was hoping to achieve. He

had eight days to find the money and leave New York, but here he was, sidetracked, derailed by the news that his sister's killer had returned. In the shadows smothering the sidewalk, he saw her body once more, broken, buckled, oozing.

He blinked and she was gone.

He started up the Delahaye and headed downtown, to the Village, to chase down his only remaining lead.

20

Wednesday 5th, 10.35 p.m.

There was nothing like the Village at night. Bebop joints, artists' lofts, fairy bars, dope pads, burlesques, cafes that never closed their doors. A panoply of venues to pop in and drop out.

Gabriel parked the Delahaye on Bedford and walked around the corner to a narrow, tree-lined street of picturesque red-brick buildings. The bar was just on the bend before Barrow Street, but Gabriel could hear the jazz music peeling out from the moment he turned the corner.

When he got there he saw the windows were painted black, and there was no signage anywhere except for a scrap of paper stapled to the front door, with the words – *Enter if you dare* – scrawled across it in pencil.

Inside the place was roaring with people, all crammed in tight. Mostly men, what the newspapers referred to as the *hands on hips* set. There were a few straight couples, artists in denim overalls, awkward-looking types whom Gabriel pegged for intellectuals, students, poets. In amongst them were a few mobsters. New York's fairy bars were where the interests of the city's homosexuals and its gangsters intersected.

Gabriel slipped through the crowd, headed for the bar, where the people were lined up three or four deep, their faces sticky with sweat and smiles, eyes dilated and drug-shined. Everything was in a terrible condition, the walls were bare brick, the tables and chairs looked like they'd been rescued from the street. The bar itself was an unvarnished plank of wood, behind which was a rickety wine rack holding all the booze, and next to it a strip of floral curtain hanging up over a doorway. A couple of young guys in tight white T-shirts manned the bar, cocking their ears over the noise to take customers' orders.

There was a gramophone at the end of the bar from which the jazz was blaring out. Old jazz, New Orleans ragtime from twenty-five years ago. There was a revival of the 'good old music' going on. Kids who'd grown up on swing wanting to go back in time and experience the real-deal. Though in this setting, Gabriel got the feeling the choice of music was ironic.

Next to the gramophone was a chubby man with a black slouch hat on his head and a pink carnation in his lapel. Jasper Ericsson was not someone who had any interest in breaking stereotypes. He sipped from a Martini as he shimmied along to the song, looked through a record box for the next selection.

'Jasper,' shouted Gabriel.

Jasper turned to look at Gabriel and his face lit up.

'Gabriel,' he exclaimed. He leaned in and hugged Gabriel tightly, spilling his Martini all over Gabriel's shoulder. Then he pulled back and grinned at him.

'You look cold. Can I interest you in a bracer?'

Gabriel nodded. Jasper waved one of the barmen over.

'This is Todd,' said Jasper, introducing the barman. 'He's an actor. He also pours drinks.'

'I'll have a whiskey,' Gabriel said.

The barman poured it, slid it over the bar.

Gabriel chinked glasses with Jasper. The song on the turntable came to an end. Jasper speedily took the record off, grabbed another, put it on. Gabriel recognized it – a King Oliver number from back in the twenties. Gabriel noted the record looked new, a re-issue maybe.

'Budget won't stretch to a live band on weeknights,' Jasper explained, over the noise of the record.

Gabriel scanned the crowd once more. The place was doing a

roaring trade. He wondered which mobster Jasper was paying, how much he was being squeezed, if the booze he was forced to serve up was legitimate stuff the Mob had stolen, or the counterfeit stuff that rotted your gut.

The New York State Liquor Authority, or any beat cop for that matter, could write up a violation and get a fruit bar closed down for *allowing undesirables to congregate*. A situation that led to a non-stop series of bar openings and police raids and court dates and re-openings.

Until the Mob had stepped in.

They offered to use the kickback-protection system they'd set up during Prohibition to allow the bars to operate without interference, in return for a cut of the profits and agreements that the bars would buy their booze from them. So the bars paid the Mob, and the Mob paid the authorities to look the other way. When the cops did decide to raid somewhere, for appearance's sake, they'd call the owners beforehand to let them know. The papers would print an article on the boys in blue busting another *daffodil den*. And so in the fruit bars and clubs of the Village, it was almost like Prohibition had never been repealed. And maybe some of the customers enjoyed it that way – the furtive, underbelly buzz, the drinks laced with a seam of danger.

'How's life in the big leagues?' Jasper asked, meaning the Copa.

'Ten times the size of this place and half the atmosphere,' said Gabriel.

Jasper laughed. 'You know, I have a theory,' he said. 'That the more expensive a night-spot's decor, the less interesting the people inside it.'

Gabriel shrugged. 'Yeah, I buy that,' he said.

'So,' said Jasper. 'To what do I owe the honor? You finally seen the light?'

'I'm here looking for info.'

'Oh?'

Gabriel lit a Lucky, offered one to Jasper, who turned him down on seeing the brand.

'Anywhere we can talk that's a bit more quiet?' Gabriel asked.

Jasper thought, nodded, led Gabriel behind the bar, through the doorway that was screened off by the floral curtain, down a corridor, into a backroom. Bare walls, a single bare light-bulb, the smell of drains backed-up. The place looked like it tripled up as staff room, kitchen and drinks store. There was a Negro woman standing at a sink, running dirty glasses through a bucket of brown water. There were crates of booze stacked up, hangers with coats, a table and chairs. The floor was strewn with broken, empty Benzedrine tubes, the ends of dope cigarettes.

'The staff,' said Jasper, following Gabriel's gaze to the litter on the floor.

Gabriel nodded. He leaned back on the wall behind him and Jasper raised his eyebrows.

'I wouldn't do that, Gabby,' he said. 'Roaches.'

Gabriel straightened up.

'Harriet?' said Jasper, turning to the woman at the sink. 'Would you give us a moment?'

The woman looked at him and nodded, turned and left the room, closing the door behind her, dimming the music.

'You got running water in here?' Gabriel asked, nodding at the bucket in the sink.

'No.'

'You should get some.'

'Everyone's a critic,' Jasper said. 'You know how much of a slice Ianniello's taking from my profits? I can barely afford to stay open, even though the place is packed every night. And the booze he stocks me with . . .'

He shook his head. Gabriel nodded. He knew Ianniello, an up-and-comer who ran protection on a number of bars in the Village under the front of a soft drinks distribution company – the Hi-Fi Beverage Corporation.

'So?' asked Jasper.

'I heard Benny Siegel paid you a visit last summer.'

Instantly Jasper's guard went up.

'Sure,' he said, relaxing into it. 'He came by one night. Then a couple of weeks later his corpse was splashed across the front page of the *Daily News*. Shame. He was a good-looking man.'

'What was he doing here?' asked Gabriel.

Jasper thought, shrugged.

'I was as shocked as anyone when he came in the door.'

Unconvincing. Jasper was hiding something. The man played the bon vivant but he wasn't soft. If he was being cagey, it was for a reason, and if Gabriel wanted to find out what it was, he'd have to bargain.

'Give me something,' said Gabriel. 'And I'll get Costello to talk to Ianniello about taking a smaller slice. Or at least stocking you with better booze.'

Jasper thought. Evaluated.

'What reason would you give?' he asked.

'That you're a friend of mine, and Costello's a friend of mine.'

Jasper evaluated once more.

'I'm here on Costello's behalf,' Gabriel added for more weight. 'Let me know. One night spot manager to another.'

Jasper stared at Gabriel and Gabriel got the sense he was being weighed up.

'You can't let anyone know what I'm about to tell you,' said Jasper.

'Sure,' said Gabriel.

Jasper nodded. 'Benny came here looking for information.'

'On what?'

'On *whom*,' said Jasper. 'A jazz musician. A Negro by the name of Gene Cleveland.'

Gabriel frowned. 'Why'd he come here?'

'Cleveland was in the band that played here Saturday nights sometimes.'

'Why was he looking for him?'

'He didn't say. And I didn't ask.'

Gabriel nodded. What the hell did Benny want with a Negro jazz musician?

'Where can I find Cleveland?'

'You can't,' said Jasper. 'He disappeared. A good while before Benny came looking for him. The disappearance was probably *why* Benny was looking for him.'

'What's this Cleveland like?'

'I hardly knew the man,' said Jasper, and Gabriel noted the use of past tense. 'He played saxophone in a jazz band. He sold dope. He hung about the Village. The bohemians delighted in him.'

'He was a pusher?'

'He hawked to his friends, to support his own habit. He was hardly Bumpy Johnson. I think the word is *two-bit*.'

'You know any of his friends?'

'Just his band-mates, but none of them have seen him since he disappeared either. It's been months since anyone saw him, Gabby. And as to why Benny wanted to find him, your guess is as good as mine.'

Gabriel nodded, started to get the feeling this was all a dead end.

'Thanks, Jasper,' he said. 'I'll talk to Costello.'

'Sure.'

They returned to the bar, said their goodbyes and Gabriel headed through the roar. As he got to the front door, he saw there was a sign stapled to its inside – *Exit if you dare*. He smiled. Stepped out into the cold, walked towards his car.

Benny had gone to the Village chasing a guttersnipe. It was strange, especially for Benny, but could it have anything to do with the missing money? Gabriel knew someone he could ask.

He got in the Delahaye and headed for the Copa, cutting north out of the Village, past the hulking mass of the Women's

Prison. He sailed through Midtown and the skyscraper canyons looked like voids in the dark. He drifted into that necropolis state of mind. The buildings like tombstones, Manhattan a graveyard, Gabriel flying through it like a wraith.

21

When Gabriel arrived at the Copa, he saw the mirage was in full swing. The dance floor was packed, the tables overflowing. The staff were gearing up for the midnight floorshow. He cast his eye over the place, made sure all was in order, headed through into the back.

Havemeyer and the others were in the office when he entered. Havemeyer gave him a sour look.

'What?' said Gabriel, sitting down. There was a stack of letters on his desk, even though he'd only been gone a day.

'You talk to him?' Havemeyer asked.

'Talk to who?'

'Genovese.'

Gabriel frowned. 'He's here?'

'Sure, he's here,' said Havemeyer. 'Been here an hour.'

They shared a concerned look. Since Vito Genovese had returned from Italy the previous year, he'd not looked in on the Copa once. It made sense; Vito wasn't a nightclub kind of guy, especially when the nightclub was owned by his rival for control of the crime family.

'He ask for me?' Gabriel asked.

'No,' said Havemeyer. 'But why else would he come here?'

'Maybe he's a Carmen Miranda fan.'

Havemeyer gave Gabriel another of those looks.

'Try *probing for weaknesses*,' he said.

'Who's he here with?'

'Half of New Jersey, by the looks of it,' said Havemeyer. 'You really didn't make him when you came in?'

Gabriel shook his head, startled that he'd missed them. Maybe all the stresses pulling at his mind were stopping him from focusing like he used to. Like he *needed* to. Now most of all.

'I gave him ringside seats and comped all the Krug he could handle,' said Havemeyer.

'Good,' said Gabriel. 'He'll like that.'

Genovese was a notorious cheapskate. Gabriel rose and headed to the restrooms. He checked his face in the mirror. Wondered what the hell Genovese was doing here. In his fourteen-year entanglement with the Luciano crime family Gabriel had seen countless vendettas and quarrels and feuds, many were of Byzantine complexity, many were left to ripen and sour over decades. The bad blood between Genovese and Costello was relatively recent by those standards, had started some time in '36, when Luciano was sent to prison and Vito Genovese became acting boss. He only held the position for a year, as he had to flee to Italy to escape a murder charge. From his prison cell in Siberia, Luciano made Costello the new acting boss. And Costello started turning round the family's fortunes. And maybe it was this as much as anything that angered Genovese – how his former underling had proved to be so much better at the job that Genovese so desperately coveted, and had so quickly forfeited.

Gabriel splashed cold water over his face. Popped two dexies and downed them dry. He left the restrooms, walked down the corridor, turned right, turned left, walked through the chaos of the kitchen, its bright lights, its French section, its Chinese section, pushed through the service door and the slam of the music filled his ears, the blaring lights, the rush and blur of the crowd.

On stage, the band was all set for the start of the show. Gabriel scanned the space, saw Genovese and a dozen goons sitting in prime seats at the edge of the dance floor, drinking up Gabriel's champagne, trying to look like they weren't enjoying themselves.

Most of them were young enough to fit into the crowd, but not Genovese. He looked fifty, going on eighty. Stocky and square-faced, wearing those odd amber-tinted glasses that gave him the air of an accountant. He was dressed in clothes that must have looked fusty even in the Sicilian backwaters he'd been hiding out in for the best part of a decade. He seemed out of his depth, in unfamiliar waters, which Gabriel hoped gave him something to play with.

He slid through the crowd towards their table. When Genovese saw him he grinned slyly.

'Vito,' said Gabriel. 'Welcome to the Copa. I hope you're enjoying yourself.'

'It's a pleasure to be here,' said Genovese. 'Thanks for making us feel so at home.'

He gestured to the men sitting around him. Gabriel scanned their faces, he recognized most of them, spotted Nick Tomasulo – Costello's mole in Genovese's clique. Gabriel made sure his eyes didn't linger on him.

'Take a seat,' said Genovese. 'Join us.'

Gabriel didn't want to, but he nodded, gestured to a captain for an extra chair. Genovese grinned, looking like he'd won some kind of victory. Just then the emcee came on stage, things shushed down, and he introduced the show. Carmen Miranda and the Samba Sirens entered to rapturous applause, dressed in chiffon, sequins and feathers.

A look of disapproval clouded Genovese's face, and Gabriel could guess why. When Genovese was hiding out in Italy, he set about ingratiating himself into Mussolini's regime. He got in with them so good, the Duce made him a *commendatore*, the highest civilian rank in Fascist Italy. It didn't take much to figure out that everything about the Copa – its Latin decor, its Chinese food, the pulsing samba music with its hint of Africa – would be distasteful to a *commendatore*.

'So how's life over in Jersey?' Gabriel asked.

Genovese shrugged. 'I'm glad to be back on American soil. A free man,' he said. 'But I come back from the war and see a lot has changed. Some good, some bad.'

Genovese waggled his head. Gabriel had to suppress a smile, Genovese was acting like a returning veteran, liked he'd actually fought in the war. The way Gabriel had heard it, when the Allies invaded, Genovese switched sides, became a fixer for the American Army, used the position to turn a profit on black-market goods. All until someone realized he was the same Vito Genovese who had an outstanding arrest warrant for murder in New York. And so he was deported back to the States.

But between his return and his trial, all the witnesses in the case either changed their statements or were killed. So in June the previous year, Genovese walked out of prison a free man, and had moved to a mansion in Middletown, New Jersey, still angered by the fact Costello had usurped him. Pretty much immediately he set about regaining control of the family, and now, seventeen months later, he was paying Gabriel a visit.

'What about you, Gabriel?' he said. 'I hear you're doing well. Here, and with the interest at the race track in Saratoga, and living on the Upper East Side with the old money.'

'I'm doing OK,' said Gabriel.

'You have a good summer this year at the race track?' Genovese asked with a glint in his eye. 'How's it working with old Albert there?'

A spike of panic stabbed through Gabriel. Did Genovese know about the skim at the race track? The cooked books? Was he going to use that to put the squeeze on Gabriel somehow?

'We had a good season,' said Gabriel, his eyes fixed on Genovese's face, looking for some clue as to the extent of what he knew.

Then another spike of panic. Maybe this had to do with the missing two million. Maybe Genovese was Benny's partner in stealing the money. Maybe Genovese had heard Gabriel was investigating. He ran through the list of people he'd seen, the questions he'd asked, wondering who could have ratted him out. Gabriel needed to talk to Tomasulo, their mole, to check if Benny had seen Genovese over the summer. Tomasulo was only sitting three chairs away, but in the current situation, there was no way Gabriel could do anything other than pass the time with the man.

'With all that money coming in,' said Genovese, 'it makes me wonder why you're still working here? Spending all night in a smoky basement with this nigger music in your ears.'

And with that statement, Gabriel realized why Genovese was there. It might still have been about the money, but it was also about something much, much larger.

'I enjoy it,' said Gabriel, eyeing him closely.

'Sure,' said Genovese. 'You look so happy.'

The skin round his eyes crinkled and a smile appeared on his lips, a cheerless smile, as if some unseen hand had pulled back the muscles of his face.

He gestured to the Copa. 'These junkie musicians and faggots and hookers. Don't you got a girl to raise?'

'I'm a night owl,' Gabriel said. 'The musicians aren't junkies and the girls aren't hookers.'

Genovese nodded, lit a cigarette and played with the lighter between his fingers.

'You're the best fixer in New York,' Genovese said. 'You got the city in the palm of your hand, and this is what Costello's got you doing? What's the sum of all this?'

Genovese waved his hand about the place again, at the mirage that disappeared each morning, highlighting the fact that Gabriel never had anything concrete to show for all his work. Genovese might have been blunt and brutish, but he knew the measure of a man. Havemeyer's words floated into Gabriel's head – *probing for weaknesses*. Genovese had honed in on Gabriel's disillusionment, had mentioned the race track, Anastasia, Sarah, Gabriel's home address. Like all the best power plays it was so subtle it almost wasn't there.

Gabriel wondered at his approach, the mix of insults and soon-to-be job offer, and while he waited for it to come, he thought about how he could use this to his advantage, if there was some way he could weave it into his escape plans, rather than see it as the complication it was.

'I got plans, Gabriel. I know it, you know it, Costello knows it. He's got the same bug Luciano and Capone had, turning themselves into celebrities. You turn yourself into Mr Big, you're putting a neon sign over your head, a flashing arrow for the Feds to follow. If there's one thing the Feds love, it's a Mr Big to go and bust. It gets them in the papers, gets them promotions and pay rises, pats on the back. You attach yourself to a Mr Big, Gabriel, you're attaching yourself to a sinking ship.'

Gabriel nodded. He agreed with Genovese on this, but Genovese created fame in another way to Costello; through ruthless violence he, too, placed a neon arrow over his head for the Feds to follow.

'You need to ask yourself,' said Genovese, 'if maybe there's more interesting work you could be doing.'

There was the job offer, the opportunity to swap sides. It wouldn't be repeated. Genovese was presenting Gabriel with a pass that, much like a bullet, could only be used once.

Gabriel nodded, signaling he understood what was going on.

'Think it over, Gabriel,' said Genovese.

Gabriel smiled and stood.

'Enjoy the champagne,' he said. 'Anything you want is on the house.'

He headed back to the office. After the job offer always came the attack. War. Sooner than Gabriel had anticipated. He needed to make sure he wasn't around when it started. They were sliding towards the solstice, to winter dark, and maybe this would be the year the light didn't return.

PART TEN

'Without exception, the young musicians today, the jazzmen who believe in modern music and appreciate the art of improvisation, pay tribute to the man they consider a real genius, the living legend of our time – Charlie "Yardbird" Parker.'

LEONARD FEATHER, *INSIDE BEBOP*, 1949

22

Thursday 6th, 2.00 p.m.

Ida milled about the benches on the corner of 59th. Behind her were the stone walls of Central Park, in front was 6th Avenue, wide and shadowed by towers, running south all the way to the horizon, cradling a roar of traffic. The sun was shining, making the city gleam, cold and hard.

After a few minutes, Louis appeared, walking down 59th. They grinned when they saw each other, hugged. They hadn't seen one another in two and a half years, and Ida was glad to see that despite the troubles she'd heard her friend was in, it hadn't affected his appearance, his smile or his manner.

'You're looking well,' he said. 'What do you wanna do?'

'I dunno,' Ida replied. 'Let's go for a walk, maybe get some food.'

'Cool,' he said.

They turned and crossed the road, heading down 6th.

They walked and talked of this and that, caught up on each other's lives – Jacob graduating from high school early and going to Berkeley to study law, Louis' new wife, whom Ida had yet to meet, how they had passed the last couple of years, news from down South. They talked of old times in New Orleans and Chicago. Remembering those shared memories, those long-gone worlds, defined the emptiness their passing had created, even as it provided consolation.

'So how comes you're in town?' Louis asked.

She gave him a breakdown of the case, of the position

Michael's son was in, of the link to a missing jazz musician called Gene Cleveland that the murders seemed to be centering on. She'd always enjoyed telling Louis about her work. She often found that explaining a case to a third person helped organize and reinforce its structure in her own mind, that the best way to learn something was to teach it.

Louis listened and nodded, and when she had finished his face assumed a sad sort of look.

'I'll be honest, Ida,' he said. 'Those clubs on Fifty-second Street ain't my world. Bebop's what the kids play. I don't know them. And they don't know me. But let me ask around. There's some people I was just on tour with who play in some of those joints. I'll speak to 'em.'

'Thanks,' she said, thinking about the articles she'd read in the press – the younger generation of jazz musicians criticizing Louis for betraying his talent, for pandering to whites, for selling out. The stream of disapproval he had to deal with just as the big band scene seemed to be floundering.

'How's it all going?' she asked. 'I heard about all the swing bands breaking up.'

'Yeah, left, right and center,' he said. 'We're all going out of business. It's getting harder to make a buck. Come Christmas, I'll have done three hundred nights on the road this year.'

Ida nodded, wondering what toll it was taking on his health, and his marriage.

'You need to take it easier,' she said.

He shrugged. 'Tell the truth, I spend more than a few days at home, I get antsy. I have to keep moving, keeping playing. It's just . . . jazz music these days is either bebop or that New Orleans revival stuff. I'm too old for bebop, and the revival feels like leaning back too long into the past.'

Ida got a sense of Louis' confusion, befuddlement. Exasperation even. When they'd met earlier, she'd thought he was his same old self, but now she was wondering if his recent troubles weren't weighing him down, if his brightness wasn't forced. In his youth Louis had been cutting edge. Now the music he'd helped define had been taken up by a younger generation, and so had been taken away from him. Ida knew his dilemma; she was facing a similar one – how did you adapt to the new without losing who you were? How did you change when you were unsure of what you might become?

'So what are you going to do?' she asked.

Louis shrugged. 'I don't know. I'll figure it out. I'm trying something new at a concert next week.'

He told her all about it as they turned off 6th and wandered through the Rockefeller Center, the sleek, monolithic towers shooting into the sky, its fountain and golden statue of Prometheus sparkling in the sun, drawing crowds.

'You should see it at Christmas,' said Louis. 'With the tree and the skating rink. Snow-globe Manhattan. How're you enjoying it anyway?'

'New York? I'm hardly getting to see it,' she said. 'But what I have seen isn't a patch on Paris.'

'Nah, it ain't. Paris was something,' he said, referring to the time the two of them had spent there before the war.

They walked down a narrow street, past the entrance to Radio City Music Hall, then on the other side of the road from it, the RCA building. Along its first-floor windows were glossy headshots of the radio personalities, the Hollywood stars, the comedians and singers who had hosted shows at the NBC studios that were housed in the building. Outside one of the windows, a crowd had formed, peering in like they were looking at a Christmas display. Ida and Louis walked over to see what the fuss was. Inside the window stood a stack of television sets, placed one on top of the other like bricks, broadcasting a small, flickering ghostly image – one of the shows being aired by the network.

In front of the screens, a gaggle of excited children and their parents watched the grainy gray image of a handsome, middle-aged white man speaking into a microphone at some kind of assembly meeting.

'Who's that?' Louis asked.

'Ronald Reagan,' Ida replied.

'The b-movie actor?'

Ida nodded. She watched him continue his address, wearing a sharp suit, wire-framed glasses, his dark hair slicked upwards and back.

'What's he doing?' one of the children asked his parents.

'He's testifying to the House Un-American Activities Committee,' said one of the parents.

'He's naming names is what he's doing,' said another voice, irate, laced with derision.

Louis gave Ida a look and they headed on down the street.

'This HUAC shit,' Louis said. 'I did a movie last year called *New Orleans*.'

Ida remembered the film coming and going in the cinemas that summer before she'd had a chance to see it.

'It was a cash-in on all that old-time revival stuff everyone's so keen on,' he said. 'Joe got me and Billie parts in it.'

Ida nodded. Louis and Billie Holiday shared the same manager, a former Capone stooge from Chicago called Joe Glaser.

'Our parts got cut down to nothing by the producers 'cos they didn't want the audience thinking black people invented jazz. Dig that shit,' Louis said. 'Then it turned out the scriptwriter was a communist, went up in front of HUAC and pleaded the fifth. Now he's one of the Hollywood Ten. The studio got scared and buried the film with a half-assed release.'

Ida thought on Hollywood, HUAC, the anti-communism hysteria that had been running in the papers over the summer. She thought of the men she'd seen in newspaper photos, standing on the steps of Congress, hunched nervously behind microphones while they were grilled by the government. She thought of the agency being set up in Washington she'd been asked to join. The war against the Germans had barely ended and the war against the Russians had started. Perhaps they were the same war. Perhaps that was the state of things. The eternal war the politicians promised would bring about eternal peace.

'You and Billie still with the same manager?' she asked.

She was a fan of the singer, had used Louis' connection to score tickets to her gigs in Chicago.

Louis nodded.

'For all the good it's done her,' he said. 'Glaser set her up on that rap she's in prison for. At least, I think he did.'

'What do you mean?' Ida asked, frowning. She'd heard Holiday had been imprisoned in West Virginia on a heroin possession charge, but hadn't realized her manager was involved.

'Billie's fella's a big-time heroin dealer,' said Louis. 'Keeps her doped up so he's got a line on her cash. Glaser figured maybe if she did time, it'd break his hold on her. So he let the cops arrest her. And when she was on trial, he didn't even send her a lawyer. She had to face a possession charge on her own while she was sick from coming off the dope. The judge gave her the full whack.'

'You know that for sure?' Ida asked, incredulous that the singer's own manager would arrange for her imprisonment.

Louis shook his head. 'Not a hundred percent. Glaser's been telling me about this hospital here in Manhattan, somewhere uptown that does something called narcotics rehabilitation. You go in there and stay for a few months and the doctors clean you up so you never wanna get high again. Glaser's saying he'll send her there. They ain't got a problem accepting Negro patients if the money's right.'

Ida nodded. She thought about Holiday locked up on a drugs charge. She thought about the men she'd seen in the soup kitchen the previous night. She wondered if they weren't all living on a knife-edge.

They carried on going, past some roadworks where men in overalls were digging into the street. Orange hazard lights had been set up, a red-and-white funnel, through which steam plumed into the icy skies. They cut south down 5th, came upon a bar and grill on the corner of 42nd. Through its sheet-glass window they saw the sandwich counter, a steam table with beef briskets, lamb and pork joints, pastrami, glazed hams, laid out across its silver top.

As they stood there staring at the food, a customer stepped out of the place with a lunch order wrapped up in grease-paper under his arm. He looked at them and guessed they were deliberating going in.

'Best sandwiches in all New York,' he said with a grin, before hurrying off down the street.

'You hungry?' said Louis, turning to look at her.

They went in and ordered thick ham sandwiches and coffees.

'How about we get these to go,' he said. 'We can eat them in the park'

'It's freezing out,' said Ida.

'Exactly, we'll have the place to ourselves.'

They got their food and walked past the library, to Bryant Park.

They really did have the place to themselves. They went to the southern edge of the park, sat on an empty row of benches that faced north, so they could take in the extent of it. It was a tiny space compared to Central Park, but it was beautiful, its grass and bare trees glittering with frost.

They ate their sandwiches and drank their coffees. Ida thought about the man who'd spoken to them outside the bar and grill, telling them the place made the best sandwiches in the city. She'd noticed on her previous visits to New York how everyone talked in superlatives, how the locals were so quick to tell her where she could find the best sandwiches, the best cocktails, the best night-club, the best hotel. It was as if New Yorkers were all involved in a collective effort to catalogue and order everything the city had to offer.

'How are you getting along now that Jacob's off at college?' Louis asked her, breaking her train of thought.

She shrugged. She confessed she didn't like it much, which was true, but that she was getting used to it, which was a lie. She told him about the job offer in LA.

'Working for the government?' Louis asked, raising an eyebrow.

Ida shrugged. Felt a pang of embarrassment, shame even, at what it would mean, becoming part of the establishment, maybe being co-opted by it.

'Los Angeles is rough on colored folks,' he said.

'I know.'

She'd heard rumors. The city had gained a reputation as a hotbed of racial hatred and violence and police brutality.

'Real rough,' continued Louis. 'You know what jazz musicians call it?'

Ida shrugged.

'Mississippi with palm trees.' He smiled, rueful, dry. 'You don't wanna run your own agency anymore?' he asked.

'Sure I do,' she replied. 'But I like the idea of leaving Chicago. A fresh start. That's kinda why I came here. See if I can hack moving to a new city.'

'C'mon, Ida,' he said. 'You moved cities before, you can do it again.'

'I was nineteen when I left New Orleans. I'm forty-seven now. It's different.'

'It ain't different,' Louis said. 'The only thing that's changed is your head.'

'Exactly,' she replied. 'The longer you live somewhere, the more that place fills with ghosts. But you move somewhere new, you become the ghost.'

Louis paused, then nodded.

He took a tobacco tin from his pocket, blew on his fingers to warm them, then opened up the tin. Ida realized that this was the reason he'd wanted to go to the empty park. He took a few pinches of tea from the tin, cigarette papers. He quickly rolled a joint in his lap.

'I haven't smoked that stuff in years,' she said.

'Lucky you. Your tolerance'll be real low.'

He finished rolling the joint and lit it and they passed it back and forth. Maybe it was the cold or the years since she'd last gotten high, but within a minute her head was buzzing, alive, thoughts whirling upwards through her mind. The wintry park, the cold hard sun, the glittering frost, the dull roar of New York in the background, all of it seemed to come alive. She saw how the city could seduce you – the buildings, the buzz, the feeling it left in you that you were at the heart of things, that none of the other parties happening anywhere else in the world were as good as the ones in New York City.

Ida looked at her friend and something passed between them, some wordless acknowledgment of a bond that was both painful and precious.

'I only ever smoke this shit with you,' she said, as if to undercut things.

'What you complaining about?' he said. 'Means you always getting it for free.'

They stared at each other and burst out laughing, and they couldn't stop, and in those moments, it was like they were twenty-one again in the Chicago summer, when there was still so much of the world to explore, and everything was full of possibility, of new and wonderful things. For that tiny slice of time, sitting in the coldness of the park, they had respite from fear and lucklessness, bewilderment and the pressing weight of things that were supposed to matter.

23

Michael descended the Third Avenue El at 129th and walked ten blocks to the Harlem Hospital on Lenox Avenue, a towering brick building set behind tree-studded lawns. At the reception desk he asked for Dr Miller and was directed to the surgery unit, spoke to the nurses there and was told to wait. There were some chairs opposite the nurses' station. He sat in one and waited, wondered again if he was doing the right thing coming here.

Tom had told him about Dr Miller years ago, how he'd studied under him at the hospital, and the two had gotten along. Michael hoped Miller might be able to shed some light on Tom's behavior, on why he quit working at the hospital. He hoped Miller might be able to provide him with something, anything, that would help the case.

After half an hour of waiting, a portly, light-skinned colored man in a three-piece suit walked into the unit and approached the nurses' station and chatted to them. A few moments later, one of the nurses pointed to Michael. The man turned and with a frown, approached.

Michael rose, nodded at the man.

'I'm Dr Miller,' he said. 'The nurses said you wanted to speak to me.'

He had a slight Southern inflection, muffled now by years of academia and living in the North. Tom had told Michael how, when Miller had been hired in the 1920s, many of the hospital's white doctors walked out in protest, and the superintendent responsible for his recruitment was demoted to the information booth at Bellevue.

'Dr Miller. My name's Michael Talbot. You know my son, Dr Thomas James Talbot. You were his superior when he worked here.'

Dr Miller frowned at Michael, trying to square the old white man in front of him, with the young colored man who'd been his assistant.

'Tom never told you his father was white?' Michael asked.

Miller paused. 'He may have done. If he did, I'd forgotten. How can I help?'

Miller raised a hand to the chairs where Michael had been waiting and they both sat.

'You heard what happened to him?' Michael asked.

'Yes,' said Miller. 'I was shocked when I read about it in the newspaper. I remember Tom as a gentle, good-natured boy. I couldn't imagine him doing something like that.'

'You haven't been contacted by his lawyer?' Michael asked. 'To come to the trial as a character witness?'

Miller shook his head.

'I see,' said Michael, wondering why the lawyer hadn't gone through the list of character witnesses he'd supplied him with, thinking again they needed to ditch the man and find someone better.

'But I'd be glad to help out however I can,' said Miller.

'I was wondering if you could talk to me about how Tom was acting before he resigned from his job here. If he spoke to you about why he left?'

'Isn't that something you should be asking your son, Mr Talbot?'

'Tom's not forthcoming on the matter.'

Miller frowned, gave Michael a suspicious look. 'Tom resigned to go and fight in the war,' he said, bluntly.

Now it was Michael's turn to frown. 'Yes,' he said. 'But Tom came back from the war, rejoined the staff here, but then resigned again, a few months before the murders in August.'

Miller looked confused. 'I'm sorry, Mr Talbot,' he said. 'May I see some identification, please?'

Michael thought about it, nodded. He took his wallet out, passed the doctor his driver's license. Miller took it, looked at it, handed it back.

'Mr Talbot,' Miller said, 'I'm not sure what Tom told you, but there was no *second time*. Tom resigned from his post here to go and fight in the war. He never came back. He never rejoined the staff. I haven't seen him since before his army service.'

Half an hour later Michael was back at 129th Street, approaching the El station, the hulking iron armature which kept both it and the train line fixed in the air. Through its strut-work came a rusted metal sunlight, patchy and hard. Michael walked up the long flight of steps that led to the platforms, his head still spinning.

If Tom had never gone back to his job at the hospital, then what had he been doing in the year and a half since he'd returned from the war? Living off his savings and wandering New York? Why had he lied? Why hadn't he gone back into employment? It was only a matter of time before the prosecution found out, and it would be another nail in Tom's coffin.

When Michael reached the platforms, he needed to sit down to regain his breath. He found a bench, sat. The wind was blowing much harder up here than on street-level, it snatched the heat from his face, left his skin smarting. But soon enough a train rattled into the station.

Michael boarded and it was only when the train was trundling downtown that he realized what it was he was feeling underneath the anger and the confusion – betrayal. Tom's lies hurt like a knife in the back. He thought about all he'd sacrificed for Tom. He remembered the night of his birth, all those years ago in New Orleans. How his son had entered the world and brought with him a trailing freight of tenderness and worry that had never lessened, and never would.

It was on Tom and Mae's behalf that Michael and Annette had moved north, rearranged their lives for the safety of their children. All he'd ever done, he'd done on account of his children, and all he wanted from Tom in return was the truth. Why was he holding it back?

He watched the city spin past in a daze, the chaotic tenement roofs of Harlem, the moneyed high-rises of the Upper East Side. He thought about Dr Miller looking at him like he was a madman.

He got off the train at 59th Street, made his way back to his apartment on 7th Avenue. The sidewalks were filled with a lunch-time crowd, office workers pouring out of towers, heading into diners, shops, running errands. Others were heading into bars, hankering after lunchtime whiskies or beers.

When Michael reached his building, he looked up at its facade and decided he needed to clear his head before going back in. He walked to Central Park, got lost in its winding paths, trying to figure out what was going on. He could make no sense of Tom's situation and wondered if it was because the situation itself was senseless, or if his brain had grown too old and slow to uncover any logic that might be running through it.

Was Tom really so traumatized by the war that he had returned from it and given up on life? If so, why hadn't he sought help? Why hadn't he turned to his parents?

It made Michael angry – at Tom, at the perpetrators, at himself. If he could just find the people responsible, he was sure he could see Tom returned to safety. He focused on the energy of revenge, even though he knew he shouldn't, and his thoughts spiraled further onwards into darkness.

He left the park and crossed to his building and took the elevator up to the apartment. He made himself a coffee, and poured a double measure of whiskey into it before placing a call to Annette back in Chicago, wondering how he'd break the news to her of this latest bewildering setback.

24

Times Square was where the city slammed against you. The blaze of neon, the blinding lights, the roiling crowds, the blast of traffic, all so strong as to feel like a physical force. It took a while for Ida to acclimatize when she came out of the subway, to take it all in, to fortify herself. Then she hurried through the night-time confusion, heading north.

She walked along streets teeming with tourists, sailors, cops, kids, vendors and hawkers of everything imaginable, a criss-cross of cabs driving through steam. She passed by all-night movie houses and seedy-looking cabarets, cafeterias whose sheet-glass windows reflected in speckles and sweeps the square's neon glitter.

She reached 52nd Street, which was lined with brownstone nightclubs, their entrances covered by ratty, half-collapsed canopies. Outside each doorway were billboard stands, set up to entice the customers in – *An Open House Jam Session – A Modern Jazz Concert – No Cover, No Minimum, No Cabaret Tax.*

Ida stopped underneath a pink neon sign that read *The 3 Deuces,* the club where she was supposed to meet the man Louis had told her might be able to help, a member of his touring band who had information on Cleveland. She smoked a cigarette, watched the crowds, the traffic, till a tall, light-skinned man approached, wrapped up in a dark blue overcoat.

'You Louis' pal?' he asked.

Ida nodded and introduced herself.

'I'm Shelton,' the man said. 'Let's talk inside. It's freezing out here.'

He nodded at the club behind them. Just inside the entrance sat an old man behind a cash till. Ida handed over three dollars for two covers and the man let them in.

'Where you from?' Shelton asked.

'New Orleans by way of Chicago,' Ida said.

'Yeah, should have figured Nawlins, what with you being a pal of Louis'.'

They descended a dark, narrow staircase then stepped through a door into a cellar the size of a shoebox, with a dozen tables arranged around a tiny stage which was empty except for a drum kit.

Shelton led her across the floor to the cramped bar. Ida took in the people sitting on the hard wooden chairs, at the impossibly small tables, or standing around the edges of the room. A strange mix – black and white, young and old, men and women. Some looked bookish, wearing loose jackets and knit ties, others looked like tea heads and dropouts, others still looked like they'd come here from uptown, brooding, dangerous. Instead of music, the audience's chatter filled the space. Ida sensed something in the air, a feeling of expectation; the crowd was excited about something.

They reached the bar and Shelton approached a man sitting on a stool, sipping a drink. He was a dark-skinned Negro, with a goatee beard and a porkpie hat slanted on his head, black suede shoes on his feet. There was something about the way he leaned back, focused on watching the crowd, the tumbler in his hand, that lent him an air of solemnity and earnestness.

'Eubie,' said Shelton.

The man at the bar looked up at them, and a grin broke out across his features. 'Hey, Shelton. What's going on?' he said.

They hugged each other, and Shelton gestured to Ida. 'This is the lady that's looking for Cleveland,' he said.

Shelton nodded and Ida introduced herself.

'Pleased to meet you, ma'am,' the man said. 'I'm Eubie.'

He spoke in a Southern drawl, yet another migrant to the city.

'Eubie's the booker at the club here,' Shelton said. 'I only know Cleveland a little bit, but Eubie played in a band with him.'

Ida nodded and explained to Eubie why she was looking for Cleveland.

'Yeah, the House of Horrors,' Eubie said. 'I recognized the name of the hotel in the papers. Figured Cleveland might be involved. You wanna get yourselves a drink?'

Ida bought whiskies for Shelton and herself.

'So, you know where Cleveland is?' she asked Eubie.

'Nah, he went missing months back. A little while before the murders. One minute he was there, the next he was gone. Had a gig and he never turned up.'

'You sure he disappeared *before* the murders?' Ida asked.

'Yeah, I'm sure,' said Eubie.

'You know why he went missing?'

Eubie paused, apprehensive.

'You can trust me,' Ida said. 'I'm not with the police. I'll keep your name out of everything. I just need to find Cleveland. A man's life is at stake.'

Eubie thought about it, sighed. 'What do you know about Cleveland?' he asked finally.

'Nothing much,' she replied. 'Just that he's a jazz musician who sells dope on the side.'

'Yeah, half the people in the scene are either pushing dope or using it. Take a look around you,' Eubie said, indicating with a nod the people crammed into the club. Ida ran her eye over the patrons and frowned; it didn't really strike her as a dope crowd. None of them displayed the stupor, the listlessness she associated with the drug.

'Before the war, Cleveland was one of the best saxophone players I ever played with,' Eubie said. 'Made music like you'd never heard. The kind of thing people'll be listening to in twenty years and still think it sounds like it's from the future.'

'But he went to fight in the war and when he came back, something had changed. He played wild. Angry. Went off on his own. Rest of the band couldn't keep up. Crowds booing. He walked off stage a few times, left us in the lurch. One time he threw his sax into the crowd, nearly started a riot. He was back on the dope then. Sometimes I think how angry he would've played without it. Maybe that's why he got high all the time. Anyway, whatever he saw out there in Europe turned him from angel music to devil music. I mean, it was still beautiful, but violent, angry.'

Ida looked again at Eubie, saw that behind the veneer of aloofness, there was anger in him, too. She wondered if he'd served in the war as well, come back to government promises that proved empty, to a city destroyed by race riots, awash with heroin and not much else. She thought of Tom, how a whole generation of young men had been affected by the war. While Cleveland came back angry and raging, Tom had come back broken, subdued, roaming the streets to ease his distress. And finally their paths had crossed in the Palmer Hotel with disastrous consequences.

'Look, I don't know *where* he disappeared to,' said Eubie. 'But I know *why*.'

'OK,' said Ida.

'After he didn't show up to that gig, no one saw him for a while,' Eubie explained. 'And we got to worrying. I went uptown, found him in that hotel room of his. Holed up. Said he was quitting music. I'd heard it before. He was like that. But this time was different. He said he had a line on someone.'

'You mean he was blackmailing someone? Who?'

'One of these guys he dealt to,' said Eubie. 'Cleveland mixed it up. Had a bunch of customers from radio stations, magazines, advertising. Midtown cats who liked to slum it. You know, do dope at parties in the Village on the weekends, then catch the commuter special to their office on Monday mornings. Cleveland used to push to them. Maybe he was friends with them too, I don't know. He used to get invites to their parties. I went along a few times. Swanky pads. Rich but trying to look poor, you know, authentic? I think they dug having colored people around. Anyway, Cleveland said he was gonna bleed this cat dry. Said he didn't need to play music no more. Once this con came off, he was set for life.'

'He say who the man was?' Ida asked.

Eubie shook his head. 'Nah. But it had to be one of those Midtowners. I figured maybe it was someone famous, from the radio or Broadway. Some Hollywood actor maybe who'd started buying dope off him. Then Cleveland figured he could switch and blackmail the guy. I wouldn't put it past him. Like I said, Cleveland came back angry.'

'You know someone in this Midtown crowd we can talk to?' Ida asked.

'Yeah, I know a guy,' said Eubie. 'Works for NBC, doing effects on the radio.'

'Effects?'

'Sound effects, background noises, atmosphere for the radio shows. Dick Tracy. Boston Blackie. All that detective serial shit. We got him a job recording some of our sessions, in return he got me and Cleveland a gig playing the background music on a few episodes of his radio show. Could have got us more, but we were the only two shines in the building and the other musicians got sore.'

'Can you get me his number?' said Ida. 'A name?'

'Sure. I probably got it in the office out back,' Eubie said, gesturing to a door at the end of the bar. 'But the number didn't come from me.'

'Course not,' Ida said. 'Thank you.'

'Ain't nothing,' he replied. 'Like you said, a brother's life is at stake.'

Ida nodded, smiled, felt a glint of hope. Cleveland was blackmailing someone influential who'd bought dope from him. Maybe that blackmail victim sent someone to the hotel to kill Cleveland and somehow it ended with a bloodbath. It was a good motive for the hit. It felt right. It fitted. Even if it meant going up against someone with pull, it was welcome news; at last they were on track to figuring out who was behind the murders. They needed to find out who Cleveland was blackmailing and, if the evidence fitted, build a case against them.

Eubie checked his watch. 'I need to introduce the band,' he said to Ida. 'Then I'll go find it.'

'Sure,' said Ida.

Eubie gestured to a kid who was loitering about at the end of the stage. The kid nodded back then disappeared through a door, and a few seconds later, five young Negro men came out of the door and walked onto the stage. They were all dressed in suits, but there was something about them, the way they hung their heads, their solemn expressions, the way they'd didn't even look at the audience, that marked them out as different to any jazz musicians Ida had ever seen.

As they got their instruments ready, Eubie walked from the bar onto the stage, and the crowd hushed.

'Ladies and gentlemen,' Eubie said, 'thank you for coming here tonight on this cold, wintry evening. Hopefully we can warm you up a bit. I'd like to present to you the Charlie Parker Quintet. On trumpet Miles Davis, on piano Duke Jordan, on bass Tommy Potter, on drums Max Roach and on alto saxophone, the one and only "yardbird" himself, Charlie Parker.'

He whisked his hand up to the band and the audience applauded. He smiled, then stepped off the stage and headed back to the bar, disappeared through the door into the office at the rear.

Ida looked at the band's leader with the saxophone in his hand. He was in his mid-twenties, she guessed, and looked a mess, his suit rumpled, his posture slumped, his eyes glazed over, staring at the boards of the stage below him. He looked disturbed, just a step away from homelessness. But the crowd all seemed to be in awe of him, leaned forward almost as one, expectant, excited.

After a moment, he looked up at the audience as if noticing them for the first time, cleared his throat.

'First tune's called "Anthropology",' he mumbled.

He nodded at his band-mates. The drummer counted time and they launched into the song.

It was unlike anything Ida had ever heard. Jazz, but played at breakneck speed. Fury and ferocity. The tune fragmented. The drummer hit the drums so fast the sticks became a blur. The ride cymbal glistened and pulsed. The horns and the piano knocked out a chorus, which quickly spun into a saxophone solo that twisted so much the melodic line kept sounding like it was going to tie itself into a knot, but always, at the last second, the saxophonist escaped in a feat of virtuosity, flipping the melody inside out, looping it round into something new, whipping it on.

Phrases shimmered about the bars in ever-shifting patterns. Solos and choruses started and stopped and started again, abruptly, juddering, jagged and tense. As chaotic and restless as the streets outside. But always, somehow, dazzling and clear. It felt like the first time Ida had heard jazz as a child in New Orleans. Bewildering.

She looked over the crowd, saw how they leaned forwards in their seats, some with grins, some with their eyes closed, some with their eyes like pins that caught the light. Those standing around the edges of the room tapped their feet and nodded to the rhythm as it twitched and throbbed.

The men on the stage played with a trance-like focus on their instruments, sweated into their shirts. Ida had never seen Negro musicians play with that kind of attitude on a stage before, disdainful, dripping with self-confidence. The saxophonist, who looked so shabby and unremarkable before the music had started, had come alive, seemed forceful now, seemed to emanate something magical.

'How you like it?' Shelton asked, shouting over the music.

Ida smiled. 'It's good,' she said. 'Reminds me of when I was young.'

He gave her an odd look. 'This is *new* music,' he said.

'I know,' she said. 'That's why.'

He thought for a second or two, then he seemed to get it.

'I've never heard people improvise like this before,' she said.

Shelton smiled. 'You free your mind and the notes come out,' he said. 'Like you don't even have a choice.'

'Doesn't sound very free if you don't have a choice,' she said.

'You've got a choice in *how* you play them,' he replied, shrugging.

Ida paused, then nodded, though she wasn't sure how true that was.

The door to the office opened, and Eubie stepped out, holding a scrap of paper. He walked round the bar and handed it to Ida. She looked at it and saw a name and a telephone number. She smiled.

'Thanks,' she said, looking up at Eubie.

He shrugged. 'Just remember, it never came from me.'

Ida nodded and slipped the paper into her pocket and they turned to look at the band.

The trumpet player, a dark-skinned kid who couldn't have been more than twenty years old, was involved in what sounded like a battle with the drummer. His solo felt like it was constantly going to be capsized by the waves of noise crashing out of the drum-kit, but somehow he always managed to surf clear, rising into the air, causing the drummer to pound the drums even more frenetically. And so they continued on, skyrocketing around one another, whirling to a crescendo.

Then just as abruptly as they'd started, the song came crashing to an end. And all that could be heard was the sound of the musicians catching their breath, the tap of their sweat dripping onto the stage.

Something rushed around the room and the audience burst into applause.

Ida thought of the big bands of the swing period, bloated and ponderous, dying now like so many beached whales. It all seemed so fake compared to these five musicians and the honesty with which they played.

When the applause had died down, the saxophonist looked around the room again, announced the next song.

'This is a newer composition,' he mumbled. 'It's called "Relaxin' at Camarillo".'

There was a smattering of applause and a few members of the audience laughed, Shelton and Eubie among them, as if the name of the song was a joke.

The saxophonist smiled wryly, then the band launched into the song, a slower number, beginning with a soothing melody that was played on the piano.

Ida looked at Shelton and Eubie.

'What's the joke?' she asked them.

Eubie nodded at the men on stage. 'Last year Parker and the rest of the band went out on tour to California. Parker couldn't score dope so easy out there so he drank. Went crazy. Set fire to his room and ran through the hotel naked. He was arrested, sent to jail, then on to Camarillo. It's the State Mental Hospital in California. Spent six months there. It's got a drying-out program for junkies. Meanwhile the rest of the band were stranded in LA, had to sleep on couches till they could afford a ticket home. I guess the song title's making a joke about it.'

Ida nodded. Turned to look at the young men on stage once more.

'Camarillo,' she repeated, and she wasn't sure why. The sound of it maybe, the way the syllables rolled off the tongue like they often did with Spanish words. She thought about Charlie Parker, heroin addiction, mental hospitals. Drew a parallel with Billie Holiday in prison on a dope charge, strung out and locked up and maybe crazy, as well. She thought about Tom and Cleveland, too. It seemed like madness and addiction followed the whole generation around.

She mentioned the thought to Shelton and Eubie.

'Sure,' said Shelton. 'Earlier this year the band had a different pianist, Bud Powell. He's in the loony bin, too, now, getting electroshock.'

Ida looked at the piano player on stage, hunched behind his instrument, sweat dripping off his face.

'Ain't a surprise,' Eubie chimed in. 'All you got to do is look around you. Something's gotten out of control and it's dangerous. World wars and people living in misery. If being rational's brought us to that, maybe we should try something crazy. Even madness makes more sense than that.'

Ida thought about this and looked around the audience again. She realized now that these were the city's outsiders, its outcasts, the people on its margins, meeting together in a smoky, dingy basement, to create something that made sense to them in a society they felt increasingly alienated from. In this light, the sharp, anxious music took on a new meaning – it was apocalyptic music, a wailing against all that was wrong with the world, the broken future this generation had inherited. They'd come here to revel in a collective bleakness, and thereby their bleakness reduced.

When the band took a break, Ida said goodbye to Shelton and Eubie, and headed out onto the street. She looked about her with new eyes, thinking torrents. She headed for 50th Street to catch the subway uptown. As she passed through the pulsing chaos of the streets, she thought again how the music she'd heard reflected it so perfectly; restless and simmering, overwhelming and fast.

She thought about what she'd learned and allowed herself a smile. They had a reason for the killings. Now all they had to do was figure out who Cleveland was blackmailing, and why.

25

Michael received a phone call from Ida in the morning. She told him how her night had gone at the jazz club, that one of Cleveland's old band-mates had supplied a reason for the killings – blackmail. It made sense, especially considering Cleveland's clientele. Michael should have felt thrilled at the news that they'd finally made a breakthrough, should have echoed the excitement in Ida's voice. But he was still brooding over what had happened at the hospital. Even after talking it through with Annette the night before he was still feeling bewildered and betrayed.

'Cleveland's pal gave me the name and number of someone we could talk to,' Ida said. 'Someone in this crowd he sold to. Edward O'Connell. Does the sound effects for radio dramas on NBC. I called his number a couple of times this morning, but no one answered. You want to follow it up while I go downtown and speak to Tom's lawyer?'

'Sure,' Michael said. He copied down the number.

'How'd it go with Tom's old boss?' she asked.

He told her about his visit to the hospital. As he spoke he could hear the disappointment in his own voice, was surprised at how strong it sounded, even to his own ears.

'It's another lie again,' he said when he'd finished.

There was silence on the line a moment.

'We need to talk to him about it,' Ida said.

'I know.'

'In the meantime,' she said. 'O'Connell.'

'Sure.'

He put down the phone, feeling no better for the conversation, and tried to focus on the task in hand. He called up the number he'd been given, figuring if there was no answer again he'd speak to Carrasco, ask him to look up the number in the reverse directory and get an address for it. But after a few rings, someone picked up, a woman with a frail, timeworn voice. She informed Michael that O'Connell had been a tenant of hers, but that the man had skipped out on her a few weeks back, in the middle of the night, owing a month's back rent. Michael thanked her and hung up.

He called NBC, asked to speak to O'Connell. Discovered O'Connell had left his job under a cloud about a month before he stopped paying rent to the landlady. The man had hit bitter days and disappeared.

A dead end.

Then Michael had an idea.

He called Ida's hotel and left a message, then he headed out. Walked to the public library on 42nd Street. In the information section, he managed to get a number for the American Federation of Labor. Called them up from a payphone in the library's lobby. Asked what union a sound-effects artist would belong to. Explained to them what a sound-effects artist was. Waited. No one seemed to know, but they narrowed it down to two – the Musicians' Union, or the National Association of Broadcast Engineers and Technicians.

He needed to pick one. Was a man who made sounds a musician or a technician? Michael thought about the Musicians' Union, its reputation for haughtiness and exclusion. Took a chance on the Technicians' Union.

He called back NBC. Thankfully, he was put through to a different person.

'Hi, there,' he said, trying to sound upbeat. 'I'm calling from the National Association of Broadcast Engineers and Technicians and was trying to trace one of our members – Edward O'Connell. He worked in your sound-effects department until recently.'

'What's it concerning, please?' said the woman on the other end of the line.

'He applied for an assistance grant when he'd lost his job a couple of months ago,' said Michael. 'The application has been successful, but the address we've got for him is out of date. I was hoping he left you with a forwarding address for his final pay check, and maybe I could try that.'

'This is a personnel issue,' said the woman. 'One moment, I'll transfer you.'

She did so and Michael spun the same lie again.

'Let me check our records,' said the man in personnel.

Michael heard himself being put on hold, then a minute or two later, the man's voice came back.

'You're in luck,' he said. 'You got a pen?'

Michael jotted down the address – somewhere in Greenwich Village. He thanked the man, hung up, sat in the lobby and waited. He'd give Ida an hour, then head down to the Village on his own.

Forty minutes later she turned up, looking annoyed.

'Well?' he asked. 'How'd it go with the lawyer?'

She shook her head. 'It didn't. Went all the way down to his office. Got told he was in court. Waited in the reception for an hour, decided to go to the court and check the dockets. He didn't have any cases on today that I could see.'

Michael took this in, felt his heart sink a little.

'I'll speak to Tom,' he said. 'Start looking for a new lawyer.'

She nodded. 'How'd it go with you?' she asked.

'The number was a bust,' he said. 'O'Connell lost his job recently and skipped out on his old landlady. But I managed to get a more recent address.'

He held up the scrap of paper with details he'd gleaned from NBC's personnel department.

'Shall we?' he asked.

They caught a taxi downtown, to a glum road of tumbledown townhouses off Washington Square Park. They rang the man's buzzer, but no one answered. They rang the buzzer for the basement, figuring there might be a super with some information.

An annoyed-looking woman opened the door to them.

'Yes?' she said.

'We're looking for Edward O'Connell,' Michael said.

'He's not in?' the woman asked. 'Why d'you want him?'

Michael reeled off the same lie he'd used to NBC about being from the union. The woman eyed them, then nodded her head down the street.

'Try the cafes on Greene,' she said. 'Where the rest of the loafers hang out.'

Greene Street was a block east of the square. It had a number of cafes on it, some on first floors, some in basements. Michael saw what the woman meant about loafers. The Village seemed like a blue-collar neighborhood, but the people in these cafes seemed anything but – they looked like college students, artists, writers, poets in training, bohemians. They were mostly young, mostly white. For all their nonconformity there was a certain uniformity in how they dressed – horn-rimmed glasses, straggly beards, baggy sweaters, suede shoes, pants cut tight and tapered at the ankles.

'Same kinda crowd that was in the club last night,' said Ida.

'You know what O'Connell looks like?' Michael asked.

Ida shook her head. They started on the corner of Greene and West 4th and went into the cafes one by one, asking for O'Connell by name. They used the union cover story again. They were met with blanks stares, apologies, and in a couple of places with hostility. In the sixth place they tried, a cramped basement that smelled of mold, they asked the barman and he nodded, pointed at a thin, slight man sitting at a corner table, reading a paperback Camus. Despite the close atmosphere in the place, he had a trench coat on over a thick woolen cardigan.

They headed over.

'Edward O'Connell?' Michael asked.

The man looked up from his book and raised his eyebrows. 'Yes?'

'My name's Michael Talbot. I was wondering if I could talk to you a minute.'

'What about?'

'We're looking for Gene Cleveland and a friend of ours told us you might be able to help.'

At the mention of the name what little color there was in the man's face drained. He shook his head.

'I don't know anyone by that name,' he said, clearly lying. 'Excuse me.'

He rose, slipped the book into his pocket and pushed past them towards the stairs that led to the street.

'Sir?' said Michael, following him.

O'Connell broke into a run, knocking over a table, spilling drinks, causing the barman to yell at him. O'Connell made the stairs and bolted up them, surprisingly quick. There was no way Michael could match a young man's speed, certainly not upstairs.

By the time they got onto the street, O'Connell was gone.

'I told you I'm too old for all this,' said Michael.

'C'mon,' said Ida. 'Sooner or later he's going to head back to his apartment.'

They found a bar a couple of doors down from the apartment where they could sit and watch its front door. As they waited, snow began falling, a flurry that left a dull shine on the street and dusted the hats and coats of the people coming up and down the sidewalk.

A couple of hours and three coffees later, they saw O'Connell heading up the street, looking over his shoulder, going inside.

They gave it fifteen minutes.

Ida went round to the rear of the building. Michael went to the front door and rang the buzzer. O'Connell's head popped out of a window on one of the upper stories. He made eye contact with Michael and immediately disappeared back inside. Michael gave it thirty seconds before he was out on the rear fire escape, heading into the alley that ran behind the apartments. In a minute he'd be on the ground, with Ida pointing her gun at him.

Michael walked round the back and it was mostly how he expected it to be.

The man was lying on his back, a hand on his face, fingers pressed against a bloody lip. Ida was standing a yard away, her .38 trained on him.

'We're not here to harm you,' she said.

'Funny, I don't believe you,' said O'Connell, moving his hand away from his busted lip to look at the blood on it. He moved his hand towards his pocket.

'Easy,' said Ida, tensing.

'I'm getting a cloth,' said O'Connell.

Ida nodded. The man pulled a handkerchief from his pocket and raised it to his lip. Ida heard Michael approaching, looked at him quickly.

'I'm sorry about this,' said Michael, holding out a hand to help the man up.

O'Connell deliberated, took Michael's hand and got to his feet.

'We're not with the police,' Michael said. 'We're not with the people who are trying to kill Cleveland.'

'Bullshit.'

'We're private detectives,' said Ida.

'And I'm the father of the man accused of killing those people in the Palmer Hotel,' Michael added flatly.

O'Connell stared at him, frowned. The earnestness in Michael's voice and demeanor had an effect; the man seemed to soften a touch.

'No shit,' O'Connell muttered, in a tone that suggested this turn of events somehow pleased him.

'We want to find the people who are after Cleveland,' said Michael. 'To clear my boy's name. We need your help. Please.'

O'Connell stared at Michael, appraising him, deciding. Michael weighed in with what he hoped would ultimately sway him.

'I know you lost your job at NBC. I know you skipped out on your last landlady and you're probably going to do the same with the new one.'

Michael fished his wallet out of his pocket, pulled out five twenties.

'I'll give you all this, if it'll help my son.'

O'Connell looked at the money, looked at Michael, looked at Ida.

'All right,' he said. 'Just put the gun down. Let's talk inside.'

O'Connell's apartment was the size of a napkin, and as joyless on the inside as its exterior suggested. It was a one-room affair, with a bed and a bedside table, a cupboard and a sink. A suitcase sat in one corner on a luggage stand. Paperbacks were piled up on a brick-supported bookshelf.

Michael wondered where the hell they were all supposed to sit.

O'Connell turned the comforter over on the bed, gestured for them to sit on it. He took the suitcase off the luggage stand and perched on it, a little precariously, to Michael's eye. He took a tobacco tin from his pocket and rolled a cigarette.

'Bum deal what happened to your son,' he said.

'That's one way to describe it,' Michael said.

O'Connell looked up at him for a moment, then got back to rolling his cigarette.

'So you two are real detectives, huh?' he said. 'I used to work on a detective serial at NBC. *Boston Blackie.* You ever listen?'

Ida nodded. 'My son used to. When he was younger. *Boston Blackie. Enemy to those who make him an enemy. Friend to those who have no friend,*' she said, repeating the show's tag-line.

O'Connell smiled.

'Boston Blackie, Charlie Chan, Perry Mason, Dick Tracy,' said Ida. 'I'd come home from work and have to listen to detectives all night.'

'I guess they must sound kooky to the real deal,' said O'Connell.

Ida shrugged. 'It's entertainment.'

O'Connell finished rolling his cigarette, popped it in his mouth, looked around, grabbed a box of matches that was lying on the windowsill, in amongst a collection of pink ticket stubs from cinemas.

'How'd you find me?' he asked, lighting up.

'We need to respect the anonymity of the person who gave us your name,' said Michael, sounding more pompous than he'd expected. 'Just like we're going to respect your anonymity and keep you safe.'

O'Connell thought on this. 'I don't know if I'll ever be safe again,' he said. 'But I'll try and help your son, if you help me with my rent.'

Michael handed him over the yard he'd shown him in the alleyway. O'Connell took the bills with a nod of thanks, slipped them into the pocket of his cardigan.

Michael turned to Ida. With a minuscule nod of the head she gestured back towards Michael, then towards O'Connell. So slight a movement only Michael would have picked up on it. He caught her meaning. He would run the questions while she would keep her eyes glued to O'Connell for twitches. It was like the old days in Chicago, when their minds worked in tandem, picking up the same cues, communicating wordlessly, with looks and gestures. An elegant partnership, underpinned by the unsaid.

'We know Cleveland was blackmailing someone,' said Michael, turning to look at O'Connell. 'We're guessing that was who attacked the hotel. The person who gave us your name said it might all be linked to your group of friends, to people who work at NBC.'

O'Connell smirked. 'Not exactly,' he said.

'Who was Cleveland blackmailing?' Michael asked.

O'Connell took a toke on his cigarette, exhaled. 'Paul J. Helms,' he said. 'Congressman Paul J. Helms.' He grinned at them.

Michael's thoughts raced, not an actor, not a radio star. A politician. A man with pull.

'Over what?' he asked.

O'Connell shrugged.

'Was Cleveland dealing to him?' Michael asked.

'Maybe,' said O'Connell.

'He was part of your circle?'

'I guess,' said O'Connell. 'He came to a few parties.'

'Narcotics parties?'

'Narcotics, sex, jazz,' said O'Connell. 'All those things the system hates. Helms was in town doing a publicity tour for some initiative he had going on. One of these things politicians do to show everyone what a swell guy they are. He did a couple of radio shows at NBC. A friend of mine got talking to him, asked him along to a party. He came, then he came to another one. We got friendly with him. You know how these things go. Then we're all at a party one night, and Gene comes around to drop off a consignment. He sees Helms there and freezes. Asks me if I know who he is. I tell him he's a congressman and Gene comes over all funny. I ask him if he knows him, and Gene says, yeah, sure, I've seen him around town.'

'A couple of days later I see Gene in the square and ask what the deal is. He says he's got some dirt on Helms, that he's going to squeeze him. I ask what dirt but he won't say. I figure Helms is a dope fiend or maybe a fairy like Gene was. I thought it was pretty low, you know. Gene doing something like that, but, live and let live, I guess.'

Michael frowned. 'Gene was a fairy?' he said. 'Cleveland?'

O'Connell paused. 'I thought you knew,' he said. 'Gene was blue-slipped out of the army. It's why he was so angry and broke all the time.'

Michael nodded. Blue-slips were handed out to servicemen who'd been discharged under special circumstances. Neither honorable nor dishonorable, the blue-slip discharge was a way for military officials to wash their hands of any servicemen they suspected of homosexuality. The slips were also disproportionately handed out to Negroes. It meant losing access to GI loans, training, jobs – the other benefits the government had promised its servicemen as part of the GI Bill. Worse than all of that, however, was the stigma. The shame. Most men blue-slipped out of the army pretended they'd never served rather than admit to it.

'How soon was this before Gene disappeared?' Michael asked.

'I don't know. A month or two.'

'You see him again after that?'

O'Connell shifted in his seat, stubbed out his cigarette, nodded.

'Saw him after the House of Horrors happened,' he said. 'He turned up one night at my old place. Standing outside in the rain, looking like death. Said he needed money, said someone was after him. Thing about Gene is, he's always been kinda . . . different. Got a loose board in his head, you know? A funny way of talking. That night he was raving, coming down off the dope and talking about how a demon was after him. Bible talk, you know? Crazy preacher stuff. I settled him down, we smoked a few joints. I gave him my bed for the night. In the morning, I loaned him some money, I was still working then. I came home in the evening and he'd disappeared. Never saw him again.'

'When was this?'

'The day after the murders at the hotel.'

'Did he say anything more about the murders?' Michael asked. 'Did he say they happened because of this blackmail plot against Helms?'

O'Connell shrugged. 'He didn't have to,' he said. 'I figured it must be. But, I dunno, killing all those people . . . I can't see Helms getting his hands bloody. He's too smooth for that.'

Michael thought of Faron, of what Carrasco had told him about the man. 'Did you ask Cleveland about this demon he said was after him?' he asked.

O'Connell shrugged again. 'I asked and he gave me this look like I was a fool. Gene can do that, cut you down with just a look. I thought it was maybe just him coming off the dope, making him crazy.'

'And that was the last time you ever saw him?' Michael asked.

'Last time I saw him,' said O'Connell. 'But I got a phone call from him after that.'

'When?'

'About a month ago, when I was still at the old apartment.'

Michael looked at Ida. A month ago meant Cleveland might still be alive.

'What did he say?'

'Just called to say thanks for looking out for him,' O'Connell said. 'He told me he was holed up somewhere safe, somewhere no one would find him.'

'In New York?' Michael asked.

'He didn't say that,' O'Connell said. 'But I got the feeling he was still in town. If he'd gone away I think he would have told me, you know?'

Ten minutes later Ida and Michael were walking towards the square to catch a cab back uptown. Snow was still falling through the sky, whirling past the crumbling brownstones that lined the street.

'We've got the name of the man behind it all,' Ida said. 'And a congressman, no less.'

She smiled at him, trying to cheer him up, but the break-through hadn't done much to alleviate Michael's gloom. He took his cigarettes from his pocket, lit one up.

'So Congressman Helms is being blackmailed by Cleveland,' he said. 'So Helms hires Faron to take care of it. Faron turns up at the hotel and murders damn near everyone in it except the one man he was supposed to kill, and Cleveland gets away and goes into hiding.' Michael paused. 'What a mess. All those people dead just to protect Helms's good name.'

He shook his head, took a toke on his cigarette.

'You think the demon he was talking about is Faron?' Ida asked.

'Must be. The man walked into a diner a decade ago and slaughtered everyone in there, and he did pretty much the same thing in Harlem this summer.'

They turned a corner onto the square, headed for a hack rank on its opposite side.

'Well, if O'Connell told us the truth,' said Ida, 'then Cleveland was still alive last month, and he might still be in town.'

She smiled at Michael once more, trying again with the cheery angle.

'This is all good progress,' she added.

'Yeah,' Michael said. 'Yeah, it is.'

'I was thinking we could ask Carrasco to pull the phone records from O'Connell's old address,' she said. 'Might give us the location Cleveland called him from last month. That's a lead.'

Michael nodded. 'Helms and Faron,' he said. 'They're our killers. All we need to do now is find them.'

PART ELEVEN

'In expansive but bulging Harlem, on the thronging Lower East Side, in Hell's Kitchen and in other districts where the scarcest commodity is living space, crimes of passion and violence flare with disconcerting regularity. Human and environmental factors produce a perpetual series of shootings, stabbings and assaults; burglaries and larcenies; robberies, rapes and murders. And aggravating the simmering volcano is that pariah, the narcotics dealer, who infests the vicinities most vulnerable to his wares.'

REPORT OF THE DISTRICT ATTORNEY,
COUNTY OF NEW YORK, 1946–1948

26

Harlem. Gabriel parked up the Delahaye and crossed 135th to the towering red bricks of the YMCA. He'd already been to Bumpy's apartment in Mount Morris Park and been told the man was out playing chess. Gabriel knew where Harlem's chess players gathered in summer – on the sidewalks outside the YMCA. But now, in the depths of fall, with winter coming on, he guessed they wouldn't be in their usual spot. When he arrived he saw he was right – the sidewalk that in the warm months was lined with rickety fold-out tables full of kids and old men and gawkers, was filled instead with nothing but an icy wind whipping down the street.

Despite the cold, two boys were sitting on the steps that led into the building. They gave him a slant-eyed look. Stared from Gabriel to the Delahaye and back again. A white man on 135th Street must either be a gangster or a cop, and judging by the car, he wasn't a cop.

'Where'd the chess players go?' Gabriel asked them, gesturing to the empty sidewalk.

The kids gave him a look like he was a moron, then one lifted a finger and pointed to the doors behind them.

Wise guys.

Gabriel peeled a twenty-spot from his roll and tossed it over.

'Keep an eye on the car,' he said. 'You'll get another twenty if I come out and the car's still there.'

He went up the steps and through the front doors. A receptionist directed him to a wide, dusty sports hall at the end of the corridor. It was chilly and dim inside the hall. There was a smell of dust, mold and boiled cabbage. On the floor was a tight grid of tables at which the chess players sat. Studious types, quiet, hunched over, engrossed. Most of them still had their coats on, hats and scarves, too. They might as well have been on the sidewalk for all the good the building's heating was doing.

As Gabriel scanned the faces of the chess players, a few people looked up, eyed him warily. He ignored them. He needed to find Bumpy, to ask him about Gene Cleveland, to maybe figure out why Benny was after him, if it had anything to do with the missing money. It probably didn't, but Gabriel was running out of more substantial leads.

At a table in the far corner he saw a colored man with close-cropped hair, dressed in a plain gray suit under a sand-colored coat. Bumpy Johnson. Playing a match against a kid who couldn't have been more than eleven years old. Gabriel headed over, slipped through the grid of tables. Bumpy looked up, saw him, frowned.

'Gabriel,' he said. 'God's most beloved angel. How's life on Earth with no wings?'

Gabriel smiled. 'I make do with a pigeon coop.'

'On the Upper East Side? I'd love to see the looks on your neighbors' faces.'

'Trust me. You wouldn't.'

'Here for a chess lesson?'

'Not exactly.'

Bumpy gave the kid a signal and the kid slipped out of the chair and slunk off to watch one of the other games. Gabriel took his place and eyed Bumpy as he started to move the chess pieces back to their starting positions. He was a hard man to pin down; ruthless leader of New York's unruliest neighborhood, drug-runner, extortionist, switchblade master, but slight of build, a conservative dresser, a reader of philosophy. He'd spent a third of a ten-year prison sentence in solitary confinement, got through it writing poetry. He'd been so successful, half the gangsters in Harlem had started copying his style, his unabashed intellectualism, his book reading, his refinement. The man had single-handedly invented a stereotype – the intelligent, black hoodlum.

'You mind if we play while we talk?' Bumpy asked. 'I don't get much time to play these days.'

'I ain't much of a chess player,' said Gabriel. 'I never had the focus.'

'No?' said Bumpy, who didn't stop resetting the board. 'You surprise me. It's all about focus.'

Gabriel lit a cigarette, organized the pieces on his side of the board. White pieces. When they were all set up, Bumpy looked up at Gabriel, nodded.

'You don't wanna pick for colors?' Gabriel asked.

'I always play black,' said Bumpy. 'I'm used to starting at a disadvantage.'

He smiled. Gabriel looked down at the board, thought about moving a pawn two spaces, changed his mind and moved it just one. Bumpy gave him a disapproving look.

'How's business?' Gabriel asked.

'Business is great,' said Bumpy. 'Can't shift enough of this new Asian shit.'

Since the end of the war Genovese and Gagliano and Luchese had moved from weak, war-time Mexican heroin back to the more powerful Asian variety. Addiction rates had spiked and Bumpy had profited. While Italian Harlem in the east was Gagliano territory, Black Harlem in the west was run by Bumpy. He'd made a fortune inundating it with heroin on behalf of the Mafia, but his value was in more than that. In a city of hot heads and cold shoulders, where every race lived at sword point to the next, Bumpy was an ambassador, a middle man, a mediator, between the two sides of Harlem, between Italian and black gangsters, between civic leaders and thugs.

'So what are you looking for, Gabriel?' Bumpy asked. He was

the only person who referred to Gabriel by his full name, drawing out the syllables in an accent that still contained a seam of Carolina in it, despite all his years in New York.

'Must be important if you're heading north of Sixty-fourth Street,' he said.

Gabriel noted Bumpy's reference to his home address, looked down at the board. Bumpy was already moving his heavy-hitters out from behind his pawns. Aggressive play. Gabriel countered as best he could.

'A man named Gene Cleveland,' said Gabriel. 'You heard of him?'

'Yeah. Why you asking? Didn't have you down as a skip tracer.'

'I heard he's disappeared.'

'Yeah, last summer.'

'How so?'

'It's a long story,' said Bumpy.

'You think you can lay it out for me before the game's over?'

Bumpy looked at the state of play. 'Not likely,' he said, with a smile.

They played another round of moves. Bumpy reacted to Gabriel's almost instantly, reacting so fast it made Gabriel wonder exactly how many steps ahead Bumpy was thinking.

'Cleveland's small time, big trouble,' he said. 'Came back from the war, started selling dope. Our veterans didn't get GI loans like the white boys did. Used to push horse out of a flophouse up near a Hundred and forty-first, and to some Midtown entertainment industry types.'Bout six months ago there was an incident in the flophouse. Four people murdered. You heard about it?'

'The Harlem Horror House,' said Gabriel. 'Cleveland was involved?'

'Seems that way to me. He was slinging dope out of the place. Then a bunch of people there got killed, then the next day Cleveland's disappeared.'

Gabriel remembered the story from the previous summer. He'd noticed similarities to Faron's m.o. at the time, but dismissed them when he saw a Negro living in the building, some veteran juiced up on voodoo, had been caught red-handed, literally.

'They arrested someone,' said Gabriel.

'Just a wrong-place-wrong-time nigger. You know how it is. Being Negro in New York is just an accident waiting to happen.'

'Not always.'

'Always,' said Bumpy. 'You think 'cos I'm doing OK I don't notice? When Costello wants to meet me for breakfast, where's he do it? The Fifty-seventh Street Diner. I still ain't got an invite to one of them breakfast get-togethers in his apartment. And don't tell me you started letting darkies in the Copa?' Bumpy stared hard at Gabriel.

Gabriel shrugged. 'We had Lena Horne performing in the lounge last year.'

'Yeah, *performing*. In the *lounge*. Your left flank is vulnerable, Gabriel. Focus.'

Gabriel frowned at the board, saw the danger and the fact that it was too late to do much about it. He thought about the murders in Harlem, felt panicky at the idea that Faron might have committed them, might have slaughtered yet more people.

'You look into what happened?' Gabriel asked, shifting a castle to the danger-zone.

'Sure,' said Bumpy. 'No one knew anything. Not even the police. I figured it was rogue cops. Maybe the Mob. Which makes you coming around here asking questions intriguing.'

'I'm as much in the dark as you are,' said Gabriel.

'Figuratively speaking,' said Bumpy.

He nodded to Gabriel to indicate it was his move. Gabriel looked down at the board, and saw he'd been completely out-flanked, that it was just a matter of time before he was in checkmate. He risked everything on a reckless counter-offensive, moving a bishop high up the board.

'So four people were murdered in Harlem and you don't have a clue what was behind it?' Gabriel asked.

'Yeah, how you like them onions?' Bumpy said sarcastically.

'You didn't hear any names floating about?'

'Nope.'

'What about a guy named Faron?'

Bumpy paused, raised his eyebrows. 'The guy that snuffed those cops back in the thirties?'

Gabriel nodded.

'Ain't heard his name in years. If he ever existed in the first place. What d'you know that I don't?'

'Just rumors. You hear about anyone else looking for Cleveland?' Gabriel asked.

'No one important,' said Bumpy. ''Cept the brother they pinned it on. He's trying to avoid an electric chair bounce and his pops used to be an investigator for the government out in Chicago.'

'His pops?'

'His pops is white,' said Bumpy. 'Now there's a state of affairs. They hired some private detective from out West to look into it, too. I heard from my boys in Narcotics they're sniffing around.'

'You got a name?'

'No, but I can get one, if you want.'

'Sure.'

Gabriel took a drag on his cigarette, tried to make connections between Benny, Cleveland, Faron, the missing money, and now the murders in Harlem. To kill four people on Bumpy's turf they must have had approval from someone. It must have been connected to one of the five families. But which one? The same one that helped Benny steal the money?

On the way over, Gabriel had thought Bumpy would provide him with some answers, instead what he'd told him had just raised more questions, confused things even further. He took another drag on his cigarette. Noticed how the sound of pieces being dropped onto boards all around him echoed about the place like raindrops.

'Guess you were right about your focus,' said Bumpy. 'You're in checkmate.'

Gabriel looked down at the board and its squares of day and night, victory and defeat.

Bumpy grinned. 'See, you were here for a chess lesson after all.'

27

Thursday 6th, 7.35 p.m.

Gabriel headed back to the apartment to catch a few hours' sleep, found it difficult on account of what Bumpy had told him about the murders in the hotel. He popped a couple of Nembutals and even then he couldn't quite manage anything more than a broken slumber. Just after sunset he gave up trying, rose, took a shower.

He called Nick Tomasulo, Costello's mole in Vito Genovese's operation. Gabriel needed to ask him if Genovese's appearance at the Copa had anything to do with the missing money. If somehow Genovese had found out about Gabriel's investigation. Even though Gabriel knew Tomasulo was probably compromised, he prayed he had something to give him, because all Gabriel's other leads were coming up short.

They arranged a meeting. Gabriel caught a cab to 47th and Broadway, entered the Mayfair Theater, bought a ticket and took a seat in the auditorium. The place was empty aside from Gabriel, a gang of boys in the front row, and a couple of teenagers at the back, eating each other's faces.

He sat through the tail-end of the newsreels and then the main feature came on, a crime flick staring Rita Hayworth and Orson Welles. Gabriel chained Luckies and ended up watching most of the film while he waited for Tomasulo to show up. As Hayworth and Welles stalked each other through a hall of mirrors, guns in their hands, jumping at reflections that may have been real, at images of killers multiplied, a man entered at the rear of the auditorium. Tomasulo. Finally. Gabriel raised a hand and Tomasulo peered at him through the blackness and the silver light flooding in off the screen. He walked over and sat next to him. He wore a thick wool overcoat with a fur collar that had caught the rain, making the fabric smell musty and stale, matching the cinema's own signature scent of moldy carpet.

'Jesus,' said Tomasulo, regaining his breath. 'Sorry I'm late. The traffic at the tunnel . . .' He shook his head.

'You've missed most of the film,' said Gabriel.

'Oh, yeah?' said Tomasulo, squinting at the screen. In flickering black and white, Orson Welles shot at one of the infinite reflections in a mirror. Glass shattered. Images dismantled.

'Any good?' he asked.

'Sure,' said Gabriel. 'Apart from Welles' Irish brogue.'

Tomasulo took off his coat. Gabriel studied him; he was looking as tired and anxious as always.

'What did you want to see me about? We're not due a check-in for a while.'

'I wanna know if Vito said anything about coming to see me at the Copa.'

Tomasulo paused, shrugged. 'He didn't say anything to me.'

'Anyone else say anything?'

'I didn't hear nothing.'

There was something pitiful in the way Tomasulo said it. He hadn't anything worthwhile to give Gabriel because Genovese had smelled a rat and was keeping things from him. Tomasulo knew it, and so knew his own worthlessness.

'Vito say anything about Benny Siegel?' Gabriel asked.

'Like what?'

'Like anything.'

Tomasulo frowned. 'I didn't hear Vito say nothing,' he said. 'But I heard some of the other guys. Last summer, after Benny had come to town begging for money.'

'What'd you hear?'

'Just the guys joking about how Vito was the only one of the bosses who didn't put money into Benny's casino. How it was a smart move, you know, after Benny got whacked.'

'Benny asked Vito for money to put into the casino?' Gabriel asked.

'I dunno if he asked him for money,' said Tomasulo. 'But they met up over the summer, when Benny was here. That's what the guys were laughing about.'

Gabriel stared at Tomasulo. It didn't make sense – Costello had told him Benny and Genovese had fallen out. But they couldn't have if Benny had gone begging to Genovese for money. With a sense of alarm, Gabriel wondered if Costello had got it wrong, or if he was hiding things from Gabriel.

'You hear anything about a guy called Faron?' Gabriel asked.

'Faron?' said Tomasulo. 'Faron?' He repeated it like he was coughing up a fur-ball. 'The guy from years back? The one who whacked that diner?'

'Yeah, that's the one. You seen him around at Genovese's?'

'What's he look like?'

'Built like a mountain. Brown hair. Dresses kinda hillbilly. Strange accent.'

'Nah, ain't seen no one like that around. But he's dead, ain't he? No one's heard from him for years.'

'You haven't heard anyone mention his name?'

Tomasulo thought, shook his head. 'What's this all about?'

'Long story,' said Gabriel. 'What about a jazz musician named Cleveland?'

'Jazz musician? What the fuck would Vito want with one of them?'

Gabriel suppressed a sigh.

'Vito been acting strange recently, doing anything different?' he asked.

'You mean like taking us all to the Copa?'

'Yeah, things like that.'

'If he had, I would have told you about it,' he said. 'It's just the usual stuff. He's working on these finocchio bars in the Village. Muscling in on them. Then there's the dope. That's it.'

Tomasulo shrugged, looking pitiful again. Aside from the information about Genovese and Benny meeting up in the summer, Tomasulo had nothing to give Gabriel, and they both knew it. Another lead was puttering out, extinguishing itself.

And just then the movie ended, on a shot of a troubled man walking through a San Francisco sunrise. Fresh and clear and full of light. The credits came up. The boys at the front started jabbering, the teenagers paid no notice.

'Nick, I want you to ask around,' said Gabriel. 'About Vito and Benny. Find out what happened between them. And ask around about Faron and Cleveland. Subtle-like. I need to know what's been going on.'

Tomasulo pursed his lips. 'I don't know, Gabby,' he said.

'What do you mean you don't know?'

The lights came up. The boys headed to the exit. The teenagers stayed put. A listless attendant came in and looked about the place, making sure no one had died. She looked at the two teenagers like they'd been there all day, then she glanced at Gabriel and Tomasulo.

'Ten-minute interval before the next showing,' she said.

Tomasulo waited for her to leave before speaking. Gabriel looked about the place. In full light it was even more rundown. The walls were coated in a layer of nicotine stains, the armrests were worn, the seat covers ripped and oozing white cotton stuffing, popcorn seemed to be strewn uniformly over every inch of the carpet. Nick Tomasulo, too, looked the worse for it in the unforgiving light, harried, agitated, old.

When the attendant had gone, he took a puff on his cigarette and looked at Gabriel, and Gabriel could see the man's eyes watering.

'I want out, Gabby,' he said, shaking his head. 'They know.

I'm sure. They're freezing me out. They don't tell me nothing. Sometimes I walk in the room and everything goes quiet.'

Gabriel could see the fear in his face, hear it in the trembling of his voice.

'You know what happens to rats,' Tomasulo said.

'Yeah, I know,' said Gabriel, feeling sorry for the man. 'But you've got Costello behind you. They won't do anything. But, please, I need you to ask around.'

'They already know,' Tomasulo said. 'If I ask around, it's just going to look even more suspicious.'

'There must be someone there you can talk to,' Gabriel said. 'Look, I'll talk to Costello. See if we can do something, send a lump sum your way, but first you need to ask around for me. Please.'

Tomasulo looked at him, hesitated, turned to stare at the empty screen in front of them. Then he sighed and nodded. 'I'll see what I can do,' he said. 'But you gotta talk to Costello. I want out, Gabby. I mean it.'

The attendant came back hoiking a tray laden with smokes, ice creams, orange squeeze.

Tomasulo stubbed out his cigarette in the ashtray in the arm-rest of his seat.

'I gotta get back to Jersey. Take care, Gabby.'

Gabriel nodded at him. Tomasulo rose and left. Gabriel stayed where he was. He felt sorry for the man. Tomasulo still hadn't realized there was no way out. Not for him, not for any of them. The only thing to do was run away, like Gabriel had planned, and hope they didn't catch you.

He tried to put it out of his mind, struggled to think everything through, figure out what his next move would be. As he tried to plan, the lights went down, the screen went bright, the newsreels came on again, and then the Columbia Pictures logo appeared, the movie started once more. Welles and Hayworth riding through Central Park, sailing to Acapulco, running through its streets, arguing in the hills above it. Gabriel wanted to watch those scenes again, to remind himself that Mexico was real, that there truly was somewhere he could escape to outside the nightmarish streets of New York; that it wasn't all just a mirage he was carrying around inside him, a mirage that was steadily dissolving.

Hayworth's figure, her sculpted looks, her blonde hair, put Gabriel in mind of Beatrice. He saw her standing in the center of her dance studio, leaning back in the chair of her office, telling him the sad, sorry tale of Benny's last days in Las Vegas, lamenting the man and his dream. And Gabriel struggled not to imagine it was Beatrice and himself atop those Mexican hills.

As he carried on watching, the plot thickened, the characters double- and triple-crossed each other, summoned up reflections of themselves to confuse and disorientate, and a new theory presented itself to Gabriel – Genovese and Benny had stolen the money together. That was why Genovese didn't put any money into the casino – he knew it was a scam. It wasn't one of the other families that had helped steal the money, it was someone within the family, Genovese. It had to be. Genovese and Benny couldn't have hated each other, they'd met up over the summer, worked it together. Maybe Genovese was responsible for Benny's death. Killed him so he could keep the two mill.

But why had Costello told him Genovese had nothing to do with it? Was Gabriel being set up somehow? And where did Faron fit in? And what did it all have to do with a down-and-out jazz musician?

28

After the cinema, Gabriel had headed straight to the Copa, had worked all night, had gone home and tried once more to get a few hours' sleep, but once more they wouldn't come. Instead he sifted possibilities, angles to a breakthrough. None came. Theories were good, but he was running out of time. He tried to construct elaborate game plans but some contradiction would dismantle them, some missing piece would send them crashing to the ground.

And then he caught a break.

A phone call. Orville Hayes, the house detective at the Savoy-Plaza, the hotel Benny stayed in over the summer, telling Gabriel he'd managed to pull the call records from Benny's room like Gabriel had asked.

Gabriel hopped in the Delahaye, rushed over. In the hotel's bar, Hayes handed Gabriel four sheets of thin paper detailing all the phone calls Benny had made and received in his room during his stay in New York. Gabriel thanked Orville, paid him, returned to the Delahaye and went through them. No numbers Gabriel recognized.

He got out of the car, found a cigar store, made change from five dollars and used the payphone there to call the numbers. He started at the top of the list, the first calls made after Benny had arrived, figuring if Benny had called a car service, he would have done it close to his arrival. And there it was, the fifth call on the list to the Manhattan Cab Company. Gabriel got the address, ran back to the Delahaye, drove.

The company was headquartered in a giant taxi-garage underneath the tracks of the Third Avenue El, the same train line that
passed by Gabriel's apartment, but at its faraway, downtown end,
an entirely different world – a dreary district of warehouses,
machine shops and saloons.

Gabriel parked the Delahaye just down the road from the
entrance, and walked over to it through the shadow slats cast onto
the street from the stanchions of the railroad above. He spoke to
the manager, explained he wanted to talk to the driver who drove
Benny Siegel around the previous summer. The manager claimed
he didn't know what Gabriel was talking about. Gabriel told the
man that he was an associate of Benny's. The man wised up, told
Gabriel the driver was a kid called Aaron Morgenstern, and his
shift finished at one.

Gabriel went back to the Delahaye and waited. He still hadn't
slept, so he took the opportunity. He opened up the Doc's package,
took out a couple of Seconals and Nembutals and dry swallowed
them. When used in combination, the two drugs amplified one
another's effects. He prayed they'd actually make him sleep. He
tipped the seat down all the way. Through the windscreen he could
see the tops of the warehouses, the underside of the elevated
tracks, the buildings below them covered in soot. In the shadows a
bar's neon light flashed blue through the gloom, on its brickwork,
faded posters for war bonds rotted and flapped in the wind.

A light snow began falling, waltzing onto the sidewalk.
Gabriel watched it a few moments, then he closed his eyes. Listened to the wind gusting down the street, making the sheet metal
of the machine shops rattle, whining as it passed through telephone wires. He fell into a weary, chemical sleep. He dreamed of
his parents, who'd died when he was a child – his mother in the
Spanish Flu pandemic, his father of the drink not long after. He
dreamed of the rattletrap tenement they'd lived in at the time,
how with their parents dead, he and his sister had no hope of
paying the rent, how they did what they could, how Gabriel's

sister was left to look after him, much as Gabriel looked after Sarah now.

They slept rough when they had to, rented when they could. They survived. They made it till Gabriel was eighteen years old and his sister twenty-four. Then she was murdered. Sarah's father had disappeared months before so Gabriel was left with the baby, and a burning desire for revenge.

They were living on the Lower East Side at the time, in a dumbbell apartment lined with moaning pipes and ancient radiators that hissed steam. They made extra money letting Mob men on the lam sleep on the studio couch in the living room, a safe house of sorts. The men came courtesy of a friend of his sister's to whom Gabriel was never introduced. They would arrive, hide out while arrangements were made for passports, berths on ships, or till the heat died down on whatever crime they had committed.

Faron was one of their guests. A mountain of a man. A six-footer with lank brown hair and crystal-clear blue eyes. He'd been staying with them a few days, waiting to travel on a ship bound for Italy, fleeing a multiple murder in a diner. When Gabriel had left that morning it was just Faron and his sister in the flat. When he returned he found his sister lying in her bed, her face unrecognizable, the sheets sopping wet with blood. She'd been raped. Sadistically. Cut up. Sliced. Left to die alone, in pain. Faron was gone.

But by some miracle, she was still alive. Gabriel got her to the hospital, where she languished, marooned in her bed. She never recovered. After months of constant pain, with a disfigured face, infections, bedsores, knowing she'd never be whole again, she managed to get to her feet one night, cross the ward to the nearest window, and throw herself out. Fourteen stories. She landed on East 17th Street, and her death sparked in Gabriel a life-long fascination with what it would feel like to jump from a tall building. Those last moments, flying through the air without wings.

Even before it happened Gabriel had set about tracking Faron down. He spoke to Benny Siegel, a friend of his from the neighborhood, older than Gabriel by a few years but the only person he knew who had Mob connections. Benny made enquiries.

What Gabriel learned was that Faron had arrived in New York from Philadelphia a few months earlier, muscle for hire, a gunman with a reputation for efficiency and recommendations from Philly's gangsters. He'd been hired by Luciano's Mob to kill a couple of crooked cops and had done so by entering a cafe at close to midnight and spraying it with bullets, killing the two cops, three customers, and an employee. Later the next day he'd turned up at Gabriel's and his sister's asking to hide out, and Gabriel had let him through the door.

Gabriel bribed someone at the Port Authority but couldn't find any ships with passenger lists that contained the name Faron. He guessed at false papers. He contacted forgers, but none of them could help him. All Gabriel had to go on was the link to the Luciano family and the link back to Philadelphia.

He asked Benny to get him a job in the family, so he might pick up any information that could help in his hunt. Benny got him a job with a night undertaker, a man who disposed of bodies for the family, bottom-of-the-ladder work. Night undertakers were looked down upon by other mobsters – it was a dirty profession, tainted, and dangerous, too.

The night undertaker Gabriel was apprenticed to was an old Neapolitan, silent and inscrutable. The old man knew the power of dissolving acid, of lime, of saws. He knew the owners of farms and garbage dumps and junkyards. He knew the backwoods and fields and lakes of New York, New Jersey and Connecticut. This was during the days of Murder Inc, of the Depression – the work came frequently and in high volume. Men were killed often, for business and for other reasons too – killed over card games, over women, over back chat, for fun, because of rumors, misunderstandings, because people were drunk and there happened to be

257

guns close by, because people were mad, and even, on occasion, simply because people were bored.

Gabriel never killed a soul, but he helped make sure the light of justice never shone on these people, he became a guardian of the darkness. He and the old man sowed the northeast with bodies. And on nights when they didn't have a body, the old man would disappear in the van. Return in the morning with mud on the wheels.

In the meantime, Gabriel continued his search for Faron. He went to Philadelphia, and from there he traced him backwards down the coast to Atlantic City, Baltimore, Washington. A pattern emerged. Faron would spend a few weeks or months in a city as muscle for hire, then go a step too far, do something too violent, too sickening, and move on to the next city. Rumors dogged him, of women killed savagely, raped and knifed like Gabriel's sister. Gabriel crosschecked the rumors with newspaper reports of unsolved murders and guessed them to be true. Faron spent the Depression travelling the country killing men for money and women for pleasure.

In Washington Gabriel heard Faron had come from Pittsburgh, and there the trail grew cold in a weight of rumors; that Faron was originally from somewhere in the Appalachians; that he'd run liquor through the mountains during Prohibition; that his father was a preacher and Faron had killed him when he was still just a boy. In some stories the father was a Catholic preacher. In others he was Lutheran. In some stories he had no parents and was a foundling. The name varied too; Feron, Farrone, O'Faron. He spoke with a German accent, with a Cajun accent, with an Italian accent. Gabriel knew he spoke broken Italian, had heard him speak it when he was hiding out at their apartment. Everyone who met him said the same thing – the man was otherworldly, distant, powerful, aloof. The man unsettled them all.

For years Gabriel looked at news reports from cities all over America and Canada, searching for reports of women knifed, or single acts of brutal violence. He found so many examples, yet none of them brought him closer to finding the man. And so Gabriel's quest went on and he disposed of more bodies, buried them in evergreen woods, dropped them off at isolated farm-houses or tumble-down wrecker's yards, and he rose higher up the family, but for all his questions and probing, he came no closer to his goal. And, meanwhile, Sarah was growing up, and Gabriel was putting her in harm's way, but still he couldn't stop.

And then came Pearl Harbor, and Gabriel, as the sole guardian of a child, was barred from being enlisted. He watched the world go to war, watched the chaos, the senselessness, and in the slaughter his own vendetta's true nature revealed itself to him – petty, stupid, selfish, a waste of a life. He realized, in his lust for revenge, he'd misguidedly fallen into a criminal life, had endangered Sarah, and so he started planning his escape. As the war raged and the world ripped itself apart, he guessed that if Faron was anywhere, he would be at the heart of the slaughter, and Gabriel was happy to leave him to it. He boxed away all his feelings.

And now Faron was back, and all those carefully constructed boxes, the ones he thought were so strong, were breaking at the first sign of strain.

He heard a tapping sound, a rapping, and awoke with a start, to see someone standing on the other side of the car window.

'My boss said you wanted to talk to me,' said a kid standing to the side of the car, peering in.

Gabriel checked the clock – 1.15. Shit. He jacked the seat upright and got out of the car. The kid looked at him. Gabriel was still half-asleep. His mouth was dry and sour. Despite the cold, he felt like he'd sweated a bucketful during his nap.

'You're Aaron?' he asked.

The kid nodded. He was still in his teens, gawky, acned, candle white. He wore a lumberjack's shirt and a brown woolen jacket, held a gray metal lunchbox in one hand.

'My name's Gabriel, I'm an old pal of Benny Siegel.'

'Gabriel Leveson?' the kid said. 'I know you, you work for Frank Costello.'

'Yeah? You know a lot, kid.'

'Benny mentioned you. Benny was my cousin.'

Gabriel paused. 'Where d'you live, Aaron?'

'Williamsburg.'

Gabriel nodded, got it. Benny had got a relative from the old neighborhood to drive him instead of using the hotel car service. Someone at a distance to Benny's usual crowd, someone he could trust.

'I wanted to talk to you about Benny,' Gabriel said.

'Benny's dead.'

'Sure, kid. Thing is, before he died he left some business unfinished, and me and some of your cousin's other pals – Frank Costello, for one – we're trying to wrap up his affairs. You answer some questions, there's a few clams in it for you.'

The kid gave him a rabbit-in-the-headlights look. Maybe he didn't buy Gabriel's story, or maybe he did and he was scared.

Just then a train roared along the El tracks above them, belching smoke and noise, making the girders holding up the tracks rattle and shudder, dispersing a cloud of soot over the neighborhood.

'All I did was drive him around,' said the kid when the train had passed. 'I didn't get involved in any business.'

'Sure, that's all I wanna ask you about. Where you drove him.'

'OK, but I gotta be getting home.'

'I'll give you a ride. You going back to Williamsburg?'

The kid nodded.

'Hop in.'

The boy thought about it, looked at the car. 'This is a Delahaye one three five,' said the kid.

'Sure.'

'I'll talk if you let me drive.'

The kid grinned. Gabriel tossed him the keys. They hopped in.

'She's a beaut. How much she cost?'

'Nothing,' said Gabriel. 'I won her in a card game.'

The kid laughed. 'Jeez.'

He started her up and they headed south, making for the bridge. Gabriel offered the boy a Luckie; he accepted.

'So where'd you take him?' Gabriel asked.

'Oh, everywhere. Every club and restaurant and bar in Manhattan, it seemed like.'

'You take him anywhere unusual, anywhere that wasn't a nightspot?'

'Not sure,' said the kid, mulling it over. 'Hotels. I took him to get his hair cut, I took him to a tailor's. A hospital, uptown . . .'

'A hospital?' asked Gabriel. 'Benny was ill?'

'I dunno,' said the kid. 'He said it was for a friend.'

'OK. Which hospital?'

'I dunno if it was a proper hospital. Maybe like a clinic or something.'

'You remember the name?'

Aaron shook his head.

'You remember where it was?'

'Sure. Riverside Drive. The first townhouse after the bridge.'

Gabriel nodded.

'Oh, we went to a talent agency too.'

'Union Square?' asked Gabriel, thinking of Beatrice.

'No. In Midtown somewhere. Swanky.'

'You remember the name?'

'Nah. But Benny said it was the agency that manages Louis Armstrong? You know, the singer?'

'Sure,' said Gabriel. He knew the agency. He knew the man who ran it – Joe Glaser, a low-level mobster who'd worked for Capone out in Chicago, running brothels and nightclubs, before he turned music-industry insider. Benny could have been trying to book talent to play at the casino, but Glaser had cornered the market in Negro talent, not the kinds of acts Benny would have at the Flamingo.

'You take him anywhere else?' he asked. 'It's real important.'

The kid frowned and took a heavy toke on his cigarette like that might help.

He looked up at Gabriel and shook his head again.

'OK,' said Gabriel. 'You take Benny to any banks or anything?'

'Banks? Sure, first day he was here. First National, just by Bryant Park. He went in with a banker's draft, came out with a roll of hundreds.'

'That's the only bank you took him to? You sure?'

The kid nodded.

'All right. You took him to the airport when he flew back to LA?'

'Oh, sure. I dropped him off.'

'He have a bag with him when he left?'

The kid thought. 'I guess.'

'Where'd you pick him up?'

'His hotel.'

'He make any stops on the way?'

'Nah,' said the kid.

Gabriel finished his cigarette. Crushed it in the ashtray on the dash. He looked out the window at the people on the sidewalk.

'No, wait,' the kid said. 'We did stop off somewhere.'

'Where?'

'Uptown somewhere. Italian Harlem. He told me to pull up and wait, and he got out and came back a while later and we headed off. I remember 'cos he was late for the plane and he was kvetching about how he was gonna miss it, and then we stopped off for all this time. I thought it was screwy, you know?'

'He take his suitcases with him?'

'When he left the car? I dunno,' said the kid, shrugging.

'You remember the address? Where he went?'

The kid shook his head. 'Nah. We were heading uptown, to La Guardia Field, it weren't much of a detour.'

Gabriel thought, ran the angles.

'OK, listen. I'll give you fifty bucks if we go up there now and drive around and see if you can find it? Whaddaya say?'

Forty minutes later they were doing laps of Italian Harlem, driving down this road and that, the kid looking around trying to jog his memory. Just when Gabriel was thinking he'd made a bad call, the kid brought the car to a stop and grinned.

'This is it,' he said.

'You sure?'

The kid nodded, grinning still, proud of himself. They were on 4th, between 118th and 119th.

'See that building down there?'

Gabriel followed the boy's finger to a store on the corner. It was one of those cellar operations that sold ice in the summer, coal in the winter, and wood all year round. There was a board outside with a pad fixed to it, a pencil on a string. An old Italian man walked past, stopped to write his order on the pad then sauntered on.

'While I was waiting for Benny to come back, two men came out the cellar with a block of ice the size of a table, all wrapped up in sacks, you know how they do it. Well, one of 'em slipped over and the ice smashed and went everywhere, all the kids in the neighborhood came rushing, and the two men were shouting at each other. I remember now. It was definitely here.'

'You sure?'

'Sure, I'm sure.'

'OK, where'd Benny go when he got out of the car?'

'Around the corner, I guess,' said the kid, pointing down 119th.

Benny had turned the corner, so the kid wouldn't see where he went: the kid who was a relative with no Mob connections, who Benny just happened to hire for the trip.

'Drive down there,' said Gabriel.

Aaron started the car and slow-rolled down 119th.

It was a nondescript street of nondescript brownstones. Unremarkable. Storefronts here and there. Certainly no banks for Benny to pay in the money. He had the cash with him. He went into one of these buildings. He dropped the money off. He got back in the car and flew to Los Angeles. A couple of weeks later he was dead.

Sitting somewhere in one of those buildings was two million dollars in cash.

29

Gabriel dropped the kid off in Williamsburg and headed straight back to the public library in Manhattan. On the third floor he received a tutorial from a librarian on how to navigate the Periodicals Reading Room, thanked her, collected a stack of celebrity gossip magazines and started going through them. Eventually, he found what he was looking for in a three-year-old copy of *Photoplay* magazine – a snapshot of Benny. It was in an article headlined *Jean Harlow Gives Socialite Benjamin Siegel Acting Lessons*. Gabriel shook his head at the word 'socialite', but the photo of Harlow and Benny was a good one. He looked dashing, his eyes sparkled. Even without the expensive suits and the charming manner, on his natural looks alone, Benny was a man who left an impression. Gabriel was depending on that.

He ripped the photo out of the magazine, then he ripped it in two, consigning the beautiful Miss Harlow to the wastepaper basket. He stepped out of the library to see that the sun had set and the city was buzzing with electric light.

He headed right back to East Harlem, but got stuck in a snarl of traffic, came to a complete standstill. As he waited, he sifted leads and evidence. He thought about Benny at the clinic, saying the visit was for a friend. He wondered if Benny had caught a disease out in Vegas. He wondered why Benny had gone to Joe Glaser's talent agency. He wondered why Benny had met Genovese, had met Jasper, how he had learned that Faron was back in town.

The traffic inched forward. Start, stop, shift.

He watched pedestrians shuffle down the sidewalks, silhouetted by the glow spilling out from shops and diners and restaurants. In front of him dual strings of taillight rubies sloped their way towards the horizon.

Start, stop, shift.

Half an hour later he made it uptown. He parked near where the Morgenstern kid had brought him, stepped out of the car, buttoned up his coat, and crossed the street carefully as the earlier snow flurry had turned the sidewalks icy.

He started at the very end of the block, he knocked on doors, he flashed the police badge he'd bought off a retiring cop a few years back, he flashed the photo of Benny Siegel looking dashing. He explained he was a cop searching for a missing person – the man in the photo – who was last seen in the neighborhood over the summer. He possibly rented an apartment in the building, or visited someone there.

He buzzed for the building superintendents first, figuring they were the ones in the know. Once he'd run the rounds, he'd start knocking on individual apartments and going into stores. Then he'd move onto the next street, then the next.

No one recognized the man in the photo as one of the country's most prominent Mob figures, a man who'd made a failed attempt at becoming a Hollywood actor.

It was well into evening when Gabriel hit gold. A building halfway up the third block he'd tried, a nondescript brownstone, with a super in a second-floor office with a sign on its door that read: *NOISEY TENANTS GET TURFED*.

'Yeah, I know him,' said the man when Gabriel flashed the photo. He was middle-aged, heavy-set, with a tobacco pouch hung round his neck on a string. 'He rented an apartment in one of the buildings I look after. I manage four buildings on this street.'

He looked at Gabriel as if he expected him to be impressed.

'What happened to him?' the super asked.

'He's missing,' said Gabriel.

The super gave him a couldn't-care-less look.

'His family are worried,' said Gabriel, trying to add some emotional weight.

'Like a wife and kids?'

'Sure.'

The super scoffed. Gabriel frowned.

'When did he rent the apartment?'

'Coming up to six months ago,' said the super. 'He took out a six-month lease. It's nearly running out. Saw him the first few days, then nothing. Didn't realize he was missing.'

Gabriel didn't buy the man's story. The super must have known the apartment was empty, must have gone in there to check what was going on.

'I need to see the room he rented,' said Gabriel. 'You open it up for me?'

The super paused. 'Sure,' he said eventually. 'It's in another building. Wait a mo.'

The super grabbed a wooly hat and a coat from inside the office, then a giant ring of keys which lent him the air of a prison guard.

Five minutes later they stepped into the living room of a sixth-floor apartment in a building a few doors down. The place smelled of dust and emptiness. The super switched on the light to reveal as unglamorous a place as Gabriel could imagine, as un-Benny a place, making Gabriel wonder if the super was confused.

The radiators hadn't been opened for fall, meaning the place was freezing.

'All these months this place has been empty,' said Gabriel. 'You didn't thinking of checking in, calling anyone?'

The super shrugged, but underneath it, Gabriel could see the man was tense. He opened up the tobacco pouch hanging around his neck and started rolling himself a cigarette.

'He'd paid the lease up front. Once I get the money what people do with the place is up to them, as long as they ain't destroying it.'

Gabriel nodded. 'Please don't step any further inside,' he said. 'Contamination.'

The super nodded, like he was au fait with the police procedure Gabriel had just invented.

'I'll let you know when I'm done,' said Gabriel.

A look of disappointment flashed across the super's face. Then Gabriel closed the door on him. Slid the door chain into place. Once he was alone, he glanced over the living room once more. There were two wide windows looking out over the rooftops of Harlem, an armchair next to them, there was a sideboard with a radio on it, a sofa-bed, folded up, and a coffee table. On the other side of the living room was a kitchenette and doors leading off to a bedroom and a bathroom.

Gabriel quickly checked the kitchenette, the bedroom, the bathroom, returned to the living room. He walked over to the coffee table. There was an ashtray on it containing some cigarette butts, mixed in with some roaches, which didn't add up as Benny didn't smoke tea, making Gabriel wonder again if he'd got the right apartment. In the under-section of the coffee table was a wire-rack filled with magazines and newspapers. Something seemed odd about it, the way the newspapers were spread out.

He kneeled down, pulled a few out – copies of the *New York Daily Mirror* from the days in summer when Benny had been in town. In the wire-rack, where Gabriel had removed the papers, the corner of an attaché case was visible. Gabriel pulled it out. It was heavy, felt like it was filled with paper. He rested it on the coffee table and sat on the sofa-bed, which was surprisingly hard and ancient. He tried the catches. They sprang back at his touch. With a sense of expectation he opened the lid.

It was filled with promotional material for the Flamingo Hotel and Casino.

Gabriel smiled, shook his head, rubbed his temples. At least it proved this was Benny's apartment.

He sifted through the contents – fliers, leaflets, prospectuses, suite lists.

He picked up one of the leaflets and studied it. There was a Disney-like illustration of the casino's front aspect. The cement work curved and swooped, made the building look futuristic, exciting. A neon sign stretched up into a night sky that was smattered with five-pointed stars. Gabriel flipped pages – architect's renditions of the casino floor, the pool, the deluxe hotel rooms, the buffet, the restaurant. There were facts and figures Benny's accountants had cooked up – projected rates of return annualized over different time periods, enticing hints at the money second-stage investors could make. Gabriel had heard the stories about Benny selling bogus shares in the project, that he'd sold the ownership of the casino three or four times over, to investors who'd all lost out when Benny had been killed and the Mob had assumed control of the operation.

On the front of one of the leaflets was a photo of the hotel. It vaguely resembled the illustration. There were flamingos on the lawn outside, the ones Beatrice mentioned that died every day and had to be replaced.

He threw everything back into the case. Closed it. Returned it to the bottom of the coffee table. He tossed the room.

In the sideboard was a cigarette tin with a hypodermic in it and some dope. Gabriel put it together with the roaches and again something didn't add up.

He tossed the bedroom next. There was a wardrobe there and it was locked shut. Gabriel jimmied the lock easily enough with a switchblade. There was nothing hanging up in the wardrobe, but at the bottom there was a drawer. It was locked too. Again he used the switchblade. Again it was empty.

Gabriel returned to the living room, looked around. Another dead end. Another day gone and no closer to the money. He put his hands on his hips and tried to think. He lit a cigarette and walked to the windows, sat in the armchair next to them, stared out over the endless rooftops of Harlem, the city lights. He smoked and thought of his dead friend, his own impending disappearance. He blew smoke rings that floated upwards, past the windows, one after the other, a parade of halos drifting towards heaven. Delicate halos, shorn of their saints. As they ascended, they trembled, then disappeared. Like they were never even there.

It made him think of all the bodies he'd buried. He imagined them rising up, too, from rivers and garbage dumps and evergreen woods that creaked in the wind. He thought of all the millions of dead, floating upwards as well. He thought of the last time he'd ever seen Benny, looking forlorn at the bar of the Copa. Almost like he was grieving. And maybe he was. But who did Benny have to grieve about?

Then Gabriel thought about the driver, saying he'd taken Benny to a clinic uptown. And then it hit Gabriel all at once and he felt like a fool for not realizing it earlier. The clinic was for Benny. Benny was grieving for himself, because he was dying. From a condition that would require a stay in a clinic and lots of money. Benny had come to set it up. Leaving the money here so he could slip in and pay for his care when the time came. Benny was in New York to check in. For a final blow-out. That explained why he was tossing away money even as he was begging for it, why he seemed so up, even as his life was collapsing all around him. Because none of it mattered. Gabriel shook his head, saddened at how his friend had chosen to deal with his impending demise. It was a lonely, dishonest way to go, but it was typical of Benny's flamboyance. Gabriel promised himself he'd raise a toast to his old pal.

He rose and walked to the coffee table, stubbed out his cigarette in the ashtray there, and as he was crushing the last of the embers, his eye landed on the sofa-bed. The lumpy, rock-hard sofa-bed. He paused.

He pushed the coffee table out of the way, took the cushions off the sofa-bed, extended it out, and there, nestled in the empty section underneath the mattress, were two bulky holdalls. He unzipped the one closest to him.

It was full of hundred-dollar bills, in ten-thousand-dollar straps. A million dollars in each bag. Give or take.

He closed the holdall. His heart raced. Again he got the feeling that something wasn't quite right. He thought about schlepping the bags down the stairs, past the superintendent, across the two blocks to where his car was parked, driving back downtown, finding Costello. He thought about calling him, getting some men up there. But Costello's phones were bugged and he'd have to leave the money unguarded while he found a phone.

Suddenly he wished he had a gun with him. He checked the front door was locked, he heaved the bags out of the sofa. Each one must have weighed twenty pounds. He lit another cigarette and went to the window to check the street in front. It all looked quiet, normal.

And then a cop car turned the corner and slow-rolled up the street.

Gabriel stepped back from the window. Watched. The police car rolled on, seemed to slow down in front of the building. Then it carried on going, heading off down the block.

Gabriel stayed where he was a moment, then he checked the other windows in the apartment, looking for a fire escape. He found one outside the bathroom window, it descended to the alleyway running along the side of the building. And beyond the fire escape, at the mouth of the alleyway, was the cop car, pulled up, lights off, waiting.

Gabriel watched it, waited too.

After a few seconds, a brown Chrysler sedan pulled up behind the cop car, and a bulky man got out and went and spoke to the cops. Gabriel couldn't see much of him in the shadows, under his hat and coat. He didn't need to. He knew something was up.

He gently lifted the window, ran back into the living room, heaved the bags onto the fire escape and crawled out, just as the two cops got out of their car and walked around the corner to the building's entrance.

Gabriel climbed up two flights to the roof with the weight of the bags pulling him down. When he got to the roof, he hoiked a bag onto each shoulder and ran as best as he could across it. How long would it take the cops to realize he had skipped out through the bathroom window? How long before they caught up with him? They didn't have a dead weight of two million dollars holding them down. And a rooftop was the perfect place to kill someone, just push them off the edge and claim suicide.

Gabriel upped his pace, jumped over the low brick walls that divided the buildings, ducked under washing lines. He reached the last building on the block. He looked over the edge. He could see his car parked up in the gloom at the next intersection. He heard a noise behind him, turned to see two silhouettes in the darkness, blurry shapes, moving fast across the black rooftops.

He found the building's fire escape, ran all the way down it. He let the fire escape's street ladder descend, ran down that, jumped into the alleyway below, stumbled, righted himself, bounded towards the corner. He looked over his shoulder. Nothing.

He ran as best he could to the Delahaye. He threw the bags into the backseat and jumped in the driver's side. His heart was beating crazily, sweat dripped down his shirt, the cold biting into his skin.

He looked in the rearview – figures running down the street. He heard car tires squeal. He hit the ignition and the Delahaye swerved off down 3rd. He took the first right onto 120th heading east. He'd just passed the intersection with 2nd when the cop car skidded into the street behind him.

They hadn't put their siren on. Bad sign. Rogue cops sign.

He dodged what traffic there was all the way to the river, cut right onto FDR Drive. Four lanes running next to the river.

He barreled it, putting the Delahaye's engine to good use. He slipped around traffic, but the car stayed close behind. He tried to think of a way out of this. If they called for backup the road would be full of cops in five minutes and he'd be in court explaining a high-speed chase, impersonating a police officer and two million dollars in the backseat. He'd be locked up when Anastasia found out about his stolen money. He'd be as good as dead.

But the cops hadn't put their siren on.

Street lights shot past above. Thomas Jefferson Park up ahead on the right, dark and empty in the freezing night. And just before the park, in a groove on the road, a patch of ice. Gabriel lurched towards it. The cop car right behind him. At the last second, he spun right. Too late, his back wheel caught the ice. The force yanked the Delahaye right, smashed it into the side barrier. Came to a halt.

Gabriel looked in the rearview, watched the cop car run straight over the ice. He prayed. The cop car veered left, smashed through the median strip, fishtailed into oncoming traffic. Brakes squealed. The cops sideswiped a Plymouth coming the other way. They spiraled, crashed dead into the railings on the thin strip between the road and the river.

Gabriel stumbled out of the damaged Delahaye. A little further back down the road, on the other side of the four lanes, the cop car was half-destroyed. The impact had pushed the railing outwards over the embankment, so that the car was now hanging precariously above the river, held up only by the railing's distended ironwork. The car's windscreen was shattered, blood sprayed all over it. The Plymouth had spun onto the median strip. Steam rose. Smoke rose. Gabriel thought again of smoke rings, halos, ascension.

He needed to check the Delahaye was still drivable and get the hell out of there, either by car or by foot. But just as he was coming to his senses, the cop car's passenger side door opened and a figure collapsed onto the ground. The figure wasn't wearing a uniform. It was the big man in the hat and coat from the brown Chrysler.

It was Faron.

Gabriel recognized him instantly. Through all the years, through all the trauma. He hadn't aged a day, hadn't a scratch on him. He was just as large and imposing as Gabriel remembered, just as strong-looking. Gabriel felt a rush of anger, confusing, dizzying, take-your-breath-away anger.

Faron pulled himself up from the ground, looked around. Cars had stopped, rubberneckers, helpers gathering. Faron spotted Gabriel across the lanes of the FDR. Their eyes met.

Through the blur of roaring traffic, through the streaks of headlights and taillights, their gazes maintained a line, held steady.

Then Faron moved, burst into action, jumped into the traffic, dodged four lanes of it, moved with litheness and agility. He hopped the barrier on Gabriel's side of the road and pulled a .38 from his pocket, pointed it at Gabriel.

Gabriel raised his hands, still stunned that the man who'd haunted him for over a decade was standing in front of him, that his gambit with the ice patch hadn't managed to inflict so much as a scratch on him.

Faron approached, walked past him to the Delahaye, gun still trained at Gabriel, and looked at the car, surveyed the damage. He saw the two bags, pulled them out and tossed them onto one shoulder, both of them at once, like they weighed nothing.

He turned his gaze to Gabriel once more. He steadied his gun arm, getting ready to shoot. Then, at the intersection, cop cars. Flashing reds and blues. Close enough to hear a gunshot. Faron turned, saw the entrance to the park behind him. Bolted towards it, disappeared over the railing into its shadows.

Gabriel ran after him. Even though Faron was a killer and was the one who had the gun. He jumped the railing, was enveloped by darkness, but he spotted a figure in the distance, heading towards the park's swimming pool. Gabriel followed. The ground was uneven from the Victory Gardens planted during the war, he had to hop over ruts and grooves in the grass, the outlines of one-time allotment plots now cradling ice.

Faron entered the swimming pool grounds. It was an open-air pool – drained for winter, nothing but a huge oblong of cement and tiles, filled for some reason with pigeons. Thousands of them. Churning like a gray foam. Faron hopped into the pool – the fastest route to the far side of the park. He disappeared from view. The pigeons burst into the air, as if they were one, in a sweeping blast of flapping wings. Pell-mell they scattered into the clouds, over Gabriel's head, across the park.

Gabriel reached the pool, hopped down into it, slipped on something, crashed to the ground, onto his knee, smacking his head, pain exploding, vision blurring, concussing, passing out, rolling onto his back. Blood from his nose slid through his sinuses, down the back of his throat. He burst into a choking fit. Realized that Faron would see him prostrate and return to finish him off. That this was it.

Through the pain he opened his eyes, looked up into the clear night sky. As he waited for Faron to return he watched the stars skate across the blackness like it was ice, the moon ferrying itself across the firmament, pulling vast oceans towards it. He thought again of halos and ascension.

He waited, but all was quiet. Where was Faron? The only noise Gabriel could hear was the rustling of the pigeons as they resettled themselves in the pool. He put a hand to his face, it was covered in blood. It didn't make sense, he'd hit the back of his head when he'd fallen, not his nose. And then he realized. The crash, he must have hit his face on the steering wheel.

He turned his head – saw the pool was teeming with pigeons once more. He rolled onto his side, blood poured out of his mouth onto the icy tiles. He tried to sit up, managed it. He was alone in the great, black emptiness of the park.

Wooziness and nausea from the concussion swirled about his

head. He tried to get to his feet, stumbled, managed it. He pulled himself out of the pool, hobbled back to the FDR. Before he even got close he could see the lights from the cop cars and ambulances carpeting the grass in red and blue.

His head and knee pounded. His heart raced. He tried to think of a cover story.

He exited the park, reached the FDR. All along the roadside were emergency vehicles, black and whites, a meat wagon, cops milling about. He headed to the abandoned Delahaye. Reached it and checked the damage. It was undriveable. Cops were approaching.

'Hey, fella? This your car?' shouted a uniform.

No way of getting out of this now, he was linked to the crash. Gabriel nodded.

'You in the crash with the other cars?'

Gabriel shook his head. 'They were behind me,' he said. 'I hit the ice and veered one way, then I saw them behind go the other way.'

'You need help? You're bleeding pretty bad.'

'Sure.'

'Sit down, pal.'

Gabriel sat on the side of the road. Someone brought a towel for his head.

'Where'd you go after the crash?' the officer asked. 'You weren't by your car.'

'I went to throw up, guess I passed out.'

'All right,' said the officer. 'We'll get a statement off you and send you to the hospital with the others.'

'Sure,' said Gabriel, hoping the others weren't either of the two rogue cops.

The officer went off to his car. Gabriel looked around. On the other side of the road, the crowd around the crash site had swelled with emergency crews. It was only then Gabriel noticed that the railing stopping the cop car from falling into the river had broken through and the cop car was no longer there. People were standing on the edge of the embankment, looking down into the river. A police launch was approaching over the waves.

Gabriel looked down, stared at the asphalt in front of him.

He'd had the money, briefly, and he'd lost it. Six days to go and he'd lost it. And now it was no longer just a case of finding it again and getting out of New York, because now it was Faron who had the money. Which meant Faron would be coming back to kill Gabriel to keep him quiet. Which meant Gabriel had to hunt down Faron first.

PART TWELVE

'The New York manipulator for Lucky Luciano, who visited him while he was held at Ellis Island for deportation, is Frank Costello. He is now the mightiest of the syndicate personnel, with an uncanny genius for mixing into highly important affairs with bigwigs in various spheres.'

JACK LAIT AND LEE MORTIMER,
NEW YORK CONFIDENTIAL, 1948

30

Friday 7th November, 12.05 a.m.

Costello stepped out of Dr Hoffman's office feeling that odd mix of deflation and hope he always experienced after a session. He looked up and down 5th Avenue. A light snow was falling. On the other side of the road, outside the offices of a company that ran sightseeing tours, an old man was selling baked sweet potatoes from a pushcart, steam rising from it into the air. Costello walked over and bought one. The man wrapped the sweet potato in grease paper and handed it over. Costello paid him, told him to keep the change. The man gawped.

Costello hailed a cab. Got in and told the cabbie to take him to the address in Hell's Kitchen where the kid was being held, the kid they were going to try and turn. As the cab pulled away Costello stared at the offices of the sightseeing company. In the windows was a giant photograph of the Statue of Liberty, the green lady standing on her island, staring across the waves, to the destroyed old world. Her classical face, her austere features, lent her a feeling of reliability, permanence, nobility. In all his decades living in the city, Costello had never once been to Liberty Island.

The cab headed south. Costello unwrapped the grease paper from the sweet potato, peeled back its skin, took a bite, felt the warmth in his mouth, but could taste none of its flavor on account of his cold. He sighed and chewed and swallowed. He thought about what Dr Hoffman had told him in their session, the same advice about how the solution to his depression lay in improving his sense of self-worth, and one way of doing that was to consort with better types, to broaden his social circle.

But Costello was already doing that. He'd made friends with writers, journalists, actors and painters, bohemians. He commissioned fine art. He went to cocktail parties in artists' lofts in Greenwich Village, and in glittering apartments on Park Avenue, where the other guests treated him as a curiosity, a streak of danger, a source of anecdotes, a novelty act. Would it really work under those circumstances? Didn't exposure to those kinds of people just highlight the gulf between them?

'Everyone started out a criminal,' Lansky used to say. 'All those big names who look down on us. All criminals. Rockefeller's father was a conman, he hired thugs to break strikes. Astor cheated Indians and got rich building slums. Vanderbilt used gunmen to strong-arm railroad contracts. Don't get me started on J. P. Morgan. Behind every great fortune there's always a crime,' he'd said. 'Give it time, Frank. All it takes is time. The crime fades away and all people remember is the money.'

Costello was the first of the mobsters to move uptown, to get an apartment on the Upper West Side. Luciano, Lansky, Siegel, all followed him. Costello was the first to get in with the politicians, renounced violence where possible, stayed clear of drugs and prostitution. But still that legitimacy eluded him. Costello thought on Joe Kennedy. They'd worked together running booze during Prohibition, but the moment repeal came along, the man wouldn't answer his calls. What if Lansky was right and all it took was time, but that time was so long, Costello wouldn't be around to see it?

The cab turned west when they'd cleared 59th, slipped through Midtown, heading towards Hell's Kitchen. Costello took more bites of the sweet potato, still tasteless, and losing its warmth. He thought of Luciano, the supposed head of the family, locked up in Siberia all those years, then double-crossed by the government, deported to Italy. That was another sign of how they were viewed. When the war came, American boats kept getting torpedoed by German submarines as soon as they'd left the New York docks. A troop carrier berthed on the Hudson mysteriously caught fire. It was only then the Navy realized they had an enemy within – the New York docks, the largest in the country, were run almost entirely by Italians. Who was to say these dockers weren't Mussolini supporters?

The Navy approached Luciano in prison, said if he kept the dockers onside, reported any mysterious characters coming and going, at the end of the war he'd be free. Lucky asked Costello and Lansky to take care of it, and they did. For the duration of the war, while half the Mafia was running a black market in rationed goods and forged ration cards, or setting up doctor's surgeries where men could have their eardrums punctured to be excluded from the draft, Costello was running surveillance on the docks, and Lansky was a regular visitor to the Navy Intelligence HQ on Church Street. He was Jewish; he wanted to destroy the Nazis more than anyone.

But even that didn't buy them what they were after. The war ended and rather than be freed, the government welshed on the deal, and deported Lucky back to Italy. While he was awaiting deportation, he was locked up on a boat docked at Ellis Island. Costello and the boys threw him a goodbye party. Copa girls, food, drink, a ring of longshoremen on the pier to stop the government from breaking it up, the press from reporting on it. The last didn't work. The next day Mayor La Guardia was in the papers complaining about it all.

And as Luciano was deported, sailing one way across the Atlantic, look who was being deported the other way: Vito Genovese. Coming back to New York to face the murder rap he'd run away from years ago. Italy and America were slinging their mobsters across the ocean like it was a tennis court.

They'd held a welcome-back party for Genovese at the Diplomat Hotel when the trial was over. Costello had walked him to

RAY CELESTIN

his spot at the head of the table. Gave a speech in his honor. It couldn't hide the fact that the cards had been dealt, the order had shifted; Costello, who'd been the number-three mobster in the family when Genovese had fled to Italy, was now Genovese's superior.

Costello asked himself again why Genovese was getting involved in the Waldorf meeting. He played mental solitaire, shifted cards around in his head, created parallel lines, structures, grids. It was a more satisfying mental exercise than mulling over Dr Hoffman's advice.

The cab pulled up at the address, an auto-mechanic's on 11th Avenue. Joe Adonis was already there, parked up opposite in his Cadillac. Albert Anastasia was with him, dressed in a plain gray suit and red tie, his fingers strewn with gold rings.

They got out when they saw the cab, stepped into the snow.

Costello met them on the street and they said their hellos.

The apartment was in a walk-up above the auto mechanic's. They filed down an alleyway and through a yard of clotheslines and garbage. Went through a door, climbed two flights, reached a murky hallway whose only illumination was the red light above a gas meter on a far wall. Adonis knocked on a door and as they waited, Costello stared at the red light, at the network of pipes it illuminated.

They entered a railroad apartment. They walked through into a living room and there was the kid, sitting at a table, smoking a cigarette, while two goons kept an eye on him. The place was cold. They'd kept the heating off, and the kid was there in his vest, freezing. He looked younger than Costello expected, mushroom pale. When the kid saw who had walked in, he went paler still, especially on seeing Anastasia, whose triple-digit body count tended to precede him.

Costello sat in the chair opposite the kid, next to a bricked-up fireplace. He blew into his handkerchief, wiped his nose. Popped

284

two cough sweets. He looked at the kid smoking. He craved a cigarette.

'You know why you're here?' Costello asked.

The kid shrugged. He knew but pretended he didn't.

'Monday night you were arrested in a basement cafeteria off Washington Square Park,' said Costello. 'Selling dope. When the cops searched your pad they found enough of it to have you sent away for fifteen to twenty. In an attempt to swerve the jail time you offered to rat out your boss, Vito Genovese.'

The kid stifled a sob. Costello wanted to press him some more but had to break off to sneeze, blow his nose. The cough sweets were making his eyes water. He got the feeling Adonis and Anastasia were sniggering behind his back. God knew what the kid thought.

'The police detective you made the offer to, he's a friend of ours. He came to me and told me what happened. You're a lucky kid. The detective could have been friends with Genovese, and then you'd already be dead.'

The kid nodded. 'Thanks,' he said. 'Thank you, Mr Costello.'

Costello waved it away, he was getting to the nub.

'Kid, you've got two choices. You can start working for us, feeding us information from Vito's camp – what he's up to, what he's talking about, who he's meeting. Or you can tell us to jump, and we'll let you walk out of here.'

The kid frowned.

'Our friend in the police force will have you brought in for further questioning. He'll grill you for a few hours, and then d'you know what'll happen?'

'I'll get charged?' the kid said.

'No,' Costello said. 'You'll be released. Which is even worse.'

The kid frowned again.

'The only bird that flies out of a jail is a pigeon,' Anastasia chimed in from somewhere behind Costello.

The kid looked confused.

'What Albert's trying to say is Genovese'll see you've been released and think you squealed,' said Costello. 'We won't even have to kill you. He'll do it for us.'

The kid's hands started to tremble, the glowing tip of his cigarette shaking in the gloom. For some reason Costello thought of the old lady's apartment in Little Italy, the phosphorescent Jesus glowing in the dark.

'No one likes a rat,' said Costello. 'Sure, you could tell Genovese we set you up, but would he believe you? And if he did, would he care? Would he be willing to start a war over a little punk selling dope?'

Costello paused. Sniffed. Crunched one of the cough sweets in his mouth, felt the pleasing shatter.

'So? You in?' he asked the kid.

The kid looked at Costello, he looked at Adonis and Anastasia behind him, who must have appeared even more menacing in the murk. It took all of five seconds for the kid to nod.

'I'm in,' he said.

Costello was glad of it. It'd take a while for the kid to rise up the ranks, for the effort they were putting in now to reap rewards, but it was all a long-game, you had to think three steps ahead, you had to arrange the lines early.

'Good,' said Costello. 'I'll talk to my friend in the police, make sure no stories get out.'

The kid smiled nervously, even though he was freezing.

'I can go?' he asked.

'Sure,' said Costello, letting him labor under the misapprehension a little longer.

'Thank you, Mr Costello. I won't let you down,' the kid said. He rose, headed for the door.

'There's just one thing,' Costello said.

The blood drained from the kid's face. 'Oh,' he said.

'How do we know you're not lying?' said Anastasia. 'You

were going to rat out Vito at the precinct. How do we know you're not going to rat us out to Vito too?'

As Anastasia spoke he moved his hands and the rings on his fingers glinted in the gloom.

'I don't . . .' said the kid, trailing off.

The boy looked at Anastasia and back to Costello, trembling. 'I don't . . .' he said, stumbling again. 'What do you want?'

'Give us something so we know you're . . . what's the phrase?' Costello asked.

'In earnest,' said Adonis.

'That's right,' said Costello. 'Tell us something important, so we know you're in earnest.'

'Something about Genovese?' the kid asked.

'Yeah,' said Anastasia. 'Something that'd get you in trouble if Vito found out. Something to prove you're in earnest.'

The kid couldn't even look at Anastasia he was so scared. He looked down at the linoleum, at his shoes, trying to come up with something. After a few painful seconds he looked up at Costello.

'I know about this coon Vito's looking for,' said the kid.

Costello frowned, gestured for the boy to continue.

'This jazz musician. He's a pusher, too. Vito's been looking for him for months now. He put the word out to my boss, if this guy comes looking to score to let him know.'

'Why does he want him?' Costello asked, trying not to sound too interested. It was the first he'd heard about it, and he didn't want the kid to think he was too clueless.

'That's the thing,' said the kid. 'No one knows. This guy's just a two-bit dealer from Harlem. We couldn't figure out why Vito's so crazy to find him.'

'What's the guy's name?' Costello asked, thinking he could pump Bumpy Johnson for information if the man was from Harlem.

'Gene Cleveland,' said the kid.

Costello turned to look at Adonis and Anastasia.

They both shrugged. This was all news to them, too.

Costello turned back around. 'All right, get out of here, kid,' he said.

'For real?'

'Scram.'

One of the goons tossed him his shirt and coat. The kid grabbed them and all but ran out of there.

Costello turned to look at Adonis and Anastasia.

'Does that make any sense to you?' he asked them.

'Maybe the kid heard it wrong,' said Anastasia.

'Maybe Vito's a jazz fan,' said Adonis.

Costello sat at the table thinking, trying to play the cards in his head, failing.

Lunchtime. Costello's cab pulled up outside the Astoria. His usual table was waiting in the Starlight Roof. He paid and got out. Walked past a row of government tail cars pulled up by the hotel's side entrance, tail cars he'd given the slip to that morning. The agents in them knew he was a creature of habit, would be back at the hotel for his lunch. As he passed them, he peered in. The agents glared. Angry, bitter men in cheap suits and cheap cars.

Dr Hoffman had told him about the theory of projection. You took the things you hated about yourself and projected them onto other people, so you could hate them instead of yourself. He'd always thought the agencies following him had a similar problem. They worked in organizations with hierarchies, with rigid, military-style structures, so they assumed the Mob was organized the same way. They didn't realize it was much looser than that. People paid for the privilege to use the family name. Once they could use the name, they could do whatever they wanted with the insurance that no one would mess with them. All the family asked was a slice of the profits in return. And so the Mob wasn't an institution, it was a franchise operation, and the authorities' failure to see that was what cost them, trying to uncover lines of command that didn't exist, in a hierarchy that was mostly flat.

Costello went to his usual booth, sat, looked at the sunlight streaming in through the Starlight's stained-glass ceiling. On Monday morning, in one of the floors below, the movie men would begin their heated discussion about what to do with the Hollywood Ten. Why was Genovese getting involved? Why was he looking for a jazz musician?

A bellboy brought Costello the phone messages that had piled up at the hotel while he was gone.

'There was also a Mr Cheesebox who came in looking for you,' the bellboy said.

'What did he say?' asked Costello.

'He said he needed to speak to you urgently.'

'Thanks, kid,' said Costello. 'Hold the lunch. I'll be back soon.'

He rose, exited the hotel, and crossed the street to Cheesebox's listening station in the office block opposite.

The room smelled even worse than the last time. The men with the headphones looked even paler.

'You came,' said Cheesebox, rising when Costello stepped in.

'Sure. What is it?'

'Those producers Genovese met with.'

'What about them?'

'The younger one's a pansy,' said Cheesebox. 'We caught him bringing a boy back to the room.'

'Caught him on tape?' Costello asked.

Cheesebox grinned.

Costello played the cards in his head and started to figure a way out of his bind.

31

Friday 7th November, 11.00 a.m.

Louis sat in the reception area of the Associated Booking Corporation and waited. He looked about the offices and noted how plush they were – crème silk wallpaper, sheer-glass partitions, the furniture all sleek and modern, walnut and chrome, the sofa you sat in and didn't stop sinking into for half an hour. This was the trick to running a talent management agency, you had to look successful to clients, but not so successful they might think you were taking too large a cut.

Along the wall opposite was a row of photos of the agency's clients; Louis had top billing, Billie Holiday was there, Lionel Hampton. All the photos were of jazz musicians, almost all of them were Negro; yet everyone working in the offices was white. That was another trick. Jazz musicians had worked in Mob-run speakeasies back during Prohibition, now they worked in a Mob-run music business. From the Musician's Union to the talent agencies to the record companies, mobsters had managed to parlay Prohibition-era nightclub jobs into professional legitimacy. From due-bill offices run by spewing threats and rubber-checks, to control of the music industry itself.

'Mr Glaser will see you now,' said the receptionist, rising from behind her desk, revealing a figure that could have made her a Copa girl. Louis rose, too, and they walked into Joe Glaser's corner office.

'Louis,' he said on seeing his client. 'I'm sorry about what happened the other night. I called the bus company; they received the check in the post yesterday. It must've got delayed.'

'Sure thing,' said Louis. 'Sorry I had to call you up.'

Glaser waved the apology away. Louis sat opposite him at the desk.

Glaser was a tall man, upright, gray-haired, thin-faced. He never drank, was in bed by ten most nights, hardly ever went to nightclubs, was more interested in sports than music, often referred to his clients as *shines* and *schwarzes*. As hard a man as Louis was accommodating. He'd raped two teenagers back in his Chicago hoodlum days, had only managed to avoid jail time by agreeing to marry the first girl, and having Capone intercede with the court when the trial came up for his second victim.

This was the man Louis had come to twelve years earlier when he was on the skids, when he was tied to a management contract with a gangster he despised and his estranged wife was threatening to sue him, as were the two records labels he'd signed 'exclusive' contracts with. At a concert in Turin Louis' lips burst, meaning he couldn't play his trumpet for six months. Besieged by lawyers and unable to work, he'd slunk back to Chicago and sought out Joe Glaser. Louis knew him from when he was the manager of the Sunset Cafe, one of Al Capone's jazz clubs that Louis had played in. Louis came to Joe with an offer – get the gangsters and lawyers off his back, take over management of his business affairs, and they'd split the profits fifty-fifty. He was smart enough to know even then that a manager with Mob connections was better than a manager without.

Glaser wasn't a music manager, the closest he'd come was a failed attempt at being a boxing promoter. But he called up some friends, the Chicago mobsters who ran MCA, the largest talent management agency in the country, and pressed them for a loan. He used the money to pay off Louis' contracts, his wife, the record labels, the gangsters, and opened a small office. Within a few years, the two of them not only turned around Louis' career, they'd made him a mainstream star.

Twelve years later, Louis was back on the skids.

'He's not here yet?' Louis asked.

'He's late,' said Glaser.

Louis nodded.

On the wall over his manager's shoulder was a painting that clashed with all the other decor in the office. It depicted the antebellum South, an Arcadian cotton field dotted with happy darkies sitting around playing banjos and singing, looking ecstatic to have been ensnared in the slave trade. Louis thought on the turkey tours of the South he'd had to endure over the years, the danger he and his bands had to navigate, the race hate, the constant threat of violence, being run out of towns simply for trying to find somewhere to eat, having to buy food from colored chefs at the back doors of restaurants, having to sleep on the bus because no hotels would offer them beds.

He stared at the painting before turning back to look at his manager.

'You've got a tan,' he said.

'I was in Los Angeles the last couple of weeks,' Glaser said.

Louis nodded. ABC had opened up an LA office a few months previously, another milestone in the corporation's expansion.

'Things are moving west, Louis,' said Glaser. 'I keep telling you.'

'Sure thing,' said Louis. 'Music and movies.'

He must have said it bitterly, because Glaser grimaced.

'Forget about that New Orleans mess,' said Glaser, referring to the turkey Glaser had put Louis and Billie in the previous year. 'I was talking to some studio bosses. We might have you in another picture soon.'

Louis nodded. Thought about Hollywood, the ongoing HUAC hearings, how they'd dented Louis' career and obliterated those of countless others. He thought about Glaser's treatment of

Billie Holiday, wondered again if he really had set her up for her prison sentence, if he really would send her to that health farm. Or if her career was over. That was always the fear in the background. The fear of black artists working in an industry controlled by white gangsters. The same fear felt by all the suckers trapped in the teeth of the Mob's racketeering machine. The dock-workers, the boxers, the market traders, the restaurant owners, the garbage haulers. Sometimes it seemed like the whole of New York was under their thumb. And it didn't matter if you were young or old, rich or poor, famous or nameless.

'How'd the tour go?' Glaser asked.

Louis gave him a rundown of the disaster.

'You see the gate receipts?' he asked when he'd finished.

Glaser nodded.

If he'd seen the receipts, then why was he asking? He knew the thing had been a bust.

'Something's gotta change, boss,' said Louis.

'Swing music's dying,' said Glaser. 'You see the article in *Time*?'

'I don't need to read a magazine to know it,' said Louis.

'There's the original jazz revival,' said Glaser. 'You sure you won't reconsider?'

Louis shook his head. 'Nah, boss,' he said. He could still feel the sting of the movie from the previous year. Louis needed a new direction. Not big bands, not revival music, not bebop. Something else. But how did you build an identity out of negatives? Earlier that year a press agent, Ernie Anderson, had approached Louis with a possible answer to that question. He'd had an idea for a concert that he said might rejuvenate Louis' career. 'Instead of earning three hundred and fifty dollars a night, you'll be earning two thousand five hundred,' he'd said.

Anderson had suggested arranging a concert with Louis playing along with five or six of the best musicians in the country – an all-star band. A small band, like Louis used to play with when he was young, instead of a bloated swing orchestra. Anderson's idea was that they wouldn't be playing revival music, they'd be playing jazz standards, but updated, mixed with the newer sounds the young musicians of the band would bring – something different, a hybrid. Neither revival nor bebop. And definitely not swing. The man had come up with a way out of Louis' dilemma. Supposedly.

He'd managed to sell both Louis and Glaser on the idea. They signed contracts and Anderson had started assembling a band, booking a venue, securing finance for advertising and publicity. As musical director he'd hired Benny Goodman's former trumpeter Bobby Hackett. The concert was due to take place in a few days' time, and they were supposed to meet Anderson to discuss the details.

As they waited Glaser told Louis about Los Angeles. Louis nodded, thought about Ida and wondered if she really would move there. She clearly wasn't over the death of her husband, seemed trapped still, in stasis. Moving to LA made sense if it would help her move on. As long as she wasn't just running away.

Glaser droned on, Louis half-listened, stared out of the window, where he could see the cliff-face of the skyscraper opposite, in whose windows people were working away. He stared at them through the snow that was drifting down the canyon, at the rows of desks, the secretaries, the clerks. They all looked young, well-turned out, fashionable. What kind of office was it? An advertising agency? A political organization?

As he stared, something nagged at him. Something to do with Ida and her investigation. Some connection he felt was in plain sight but also obscured. Maybe to do with the office workers, with Glaser, with Billie Holiday and LA, with the slaves playing banjos in the picture. What?

As he was trying to find a thread to sew it all together his thoughts were disrupted by the receptionist entering, bringing with her a harried-looking Anderson.

'Sorry I'm late,' said the man. 'I left my cab because of the traffic, ran three blocks up the Avenue. Mr Armstrong, sir.'

He held out his hand. Louis grinned, stood, shook his hand. The man held out his hand for Glaser too, who didn't stand, and shook it coldly.

'Take a seat,' said Glaser.

Anderson sat, smiled at them both, his enthusiasm undimmed.

'Everything's arranged,' he said, beaming. He had a strangely adenoidal tone, like the source of his voice was located somewhere in the depth of his sinuses.

'Posters have been up in venues two months now. Adverts have been running in the trade press the last six weeks. The venue called me yesterday – it's a sell-out. We've already had confirmed the jazz critics will be there from the *Times* and the *Tribune* and the *Washington Post*, *Time* Magazine and *Newsweek*. And this morning I finalized the details of the band with Bobby.'

He turned to grin at Louis and passed him a sheet of paper: *Jack Teagarden (trombone), Dick Cary (piano), Bobby Hackett (second trumpet), Peanuts Hucko (clarinet), Bob Haggart (bass), Sid Catlett (1st drums), and George Wettling (2nd drums).*

'Like I promised you, Mr Armstrong,' he said. 'The best band you've played with in twenty years.'

The man grinned again. The musicians really were the best he'd played with since his heyday in Chicago in the twenties. All of them first-rate and forward-looking. Hucko and Bobby Hackett had played with Benny Goodman, Catlett and Teagarden had worked with the bebop bands in Midtown. The band was a perfect mix of the current and the future.

A warm feeling came over Louis, a feeling he hadn't had in years – excitement. He grinned, passed the list to Glaser.

'All that's left now is deciding on the set list and rehearsals,' said Anderson.

He pulled a ragged sheet of paper from his pocket. 'I've got some ideas.'

Twenty minutes later, Anderson and Louis walked out of the office and through the reception.

'You know,' said Louis, 'I wasn't sure you'd pull this off.'

Anderson laughed. 'I haven't, yet,' he said.

They stepped into the elevator, it shivered, then began its descent.

'You might have already gathered,' Anderson said, 'but I'm a fan.'

'Yeah, I kinda figured on that already.'

'I grew up listening to your Hot Five and Hot Seven records. Best jazz ever recorded.'

'Yeah, thanks, pops. They weren't too shabby.'

They reached the first floor, exited the building. Anderson hailed a cab and hopped in. Louis watched him go then looked about the crowds on the street, hurrying through the whirling snow. He looked up at the building opposite, felt that same nagging sensation he'd experienced before Anderson had turned up, that something related to Ida's investigation was maybe connected to the meeting he'd just had, or to the building opposite, or to the people inside it, or to the sky whirling with snow.

PART THIRTEEN

DAILY NEWS

NEW YORK'S PICTURE NEWSPAPER

City Edition Final Saturday, November 8th 1947

LOCAL NEWS

HOUSE OF HORRORS HOTEL OWNER KILLED

David Newark—Crime Correspondent

Manhattan, 7th Nov. – Milton Eldridge, 54, the owner of the hotel at the center of last summer's 'House of Horrors' murder sensation was killed today in a hit-and-run accident on 128th Street, Harlem. Mr Eldridge was crossing the intersection with 7th Avenue shortly after 10 a.m. when he was knocked down by a passing vehicle. He was found unconscious but alive at the scene by two patrolmen. He succumbed to his injuries, however, before the arrival of paramedics. No witnesses to the accident have so far come forward, leading police to make an appeal. Those with information are asked to contact the 28th Precinct on 8th Avenue between 122nd and 123rd, or to call the precinct emergency crime hotline number on *UN ivrsty 4-8783*.

32

Saturday 8th, 11.00 a.m.

The fund-raiser was being held in the meeting rooms of a grandiose Anglican church on the Upper East Side, one of those opulent, gilded buildings whose walls were made of money. The ticket had cost fifty dollars and helped fund a charity that sought to alleviate the plight of the city's poor. Michael and Ida had read about the event in a newspaper when they were researching Congressman Paul J. Helms the previous day. Michael had called the organizers and was told there were still tickets available. He'd bought one and headed down there. He wanted to see him in person, to get the measure of the man, to see if he might be hiding a secret dope addiction that Cleveland was blackmailing him over, or if the blackmail concerned something else.

Michael arrived early, sat in an aisle seat in one of the middle rows. The rest of the audience was elderly and wealthy-looking – bejeweled matrons with perfectly fussy haircuts, old men who seemed to have been dragged there against their will, who couldn't see the angle in helping the city's poor.

On the stage in front of Michael sat six people – the five speakers, all in a row, and a master of ceremonies who stood at a lectern in the center of the stage, introducing the speakers. She gave brief bios of each one, and what she said about Helms tallied with what Ida and Michael had learned of him – a young congressman from upstate New York, a war hero, a campaigner for social change, a rising political star, someone we would all be hearing a lot from over the next few years.

When she'd got to the end of the introductions, she asked the first of the speakers up to the lectern, a Catholic preacher with a parish in Harlem, there to explain to these people who lived in the wallow of wealth how heroin was ravaging the community that lived a ten-minute drive uptown. The preacher, a red-faced Irishman, extolled the evils of the narcotic in a fire-and-brimstone oratory style that wouldn't have been out of place in nineteenth-century Dublin.

While he made his points, Michael studied Helms. He was young and handsome, tall and broad-shouldered. He projected an aura of good health, of cornfield freshness, a cleanness that in politicians and salesmen made Michael suspicious. If what the sound effects artist had told them was true, this was the man whom Cleveland was blackmailing, the man ultimately responsible for Tom's imprisonment. Somehow Helms provided a link that descended from the political class at the top of society down through the world of the entertainment industry, to the city's bohemians, to its underbelly of criminals, murderers and addicts. The question was *how*. One thing was for sure – Helms was not a junkie, he was much too healthy-looking for that. Whatever Cleveland was blackmailing him over, it was not a secret dope addiction.

The Irishman finished up his speech and was followed by a woman who ran a shelter for battered wives. Then Helms took to the lectern, talked about the charity's schemes to help servicemen coming back from the war. He talked about his time in the Eighth Army during the Invasion of Italy, the horrors and destruction he had seen in Sicily and Naples. He played the war hero, capitalizing on the social currency it gave him without ever overtly sounding like he was doing so. He played it to perfection.

And it grated. The way Helms used the war to score points, the way Michael could see through the sheen to the self-serving man on the inside. Helms seemed to be one of those people who mistook entitlement for confidence, who was best-adapted to do well in a superficial culture, and took that as a sign of something great and good inside them, rather than as a sign of something wrong in society.

Michael's thoughts drifted off on a sea of resentment and before he knew it, the speeches were over and the emcee returned to round things up. A smattering of applause finally brought things to a close. People rose, milled about, opened check books. The speakers descended the stage and mingled.

Helms worked the crowd, shaking hands, smiling, chatting, in a patter that was smooth and oiled. Michael got lost in contemplation again. Here was a guilty man being lauded, there was Michael's innocent son in Rikers, beaten, broken, surrounded by killers, the electric chair waiting in the darkness. Michael had always been honest, had always put himself last. Helms seemed to be his opposite. Maybe this was why Helms was a rising star and Michael was fighting to free his son. Maybe it was Michael's morals that had got him into this mess. Maybe more selfishness would have served his family better.

Without his really realizing it, Helms had approached while Michael had been brooding over things, was standing in front of him now – beaming smile, not a strand of hair out of place, not a fiber of lint on his suit.

'Sir,' said Helms, holding out his hand. 'Thank you for attending.'

Michael glared at him.

Helms waited, his hand in the air between them. Michael wanted to swing a punch at him, bruise his face as Tom's had been bruised. But he wasn't sure he could still do it. He couldn't even remember the last time he'd been in a fight. And more importantly, he couldn't make a scene for Tom's sake. If Helms found out they were on to him, Tom was in even more danger of being taken out in a jailhouse hit. Michael was supposed to have gone to the fund-raiser incognito, to have melted into the crowd, to have left after the speeches.

Helms continued to wait, his hand still hovering, confusion spreading across his features.

'You're welcome,' said Michael, eventually. He shook Helms's hand. It was cold and clammy, but his grip was strong.

Helms nodded. Michael prayed he hadn't raised Helms's suspicions. But he couldn't see any trace of it in the man's blank face, and soon enough Helms had moved on. Ushered towards the door by his advisors, whisked through the fawning crowd.

Michael watched him go. He suddenly felt weary. Old and tired and powerless and stupid. Why had he even come here? To get an inkling of what dirt Cleveland might have had on Helms? To get the measure of the man? Or to stupidly risk it all?

He walked out of the hall, down the stairs, out into the New York morning. Helms and his entourage were on the sidewalk, a pair of black Cadillacs waiting for them in the road. They stopped to talk to a gushing mother, who held the hand of a little girl in a blue-and-white winter coat. Michael stopped and watched them. Helms leaned down, talked to the girl. The wind blowing down the street made the fur which trimmed the girl's coat dance and sway. Helms chucked her under the chin. Something about the gesture filled Michael with resentment once more. This man who was responsible for the deaths of four people in Harlem, who might well see Tom electrocuted, playing the nice guy with this mother and daughter.

The entourage moved on, disappearing into the Cadillacs, into traffic, into New York.

And as the girl and her mother turned to walk away, Michael realized why he had come. It wasn't every day you got to look the devil in the eye, and shake his hand.

In the cab heading downtown he tried to fight his despondency. He watched the Saturday afternoon shoppers on 4th Avenue, pressing on despite the wind that was whisking through the city. The cab stopped at an intersection and through the crowds and the snow that had started to fall, Michael saw a billboard affixed to the side of a building. Posters advertising laundry services, car tires, costume jewelry. Some of the more recent posters were peeling at the edges, revealing the older posters behind, including one for war bonds. It showed a smiling GI walking through a gate in a white picket fence towards a perfect American house. At the bottom of the image were emblazoned the words *Bring him back sooner, buy war bonds.*

Michael stared at the poster, annoyed by it. He thought of Helms returning home to a glittering political career, and Tom returning home to wander the streets and into a prison cell. Cleveland too, coming back damaged, picking up a drug addiction. Even Bucek fought in the war, to come home and be slaughtered in a Harlem flophouse.

The cab drove on and the image of the GI and the white picket fence disappeared from view, but Michael kept thinking about it, something jarring. All down 4th Avenue the image tugged at his subconscious, snagged on something in the shadows of his mind, something that demanded attention.

And then it all fell into place.

The war.

Cleveland, Bucek and Helms had all fought in the war.

What if they all fought together?

What if that was what connected them?

Michael thought back to Helms's speech, how he talked about fighting in Italy with the Eighth Army, and something else clicked into place. Faron. Carrasco saying there was a rumor Faron had fled to Italy before the war. Maybe Faron had been in Italy too.

Faron, Cleveland, Helms. Maybe all their paths crossed during the war. How else would a Negro jazz musician and a young politician and a mobster meet if not during the great leveling of status that happened during war-time?

If Cleveland was stationed in Italy with Helms, then maybe Cleveland had been blackmailing Helms over something that happened during their time there. Not anything to do with dope, or homosexuality, or louche parties in Greenwich Village.

And maybe Bucek was stationed in Italy too. And he and Cleveland were in the blackmail plot together, and that's why they both ended up at the Palmer Hotel.

'Pal?' Michael heard a voice say.

Michael looked up, saw the cab had stopped, the cabbie was turned around in his seat, staring back at him, the toothpick in his mouth bouncing up and down.

'We're here,' he said, looking at Michael like he was a fool.

33

Saturday 8th, 1.45 p.m.

Michael stumbled off the street and into the bar, still dizzy from the breakthrough, looked around. It was an old-fashioned place, with butcher-shop sawdust on the floor, barrels behind the bar, metal spittoons between every other stool. He slipped through the crowds looking for Carrasco and Ida. The place was busy with workers who'd just finished their five-and-a-half-day work week, and were already spending their wages.

Michael found Ida sitting alone at the bar.

'Sorry I'm late,' he said. 'Where's Carrasco?'

'Came and went,' she said.

They'd arranged to meet him there to pick up the call logs from the payphone at the Palmer Hotel. Ida slipped a few folded-up sheets of paper from her jacket's inside pocket, to show Carrasco had come through.

'You want a beer?' she asked, gesturing to the schooner in front of her.

He shook his head.

'I think I figured out what's going on,' he said.

He told her what had happened with Helms, the mention of fighting in Italy. The link with Bucek, Cleveland, Faron.

She looked puzzled for a moment, then her eyes lit up.

'At the nightclub,' she said, 'Cleveland's friend said he fought in Europe. It could be they were all stationed in Italy.'

'It fits with Faron,' said Michael. 'He flees to Italy in '33 to avoid the heat from the diner attack. A few years later the war in

Europe starts. He's stuck there. The war ends, he heads back stateside.'

'I'm not sure I buy that,' said Ida. 'Faron would be an American in Italy during the war. He'd have been locked up or shot.'

'Who's to say he's American?' said Michael. 'No one knows where he came from.'

Ida thought, conceded the point, nodded.

'So the war ends and he comes back to America to pick up the old trade,' said Ida. 'Helms is being blackmailed by Cleveland, wants a killer to take him out. Maybe he knows Faron from the war and asks him.'

'Or he asks around,' said Michael. 'And someone suggests Faron.'

'Helms hires him 'cos he doesn't know about Faron bungling the diner job.'

'Maybe,' he said.

'Maybe.'

They looked at each other, both of them excited to be bouncing theories around like the old days.

'We still don't know for sure Cleveland and Bucek served in Italy,' said Ida. 'We need to check. And Cleveland's colored, he couldn't have been in the same battalion as the others.'

'We need to find out where they served,' said Michael.

'We can go back to speak to O'Connell,' said Ida. 'He was friends with Cleveland, he'll know. What about Bucek?'

Michael thought. 'His parents,' he said. 'His home address is in the police reports. It was somewhere in Queens.'

'Who d'you wanna take?'

'I'll take O'Connell,' she said. 'I reckon you'll have better luck in Queens.'

They rose and headed to the door.

Michael hailed a cab and Ida jumped into it.

'I'll come by the apartment when I'm done,' she said.

The cab sped off, Michael waited for another, hopped in, told the driver to head uptown. He popped back to the apartment and checked the case file, found Bucek's address in Astoria, Queens.

Back on the street it took him three tries before he found a cab driver willing to take him. They headed east. They hit the bridge. It whisked them into the sky, high over the river. Above them the strut-work of the bridge shuttered past, stanchion after stanchion. All around snowflakes rushed in the wind. To the south he could see all the way down the curve of Manhattan, the river flat and gray, studded with a weight of boats and ships. The tip of Welfare Island poked out of the water, its trees and rooftops spitting past underneath them, almost as if they were flying.

Then the bridge tapered downwards, and they descended into Queens. Passed through nameless neighborhoods. Arrived in Astoria, and finally stopped on a pleasant, tree-lined street of small box houses.

Michael paid the cabbie and got out into the snowfall. Walked up to the house, his earlier excitement tempered by the fact that he had to go and talk to the parents of a murder victim. He thought back to his years as a cop, how these kinds of visits had been routine. How had he ever managed it?

He stepped onto the porch, rang the bell and waited.

A middle-aged woman opened the door, dressed in an angora sweater and a pleated skirt.

'Yes?' she said, looking at Michael warily, at the smallpox scars across his face.

'Mrs Bucek?' Michael asked.

'Yes?'

'My name is Michael Talbot,' he said. 'I'm a private investigator. I wanted to talk to you about your son, Arno.'

For an instant she gave no clue as to what was going on in her head. Then her eyes clouded over, became dim, suffused with pain and loss. He thought what the woman must have gone through, the worry she must have experienced for all those years her son was fighting in the war. Only for him to return and within a few months be slaughtered at home.

'Talbot?' she said.

The same name as the accused.

'Ma'am,' Michael said, 'I know this is difficult. My son is the boy accused of the crime. I'm trying to clear his name. I think the murder had something to do with your son's war service. I was wondering if I could ask you some questions.'

She frowned, looked puzzled.

'That's not possible,' she said. 'The man accused is a Negro.'

'He's my son.'

She continued staring at him, couldn't seem to understand it.

Michael took the family photo out of his wallet, handed it to her.

She took it. Looked at it.

A moment passed.

Then a look of revulsion spread across her face.

'Leave me alone,' she hissed, and slammed the door shut.

Michael watched the photo fall to the ground, into the snow.

He listened, didn't hear her footsteps receding from the other side of the door.

'Ma'am,' he said, 'they lied about my son, just like they lied about yours. I know he wasn't a drug addict. He didn't have a single needle mark on him. They killed your son, ma'am. Please don't let them kill mine.'

He waited, prayed it would do the trick.

It didn't.

He sighed.

He kneeled down and picked up the photo from the front step. Wiped the snow-water off it. Looked at the faces of his wife and children. He wondered how much of the woman's reaction was due to the fact that he was claiming to be the defendant's father, and how much was simple disgust at the nature of Michael's family. All his life he'd been aware of prejudice, had seen how it affected Annette, but it wasn't until he'd had colored children that he had really understood, only when the gun was turned towards them did he really feel its presence, there, every day, the baseline of race hate that could rear up from the background at any moment. Annette had told him years before that the color of her skin was the first thing white people saw, and often the only thing they remembered, and eventually, sadly, he knew it to be true.

It would have been hard for Mrs Bucek to let him into her house, the father of the accused, but Michael couldn't help but feel that maybe, if his family had been white, the woman might just have been a little more willing to hear him out. Maybe.

Just as he was putting the photo back in his wallet, he heard a noise. He looked up to see the door opening, Mrs Bucek standing there with tears in her eyes.

'I spoke to the police,' she said. 'Told them he wasn't an addict. They told me I was hysterical.'

'Ma'am,' said Michael, tears welling up in his eyes too. 'I'm sorry for what happened to your boy. Please don't let them do the same to mine.'

Forty minutes later he was on the subway back to Manhattan. Thirty minutes after that he returned to the apartment. He poured himself a measure from a bottle of rye. He thought. He went through his wallet. When he'd walked into the fund-raiser that morning, he'd been given an information sheet. Among the details was the number for Helms's office in Washington.

Late on a Saturday afternoon. He wondered if it was too late.

He went to the phone and dialed the number.

After a half-dozen rings a man picked up.

'Congressman Helms's office.'

'Afternoon,' said Michael. 'My name's John Brown. I'm calling from the *Times* in New York. I was at the fund-raiser Congressman Helms spoke at this morning.'

'Yes?' said the voice. 'How can I help?'

'I'm writing up a piece about it, and I just wanted to check the Congressman's war record.'

'What would you like to know?'

'When was he stationed in Italy. He mentioned Naples but I'm not sure I got the dates.'

'One moment, please.'

There was a minute or so of rustling on the other end of the line and then the voice came back.

'He was stationed in Naples for eighteen months, from 1944 through to 1945.'

'Thank you, sir,' said Michael.

He hung up and allowed himself a smile.

He moved a chair to the window and sat. It had a decent view: the intersection of West 58th and 7th Avenue, the trees of Central Park to the north. Postcard Manhattan. He watched the snow falling, watched the people on the sidewalks, watched the sun setting, night come on.

At twenty past six, he heard the keys in the door. Ida entered, shaking snow off her coat.

'Cleveland served in the Eighth Army,' she said. 'He was in a Negro battalion so they weren't allowed to see active duty, they were given quartermastering duties in the Naples docks from '44 through on to '46.'

'That's where Bucek served too,' he said. 'His mother told me. He was assigned to the Allied Military Government in Naples. It's also where Helms was stationed. I called his office earlier.'

She grinned.

'That's where they met, then,' she said. 'Naples. That's how they knew each other, that's how Bucek ended up hiding out in a flophouse in Harlem.'

Michael smiled. Nodded. 'You look freezing,' he said. 'Come sit by the radiator. I'll fix you a drink.'

She crossed the room and sat on the sofa, put her hands up above the radiator.

Michael poured her a glass of rye, passed it to her.

'What's your take?' he asked.

She took a gulp of the drink, looked at him.

'Bucek and Cleveland were out in Naples during the war,' she said. 'And they saw Helms, and maybe Faron, do something bad. And then they all got back to the States and went on with their lives. And then out of nowhere Cleveland bumped into Helms at a party, recognized him, realized he was the same Helms from the war, realized he was a congressman now, realized he could black-mail him over whatever the hell happened back then. So he tried to blackmail him, along with help from Bucek. Then Helms and Faron retaliated. Bucek bought it in the hotel, but Cleveland got away.'

Michael looked at her. 'I guess that's the shape of things,' he said.

'We need to figure out what the hell happened in Naples,' she said.

'There's something else,' he said. 'What if it wasn't just Cleveland and Bucek? What if there were other blackmailers? Or just other people who know what happened in Naples. If Helms and Faron have been going around tying up loose ends . . .'

'Then there could have been more murders,' Ida said, finish-ing off Michael's thought.

He nodded. 'We need to find out exactly how many they've killed.'

PART FOURTEEN

'The judicious policeman most correctly reflects the policy of the Department. To transients and visitors he is the public representative of the city. His demeanor and deportment in dealing with the public create impressions either favorable or unfavorable to himself, the Department, and frequently to the city.'

NEW YORK CITY POLICE DEPARTMENT,
MANUAL OF PROCEDURE, 1949

34

Friday 7th, 8.14 p.m.

After the crash, Gabriel gave a statement to the cops, then, when he was supposed to have been going to the hospital, he skipped out. He wanted to go home, take a bucketful of pills and sleep off the concussion, the shock, the adrenaline. But he didn't want Sarah or Mrs Hirsch to see him bloodied and bedraggled, and he knew it would be impossible to sleep, despite his tiredness. He was too wired, too amped up, so instead he made plans.

He went to a bar and washed the blood off as best he could in the restroom, then he called a mechanic to pick up the Delahaye from the pound the police had moved it to. Then he called up Salzman and arranged to meet him later that night, called Havemeyer and told he him he wouldn't be going to work. Then he caught a cab downtown, went to a car service he knew and rented a car – a black Cadillac Series 62.

Then he drove back uptown to meet Salzman.

Clear skies, a splash of stars. The moon sweeping silver over the city. He wondered what the hell he was going to tell Costello. That he'd had the money and lost it? That Faron had it now? Would Costello buy the story? That a man almost everyone thought was a myth had jumped out of a police car and taken the money off Gabriel? Or would Costello just assume it was a ruse?

Gabriel parked up on the same East Harlem street he'd met Salzman last time. Waited. Smoked. Waited some more. Wondered how long it would take for the adrenaline to work its way through his system, for his pulse to slow, his heart to stop smashing against his ribs like a caged animal. Now and then a pedestrian ran down the sidewalk with their coat buttoned-up, seeking shelter, a car slow-rolled through the gloom. Gabriel watched every movement like it was a potential threat, edgy and anxious and paranoid.

After a few minutes Salzman's cruiser pulled up, and the man hopped out of it and into the passenger seat of the Cadillac.

'What happened to the sports car?' he said.

'Don't ask,' said Gabriel.

Salzman eyed him.

'What happened to your face?' he asked.

'Don't ask that either.'

Salzman frowned, working things out, making connections. When Gabriel had called him earlier, he'd told him he wanted info on the cops involved in the crash that afternoon.

'Shit,' he said. 'It was you they were chasing?'

Gabriel gave him a *change the subject* look and Salzman caught it and whistled through his teeth.

'So who were our two friends that took a dive in the river?' Gabriel asked.

'Lieutenants Doyle and Higgs,' said Salzman. 'Irish. Low-level. From the precinct chatter sounds like they used to be bagmen for the Gaglianos in East Harlem before they moved on to better things. You wanna tell me what this was all about?'

Gabriel drummed his fingers on the steering wheel. 'They tried to stick me up,' he said.

Salzman stared at him through the gloom, unsure what to say. 'Maybe the Gaglianos put them up to it,' he said eventually.

Gabriel tried to draw connections between the Gaglianos and Faron and the missing money. Were they the family behind the conspiracy? Them and not Genovese? Italian Harlem was where Benny had stashed the money after all, Gagliano territory.

'They still alive?' Gabriel asked.

'Doyle and Higgs?' asked Salzman with a frown. 'No chance.

One of them cracked his skull in the crash, the other one drowned.'

Gabriel nodded. Let the news of their deaths sweep through him. The guilt would come soon, when the shock wore off. In the meantime he assessed the angles, how their deaths complicated matters in some ways, made them easier in others.

'How'd you get on looking into those murders?' he asked Salzman.

'Still working on it, buddy,' he said. 'Gimme a couple more days.'

It was Friday night. Gabriel was supposed to be leaving on Thursday. Six days and counting.

Salzman eyed him. 'You OK?' he asked.

'Fine,' said Gabriel.

'You seen a doc?'

'No need.'

He could tell by the look on Salzman's face he didn't believe him, but he nodded.

'Well, take care, Gabby. I'll be in touch.'

He opened the door, walked back to his car.

Gabriel watched his cruiser drive off and he lit another cigarette.

He wondered if the two dead cops had been following him, or if it was the building super who'd tipped them off. If they had been following him, he wondered who they were working for and how long they'd been at it. He wondered if they'd seen him pick up the passports from the forger; if so, his plan was compromised. He made a mental note to call the clinic in Toronto and make sure the man had actually checked in.

It was Friday night and he had a chest full of anxiety and fear to burn off. He put the Cadillac into gear and sailed through New York. Did what he hadn't done in years. He cruised the city looking for Faron, cruised the necropolis, a wraith in search of a wraith, his way lit by the glowing billboards that filled the city's

317

skies each night, guiding lights to the consumer promised land. It was the billboards that split the city, into haves and have-nots, into those who lived in the neon Olympus above, and those who lived in its shadows, the criminal underworld in which Gabriel, fallen angel, had found his home. Faron was out there too, somewhere in New York's hinterland of factories and alleyways and tenements, in amongst the poor, the exploited, the outsiders. He was figuring out who Gabriel was, where he lived, when to attack. It wouldn't be tonight or tomorrow, but at some point in the next few days.

Gabriel cruised the strips in Hell's Kitchen, Chelsea, Midtown. The East Side docks. He checked the red-light zones where Faron picked up his victims, the wastelands where he dumped their bodies. He crossed the bridge to the Brooklyn waterfront. There were other places he could have gone, in Long Island, the Bronx, Jersey. But there weren't many people out; an icy cold was keeping the streets unusually empty. Even the skyscrapers, those giants whose shoulders made up Manhattan's skyline, seemed to be huddling together for warmth. A few shivering hookers, telegram messengers, cops, ragged vagrants hunched around trash-can fires, looking for sunrise in paper bags. Gabriel knew there was no chance of finding him just by driving around, not unless he was amazingly lucky. But he felt he had to do something to kill the time while his head was reeling. Pay lip service. Conduct a ritual. Ward off a demon.

After a couple of hours, he pointed the Cadillac west, and crossed the city once more, back to the apartment.

He crept in. Sarah and Mrs Hirsch were asleep.

He went into his bedroom, stripped out of his bloody clothes. Studied his bloody nose, his bruised knee. He took a shower. He put on clean boxers and a vest. He walked around the apartment, checking the locks, checking the windows, checking all the guns in all the stash spots.

He drank a whisky and downed two Seconals and two Nembutals. He slipped into bed. What he craved now was sleep. Dreamless and black. He stared at the white ceiling of his room, and in the frame of the sconces a film of his sister being murdered played out, of Faron attacking him, of the crash, of Sarah being murdered, too. A horror show, laid on by his fear. As he watched the ghostly images, he wondered if this was what he had led Sarah into. He tried to think of plans to avoid them becoming real and realized that maybe it was all his plan-making that had got him into this mess in the first place.

When he awoke it was daylight and something about that lifted his spirits. Some winters, when the days were short and Gabriel was working long hours at the Copa, he didn't see the sun for weeks.

He heard Mrs Hirsch in the kitchen. He got up and stepped into the living room. Sarah was in there, sitting on the sofa, sipping an orange juice.

She stared at him, froze. 'What happened?' she asked.

'I crashed the car,' Gabriel said. 'I'm fine.'

She continued staring, not sure whether she should believe him or not. Then she got up, rushed towards him and hugged him, and he felt her warmth against him, her tender arms. He hugged her back and they stayed like that and she was a little girl again, and it made him want to cry. The urge to keep her safe ran through him and reminded him that this was the point of it all, and only a fool could be discontented living in a world such as this.

He heard Mrs Hirsch come in from the kitchen and stop. The silence thickened. Then he heard her retreat.

Sarah let go of him and he held her out at arm's length and they looked at each other.

The phone rang.

Gabriel smiled at her, then she picked up the receiver, turned back and held it out to him.

'It's for you,' she said. 'It's Uncle Frank.'

35

Saturday 8th, 12.30 p.m.

The Astoria was packed – guests checking in, checking out, heading to the Norse Grill, the Starlight Roof. The hat-check girl was doing a steady trade in minks and cashmere overcoats, silk scarves, leather gloves. Gabriel crossed the marble floor and walked through the arch into the bar.

The tables and booths were overflowing. He spoke to the maître d', was directed to an empty booth, and the 'reserved' label was whisked away. He scanned the crowd – well-heeled young women in New Look dresses, old-money matrons in black and pearls, suited men from conglomerates and advertising agencies. These were the people who designed the billboards that floated over the city. And everywhere they were knocking back drinks, chatting, laughing. The whole place seemed to gleam with light, the chrome and leather, the linen, the silver service, all of it sparkling in the sunbeams blasting in from the giant windows.

And here he was, with five days to find the money, and Faron on the loose, and Costello about to grill him.

A waitress approached and asked if he'd like a drink. Gabriel looked around the crowd once more and ordered a Martini for propriety's sake. The waitress flitted away and he lit a smoke, tried to think what he'd tell Costello. What could he say? He tried to put himself in Costello's shoes, wondered what he'd think if he were a Mob boss and an underling told him he'd lost two million dollars ten minutes after finding it because he'd been robbed by a man who hadn't been seen in over a decade. He'd probably have the underling whacked, either for lying or for stupidity. Meaning Gabriel had to lie about having lost the money. He shook his head at the thought of it. He'd been walking a tightrope for way too long, and now, five days before he reached its end, a gale force wind had blown in.

A minute or two passed and Costello entered the bar, with his usual perfect suit, perfect haircut, perfect shave and manicure.

'What happened to your face?' he asked, sitting down.

'I crashed the Delahaye.'

'You all right?'

'Fine except now I got to drive a Cadillac.'

'It's a hard life, Gabby. You eating?'

'Yeah, I ordered a Martini olive. You drinking?'

'Always.'

The waitress reappeared with Gabriel's drink and Costello ordered a whiskey sour.

She left. Costello took a handkerchief and a bottle from his pocket. He poured oil from the bottle onto the handkerchief and the booth filled with eucalyptus fumes. He stuck the handkerchief under his nose and inhaled like he was trying to chloroform himself.

'This goddamn cold,' he said.

'It's the season,' Gabriel said.

'How you getting on with the money?'

Gabriel squirmed. 'Not great,' he replied. 'I don't think Benny put the money into a bank. I checked with his driver. He stashed it somewhere, I'm honing in on it. He made a few stops that don't make sense.'

'Like?'

'Like he stopped off at a clinic to arrange booking in "a friend". Benny mention anything to you about being ill?'

Costello shook his head. 'Maybe he caught the clap off one of them showgirls.'

'And he stopped by Joe Glaser's talent agency.'

'Maybe he was booking singers for the Flamingo.'

'Glaser's is all-Negro,' said Gabriel. 'Benny'd only be hiring whites.'

Costello thought, tapped his fingers on the tablecloth, on the shining linen.

'There's something else,' said Gabriel. 'I checked in with Tomasulo. He said Benny and Genovese had a pow-wow in the summer when Benny was in town. Said Genovese didn't invest in the Flamingo, and he was bragging about it after Benny got whacked. You sure Genovese isn't involved in all this?'

'Sure I'm sure,' said Costello. 'Like I told you, they hated each other.'

The waitress arrived with Costello's drink. Gabriel studied him, wondered why he was so convinced that Genovese wasn't involved. Wondered if Costello had got it wrong or if there was something else he wasn't telling him.

'Tomasulo's nervous,' Gabriel said. 'Told me he wants out. Told me he thinks Genovese's onto him.'

Costello shrugged. 'He knew what he was getting into.'

He downed half his drink in one go and ordered another.

Gabriel told Costello about Jasper's bar in Greenwich Village, how the man had given up information in return for Costello arranging a better deal with the mobster to whom Jasper was paying protection money. Costello said he'd take care of it.

His drink arrived, he took a sip. Then he sighed, turned to look at Gabriel.

'You ever hear of a pusher called Gene Cleveland?' he asked.

Gabriel's heart jumped. He thought of lying, saying no, then he realized that if Costello spoke to Bumpy he might find out Gabriel had been asking about him.

'I saw Bumpy the other day,' Gabriel said. 'He mentioned something. Why you asking?'

'We braced this kid dealer yesterday, some punk selling dope in the Village. He said Vito was all het up looking for this Cleveland character but no one knew why.'

Gabriel's thoughts raced. Genovese was looking for Cleveland, too. First Benny and now Genovese. Gabriel tried to stay calm, lit another cigarette, told Costello a condensed version of what Bumpy had told him about Cleveland – that he was a two-bit dealer from Harlem who disappeared after a bunch of people got killed in the hotel he dealt from. Costello nodded and frowned, understanding about as much as Gabriel.

They finished their drinks. Costello caught the elevator to the roof for his lunch, Gabriel wandered back into the cold outside.

He sat in the driver's seat of the Cadillac and stared ahead, at the traffic backing up at the intersection with Park Avenue, trying to figure an angle through it all. The car was freezing, but still he felt hot. He scrabbled a cigarette from his pack, lit it up, sucked it down.

Benny and Genovese had met over the summer and despite what Costello said, they were possibly in on the scam with the money together. Had they been looking for Cleveland together as well? And what about Faron? Maybe Genovese had hired Faron to find Cleveland. And that's how Benny knew Faron was back in town.

Gabriel wondered if, after Faron had stolen the money, he'd kept it for himself, or passed it on to his boss, Genovese. Either way, Genovese and Faron would be coming after him, separately or together.

He continued smoking and thinking and fighting the dread that was gnawing its way through his chest. He needed to act, but all his leads had stalled. He was waiting for Salzman to get back to him with details of any killings Faron might have been involved in. He was waiting for Tomasulo to get back to him with any info from inside Genovese's camp. What else could he chase? What other angles were there left?

Doyle and Higgs. The two dead cops. They'd been in the car with Faron. They used to work for the Gaglianos. Gabriel tried to think who he knew in the Gagliano family he could brace for information, who was weak, who he could squeeze, and who wouldn't spill.

Time passed. Or maybe it didn't. He couldn't tell. The hands of the giant clock on the First National building were playing tricks on him. He stared at the clock impossibly high in the sky, noticed above it a row of gargoyles peering down at the city with contempt. He thought of Mrs Hirsch. He thought of Sarah. He got back to thinking about the money.

The two detectives from Chicago. Bumpy had said they were investigating the killings at the hotel. Maybe they had found something out about Faron he could use. Maybe he could find a way to bargain information from them, brace them if he had to. That made a second lead, in addition to the Gaglianos. He tried to come up with a third. Failed.

At some point he looked around and noticed the sun had dropped low in the sky, was setting behind the finials of the towers to the west. The yellow orb seemed to be sucking light from the land instead of dispersing it. Sucking it first from the buildings, then from the streets, then from the sky itself, siphoning off every speck till the surroundings became a landscape of shadows.

On the sidewalks the deluge of people continued unabated through the gloom, and the scene seemed so strange to him now, had as much sense to it as a battlefield. There was something alien, unnerving, about the way this mass of people were so in step with their surroundings, like the city was marching to some grand music Gabriel could no longer hear, some dissonance that underpinned it all.

He rubbed his temples. He slow-breathed.

He had two million dollars to find, and five days to do it. And now he had a killer after him, and maybe a Mob boss, too. He had to get his head straight. He opened the window a crack and let the air cool his face.

He only had two leads left to pursue. He started up the Caddy and pulled into traffic.

36

The first floorshow of the night was under way and the sound of it seeped into the backroom, where Gabriel and Havemeyer and the others were counting up cash. There was a knock at the door. One of the runners opened it and another entered, holding a cloth bag. He tossed it onto the table and Havemeyer loosened the drawstring and a rain of dollars fluttered onto the table.

The runner yawned, then looked at Gabriel.

'There's a girl out there asking after you,' he said.

'Who?'

He shrugged. 'Leggy blonde. Looks like she walked in off a movie screen.'

Beatrice. An image of her flashed in his mind's eye, sitting in the office of her dance studio, smoking, staring at him through her lashes, eyes of slate gleaming in the red gloom.

He rose and headed out of the room. Havemeyer watched him go, that fatherly concern look on his face. Gabriel went to the washrooms and checked his appearance. He still looked haggard, still had the bruised face. He'd spent all day chasing down information on the Gaglianos, if they had any links to the two dead cops. It was tricky work, having to ask about the crash without implicating himself, having to ask about the money without revealing it was missing, having to ask about Faron without letting on the man was back in town.

Everything he'd tried had come up blank. No one knew who the dead cops were working for, no one knew what they were working on, no one had seen or heard of Faron, and people looked at him strangely when he asked. So he'd given it up after a ten-hour stretch and had gone to the Copa for the start of the night, anxious about the fact that he only had one lead left now – the detectives from Chicago.

He left the washroom and walked through the corridor, approaching the rumble that was Carmen Miranda and her floorshow. He stepped into the chaos. He peered through the columns and the fake palm trees, across the mezzanines, to the bar, which took up one whole side of the space. And there was Beatrice, in a black dress, flaxen-haired and long-legged, looking indeed like she'd just stepped out of a movie.

He headed over.

On the wall behind the bar was a long mural of Rio's beachfront at night. An illuminated mural, with fairy-lights poking out of the plasterwork where the lights of the boats and hotels and stars were supposed to be. Gabriel thought of the film he'd watched in the cinema a few days earlier, Rita Hayworth adrift in Acapulco.

Beatrice saw him and smiled.

'You kept your promise,' he said, over the sound of the band.

'I always do. What happened to your face?'

He shrugged.

'I crashed my car,' he said. 'I'm fine. You here on your own?'

She nodded, took a sip from her drink. She was acting cool and composed, but Gabriel could tell underneath it she was flustered. She hadn't just dropped by for old time's sake. For Beatrice to be agitated something big had to be going on.

She nodded at the floorshow. 'Carmen Miranda's quite something,' she said.

'She's a Brazilian in a million.'

Beatrice laughed.

They looked at Carmen Miranda and The Samba Sirens. He studied the girls and thought there was something off. It took a moment but he realized what it was – one of the dancers was missing. Miranda had eight girls normally, now there were only seven. No one had said anything about it. He needed to go backstage and see what had happened.

He turned to look at Beatrice. Saw her expression had changed, she was staring off into the distance with a look of concern. Gabriel followed her gaze to somewhere beyond the floorshow: a table full of Gagliano goons. The family that had put the contract out on her junkie brother. The family the two dead cops used to work for. The family he'd spent the day investigating.

One of the goons made eye contact with Gabriel, a wiry kid with a scowl on his face. The kid acted like he hadn't seen Gabriel, got back to his drink.

Beatrice turned towards Gabriel like nothing had happened too. Gabriel tried to run the angles, wondering what the chances were Beatrice's appearance and that of the goons was a coincidence. All of them turning up so soon after the two cops went for a dip in the river and Gabriel started sniffing around.

'So what are you *really* doing here, Bea?' he asked.

She paused, frowned.

'Don't tell me you came down here for old time's sake,' he said, sounding colder than he meant. 'You've avoided this place since the day we broke it off.'

'Since *you* broke it off with *me*,' she said. 'Let's not re-write history.'

Almost as soon as she'd said it she sighed, regretting the outburst.

'Something's happened,' she said. 'I need to talk to you.'

As she spoke, Gabriel scanned the room. From the corner of his eye he saw the wiry Gagliano goon get up and disappear through the crowd. A second later one of the club captains approached.

'Gabriel, we need you backstage,' he said.

'What's up?'

'Some kind of commotion in the dressing room. One of the girls,' he said.

Gabriel looked at Beatrice.

'It can wait,' she said. 'Till we find somewhere private.'

'OK,' he said. 'Wait here. I'll be back in two minutes.'

She nodded.

He headed off towards the door that led backstage. He turned off the corridor and walked through the kitchen, arrived at the dressing rooms, knocked, stepped inside. The place was mostly empty on account of all the girls being out on the floor, except one. A brunette, sitting on a chair, bawling her eyes out. Kneeling in front of her, patting her hand was Vera, the club's seamstress, responsible for all the gowns and outfits, and often the girls, too.

Next to them both was one of the club's bouncers. The dancing girls had their own entrance to the building, away from where the customers lined up, and the bouncer was supposed to be guarding it.

'What's going on?' Gabriel asked.

'Ah, jeez,' said the bouncer.

'Joan's ex-feller's been hanging about the stage door,' said Vera.

'We warned him, Mr Leveson,' said the bouncer, full of remorse.

'Three nights in a row now,' said the crying girl. 'Ever since I ditched him.'

'What did you do?' Gabriel asked, turning to look at the bouncer.

'He beat him to a pulp,' screamed the girl.

'He was threatening to come back with a gun,' said the bouncer.

'You didn't come and get me?' Gabriel asked.

'I'm sorry, boss.'

'When did all this happen?'

''Bout a quarter of an hour ago,' said Vera. 'Just as the girls were going on stage.'

'Where is he now?' Gabriel asked.

'We put him in a taxi for the hospital,' said the bouncer.

'Cops?' Gabriel asked.

They shook their heads.

'All right,' said Gabriel. He thought. He turned to look at the crying girl. 'Joan, you got the rest of the night off. Here's money for a taxi.'

He peeled off some bills. 'You live alone?'

She shook her head.

'Good,' said Gabriel. 'I'm going to send Havemeyer over to the hospital, keep an eye on your fella, make sure he gets the best care and Havemeyer'll call you when he's all right. OK?'

The girl nodded.

'Everything's going to be fine,' he said to her.

'Don't worry, Joanie,' said Vera, patting the girl on the knee. 'It's all gonna be fine.'

The girl nodded.

Gabriel turned to the bouncer. 'Was it just you?'

The bouncer paused.

'Me and Pete,' he said.

'Come see me at the end of the night.'

The bouncer nodded once more.

Gabriel shook his head and just as he turned to leave a flash-bulb popped, blinding him for an instant. He turned to see a photographer in the corridor behind him. Gabriel had left the door open. The photographer was a gangly kid in his early twenties, dressed in slacks and a cardigan, holding a camera aloft.

'Who the hell are you?' asked Gabriel.

'I'm from *Look*, sir. The photographer from *Look* magazine.'

The boy was stammering, scared, clearly he hadn't recognized Gabriel from behind when he'd taken the photo. Gabriel frowned, he didn't remember anyone having told him about a photographer visiting.

The boy rummaged around in the pocket of his cardigan, and passed Gabriel a business card: *Stanley Kubrick, photographer, Look Magazine, 488 Madison Avenue.*

And only then did Gabriel remember. A chat with an editor weeks ago, a pitch for a puff-piece photo story – *Backstage at the Hottest Club North of Havana.* Gabriel was overcome by weariness. Things like that never used to slip his memory. There were punch-ups going on, girls not taking the stage, photographers in the club, and Gabriel didn't have a lid on any of it. He was starting to lose his edge just when it mattered most.

'Kid,' said Gabriel, 'you can take all the photos you want, just two exceptions. No shots of anyone crying. OK?'

'Yes, sir. Sorry, sir.'

'And absolutely no photos of me.'

The kid nodded again.

Gabriel headed off down the corridor. Through the roar and heat of the kitchen into the roar and heat of the floor. The band filled his ears, the blaring multicolored lights, the rush and blur of the dancers.

When he got back to the bar, Beatrice was gone.

He looked about.

Miranda was halfway through the finale of her act – 'Let's Do the Copacabana'. Where the hell was Beatrice? Then something else caught his eye – the table full of Gagliano goons had emptied, just before the climax of the twelve o'clock show. They hadn't even stayed to drink out their minimum.

Worst-case scenarios streaked through his mind. Beatrice came here to tell him something, and the Gaglianos had stopped her. He imagined Beatrice dragged out of the club into an alley by Faron, cut up, sliced, bloodied, ripped open by blades.

He pushed through the crowd, up a ramp, past mirrored columns, through the shafts of blue unfurling from above. The band had dropped out now, all but the congas, driving Miranda on, her hips vibrating, shimmering as rapidly as the drums. He reached the Gaglianos' empty table.

'Where'd they go?' he shouted to the captain who was overseeing the waiters clearing it. The captain shrugged, pointed to the exit. Gabriel turned and barreled off.

Miranda finished shimmying. The band came back in and crescendoed in a crash and swoop of horns and drums and the crowd went wild.

Gabriel burst into the foyer, out onto the street. The bouncers turned to look at him, the line was a block long, taxis parked up, limos, the van with the antennas on its roof from the radio station broadcasting out of the Copa Lounge.

No Gaglianos, no Beatrice, no Faron. He spun about. The alley at the back. The fastest way was through the lounge. He turned. He ran up the steps, past the bouncers, into the bar. The Lounge was different to the Copa, all chrome and black leather and a more fashionable crowd.

Gabriel pushed past them, skirted a ringed-off area from where the radio show was being broadcast. Jack Eigen interviewing Walter Winchell. Both holding cocktails. Both looking drunk. Gawkers watched. Cables trailed to the van outside. The show's tag-line boomed: *The later the greater, now there's a late show in the Copa Lounge*.

Gabriel rushed past them, into the store room, out the fire exit, into the alley behind.

Nothing.

He kept going, turned onto the alley that ran along the side of the club. A cleaner was mopping up blood by the stage door. He froze a moment, then realized it was the blood of the dancing girl's ex-boyfriend. He stared at the size of the puddle, looked at the cleaner.

'Mr Leveson,' said the cleaner.

Gabriel needed his gun, and the keys to the Cadillac, both of which were in the backroom.

He rapped on the door. The bouncer from earlier opened up.

Gabriel ran down the corridor. The dancers were heading back the other way now that the floorshow was over. That post-show buzz in the air. Excited chatter. Carmen Miranda glowing. Gabriel turned the corner and saw her – Beatrice, sharing a cigarette with one of the Samba Sirens.

'Jesus,' he said, exhaling.

He approached Beatrice and the girl. They looked up at him.

'Where the hell did you go?' he said.

'I came back here,' said Beatrice.

'You said you were going to wait for me.'

'I saw Selma in the chorus,' said Beatrice, flinging a thumb at the girl next to her. 'She's one of my old students. She invited me back.'

Beatrice frowned at him. So did Selma. Staring at him like he was crazy. Because, of course, he was. The missing money, the drugs, the stress, the crash, the sleeplessness. All of it driving him crazy.

'I thought,' he said, and stopped. Realized he hadn't thought, he'd simply jumped to conclusions.

Beatrice turned to Selma.

'I'd better go, honey,' she said. 'It's lovely to see you doing so well.'

The girl glowed, headed off to the dressing rooms. Beatrice turned to look at him.

'You don't look too good,' she said. 'You wanna have that chat now?'

'Sure,' he said.

'Anywhere quiet we can go?'

Five minutes later they were sitting in Gabriel's Cadillac a half-block from the club. They'd gone via the cloakroom for Beatrice to pick up her coat, but even though she had it on now, she still looked cold. Gabriel switched on the car's heating, but it would take a while to kick in.

'So?' he asked, his breath steaming in the icy air.

Beatrice sighed. 'I'm not sure where to start,' she said. 'I had a visit last night.'

'From?'

'Two thugs I'd never seen before. They told me they had pull with the Gaglianos. They told me if I did them a favor they'd get the contract on my brother torn up.'

'What was the favor?'

'To lure you back to mine,' she said. 'And they'd take care of the rest.'

'What did you say?'

'I said I'd think about it. Then I came to tell you.'

There were tears glistening in her eyes. She'd had to choose between her brother and Gabriel, and she'd chosen Gabriel.

'Thanks,' he said.

She paused, then nodded.

'They were here tonight,' he said.

'I know. Did you see the goon? The wiry one?' she asked. 'He's the one who's got the contract out on my brother. You think it was a coincidence?'

He shook his head. 'They come down here a lot. But if it's a coincidence, it's a hell of a strange one.'

He couldn't tell her about the crash, about the two dead cops who used to be connected to the family.

'So what are we going to do?' she asked.

He thought. He wondered why they had approached her of all people. Everyone knew they'd been split up for years. Had someone been following him when he'd visited her dance studio on Tuesday? Had someone been following him when he'd picked up the passports? How much did they know? He tried to find an advantage. He rubbed his temples.

'They have it planned for tonight?' he asked.

333

She nodded.

'They say where they'd be waiting?'

'Outside my apartment.'

'Where d'you live these days?'

'West Fourteenth. Near the dance studio.'

'Give me your address and phone number,' he said.

She wrote them down on a scrap of paper for him.

'OK,' he said. 'You get a cab back to yours. They'll probably call you to see what happened. Tell them I'm coming to yours, this morning, when I've closed up the club. About six. Then just wait in your apartment.'

'What are you going to do?' she asked, concern writ large all over her face.

'Get them before they get me.'

She stared at him. Nodded.

They got out of the Cadillac, crossed to the line of taxis outside the club and Gabriel watched her get in one of them and head off to West 14th.

He went round the corner to the side entrance, knocked on the stage door. The bouncer opened up. 'Mr Leveson.'

'Any other night,' Gabriel said to him, 'you'd get sacked for what you and Pete did to that girl's fella. But you're in luck. I need help with a job this morning when the club closes. You and Pete help me out and keep your mouths shut, you get to stay.'

'Anything, Mr Leveson.'

'You two have guns?' he asked.

'We can get them,' the bouncer said.

Gabriel nodded, explained what he wanted them to do.

334

37

The exhibition opening was being held on East 57th, in a newish gallery in one of those buildings with cast-iron fronts and giant windows. Costello had caught a cab over there alone, wandered in. The place was packed with people in evening dress. Although he didn't recognize any of them, he recognized the types. Wall Street bankers, industrialists, Madison Avenue ad execs, young heirs to great fortunes, all of them there to catch an art-scene buzz. Waiters and waitresses sifted through the crowd with trays of champagne flutes. There were tables dotted about with canapés on them, dainty, elegant-looking, even by Upper East Side standards.

The place itself looked clinical in that way a lot of the art galleries Costello visited did. All white walls and bare floorboards with no decorations. Costello picked up a champagne flute from a passing waitress, put it down, blew his nose, picked it up again.

He looked at the crowd, chatting and laughing and schmoozing and he had that feeling he got sometimes, that this was it. The center of things.

People liked to say the heartland of America was in its middle, in hick towns in the mid-West populated by a farmer and two cows, some muddy fields where salt-of-the-earth types tended the land. It wasn't. The heart of the country was here. This was where the nation's economy was based, where its corporations were, where its ideas and innovations came from. These were the people the rest of the country relied on for its products, its imports, its radio and music, its novels and magazines, its ads, its art, its culture. New York created it all, and the rest of the country sucked it up. This was the center, the heart within the heart.

Costello relished the feeling, let it warm him a moment.

Then he searched the crowd, but couldn't find who he was looking for, so slipped through into the exhibition itself.

The first room he entered contained five giant paintings. A smattering of people staring at them, sipping champagne, discussing. Costello looked at the paintings. Each of them was just a big blob of color, with a few strips of other colors here and there. What were they supposed to be paintings *of*? He looked at the titles for a clue, but each title was just a number. He looked at the name of the artist. Rothko. What the hell kind of name was that? It sounded like a Jew name cut in half.

A doorway led into the second room. Costello walked through it to see another set of blobs. There were fewer people in here and the party noises from the reception sounded more distant. Then he noticed something odd, a door leading to a third room, this one almost completely dark, lit only by a murky orange light, as if the room was illuminated by candles.

Costello walked over and peered in. There were more of the same paintings, these ones in dark blues and reds, and standing in front of them, a young man in his twenties, wearing a suit in a Hollywood cut, horn-rimmed glasses, black suede shoes. Costello looked around for candles. Couldn't see any. Saw the ceiling lights had been dimmed all the way down.

He wandered in. He stood next to the young man, looked at the painting he was staring at – a deep-blue blob, a few streaks of yellow and black around the edges.

The young man seemed to be lost in the painting, like he was staring at a cinema screen.

'I don't get it,' said Costello, breaking the silence.

The young man jolted, as if woken from a trance. He turned to look at Costello with an annoyed expression. Costello felt the young man take him in, imagined what he saw – an older Italian

man in an expensive suit, who didn't quite fit in with the surroundings or the crowd.

'It's just a blue blob,' said Costello. 'What's the point?'

He turned to look at the man with an open expression, seeking
guidance, genuine in his desire to learn. Perhaps this disarmed the
young man.

'They're multiform,' he said. 'Fields of color. Why start a
painting with sketches, with lines, when you can start with color.'

The man gave Costello a superior sort of look.

'But they don't look like anything,' said Costello.

'They don't *need* to look like anything,' the young man sighed.

'They don't?' Costello sneezed, blew his nose, popped two
cough sweets. 'You'll have to excuse me,' he said. 'I can't shake
this cold. How comes the room's so dark?'

'The paintings are supposed to calm you down. The dimness
helps. That's how the painter wants them exhibited. In a dark
room.'

Costello thought about this, turned to look at the painting
once more, appraised it as a psychological aid, wondered what Dr
Hoffman would make of it. He forgot about the cough sweets in
his mouth and took a sip of champagne and the two tastes curdled
instantly on his tongue. He winced. He swallowed.

'I've got a Howard Chandler Christy at home,' he said,
proudly.

The young man's face soured. He gave Costello a contemptu-
ous look and turned to leave.

'Don't go, kid,' said Costello. 'I wanted to talk to you.'

The young man turned around, frowned. 'Do I know you?'
he asked.

'No, but I know you. Come back and explain the painting.'

'Who are you?'

'Frank Costello.'

It took a second, then the color drained from the young man's
face.

'Come on back and let's look at the painting.'

The young man considered, then returned to Costello's side.

'How are you enjoying New York?'

'Fine,' he said, and Costello could detect the first traces of fear in his voice. 'What did you want to talk to me about?' the young man asked.

There was a pause, then he added a 'sir' to the end of the question.

'I wanted to talk to you about the price tag on this painting and why anyone would pay that kinda money for it.'

'I don't know. You'd have to talk to the gallery owner.'

'I'm just joking,' said Costello with a grin. 'I couldn't give a shit how much someone paid for a painting. Excuse my French. I wanted to talk to you about Vito Genovese.'

'Genovese?'

'Sure. You're a movie producer, right? A junior executive.'

'How do you know that?'

'I know things. I know you and your boss flew in early for the producers' meeting that's going to happen at the Waldorf on Monday, and after you got here, you both went and met Vito Genovese. An old friend of mine. I just came down here today to ask you why you two met him and what you talked about. I'm intrigued. Of course I could ask Vito himself, him being an old friend of mine, but he's a busy man and I don't like to bother him.'

Costello turned to look at the young man, kept his expression flat. He desperately wanted a cigarette, but he still had the god-damn cold.

'I . . .' the young man stammered. 'How do you know all this?'

'It's my town, son,' said Costello. 'I know things.'

'I don't think I can reveal what we spoke about.'

'Sure you can.'

'Mr Genovese spoke to my boss, sir. I didn't hear what they spoke about. I'm sorry. I can't help you.'

He turned to look at Costello through the gloom and smiled, as if he'd found a way out of his bind.

'Too bad,' said Costello.

The young man smiled again.

'I have to go now, sir,' he said, turning to leave.

'Oh, say. How's your friend?'

The young man paused, turned back round. 'Sir?'

'Quit with the *sir* shit. Your friend that you took back to your hotel the other night. What was his name? Peter? It was Peter, wasn't it?'

The young man trembled.

'You picked him up outside one of those cinemas on Times Square. With all of the other chicken hawks. Personally, I find these things, what's the word? Disreputable? But that's just me. What happens between two consenting adults, it's none of my business. Like if someone wants to spend enough money to buy a house on a painting of a blob, it's none of my business. Same thing. You're a young man. Peter's a young man. These things happen. But when one of the young men is in his twenties, and the other young man is only sixteen. Well, when that happens, the courts, they don't have the same laid-back attitude I do. And let's say they did, you'd never work in Hollywood again. Best job you'd end up doing with that kinda rap is spotting pins in a bowl-ing alley.'

The young man lifted a hand up to his face, seemed to freeze for a few moments, then he sobbed into his palm.

'Come on, kid. Don't cry,' said Costello. 'What are you crying for? We're at an art exhibition, half the guys in here eat pillows.'

The man tried to say something, but it wouldn't come up.

'Look at the blob,' said Costello. 'It's supposed to calm you down, right? Look at the blob.'

The young man paused his sobbing, was about to say some-thing then let out a wail.

'Oh, Jesus,' said Costello. He put an arm around the young man. The young man continued sobbing.

Two people walked into the room, appraised the scene, turned and headed back out again.

'Come on,' Costello said. 'It's gonna be all right.'

The man's sobbing eased down a little.

Costello craved a cigarette.

'Look at the blob, son. Look at the blob.'

The young man's crying subsided enough for him to speak. 'What do you want?' he stammered.

'I just want to know why Vito spoke to you and your boss.'

'I wasn't there when they spoke,' said the young man. 'But . . . but I spoke to my boss about it after.'

'What did he say?'

The young man sniffed a couple of times, composed himself, turned to look at Costello. The tear trails running down his cheeks glistened in the gloom.

'Genovese was trying to get us to vote against blacklisting,' the young man said.

'*Not* to blacklist?' Costello asked. 'You sure?'

The young man nodded. 'We couldn't understand it,' he said.

'You're not the only ones, kid.'

Why would Genovese be trying to get them to vote that way? Bringing down government heat onto the unions the Mob controlled in LA? Why would he want to sabotage everything?

'He say anything else, kid?'

'My boss said it had something to do with Ronnie Reagan.'

'The b-movie actor?'

'He's the president of the Screen Actors Guild,' the young man said. 'He got voted in with MCA campaign money. My boss thought it might have something to do with that.'

MCA. The Music Corporation of America. The talent management agency started by a bunch of Chicago mobsters who used to work for Capone. People Costello knew well. People who could help him figure out what the hell was going on.

'All right, kid,' Costello said. 'You did good.'

'I can go now?'

'Sure. You can go.'

A strange look crossed the young man's face and he began to walk away.

Costello tried to play the cards in his head, couldn't. These were the golden days. And Genovese was trying to rip them all up. Why?

Then he had a thought.

'Kid,' he said, just as the young man was stepping out of the room.

The young man turned to look at him, fearing another grilling.

'You don't got a spare cigarette on you?'

38

Gabriel and Havemeyer stepped out of the club into an ashy dawn. Havemeyer headed to the subway, Gabriel got into the Cadillac and drove south. When he reached West 14th he parked up a half-block away from Beatrice's address, on the opposite side of the road.

There were five cars between him and the building's entrance. Gabriel scanned all of them, spotted three heads crouched down in a Plymouth. Spotted the two bouncers in a Studebaker further up. He assessed angles. Lines of fire. He got out of the car and crossed the street at the worst point for the men in the Plymouth.

As he approached Beatrice's door he heard a voice behind him. 'Gabe Leveson?'

Gabriel turned to see a kid standing on the sidewalk. He looked young, a teenager, skinny, pale, trembling in a thin leather jacket.

Just then there was a noise – the two bouncers running up the street, pulling .38s. The kid looked from them to Gabriel, realized what was going on. Then a screeching noise – the Plymouth peeling off. The kid's partners ditching him.

The kid turned and ran, heading east towards Union Square. Gabriel chased him. The bouncers did too. Gabriel turned to them and shouted.

'Follow the Plymouth,' he screamed.

The bouncers turned and headed for their Studebaker. Gabriel looked ahead. The kid might have looked unhealthy, but he was fast. Way faster than Gabriel.

They crossed a block to the square, then just outside Ohrbach's the kid jumped into the road. There wasn't much traffic, but enough for a chorus of horns and screeching brakes to smash the peace, causing birds to burst from the trees in the square.

Gabriel jumped through the path the kid had cleared. The kid reached the subway station, jumped down its steps five at a time. Gabriel followed. Through the ticket hall. Hopped the turnstile. Ran along the platform of the Eighth Avenue line. The kid getting further and further away.

Then Gabriel spotted a set of stairs at the end of the platform. The kid was heading towards them. The steps led to a bridge over the tracks. It'd bring the kid out on the opposite platform, where a Bronx-bound train was pulling in.

Gabriel could cut him off.

The kid reached the stairs, disappeared up them.

Gabriel inhaled, jumped off the platform, onto the tracks. People screamed. He stumbled, the third rail loomed. He put out a hand and grabbed a sleeper. He stopped himself falling less than an inch from the electrified rail.

On the platform people were calling him a madman, others were shouting for the police.

Gabriel righted himself. Saw the train approaching, hopped over the remaining rails and pulled himself onto the platform to see the kid running down it towards him, looking over his shoulder at the stairs behind him, where he thought Gabriel would emerge. Gabriel ran towards him. The kid turned. Gabriel swung his fist at the kid's face. Connected sweetly. Bone to bone.

The kid went flying, landed hard, smacked the back of his head. More screams. The train rushed into the station. The kid sprawled, rolled about, dazed, concussed. Gabriel kneeled and frisked him. Plucked a .38 Smith & Wesson from one pocket, the kid's wallet from another, a stiletto strapped to the inside of his boot.

The kid came to, looked at Gabriel, patted himself, realized he'd been fished.

'Head for the exit,' Gabriel said. 'Or I kill you here. With your own .38.'

The kid stumbled to his feet.

They made it out of the station before the cops arrived. Gabriel walked the kid through the square, putting distance between them and the scene of the fight. He threw the kid onto a bench, stood in front of him.

'Talk,' he said.

The kid looked at him blankly, woozily.

Gabriel took the kid's wallet from his pocket. Found a driver's license.

'John Stanley Jones,' he read. 'Start talking, kid, or I'll take you to the address you've got in here and make it look like suicide.'

The kid considered his options. 'What do you want to know?' he said, his voice dripping with feigned menace.

'Who sent you?' he asked.

'Al Rocca.'

Gabriel knew the name. A middle-man who farmed out muscle-work for Genovese. Not for the Gaglianos.

'Who'd Rocca get the job from?'

The kid leaned forward, tested the bruise on his face with his fingertips.

'Genovese,' he said. 'Who'd you think?'

'Why'd he send you after me?'

'I don't know.'

The kid looked up at Gabriel, blood dripped out of his nose, onto his fingers. Gabriel tossed him a handkerchief.

'Don't lie to me, kid,' he said.

He lit a smoke and looked about the square. It was empty on

account of the early hour, the benches and lawns were covered in dew. Even the giant Coca-Cola sign above Beatrice's dance studio, switched off now, was covered in it, its bulbs and iron scaffolds glistening and dripping.

Gabriel looked back at the kid. He had the handkerchief pressed up to his nose.

'It's something to do with this pusher called Cleveland,' he said. 'Genovese's been looking for him. Then he heard you were looking for him, too. That's all I know.'

Gabriel frowned. He knew the kid was telling the truth, but what he was saying didn't fit. Gabriel imagined Genovese coming after him over the missing money, over Faron, over the rejected job offer. Instead he tried to whack Gabriel because he'd been asking after Cleveland?

'Why's he looking for Cleveland?'

'I told you all I know.'

'What do you know about the two cops who got killed yesterday?'

'The ones that drowned? They were working for Genovese. He asked them to look for Cleveland.'

There was the link again. The cops, Faron, Genovese. Beatrice had said the men visited her the previous night, just hours after the crash. Genovese had wasted no time in coming after him. It was just a matter of time now before he came again. Sunday morning now. Gabriel's escape was planned for Thursday night. Would he even be able to survive till then? Especially as he only had one lead left now – the two detectives from Chicago. He had to track them down, follow them maybe, break into their office to see what information they'd gathered.

He stared at the kid. He had to kill him. Every shred of logic said he had to. But in the open light of the park, the kid looked even younger than he had on the street. Gabriel checked the date of birth on the driver's license. Seventeen. Four years older than Sarah. Gabriel looked at him again.

'I'm going to let you go,' said Gabriel. 'You tell your boss you got away from me. We never spoke. Got it?'

The kid nodded. Gabriel threw him back his wallet.

'If you do say anything, and I find out,' said Gabriel. 'I'll hunt you down. Got it?'

The kid nodded again, got off the bench and ran through the square. Gabriel watched him go, stared a moment at the cold sunrise. Then he headed south, to Beatrice's apartment.

He rang her bell and she buzzed him in. He caught an elevator up twenty-four stories, knocked on her door. She opened up looking tired and concerned, dressed in trousers and a baggy wool sweater.

'Well?' she asked.

'I took care of it.'

She walked him down a hallway into a spacious lounge with windows looking north. The place was crammed with pot plants and paperwork from Beatrice's agency.

'Nice place,' he said.

'It's overpriced,' she replied. 'But it's close to the studio. You want a drink?'

He nodded.

She crossed to a drinks cabinet and poured him a rye.

They sat on the sofa and Gabriel told her what had happened with the kid, told her to expect a call from the two bouncers maybe.

She rose and put the radio on, tuned it to a station playing ballads. They drank more, waited for the bouncers to call. They stared out of the windows, watched New York waking up to a cold, bright Sunday morning. From the windows they could see Broadway snaking up through Union Square and onwards towards 42nd Street and Midtown.

'You got a nice view here,' he said.

'Thanks,' she said, taking a sip of her drink. 'I like looking out over Broadway. I like how it cuts through everything.'

Gabriel looked at the rigid grid of streets laid out below them, noted how Broadway sliced across it diagonally, haphazardly, intersecting the framework that covered most of the island, a single line of chaos through the order.

'What's so great about that?' he asked.

'I dunno,' she said. 'It used to be an Indian trail, runs along a natural ridge. That's why it's got the shape it has. Why it messes up the grid we tried to put in place. There's something nice about that. One last fuck-you from the Indians who used to live here.'

She smiled. The phone rang.

She picked it up and passed it to Gabriel. He listened to what the bouncers had to say, hung up.

'They chased the Plymouth for a bit,' Gabriel said. 'Then they lost it.'

He returned to the sofa. Tried to think, but couldn't make much headway. Not just now. So he returned to drinking and smoking. And the time slipped by.

'You know,' Beatrice said at one point, 'even if those men hadn't visited me, I still would have come to see you.'

He gave her a look.

'Don't get the wrong idea,' she said. 'I know we'd never make it. There's no happy endings when two people are in love. And we do love each other, Gabriel.'

'We had to split up,' he said.

'To protect me from the world you live in?' she said. 'You still believe that?'

'Sure.'

'You split up with me because you wanted to maintain control, Gabby. And you know it. But the more you do that, the lonelier you get. I thought you'd have realized that by now.'

Something stirred inside of him and he looked away from her. He thought of Mrs Hirsch and the Doc and all their warnings.

'I would have come because I was worried,' she said. 'When you turned up at the studio, you looked like my brother did before

347

he disappeared. Haunted, pale, anxious. What the hell's going on with you?'

Something about what she'd said panicked him. Did he really look haunted? Was that why Sarah gave him that hug out of nowhere? Was there really such a big disconnect between his self-image and how others perceived him? And if he was so wrong about something so basic, what other things was he wrong about? How deep did the self-delusion run?

He swallowed and stared at the city outside. Eight million souls in it and who could he trust?

He told her everything.

About the Saratoga racetrack and the cooked books and stealing the money. About running away to Mexico. About Bennie's missing millions, about Genovese and Cleveland. And in telling her it was like all the weight he'd been living under the last few months lifted, the stress and the anxiety poured out, like a valve had been opened.

She didn't offer solutions because there were none to give. She didn't offer sympathy either, because she knew it was no good. She just listened, tears in her eyes. They drank more. They melted into the sofa, listened to the ballads on the radio, watched the specks of traffic move about the streets far below them.

'You gonna miss it?' she asked. 'New York?'

Gabriel thought. He wouldn't miss the claustrophobia of it, things always pressing down on him. New York was a city without oases. Maybe that was why he dreamed of jumping off buildings, the need for wings, a way of reclaiming power over the environment. But still he'd miss it.

'Sure,' he said. 'These last few months I've been walking around. I've been making a list in my head, of all the things I'm going to miss. And it seems like I'm adding something new every day.'

'What are you gonna miss?'

'Mainly, the buzz,' he said. 'That feeling there's always something going on, that you're living somewhere big. How the city's big and it makes you feel big. How everyone walks fast and talks fast. How every cab driver and bellboy and kid running an elevator's got an angle, a story to tell. How when a train leaves Grand Central the sidewalk on Park Avenue shakes. How when the wind blows west the smoke drifts over Jersey and it makes the sunsets red. How you can tell how the Yankees did just by looking on the faces of the old-timers catching the Eighth Avenue Line back from the game. How when it's foggy the skyscrapers disappear and all you can see are the windows glowing in the sky. How when they fill the swimming pools at the start of summer all the neighborhood kids run to the parks, like they know, like there's a siren only they can hear.'

He turned to see her smiling. He really would miss it all. Lament it. The shadows and the gleam. Most of all, though, he would miss walking the streets he walked with his sister, all those years ago. Seeing the sights she saw, living in the city she called home.

'Remember when we used to take Sarah to the skating rink at the Rockefeller?' Beatrice said.

They both smiled.

Remember when.

They talked about old times. Awkwardness gave way to tenderness. They fell asleep. In their clothes, in the sunlight, in front of the window.

At one point Gabriel stirred, his mind emerged briefly from the waters of sleep, bobbed along the surface unsteadily. He thought about Beatrice and Benny and all the other people who had passed out of his life, and all the people who would pass out of it when he ran away. He mused on what Beatrice had said, how it echoed the advice of everyone else in his life. His inability to change was costing him relationships. By imposing himself on the world around him, he might have maintained his identity, but he'd lost something more important.

He realized the weight of the revelation, felt if he could remember it when he woke, all his problems would be fixed. He tried to hold onto the thought, but his mind was too battered, too fuzzy, too ragged, too close to unconsciousness. Before he could really tighten his grip on it, he submerged into sleep once more.

PART FIFTEEN

'I don't know how I made it through those years. I became bitter, hard, cold. I was always on a panic – couldn't buy clothes or a good place to live . . . The mental strain was getting worse all the time. What made it worst of all was that nobody understood our kind of music out on the Coast. I can't begin to tell you how I yearned for New York.'

CHARLIE PARKER, *METRONOME*, 1947

39

Michael exited his apartment building into a bitterly cold wind. He stood on the front step, buttoned up his coat and headed towards the subway stop. The streets were quieter than they were on weekdays, giving the surroundings an emptiness that Michael found un-nerving. A block or so from his apartment, he got the feeling someone was following him. He paused to look in a shop window, and in the corner of his eye, he saw a man stop at a window a few stores down. Amateurish.

Michael had his Browning in his pocket. He came up with a plan.

He carried on walking down the block, found an alleyway and stepped into it, took the gun from his pocket. About halfway down the alleyway was the service entrance to one of the stores on the street. He ducked into the alcove of the entrance and waited.

A half-minute later, the man walked past.

Michael stepped out from the alcove when the man was a few feet past him and raised the gun.

'You flat-footing me, son?' he asked.

The man stopped, turned round to see Michael holding the gun, raised his hands. He was tall, good-looking, had that gang-ster cockiness. But there was tiredness around the man's eyes, a bruised face, a slight tremor, a haunted quality.

'I'm just on my way to meet a pal. This a stick-up?' the man asked.

'You're following me. You've been following me since I left my apartment. How about you tell me what you're up to and no more lies.'

The man thought. Michael could see behind his eyes he was evaluating the situation.

'I wanted to talk to you.'

'Well, you got a damn strange way of going about it, son,' said Michael.

The man didn't look het up, coiled, like he was following Michael to attack him. Something else was going on. Maybe he'd followed Michael to see how long he'd be gone – if he saw Michael disappear down a subway entrance, hop in a cab, maybe he would have gone back to the apartment and ransacked the place.

'Can I put my hands down at least?' the man asked.

''Fraid not,' said Michael. 'I'm not as fast with one of these things as I used to be. You're gonna have to keep 'em up. Now you going to tell me what you're up to?'

The man paused.

'You're looking for a drug pusher named Gene Cleveland,' he said. 'So am I. I was thinking we could compare notes.'

'That'd depend on why you're looking for him.'

''Cos I'm really looking for one of the other men who's after him. A hired gun called Faron.'

'And why are you looking for him?'

'He killed my sister.'

The man stared at Michael a moment before continuing.

'It's a long story,' he said. 'Could we talk about it somewhere warmer?'

Michael wondered if this wasn't all a ruse, if the tailing was deliberately sloppy, if the man didn't already have associates breaking into Michael's apartment, stealing the case documents. But something about this man suggested he was working alone, and that he was desperate, and that he really did need Michael's help.

'You got a name, son?' Michael asked.

'Gabriel,' the man said. 'Gabriel Leveson.'

There was a bar just around the corner. They stepped inside and Michael was glad to be back somewhere warm. The place was mostly empty, and the few people in there were slumped in front of schooners watching the television the owner had set up at the end of the bar. Michael stopped to stare at it; a television set was a strange enough thing, but one in a bar seemed ludicrous.

They ordered beers, sat at a table, turned to look at the tiny gray screen. It was filled with the image of a wrestling ring; two gray blobs in the center of the ring circled each other, lunged.

'Do the bars in Chicago have TV sets in them?' Gabriel asked.

Michael shook his head. 'No. But they will do. How'd you know I'm from Chicago?'

'I know all about you and your partner,' said Gabriel. 'I asked around. The two best detectives ever to work Chicago. The First National heist, the Brandt kidnapping, the McCulloch murder.'

'That was all a long time ago.'

Michael took his cigarettes out, offered one to Gabriel. They lit up.

'How'd you find out I was looking for Cleveland?'

They'd done their best to keep their tracks covered, yet clearly there'd been a breach. And a breach meant they might have put Tom in further danger.

'Friend of a friend that works Narcotics,' said Gabriel. 'He heard you were making enquiries. I put two and two together.'

Michael thought about what Carrasco had told him, that he'd asked someone in Narcotics for info on Cleveland. He wondered how wide the breach was. He needed to speak to Carrasco about it.

'I think I know who killed those people in the hotel,' said Gabriel finally.

'And who would that be?'

'A gun for hire by the name of Faron.'

'The man who killed your sister?'

Gabriel nodded.

Michael could see he was summoning up the resolve to dredge up something awful. He took a long drag on his cigarette and told him a long tale about his sister being murdered by Faron, of Faron disappearing, of Gabriel spending years looking for him, and how a few days earlier, he'd heard Faron was back in town. Had been hired to kill Cleveland.

Gabriel told him a lot of things, but none of them helped Michael out much except confirming the timeline of Faron's movements that he and Ida had already established.

'So, that's what I know,' said Gabriel. 'Maybe you can repay the favor.'

Michael paused, sighed. 'I'm not sure I can do that,' he said. 'Not just yet. We think the police colluded in covering up the hotel murders. Which leads us to think there might have been Mob involvement, too. So you can understand I'm a little wary when a mobster turns up in the middle of it all offering assistance.'

'Who's to say I'm a mobster?' Gabriel said.

'Son, I've worked in the underworld more than fifty years. You've got it written all over you.'

For a second Gabriel's veneer disappeared, that sense all mobsters had of being comfortable in their own skin, at ease in the society they had rebelled against.

'Unless you give me something more than I already know,' said Michael, 'I'm still not sure I can trust you.'

Gabriel nodded, took a sip of his beer.

On the television at the end of the bar, one of the gray blobs was counted out and a tinny cheer rose up.

'The man behind the Palmer Hotel hit was Vito Genovese,' said Gabriel.

'Genovese employed Faron to kill Cleveland?'

Gabriel nodded. 'Find and kill him,' he said.

Michael thought. Faron had been employed by Congressman Helms, not Vito Genovese. What Gabriel was saying completely contradicted everything Michael and Ida had come up with.

'You sure about that, son?'

'I ain't got proof,' he said. 'But that's how it's looking from here.'

'And why does Genovese want Cleveland dead?'

'That's what I don't know.'

Michael took a drag on his cigarette. 'Which of the five families d'you work for?' he asked.

'I work for Frank Costello.'

'Costello and Genovese are both in the Luciano crime family,' said Michael. 'That puts you on the wrong side of the fence.'

'They may be in the same family, but they hate each other. Genovese's planning a takeover. Ask anyone in NYC. All this with your son is linked. I'm not sure how, but it is. I may be a mobster, but I'm sure as hell not working for Genovese. I can't stand the guy.'

Michael took a sip of beer. Wondered if it was all a ruse. If Gabriel was working with Faron. If he'd come fishing for information, to find out exactly how much Michael knew, to see if it was worth their while arranging a hit on Tom in Rikers.

He wondered if he was being sucked into a gangland war, was being used as a pawn in a chess game whose players he could only guess at. He thought back to the Van Haren case twenty years earlier, to the Axeman case ten years before that. How the lines of command and conspiracy always stretched further than was fathomable. He needed to talk to Ida, to see if they could trust Gabriel, if maybe they'd got it all wrong with Helms, or if they needed to reject the man's offer.

'Stop Genovese, catch Faron,' said Gabriel. 'That's all I want to do.'

Michael could sense something else though, an ulterior motive in there somewhere. Gabriel seemed anxious, edgy, pressured. And none of that fitted with everything else he was saying. He wondered if Gabriel was as pressed upon as Michael. If he was as desperate.

'And if you catch Faron,' Michael said, 'what'll you do with him?'

'What do you mean?'

'I've seen men like you before, son. Men with revenge on their minds. You want to kill him. If you do that, where does that leave our case? You'll be killing the alternate suspect we need to see my boy freed. That doesn't make us allies, it puts us in a race against each other. We need to catch Faron alive.'

'Not necessarily.'

'No, but it would help.'

'Faron's an animal,' Gabriel said. 'A force of nature. All I want is him stopped, and the only way to do that is to kill him. You need to realize that. If Faron dies because I shoot him, I'm happy. If he dies in the electric chair, I'm happy too.'

Michael deliberated, not sure if Gabriel had said the last because he knew it was what Michael wanted to hear.

'Maybe we can work together on this,' Michael said. 'But I'll have to talk to my partner.'

'Sure,' said Gabriel. 'But I need an answer soon. I don't have much time.'

'Neither do we, son. Neither do we.'

40

Sunday 9th, 10.00 a.m.

Ida wanted to start investigating if there had been any other killings. If Helms and Faron had murdered any other people in their
attempt to hide what had happened during the war. But it was
Sunday. Offices were closed, businesses were closed, even the
library was closed. People were away.

She spent a couple of hours going through the call logs from
the Palmer Hotel that Carrasco had gotten for them, matching up
the addresses and names to anyone who might be related to the
case, trying to spot patterns in the calls, the numbers, the area
codes, the times. She came up blank.

She called Michael and Louis but they were both out, so she
went for a walk, a long one that took up most of the day, that led
her all the way downtown, to the Brooklyn Bridge. She walked to
its middle and stood watching the boats passing across the surface
of the river below, ocean liners and pleasure craft, tugs, ferries
and lighters. In the distance the giant cranes of the Brooklyn
Naval Yards towered into the sky, the scores of ship-builders'
yards that ran the length of the waterfront.

She watched the couples strolling past on the bridge, the
cyclists, the people in their church clothes, the gulls arcing above.
The city seemed to be alive with a different energy, a more relaxed
Sunday spirit. She wondered if this was what her weekends would
be like if she moved to California.

She returned to Midtown, through the multicolored confetti
of Times Square, dull and shimmering in the cold. She watched a

RAY CELESTIN

movie on Broadway. A crime film. One of a dozen on at the cinemas there.

She came back to the hotel late, to a message that Michael had called.

She called him back.

'I had a visit this afternoon,' he said. 'From a Gabriel Leveson. You heard of him?'

He told her all about it and they discussed what to do, whether they should trust the man. Michael seemed like he wanted to. Ida urged caution, not sure if they were desperate enough just yet to start comparing notes with a mobster. They talked about the breach in Narcotics and how much danger that put Tom in. They talked but came no closer to an agreement, deciding only to reconvene in the morning.

She called Jacob over in Berkeley and managed to get through to him.

'How's it going?' she asked.

'Good, Mom. But busy. Real busy.'

They chatted a while and she was warmed to hear his voice, but the warmth cooled almost as soon as she put the phone down, and the distance reasserted itself.

She took a bath, got into bed, stared at the ceiling, thought about her day spent adrift in New York. Untethered as a ghost. The loneliness both kept her awake and made her feel tired. How was that possible?

She must have fallen asleep at some point because she woke to the sound of ringing, to daylight streaming in through a gap in the curtains.

She picked up the phone.

'Hello?' she said, groggily.

There was a rustle of static then a male voice came on the line.

'Ida? It's Adrian.'

The man who'd offered her the job in LA.

'Adrian, hello.'

360

'I woke you, I'm sorry.'

'It's fine.'

She checked her wristwatch on the bedside table.

'I was calling with good news,' he said. 'You passed security clearance. You're in. I had to pull some strings, but it happened.'

Ida wasn't sure how to reply. 'That's great. Thank you.'

'You don't sound all that pleased.'

'I'm sorry . . . I just woke up.'

'No problem.'

There was silence on the line for a few seconds.

'I've still not got a firm acceptance from you,' he said.

'I'm sorry, Adrian. I still haven't decided. The case I'm working on has taken over and I've just not had time.'

'I see,' he said.

There was another silence, even more awkward this time.

'The job sounds great,' Ida said eventually. 'It really does, but . . . just give me some more time to think about it?'

'Sure,' he said. But she could hear the wariness in his tone.

After she put down the phone a sense of panic gripped her, of things spinning out of her control. She quickly called the office in Chicago to see how things were going, was disappointed when they told her everything was fine.

She got dressed and headed downtown.

An hour later she was walking through the lobby of the Manhattan Criminal Court. It was full of people, their footsteps and conversations filling the space with an echoing noise that was at once shrill and diffuse. The bustle reinforced Ida's belief that law courts were not so much spaces where justice was dispensed, as they were market places; great bazaars where the economics of the legal system were worked out. Where the people who profited from crime, *really* profited – the judges, lawyers, DAs, police, bond-makers, bailiffs – descended like a flock of gulls to feast on the unfortunates caught in the net, where the first order of business was to process the money, and then the paperwork, and last of all the people.

She checked the calendar, found Tom's lawyer's name. Len Rutherford, counsel for the defense in an arraignment. The lawyer who was refusing to answer her calls. The lawyer they were about to sack, regardless of how close they were to a trial date.

She walked through a maze of corridors, found the courtroom, sat in the public gallery. The case involved a stabbing at a bar on the Lower East Side. Rutherford's client, a sullen-looking Irishman, pled guilty. Rutherford made no attempt to convince the judge his client wasn't a flight risk; he spent most of the time looking at his watch. The judge set bail. The defendant shuffled out. It was all over in the space of a few minutes.

Ida left the court, waited for the lawyer in the corridor outside.

'Mr Rutherford,' she said.

He turned around, looked her up and down, smiled. 'Yes?'

'My name's Ida Young,' she said. 'I'm the private investigator hired by the family of Thomas James Talbot.'

The man looked blank before realizing who she was.

'Of course,' he said. 'If you don't mind, I have another hearing to go to. Please call my office and we can arrange a meeting.'

He turned and strode down the corridor.

Ida followed.

'I've left numerous messages at your office,' she said. 'And I checked the dockets, your next court appearance isn't till this afternoon.'

'I see' he said, the irritation plain in his voice. 'What do you want, Mrs Young?'

'I wanted to discuss the case with you,' she said.

'My duty is to my client,' he said. 'I don't have to share information with you.'

'You don't have to,' she replied. 'But it would help.'

'Hardly.'

They reached the end of the corridor. Rutherford stopped and opened the door for her.

She nodded her thanks and they stepped through into the echoing lobby.

'The boy needs to plead guilty,' said Rutherford.

'He's innocent.'

He scoffed. 'I was almost of that opinion when I took on the case, now I'm convinced of his guilt. Regardless, it's beside the point. A guilty plea and I can bargain down his sentence. He'll leave prison with some of his life still left. I know the juries in this town, Mrs Young. He gets in that courtroom with a not-guilty plea, he's as good as dead.'

'There's enough there to see him freed.'

'Such as?'

'Such as the prosecution has failed to find a single eyewitness or establish a coherent timeline,' she said. 'Their versions of events is far-fetched, bordering on ridiculous, and completely undermined by the fact that the murder weapon was never recovered. The evidence gathering was incompetent at best, and prejudicial at worst. The chain-of-evidence brief is riddled with inconsistencies. The whole case is based on supposition, secondary evidence and race bias. Any half-competent defense lawyer with enough funds and time could have this case thrown out before it even reached trial.'

The last wasn't true, and both of them knew it, but Ida had gotten carried away; something about Rutherford irked her, his indifference, his sense of superiority.

He arched an eyebrow. 'That's all as maybe,' he said. 'But none of that matters, Mrs Young. Because when it gets to trial, all the jury's going to see is a Negro who killed a woman and a white boy. A Negro who was caught red-handed. Literally. A thoroughly unsympathetic character.'

'A war veteran and a doctor,' Ida countered. 'A man who spent his life helping people and was damaged by his service.'

Rutherford scoffed. 'It seems you're not in possession of all the facts.'

They reached the exit. He held up a hand and they stepped through the doors onto the steps outside the courthouse. He put his briefcase down, pulled a pair of gloves from his pocket. Ida buttoned up her coat against the cold.

'I spoke with a friend of mine on the prosecution. They managed to get hold of Thomas's army service record. Late last week.' Rutherford spoke slowly, sliding the black leather gloves onto his hands. 'Thomas was blue-slipped out of the army. You're aware what that's a euphemism for? Homosexuality.'

He stared at her. Ida felt a sickening mix of disappointment and bewilderment rush through her.

'They also added his former landlady to the witness list. I had a look at her statement. He was thrown out of his last apartment after being caught indulging in his vices. That's how he ended up at the Palmer Hotel,' Rutherford said.

'Can you imagine what the prosecution will make of all that? A man of his proclivities cutting up a woman and a young, white boy? They'll say he was a pervert. Twisted. A drifter. Thrown out of the army and out of his apartment he decided to take his revenge on society. Or how about another motive – the hotel worker found him *in flagrante delicto* and at the prospect of being thrown out once more, he flew into a murderous rage. They can twist this a million ways, Mrs Young, each scenario worse than the next.'

Rutherford stared at her, letting the silence press home his victory.

'So you see,' he said, 'it's in everyone's interest for him to plead guilty. May I offer you some advice?'

Ida didn't know what to say. She nodded.

'You're not on home ground. Neither you nor Thomas's father. This is New York. You don't know how things work here. You're far from home and that makes you powerless. My advice to you is to head back to Chicago before you do any more damage and see a boy lose his life unnecessarily.'

'I'm here to save the boy's life.'

He let out an exasperated laugh. 'Did you see the newspaper this weekend?' he asked. 'Milton Eldridge, the owner of the Palmer Hotel. He was killed in a hit-and-run accident. Now, Mrs Young, are you naive enough to think it really was an accident? Or do you truly understand what we're dealing with here? The sooner Thomas pleads guilty, the sooner he's out of danger. I'm trying to save his life.'

'I see,' said Ida.

'Do you?' He looked at her, then he sighed, wearied by it all. 'Now if there's nothing more,' he said, 'I have work to get back to.'

He nodded at her and trotted down the front steps. She watched him go, feeling thoroughly beaten.

She waited a moment, then descended the steps herself, found a bench, sat on it, took her cigarette case from her pocket and lit up, stared at the traffic slipping past. She'd let herself get swept up in the quarrel, had forgotten her usual policy of never arguing with lawyers. The wind blew against her, its coldness numbing the skin on her hands and face, making her eyes water.

Rutherford's news explained why Tom had moved to the flophouse in a hurry, why he had lied about what he was doing there. It explained why he never returned to the hospital to get his old job back – they would have asked to see his discharge papers. Rather than shame himself, he never reapplied. He used his savings to wander New York, to help out at a charity. He'd lied because he was ashamed.

Then it dawned on her. She'd have to tell Michael. Before Rutherford did. She wondered how he'd react. She thought about Cleveland and Tom ending up in the same hotel, both of them blue-slipped out of the army. A thought came to her – what if it wasn't a coincidence? What if Tom and Cleveland knew each other? What if she'd got it all wrong and Tom *was* somehow involved?

She thought about Eldridge being killed and Rutherford's acknowledgment that Tom was in danger. Offered up as if it were common knowledge.

She exhaled wearily. Rutherford had shaken her faith, made her doubt everything. And then a worse thought struck her — what if Rutherford convinced Tom to plead guilty? He'd done a good enough job of convincing her. She summoned up the energy to rise, headed to the subway as a light snow started to fall. How on earth would she break the news to Michael?

41

When Ida got to 5th Avenue to meet Michael she found him standing under the library's portico, looking small against the giant facade, the beaux-arts columns and sculptures and towering Vermont marble.

'How'd it go?' he asked when he saw her approaching.

His breath steamed in the cold. She saw a wooden bench just next to the entrance and led him over to it. They sat. She told him everything. He listened and nodded and kept his eyes on the trees and lawns that encircled the building, the traffic skating up the avenue, the falling snow.

'I see,' he said, when she'd finished speaking.

His expression was blank, and she wasn't sure if it was because he was keeping something in, or was still too shocked to register an emotion yet.

'What do you want to do?' she said.

'Tell Tom to get a new lawyer.'

'I mean about Tom.'

'I don't know,' he said, shaking his head. 'Why didn't he say anything? He lied and now it looks even worse.'

'He was ashamed, Michael,' Ida said gently.

Michael paused, rubbed his temples. 'All I've ever done is tried to do right by the boy, and his sister.'

'I know.'

'Blue-slipped. The boy went out there to be a medic.'

'I know.'

Michael stared once more at the snow-dusted cars and taxis heading down the avenue.

'We need to speak to Tom,' she said.

Michael checked his watch.

'We've missed the boat to Rikers,' he said. 'I'll head on over there tomorrow. Come on, let's work.'

He rose and headed towards the doors. Ida watched him go, feeling a sense of disquiet, of things being bottled up for the worse.

The library's Periodicals Reading Room was located on the third floor, in a room which looked more like something from a belle époque mansion than a library. They requested copies of the *Times*, the *Daily Mirror* and the *Daily News* since the start of the year. They went through the homicide reports, looking for other murders Faron and Helms might have committed. They'd asked Carrasco to do a search, too, but knew it would take him a few days, so here they were trying to get a jump start. As they worked, Ida kept an eye on Michael, and felt stupid for doing so.

They compiled a list.

Dozens of murders.

None of them looked like they had been committed by Faron, though. None of them linked in any way to Bucek or Cleveland or Helms or the Palmer Hotel or even Vito Genovese. The murders were, for the most part, mundane. Bar fights, muggings, burglaries gone wrong, brawls over money or women.

The day wound wearily on.

They went out to lunch, came back, continued. The sun dipped behind the skyline and the library's lights came on with an electric mosquito buzz. The desks around them emptied one by one, but still nothing connected back to their case. They stayed till the library closed and as they stepped out into the bitter cold that lay like an anvil on 5th Avenue, Ida felt the sinking regret of a lost day. A day that had started badly and had gotten steadily worse.

'I think I'll walk back to the apartment,' Michael said.

Ida could see beneath his words the need to be alone, to wander the city and try and make sense of things. Just like her. Just like Tom.

She nodded, and Michael walked off through the snow and she caught the subway up to Harlem. The express train was packed even before it reached 59th, so she had to stand all the way as it rattled and roared its way uptown, swinging passengers and lights this way and that. She tried to take her mind off the case. She scanned the headlines on the papers of her fellow commuters – snatches of information about the ongoing saga of the UN building, Jackie Robinson, the plan to partition Palestine, the HUAC hearings.

Against her will her mind drifted to Washington, to the CIA, to the job in California that was hers now, the job helping protect America, the eternal war. She turned away, feeling that same anxiety she'd felt ever since Nathan had been drafted, of powerlessness in the face of history, of being beaten by the cavalcade thrown at her from the future.

She got out at 125th Street and hurried through the snow and the sickly orange of the street lights back to her hotel. She walked past the notion stores full of cheap, flimsy clothing and trinkets, past the five-and-dimes, past a hall holding a revival meeting, past a bar on the corner from which emanated blues music, shaking the sidewalk. She thought of the bebop club. The saxophonist with all that fire inside him, the instrument just a tool for getting it out, a gasket, a safety valve. She heard the sound of his saxophone once more, skating through the air, fragile and lonely, but beautifully so.

It was only when she got into her hotel room that she realized she hadn't eaten dinner again. She'd have to call down to reception or go out for food. She lay on the bed to get a moment's rest, her coat still on. The murders she'd spent all day reading about ran through her head. All those dead men. Killed so senselessly.

So much pointless loss of life. She thought of Nathan and that silent time after he'd died. She thought of Jacob's father. She thought of Michael burying his pain with work, and how foolish that seemed.

And then she realized with a corrosive dismay that burying herself in work was exactly the tactic she used for dealing with distress, too. She'd been ready to lecture Michael for something she herself was guilty of. Did she look just as foolish when she did it? Why did it look so bad when she saw it in another person, yet feel so natural to her? She felt her emotions welling up, and she closed her eyes and let them come, let them overflow.

After a while she noticed that she was sweating. She was still wearing her coat on and the room's heating was on. She opened her eyes, sat up, pulled her coat off. She rolled over and saw the call log from the hotel poking out of her handbag. She grabbed it, used it to fan her face. She figured she'd kill time going through it once more. She set it down on the bed. All the names and addresses and numbers blurred for a second, then came into focus. She ran her eye down the list and a name popped out at her.

John Marino.

She stopped, frowned, thought as to why the name tugged at her memory. Someone at the Palmer Hotel had called his number three times before the murders. Two incoming calls from his number as well. The calls all happened in the evenings, between eight and eleven.

Then it clicked.

The murders.

Ida scrabbled through her handbag for the notes they'd made in the library, flicked through them. There he was. John Marino. Twenty-eight. A worker on the Brooklyn docks, disappeared six weeks before the hotel murders, the day before Bucek went into hiding. His body had turned up a few days later in the Hudson. He'd been stabbed in the torso multiple times, thrown into the river.

Someone at the hotel had been calling Marino. Marino had been murdered, and the next day Bucek had gone on the run. Marino was the third blackmailer.

Were there any more?

Ida sat up and grabbed the phone and dialed Michael's number. A new victim, and with the call logs a direct link to the Palmer Hotel. Evidence that might stand up in court. And, more importantly, a new lead to pursue.

PART SIXTEEN

'The business of carrying on crime today has been extraordinarily complicated by the use of front men, cash transactions, high-priced lawyers who know how to cut the legal corners, corporations and partnerships, and by concealed ownership of real estate and other assets. Cartels and corporations, with all their interlocking directorates and their legal and financial shenanigans, are miracles of simplicity by comparison.'

HERBERT ASBURY, *COLLIERS*, 1947

42

Monday 10th, 1.25 p.m.

Costello got out of the cab and looked about the Midtown spires rising high into the icy sky, the snow pirouetting between them. He found the number of the building, walked over. The door-man let him in; Costello slipped him a twenty. He approached the reception desk, asked for the ABC offices and was directed to the elevator bank.

All the way up, the elevator boy shot him looks through the dull reflections in the fake gold panels on the back of the doors, wondering if it was *the* Frank Costello he was riding with.

When they reached Glaser's floor, he slipped the kid a twenty and walked down the red carpet to the office, stepped inside. The decor was sleek and plush. Cutting edge. Costello recognized some of the furniture from the design magazines Bobbie left strewn about the house – Scandinavian things she was pestering him to fill their own apartment with.

He spoke to the receptionist, a girl he thought he'd seen some-where, in a Broadway show maybe. She ushered him over to the sofas to wait for Joe Glaser. He sat. He waited. He blew his nose. He munched on cough sweets.

He looked at the photos opposite, all the Negro musicians on whose backs Glaser had ridden from washed-up Capone stooge, to swanky Midtown respectability, to satellite offices in LA, to the mainstream. Glaser had started the agency with a loan from Jules Stein, the Chicago mobster who ran MCA, the Music Corpor-ation of America, the talent management behemoth. Stein had run whiskey with Capone during Prohibition, had helped refine Capone's book-keeping model. With Capone's help, Stein had hired mobsters to scare nightspots into booking MCA artists, used stink-bomb and fire-bomb tactics. He cut sweetheart deals with the Mob-run Musicians' Union. Stein and his associates had made MCA the largest talent agency in the country, representing not just musicians, but most of Hollywood, too.

It was quite something, how a bunch of poor Russian Jews from Lawndale, Chicago had come from nothing to run much of the entertainment industry. And down through the years, Costello had worked with them on this and that, whenever the need arose. He'd never had a problem working with Jewish gangsters. He'd come up with Rothstein and Lansky and Siegel. Trusted Gabriel more than all his other fixers.

Costello had always been like that. When he was seven or eight years old, he wandered one Saturday morning into the Jewish neighborhood in West Harlem that adjoined the Italian slum he lived in. An old bearded man approached him, pegging him for an outsider, offered him a penny to light his stove for him. Costello thought the request a strange one. The old man explained that it was a sin for an Orthodox Jew to light a fire or do any kind of work on a Sabbath. Costello went back the next Saturday, and the one after that, and soon he was the neighborhood's *Shabbas goy*. He learned more about the religion, and on the dates of the Jewish holidays he upped his price to a nickel. Eventually, he married a girl from the neighborhood.

The receptionist walked over to Costello and smiled.

'He's free now,' she said.

She led him through into a corner office. Joe Glaser didn't look pleased to see him.

'Frank,' said Glaser.

'Joe,' said Costello.

Glaser offered him a seat. A bizarre modernist confection of upholstery and strange angles.

'What the hell is this thing?' said Costello.

'It's a chair, Frank,' said Glaser.

'Looks like it should be in a b-movie about flying saucers.'

Glaser scowled. Costello sat. They stared at each other.

'How's business?' Costello asked.

'Good.'

'You got a tan.'

'I was in LA,' said Glaser. 'We're setting up a West Coast office.'

'Is that so?' said Costello.

'America's moving west.'

'It's always been moving west, Joe.'

Costello sneezed. Chloroformed himself again with the eucalyptus-oiled handkerchief.

Glaser eyed him.

'I'm glad to hear business is good,' Costello said, moving the handkerchief from his nose.

Glaser gave him a *get on with it* look.

'You hear about the meeting in the Astoria?' Costello asked.

'The movie men? Sure.'

Costello thought of a delicate way to put to Glaser what the movie producer had told him in the art gallery.

'MCA's name came up,' he said. 'Ronnie Reagan's name came up. I wanted to speak to Stein about it, but my phones being what they are, I thought I'd talk to you first.'

The mobsters in charge of MCA were the same men behind Glaser's own agency and Glaser was in close contact with them. So rather than picking up a bugged telephone to call them out in LA, Costello had come to see Glaser, to see if he might shed some light on what was going on.

Glaser gave Costello a suspicious look, leaned back in his seat.

'In what context did their names come up?' he asked.

Costello told him about the two movie producers, about Vito

377

Genovese trying to swing the vote, about the producer saying it had something to do with Reagan and MCA.

Glaser listened to what Costello had to say, put his fingers together in a steeple.

'I think I know what this is to do with,' he said eventually. 'I'll let you know, but you need to talk it over with Stein when you can.'

Costello nodded.

'Reagan's an informer for the FBI,' said Glaser. 'He joined a couple of organizations a few years ago with links to the communist party he didn't know about. He's so scared of being accused of being a red, he's gone on an anti-communist tirade to cover it up. He contacted the Feds out in LA, told them he could give them names of actors he knew were commies, gave them a whole list. Ratted out his own friends.'

'And what's that got to do with MCA?' Costello asked.

'Up till a few years ago Reagan was washed up,' said Glaser. 'A string of b-movie turkeys and too much carousing. MCA offered to rejuvenate his career, gave him the nudge to put himself forward for president of the Screen Actors Guild. They figured with Reagan in charge of the guild they could cut sweetheart deals.'

Costello waved his hand in the air. 'I already know all this,' he said.

Costello had heard about it from Jack Warner. Having an MCA stooge as the president meant the union was effectively being run by their members' largest employer. It was a conflict of interest in the most brazen, glaring way imaginable, but Reagan was voted in regardless, on an anti-communist ticket. Much like the other unions in Hollywood, the Mob had used red-baiting to take control.

'Well, if Reagan's naming names,' said Glaser, 'and the studios are worried about witch-hunts, then maybe Genovese's setting himself up as a solution.'

Costello nodded. That was it. That was why he was getting

involved. Genovese, like Glaser, like MCA, like many of New York's broadcasting companies, was moving west. The Mob was supposed to be helping the industry, getting Communists and FBI probes and Congressional Committees off the studios' backs. Genovese was making sure that didn't happen. He was making things get worse, making it look like Costello and his men were failing to offer the protection they had promised, so he could step in when things were really bad and offer himself up as an alternative, and effective, solution.

'Oldest trick in the book,' said Glaser. 'Start a shit-storm and sell people mops.'

'If Genovese's offering himself up as a solution,' said Costello, 'he must have something concrete to offer them.'

'An ace up his sleeve?'

Costello nodded. 'You know what it is?'

Glaser paused, shrugged. 'Maybe he's got a man on the inside.'

'Inside HUAC?'

Glaser considered it. Shrugged. 'Maybe,' he said.

Costello mused, looked up, saw Glaser staring at him, hawkish, ravenous.

'Well, it was nice talking,' said Costello. 'I'll speak to Jules somehow. I'm sure we can all figure out a way of dealing with this.'

Costello rose from the space-ship seat with a groan, slipped his hat onto his head. Paused. Looked at the bizarre painting on the wall, a field full of spades in white smocks playing banjos and singing. He was reminded of the blue blob painting he'd seen in the gallery the other night.

As he rode down in the elevator, he thought about Los Angeles and Chicago, Genovese and the studios, the FBI, all of it, and he tried to think how he could use the information he'd gleaned, and what way it could be used to give him greatest advantage in the war that now seemed inevitable with Vito Genovese.

PART SEVENTEEN

'The waterfront now competes with the city's most depressed slum areas as a spawning place of crime. This unhealthy condition, qualified authorities agree, results largely from the antiquated method of hiring labor, long since abandoned in the world's other great ports but still in use on New York's docks. The lack of any assurance of regular employment and the complete dependence of the men on the favor of gang and dock bosses who do the hiring perfectly "set up" the industry for control by racketeers.'

REPORT OF THE DISTRICT ATTORNEY,
COUNTY OF NEW YORK, 1946–1948

43

Four days left till he was supposed to be leaving town and Gabriel was still no closer to finding the money. All his leads had come up short, petered out into dead ends and frustration, anxiety and waiting games. Waiting for the detectives, waiting for Salzman, waiting for Tomasulo, waiting for his own drug-addled, jittery brain to conjure up a breakthrough.

And then, just as he was heading out to the Copa, one of his leads sputtered back into life via a phone call from Salzman.

'I looked into those murders for you,' Salzman said. 'Girls cut up over the last six months that match Faron's style.'

'And?'

'I found something,' he said. 'Plenty of cut-up girls. I'm surprised there's any left on the streets. But there's one – a hooker by the name of Pearl Clayton. Her body turned up in a wrecker's yard out in Hell's Kitchen back in July. Sliced up. Matches Faron's MO. The interesting thing is what happened next. Two homicide cops working the graveyard shift caught the case 'cos her body was found early morning. When the shift change happened a few hours later, the case was re-assigned.'

'To who?' asked Gabriel, though he already had a feeling on the answer.

'To Detective Lieutenants Doyle and Higgs,' said Salzman. 'Lately of the East River.'

The two cops who died chasing Gabriel in the car. The ones who were partnered up with Faron.

'From the bureau squawks it sounds like they were the ones that pushed for the re-assignment,' added Salzman.

'Figures,' said Gabriel.

Faron had killed the girl. The two cops he was working with asked to take over the case so they could make sure Faron didn't get pegged for it.

'How did the investigation work out?' Gabriel asked.

'They shit-canned it.'

'Can I have a look at the case files?'

'Sure,' said Salzman. 'But there's something else. I checked to see if the girl had any raps of her own. She did. She'd been picked up in street-walker sweeps a couple of times, and again a month or so before she disappeared, this time the victim of an assault. I spoke to some friends in Vice. Looks like the perpetrator of the assault was John Bova. She didn't press charges and it was dropped.'

Bova. The rat in Costello's organization, the scar-faced pimp. Gabriel thought back to the last time he'd seen the man, at the breakfast at Costello's when Gabriel had been given the job of finding the missing money. He remembered Bova fishing for information, pointing at Jack Warner, making Jew jokes.

So much for going to the Copa. Gabriel had four days left, and finally, a lifeline.

'Where can I meet you?' he asked.

He was uptown in twenty minutes. He was sitting in his car flicking through the case files in thirty. Salzman was right, Doyle and Higgs had hardly bothered investigating the murder, although there was not much to go on from the start. Pearl Clayton, twenty-three, identified by an ID card in her purse, a prostitute of no fixed address. The photos showed a young, skinny red-head. Pretty. Her naked torso was found mutilated and dumped between two wrecked cars in a breaker's yard. Cut marks everywhere. Faron hallmarks. Aside from the ID card there wasn't much else on her. Some change, a handkerchief, a packet of gum, a ticket stub from a diner.

Gabriel paused on the last. The Greenspot Luncheonette. He knew it. An all-night diner just south of Columbus Circle. Not far from the breaker's yard where the body was found. Opposite one of John Bova's cathouses. Popular with the local streetwalkers.

It was worth a shot.

He thanked Salzman. He handed over the wedge of money he'd promised the man. Salzman whistled through his teeth. Gabriel headed back downtown. Through the cold and ice. Through Times Square's neon sweep to the Greenspot Luncheonette. The road was quiet, dark. The diner seemed to be the only place open. On the street opposite, walking up and down, or in groups at the corners of the blocks, were the girls.

Gabriel parked up near the diner and headed over to talk to them, to ask if they knew Pearl. Some pretended they didn't know her, some pretended they did. When he offered them money some of them gave him scraps of information that all contradicted each other. Pearl worked for Bova. Pearl didn't work for Bova. Pearl was OK. Pearl was a troublemaker. It was Pearl's fault Bova had assaulted her. It was Bova's fault. Bova had cut Pearl loose after the assault. Bova hadn't cut her loose.

When he asked about who might have killed her, he hit a wall of silence. Girls clammed up, walked away, shook their heads. He was at it about an hour, tried corners blocks away from the Greenspot, even the diner itself. He could find nothing definite so weaved together the conflicting strands as best he could, came up with a story that might explain it all – Genovese and Faron. Faron wanted a girl, Genovese got him one via Bova. Bova picked a trouble-maker girl from his stable he'd had a recent bust-up with, a girl he was going to cut loose anyway, a girl he wasn't bothered about. He tossed her to Faron like he was throwing a steak to a lion. The idea of Faron being fed girls by his partners in crime reminded Gabriel of something, some story or myth maybe he couldn't quite put his finger on.

When he'd done as much as he could, he headed back to the Cadillac, sat, smoked, planned. Decided not to return to the Copa. He was sick of the place. Instead he drove through the city, going to places he thought Faron might be, New York's underbelly, its hinterlands.

Time passed. Anxiety swelled. By Thursday night he would be on the run, one way or the other. If he survived till then. It was enough to induce terror and madness in anyone, running away from the Mob's extermination machine. A fear manifested in him, an anxiety-rattled realization that if he didn't make it to Mexico, he'd be going to hell.

He checked his watch. It was nearly four. In a few hours eight million alarm clocks would rattle the city from sleep and the empire of night would relinquish the sidewalks for another shift, and Gabriel would carry on being out of step with it all, another few hours closer to perdition.

He drove back to the apartment and took two Nembutals and tried to sleep, and in the moments before the blackness, the myth he couldn't remember came to him – the minotaur, the beast at the center of a maze who was fed with girls. Then he slept, and dreamed of Manhattan as a giant labyrinth, the skyscrapers its walls, Faron at its center, roaming, bloodthirsty.

The phone woke him. How long had he been asleep? He looked out of the window and saw snow falling through the darkness. He checked the clock on the bedside table and was shocked to see it was late evening. The Nembutals had knocked him out for over twelve hours. Panic and fear pulsed through him. Four days left and he'd wasted half a day of it passed out. How stupid was he? How careless? How sloppy?

The phone continued its clamorous ringing; he tried to move

and all his muscles felt weak. It was a strain just to turn, to move his arm over to the phone.

'Hello?' he said, finally picking up the receiver.

His voice sounded groggy, his mouth felt like it had been glued together.

'It's Michael Talbot,' said a voice on the other end. 'I've spoken to my partner.'

Gabriel tried to get his head straight, tried to concentrate.

'And?' he said.

'Maybe there's something you could help us with,' said Michael. 'We've traced another victim. An Italian who worked on the Brooklyn docks. We figured, things being what they are on the docks, it'd be hard for us to get anyone around there to talk.'

The detectives needed information from the docks. The Mob-controlled docks. And they were smart enough to know the only way they'd get it, was by asking a mobster to help them.

'You'd like me to find out what happened?' Gabriel asked.

'Sure. See what comes up.'

Gabriel tried to think through the sleep and the last wisps of the Nembutal.

'What's the angle with the docker?' he asked. 'Give me something.'

There were a few seconds of silence.

'We think there's a connection to the war in Italy,' Michael said. 'Cleveland and one of the other victims were both in Naples during the war. Maybe Faron was too. So was this docker.'

Gabriel processed the information. A war connection. A link between Cleveland and two other victims. Faron in Italy during the war. The chain of information unearthing in his mind woke him up.

'Hello?' said Michael. 'Are you still there?'

'Sure,' said Gabriel. 'But if there's a connection to the war and Naples, you're gonna have to tell me more.'

'Why?'
'Because there was someone else in Naples during the war.'
'Who?'
'Vito Genovese.'

44

Ida waited at the port on 134th Street and watched as the ferry approached from Rikers Island, navigated the choppy waters, docked. The passengers exited over a jetty made slippery by the snow. Michael was the last to emerge.

'What happened?' she asked.

She'd been hoping Michael would have talked to Tom, that they'd have settled their differences, Tom would have told Michael the truth, and they'd have decided on getting a new lawyer.

'He wouldn't see me,' said Michael. 'I turned up there and sat in the hall for an hour to catch the boat back.'

Her hope evaporated, was replaced by a sinking feeling.

'I guess Rutherford got to him first,' she said.

Michael didn't reply. She saw the frustration and disappointment on his face, the desperation. She felt it, too. They were running out of options. They'd progressed on finding an explanation for why the crime had happened, but they'd gathered no evidence that might see Tom set free. Maybe the meeting with the witness at the docks would give them the breakthrough they so badly needed.

'Come on,' she said. 'We've got to meet your man in Brooklyn.'

They walked through the snow to Cypress Avenue, caught the Lexington Avenue line all the way downtown, then the 14th Street-Canarsie line out to Williamsburg. They exited the Bedford

Avenue stop onto a tree-lined street of low-rise buildings and down-at-heel store fronts. Michael looked around, nodded to a man on the other side of the street, standing under an awning, pacing about in the cold to keep himself warm. They crossed and Michael introduced her to Gabriel Leveson. He was good-looking in a ruffled, scruffy way.

'Mr Leveson,' she said.

'Gabriel, please,' he replied. 'Or Gabby, if you want. Shall we?'

He gestured to the road behind him, which led back towards the docks. They turned and walked.

'After you called me yesterday,' said Gabriel, 'I spoke to some friends. They said the murder victim had a brother-in-law called Vinnie Ferrara who we could talk to. They told me where he worked on the docks. They said he's hard up. I figure if we offer him some money he might talk. Tell us what the murder victim was up to.'

Ida nodded. He'd turned it around quick, making her wonder why he was in such a rush, and who these friends were he could get the information from so quickly.

'You told Michael you thought Vito Genovese might be behind everything?' she said.

She wanted to square their own theory about Congressman Helms being behind the murders with Gabriel's angle on Genovese, wanted to make sure she and Michael weren't wrong about the whole thing.

'Like I told Michael,' Gabriel said, 'Genovese was over in Naples during the war. He'd run away there back in the thirties to escape a murder warrant here in New York. He got in with Mussolini, then when we invaded, he switched sides. Got a job as a fixer for the army. Used the job to siphon army goods out of allied bases to his contacts in the Camorra. Eventually someone realized he had an outstanding warrant back here and he was extradited. All the witnesses in the trial disappeared, or died, or changed their stories, so he was freed. I was thinking maybe all these deaths are linked to that black-market scam he had going on.'

Ida thought. A black-market operation. She tried to slot it in with what they already knew. Maybe Helms was involved in the black-market operation, too. Had been inveigled into it somehow. Cleveland knew him as a racketeer out in Naples. Then he bumped into him at a party in New York and realized he could blackmail him over it. Had some evidence he could use to squeeze him.

She looked at Michael to see if he was thinking along the same lines. He gave her a nod, but she could see he was still distracted, still mulling over Tom's refusal to see him at the prison that morning.

'Makes sense,' she said, turning back to Gabriel. 'Cleveland was in a colored platoon, they weren't allowed to fight so got given quartermaster duties in the docks. In charge of supplies and warehouses. Maybe Cleveland, Bucek and Marino were all working for Genovese's black-market operation out there.'

'Maybe Faron, too,' said Gabriel. 'We just need to figure out why Faron and Genovese have started going around trying to kill the people involved in it.'

Ida nodded, stayed silent. She and Michael had agreed not to reveal what they knew about Congressman Helms till they could trust Gabriel more.

As they walked the sounds of the docks grew ever louder. Then after a few blocks, the buildings petered out, gave way to a sprawling industrial site, ringed by a set of long barbed-wire fences on which there was affixed a rusting white sign – *The Brooklyn Eastern District Rail-Maritime Terminal*. There were two gates in the fence, one through which railroad tracks passed and another for cars and pedestrians, where two men in lumberjack shirts stood sentry.

'Here to see Nicky Impellezzeri,' Gabriel said to them.

'Who's asking?'

'Gabriel Leveson.'

The sentries shared a look, opened up the gate. Gabriel held up a hand to let Ida and Michael enter first. They stepped into a vast concrete enclosure which was crisscrossed with train-tracks, heading towards a row of giant hangar-like buildings which lined the waterfront. They walked to the second one along. Its gates were open, trains were moving up the tracks to its interior, where armies of stevedores were loading them with cargo from the freighters which floated on the sparkling river beyond. Inside the hangar, Ida could see cranes, cargo stacks, lines of trucks, seagulls swooping about, all in the shadows beneath the structure's colossal walls.

To the side of its doors was a fenced-off yard, in which a few dozen men were loitering, smoking, chatting, playing cards on the concrete. Behind the men was a small wooden hut, its metal flue pipe emitting thick black smoke into the air.

Gabriel led them through the crowd of men to the hut, rapped on the door. A lean-faced young man in a sack coat opened it, looked them up and down.

'Yeah?' he asked.

'Nicky Impellezzeri?' said Gabriel.

'Who's asking?'

'Gabriel Leveson.'

The man paused, tensed, nodded. 'I'll go get him.' He disappeared back into the hut, closing the door after him.

Gabriel turned around to look at Ida and Michael. Ida watched the crowd of men hanging about the concrete yard.

'They're waiting to get picked for work on the pier this afternoon,' Gabriel explained, nodding at the crowd.

'There's more men than work, so the men pay kickbacks to the ringleaders to get picked. See the ones with toothpicks behind their ears? It means they're willing to pay kickbacks to get selected. By the time they've paid the kickbacks, and their Mob-inflated union dues, they're lucky to take home a third of their actual pay.'

The way he spoke about it seemed odd to Ida. She sensed he disapproved of how these men were being exploited and robbed, but he didn't expressly condemn it. He seemed to be at peace with it as some facet of the natural order; here were the herds and predators, here was the food-chain in industrialized form.

The door to the hut opened, revealing an obese man in a black suit – Impellezzeri.

'Gabriel?' he asked.

Gabriel nodded.

'Yeah, Albert said you might be coming,' Impellezzeri said. 'You're after Vinnie Ferrara, right?'

'He working today?'

'Nah, he didn't get picked in the morning shape-up. You can probably catch him at the dog-fights. In the warehouse behind the old Chesterfield factory.'

Gabriel nodded.

Impellezzeri eyed him a moment then closed the door.

'Come on,' Gabriel said, turning to Ida and Michael. 'I know where he meant. We can walk there.'

They followed him back the way they'd come, passing by the sorry-looking dockers in the yard.

'Who's Albert?' Ida asked.

Gabriel paused, almost looked embarrassed, as if the question had touched a nerve. Above them a seagull flew by, squawking, arcing through the gray autumnal sky.

'Albert Anastasia,' Gabriel said.

'Of Murder Inc?'

Gabriel nodded. 'He's a business associate. What do you know about the docks?'

'Not much,' said Ida.

'It's the biggest Mob operation in the city,' he said. 'Manhattan's waterfronts are run by the Irish gangs, but Brooklyn's all Anastasia's territory. He catches a slice of all those kickbacks the workers pay, catches a slice of the union dues, too. And if the men don't get picked for work, he has his loan sharks lend them money. And when they fall behind on repayments, he has them steal cargoes for him.'

He took out a cigarette, lit up. Ida sensed again his disapproval of what was going on, but stronger this time; he wasn't trying to conceal it anymore.

'Anastasia and I have some business dealings together,' he said. 'Nothing to do with the docks. I spoke to him yesterday after you called. Got his OK to come down here and ask questions. We couldn't do it without his say-so.'

From the look on Gabriel's face, his sour tone, Ida sensed there was some animosity between him and Anastasia, and she wondered what form their mutual business dealings took.

They reached the end of the terminal, stepped through the gate back onto the street, turned north and walked along desolate sidewalks, next to a road that was empty except for the occasional truck that rattled past from the docks. On one side of the road were wall-to-wall warehouses, squat, dark, uniform. On the other was a hinterland of empty lots. After a few minutes, they turned and walked across one of these empty lots; a muddy tundra of razor wire and ditches, spotted here and there with patches of cement on which children had scrawled in pastel chalk the boundary markers for the games they played.

When they reached its far end, Ida could hear angry shouts, snarling and barking, carried on the howling wind. They passed a half-collapsed brick wall, and there, in the emptiness of the adjoining lot, was the dog-pit. A great circular ditch, muddy and frosted and covered in blood. Around the edge of the pit, some forty or fifty men were eagerly watching the dog-fight, money was changing hands, burly mobsters loitered.

Ida paused to watch what was happening in the pit. The two dogs were of the same breed, both blocky and thick-legged, all muscles and teeth. They were about the same size and age, one had black fur, the other a muddy brown. Both were spotted with blood and cuts.

She turned to look at Michael, who was also staring into the pit. Gabriel, however, was scanning the crowd. Ida watched him walk over to a bookie who seemed to know him. They chatted and the bookie gestured to a man in the crowd. A young Italian with a five-day stubble, wearing a zipped-up docker's jacket and a woolen hat, kneeling at the edge of the pit, his eyes focused on the fight below him.

Gabriel returned to Ida, nodded at the man the bookie had indicated.

They approached. He felt their presence and turned to look at them.

'Vinnie?' Gabriel said.

The man sensed Mob, or maybe police, and shook his head.

'You got the wrong guy, buddy,' he said, turning his gaze back to the dogs.

'I don't think I do,' said Gabriel.

There was a sickening noise from the pit, and Ida looked down to see the black dog lying dead in the dirt, the brown dog ripping into its neck. Cheers and curses rose up from the crowd. Winners went to their bookies to collect.

Ferrara waited for the crowd to move. Then he burst into a run. Shoving past people, darting into the wasteland adjoining the pit. They dashed after him, across the empty lot, into a maze of rundown tenements beyond, over ground made slippery by snow and frost. Ida and Gabriel just about managed to keep up, but Michael was left far behind.

They turned a corner and Ferrara slipped into an alleyway between two derelict buildings. They followed him, came out into a courtyard filled with wagons, drays, coal carts. Ferrara darted through them all, came to a stables at the end of the courtyard, where horses were lined up, eating hay from bags hooked to the walls. He scurried in amongst them, disappeared into the shadows.

Ida and Gabriel ran in after him, looked around. The horses were glistening with sweat, releasing steam into the air. Everything was quiet, the sound of gulls in the distance. Then Ida heard scrabbling at the end of the stables. Just as she was getting her .38 from her holster, Ferrara appeared in front of them, a shotgun in his hand, pointed right at them.

'Don't,' he said to Ida.

She moved her hands away from her holster, raised them in the air. Ferrara gestured for Gabriel to do likewise and he did. Ida wondered where Ferrara had gotten the shotgun from. If he used the stables as a stash spot.

'You got the wrong guy,' he said.

'We just wanted to talk to you,' Gabriel said.

'Well, I don't wanna talk to you. Now I'm gonna leave, and if you follow me, things'll get ugly.'

He gestured with his gun for them to move up against the wall, so he could leave the stables from where they'd entered. They did so and he took a few steps backwards in the direction of the entrance, his gun trained on them. As he stepped past the last of the horses and out into the courtyard, Michael appeared behind him, gasping from the run, sweating. He raised his own gun to the back of Ferrara's head.

'Drop the gun, kid,' he said, between breaths. 'I'd hate to startle all these horses with a gunshot.'

Ferrara hesitated, then dropped the shotgun into the mire at his feet. Ida picked it up.

'Turn around,' said Michael.

Ferrara did so. Michael sized him up, waited a few moments for his breathing to steady.

'Now we don't mean you no harm,' he said eventually. 'We're

not with the people who killed your brother-in-law. We're not with the police. We just want to ask some questions. And we'll pay you to do that. Pay you enough so you don't have to go betting the wages you don't have on fixed dog-fights you're always going to lose. Now how about we go somewhere and talk?'

45

Ten minutes later they were on the roof of a tenement, just a couple of blocks from the stables. Snow was falling on the clotheslines which cross-crossed the roof, on the chimney stacks, the rickety old chairs scattered about. Ida wondered why Ferrara hadn't taken them inside, to his apartment. Wondered if there was perhaps a wife, a family, he wanted to keep in the dark.

Ferrara walked to the roof's edge, wiped the snow-melt from one of the chairs and sat. Ida, Michael and Gabriel did likewise. Below them was a view of the empty lots, and beyond, the rooftops of Brooklyn, the docks, the river in the distance, the bridge, the giant cranes of the Naval Yard. Here and there the icy landscape was dotted with the orange specks of barrel-fires lit by hobos.

Gabriel took his wallet out, peeled five twenty-dollar bills from it, and held them out for Ferrara to take. Gabriel told Ferrara how the man who probably killed his brother-in-law was the same man who had killed Gabriel's sister. That they wanted the information to try and find him before he killed anyone else. As Gabriel spoke, Ferrara took a tobacco pouch and a pipe from his pocket, packed the pipe.

When Gabriel had finished speaking, Ferrara sighed.

'What do you want to know exactly?' he asked.

'Why John died,' Gabriel said.

Ida had decided beforehand to let Gabriel ask the questions, figuring Ferrara would relate to him best. It also meant she could watch Ferrara for signs he was lying.

'John was killed by Vito Genovese's boys,' said Ferrara.

Ida wondered if he meant Faron in particular.

'You sure of that?' Gabriel asked.

'I mean, I didn't see them do it, but it must've been them.'

'What happened?'

'He never finished his shift is what happened. When the quitting bell rang he never turned up. I went home, went to his house. I asked around. Some of the guys on the pier saw some Genovese goons hanging around. Two days later Johnny's body turned up in the river. What do you want me to think?'

'You know why Genovese wanted to kill him?' Gabriel asked.

Ferrara took a puff on his pipe.

'It was that stupid nigger from Harlem,' he said. 'I told 'em not to listen to no nigger.'

Ida said nothing. She'd been dealing with it all her life, had spent much of her career turning it to her advantage – white people thinking she was one of them, assuming they could talk freely in front of her. And even though she'd learned to expect it, knew how casual and ubiquitous it was, it still stung when it came.

'Listen to them about what?' Gabriel asked.

'Blackmailing that congressman. Helms,' said Ferrara.

Gabriel frowned, turned to look at Ida and Michael. She nodded at him, suggesting she already knew about this. The one piece of information they'd hidden from Gabriel was out, and it was clear from his surprise that he hadn't known it. If he was offended by their having hidden it, he didn't show it. He turned back around to Ferrara.

'I told 'em not to do it,' Ferrara said. 'I told 'em it was a stupid idea, that someone like that would have mobsters behind him. But they wouldn't listen. They said it was worth a shot. They said he might not have Mob backing any more, and even if he did, it was worth a shot. That's how desperate they were.'

He raised his hands into the air, shrugged.

'You know what happened out in Naples?' Gabriel asked. 'How Cleveland and Bucek and your Johnny all met?'

'Sure. I was there,' Ferrara said. 'Eighth army. Operation Husky. We invaded Sicily, moved up to Naples, set up base. Was there for four months before I got moved north. Bucek and Johnny got a gig driving trucks of stolen supplies for Genovese – food, clothes, medicine, all these emergency packages that were supposed to rebuild the country. They'd pick 'em up from Cleveland and the rest of the shines in the quartermasters on the docks, drive 'em out to the hills. They did good off it, but they weren't that smart – made money one week, lost it in card games and whorehouses the next.

'Then the war finishes and we come home. Me and Johnny get jobs back in the docks. Bucek goes back to Queens. Everything's fine. We were even looking to get some of those free college courses through the GI Bill. And then Cleveland turns up. He says he's seen Helms in Manhattan and he's a congressman now, and he thinks he can put the squeeze on him, get him to cough up some dough. But Cleveland doesn't want to do it alone, reckons he wouldn't get taken seriously 'cos he's just a nigger and a junkie to boot. He wants some white boys to help him out with it.'

'I told 'em not to do it. I told 'em Genovese was back in town and chances were Helms would go to him for protection and that's what's happened. First Johnny got bumped off on the docks, then they tried to take out Bucek, he ran away to hide with Cleveland in Harlem, but they got him there. Only Cleveland got away. The one who started it all. Where's the justice in that?'

Ferrara took a puff on his pipe, saw it had gone out while he'd been talking and relit it. Gabriel turned to look at Ida, she gave him a slight nod of the head. It made sense with what she knew.

'They'll find Cleveland if they haven't already,' Ferrara said. 'And that'll be that. Helms'll move on up through congress and Genovese'll have his claws in him. Meanwhile, Johnny's widow and two kids are going hungry, and Bucek's parents are sitting around wondering how the hell their kid ended up getting slaughtered in Harlem.'

He shrugged, stared at them indignantly. In the wasteland below, a cold wind howled, swirled about, made the flames of the barrel-fires flutter.

'When you were out in Italy,' said Gabriel, 'you hear of a man named Faron working for Genovese?'

Ferrara thought about it and shook his head.

'You sure about that?'

'Yeah, I'm sure.'

Ida wondered how Cleveland had hoped to work the scam, how he would have been so sure he could pressure Helms into handing over money, how he could have roped Bucek and Marino into it.

'Did any of them have any evidence that Helms was involved in the black-market operation?' she asked. 'Beyond their eyewitness accounts, I mean. Did they have paperwork or anything to prove Helms had done something wrong?'

Ferrara looked at her, confused.

'Helms wasn't involved in the black-market operation,' he said.

Ida frowned. She and Gabriel shared a confused look.

'So what were they blackmailing him over?' Gabriel asked.

Ferrara shrugged.

'Johnny never told me what dirt they had over Helms. Just they'd found out something out about him while they were driving those vans through the countryside to Genovese. Whatever it was happened after I'd already left Naples.'

'I thought this was about the black-market operation,' Ida said.

Ferrara shook his head.

Gabriel turned to look at her and Michael, raised his eyebrows. Ida nodded in response – they'd got what they'd come for. Gabriel turned back around to Ferrara.

'Thanks for telling us all this,' he said.

'Thanks for the money.'

They all rose and Gabriel took more money out of his wallet, held it out.

'That's for Johnny's wife and kids.'

Ferrara took the money. Ida cast a last look at Manhattan in the distance, the river, the shipyards, the tumbledown buildings of Brooklyn, the people living their hinterland lives in the empty lots below.

They headed back inside. Walked down the stairs. When they got to the second floor, Ferrara stopped at one of the doors, indicated this was his apartment. They said their goodbyes, but just as he was opening the door, he paused, turned back around.

'Say,' he said, addressing Michael, 'why'd you say the dog-fight was fixed?'

Michael shrugged. 'One of the dogs was juiced up,' he said. 'You could see it in his eyes. Dilated.'

Ferrara paused to contemplate this, then he exhaled, shook his head, and disappeared into his apartment.

They walked through the snow back to Bedford Avenue.

'Thanks for saving me in the stables back there,' Gabriel said, turning to look at Michael.

'You would have done just fine without me.'

'I'm not so sure,' said Gabriel. 'You both knew about Helms?'

'Yeah,' said Ida.

Gabriel stared at them, his eyes ever so slightly narrowed, suppressing any annoyance he might have felt at them for having hidden information from him.

Ida gave him a rundown on their investigation into Helms, told him why they'd kept it from him, hoped her honesty might rebuild his trust. Gabriel listened and rubbed his eyes and Ida saw that weariness that she'd noticed before was dogging him once again, a sense he was under pressure.

'While you were looking into all this,' Gabriel said, 'did Benny Siegel's name crop up?'

Ida frowned, shook her head.

'No. Why?'

Gabriel paused. 'Because I heard Siegel was looking for Cleveland too.'

'Siegel died last summer,' said Ida. 'You sure?'

'Yeah, I'm sure. Before Siegel died he came to New York. And while he was here he was looking for Cleveland.'

Ida tried to process the information. Was Siegel working with Genovese? Had he been involved somehow in covering up the blackmail too? She wanted to ask Gabriel more about it, but when she looked at him she saw from his expression that he was as perplexed as she was.

They walked on in silence for a while. An icy wind whipped down the street, picking up trash and snow, sending it tumbling down the sidewalk.

'So what do we do now?' Michael asked. 'We're still no closer to finding Faron.'

'You can't use your contacts to look for Faron?' Ida asked Gabriel.

'That's what I've been doing since I learned he was back in town,' he said. 'No one's talking. No one knows where he is. Half the people I talk to think he's a myth.'

'You can't go straight to Genovese?' she asked.

'Not without starting a war.'

They turned the corner onto Bedford Avenue and when they reached the subway station, they stopped, looked at each other.

'I've got an idea,' Gabriel said. 'How about instead of chasing them, we let them chase us.'

'How are we going to do that?' asked Ida.

'They're still looking for Cleveland. We put the word out Cleveland's going to be at a certain place, at a certain time, and we lie in wait. For Faron or whoever the hell else comes after him.'

'That's a risky plan,' said Ida. 'Not a minute ago you were talking about not starting a war.'

'Doesn't mean a war,' said Gabriel. 'Not if we do it right.'

'OK,' said Ida. 'Let's say you do smoke out Faron. That doesn't help us get the evidence we need.'

'No, but you'll have a suspect to question.'

'If you catch him alive,' said Ida. 'That's a big if.'

Gabriel rubbed his eyes again, sighed.

'I know that,' he said. 'But I don't have much time. I need a solution quick and this is the best one.'

'Why don't you have much time?' Ida asked. 'What's the rush?'

'Let's just say this is my last chance,' he said. 'Look, I'm going to do this. With or without you. What do you say?'

Ida turned to look at Michael. He gave her a look back.

'We'll have to discuss it,' Ida said.

'Let me know by the end of today,' Gabriel said. He pointed to a black Caddie parked up a little way down the street. 'You two need a ride?'

They shook their heads. He tipped his hat at them, got in the car and drove off, heading west. They watched him go, then headed into the subway.

'What do you think of his plan?' Michael asked as they walked down the steps.

'It might work. But more likely it'll get us all killed. He's only doing it 'cos he's backed into a corner and desperate as hell. That's not the right way to go into these things.'

'And we're not backed into a corner and desperate as hell?' Michael asked.

'We're level-headed,' Ida said. 'He's an unknown quantity.'

They came out into the ticket hall, pushed through the turnstiles and walked down to the platform. As they stood there waiting for the train, Ida stared at Michael, saw how old and weary he looked.

'Time's running out for us as well as Gabriel,' he said. 'We know all the reasons why everything happened, but we've got no evidence to set Tom free.'

'You're saying we should go along with what he's suggesting?' Ida said. She was surprised and concerned Michael was feeling hopeless enough to consider it. 'Setting a trap for a gang of killers with made-up bait? Either one of us gets killed or one of them gets killed, or we all get killed, and none of that helps any of us much.'

Michael nodded, but she could see her words hadn't had any effect on him. Down the line, a train was rattling towards the station, its lights flickering in the gloom.

'Two things,' he said. 'First, we don't know what's going on with Tom. For all we know, his lawyer could have got him to change his plea to guilty. And we both know the longer this goes on for, the more likely Genovese or someone plans a jailhouse hit. So maybe acting fast is the safest way to go.'

'And two?'

'And two,' said Michael. 'Gabriel's going to do this with or without us. You heard him. Whatever it is that's haunting him, whatever pressure, whatever bloodlust – it's going to push him all the way. Let's say he does it and kills Faron. There goes our alternate suspect. Don't you wanna be there to make sure he doesn't mess it all up?'

He stared at Ida, and she saw a reflection of the same desperation she'd seen in Gabriel's eyes, the same disturbing anguish, and as the train roared into the station, she wondered at the power that was motivating them both.

PART EIGHTEEN

'Why should music stand still? Nothing else stands still. Who can say that the whole United States and the musical mind should stand still? Music now is in skilled hands. It's going to move along.'

DUKE ELLINGTON,
CARNEGIE HALL PROGRAM NOTES, 1947

46

Costello was in the Astoria's barbershop having his daily shave and hot-towel treatment when Gabriel walked in. He motioned for Gabriel to wait while the barber finished the job. Gabriel sat in one of the leather armchairs lined up along the back wall and Costello watched him out of the corner of his eye. The outfit's best fixer was in a sorry state. The same jitteriness Costello had noticed in Gabriel the last time they'd met had exploded all over the man. He looked edgy, distracted, exhausted. What the hell had happened to him?

The barber threw a hot towel over Costello's face and everything went black. The steam started to soothe his still-inflamed sinuses. He tried to think relaxing thoughts but couldn't quite manage it. Five minutes later the towel was whipped off, the barber patted him with cologne and Costello rose. He slipped the barber two twenties and walked over to Gabriel.

'How's the cold?' Gabriel asked, rising.

'Still got it,' said Costello. 'Nearly two weeks now. Can't seem to shake the damn thing.'

They headed through the exit and down the corridor that led to the hotel's reception. It was a long, echoing corridor, made of rose marble that the cleaners kept perfectly shining.

'What did you want to see me about?' Costello asked. His voice rebounded off the marble walls, the reverberations making it sound hollow, flat, airy.

'Can we talk here?' Gabriel asked.

'We're the only two people in a marble corridor,' said Costello. 'Yeah, we can talk.'

'I need you to give me the OK for something.'

'Shoot.'

'Faron,' said Gabriel. 'He's got your money.'

Costello stopped walking, turned to look at him. Costello knew all about Gabriel's obsession with Faron, how he'd spent years looking for the man, how he'd initially got a job with the family to trace him. And now Gabriel was claiming this same man was back from the dead and had stolen Costello's money. He wondered if Gabriel's problems were deeper than he'd thought. He wondered if Gabriel was cracking up.

'How's Faron got my money?' Costello asked.

'Benny stashed it at a spot in East Harlem. I got there a few days late. By the time I arrived, Faron had turned up and already stolen it. Faron's after that drug pusher, Cleveland. The same guy Genovese's after. Which is making me think they're working together.'

Gabriel told Costello a story about a congressman Genovese had his claws into, a congressman who was being blackmailed for something he'd done out in Italy during the war. Costello had heard the man's name. A rising star. He put it together with Genovese's plan to infiltrate the unions out in California, and it all clicked. This must be the other part of Genovese's plan. This congressman was going to be the key to how Genovese would offer the studios protection.

'I've been hunting Faron down these last few days and I can't find him. No one's talking. No one knows anything.'

'You want me to ask around?'

'No,' said Gabriel. 'I want to smoke him out.'

Costello eyed him, noted once more what a state he was in.

'What have you got planned?' Costello asked.

'I've got a pal in the Narcotics Division. He's let slip that I've been asking for passenger lists out of Liberty Airport, looking for a guy named Gene Cleveland. Genovese's men in the division'll check the passenger lists themselves. They'll see there's a Gene Cleveland booked on a Pan-Am flight out to France tonight because I've already bought a ticket in his name with a fake ID. They'll pass the information on. Faron and whoever else'll come down there. We'll be waiting.'

Costello searched for weaknesses in the plan, oversights. He assessed the risks.

'An airport sounds dangerous,' he said. 'Lot of heat. Lot of witnesses.'

'Not if he's catching a red-eye flight,' Gabriel replied. 'Place'll be deserted. You know what the roads leading up to it are like. Nearest precinct's a fifteen-minute drive. You give me the say-so, and I'll go down there.'

Gabriel stared at him, waited for an answer.

'You think Genovese stole my money?' Costello asked.

'No,' said Gabriel. 'I think Faron stole it, and he's keeping it. It's just we can use Cleveland to lure him out. Otherwise, I don't know how the hell we're going to find it. No one knows where Faron is, where he's hiding. Unless you wanna go and beat it out of Genovese?'

Costello weighed up the two million dollars against Gabriel in a shoot-out with a bunch of muscle hired by Genovese. Getting the money back versus starting a war.

'If you get caught,' said Costello, 'this comes straight back to me. It'll look like I sent you out there to attack Genovese's men.'

'I know,' said Gabriel. 'That's why I came here to get your permission.'

Costello was torn. He took his cigarettes out of his pocket, lit up. He assessed the variables. He could evaluate everything in the equation except Genovese and Gabriel, the two most important variables of all.

'I can't give it to you, Gabriel,' he said. 'I'm not going to risk it. Not when you've got your blood up about Faron. I know he killed your sister, but you can't start a war over it.'

'I'm doing this to protect us,' Gabriel countered. 'It might get your money back too. Sooner or later, Frank, you're going to have to face up to Genovese. Better do it now, while City Hall is on your side. While your two million might still be out there.'

Costello knew that Gabriel was right, that at some point he'd probably have to face up to Genovese, or risk losing everything. But he also knew the longer he put that day back, the more chance there was of Genovese somehow destroying himself before it ever came. Sometimes procrastination was the surest bet.

'No wars, Gabriel,' he said. 'War is how you get in the newspapers for all the wrong reasons, wars is when the Feds come after you. Right now all they care about is Commies. Let's keep it that way.'

'Appeasement?'

'It'll work till I don't need it to work no more,' said Costello.

He watched as Gabriel tried to suppress his anger, that same anger Costello had noticed in the man over a decade ago, when he was still burning with hatred over his sister's death.

'So be it,' Gabriel said finally.

There was a grim determination on his face. Gabriel might have come here for permission, but Costello could see that if he didn't get it, he'd go ahead with his plan anyway.

'If you need to kill Faron to protect yourself,' said Costello, 'I understand. But if you go up against any of Genovese's men, I'll have to cut you loose. You'll be running for the rest of your life.'

'I know.'

Costello nodded. 'Then go do what you gotta do.'

They walked down the rest of the corridor, their footsteps shrill against the marble. When they reached the hotel's lobby they nodded at each other and Gabriel headed for the exit. Costello took a toke on his cigarette and watched the man disappear among the crowds. Then Costello walked through into the bar, asked the bartender for the phone, stubbed out his cigarette.

There'd be a lot going on in New York that night. Glaser had sent him complimentary tickets to a Louis Armstrong gig, the papers would go to press with the decision the movie producers had made, and over the river in Jersey, a battle would be played out that might start a war.

Costello got his black book from his pocket, found Vito Genovese's number over in Middletown, picked up the receiver and dialed.

He felt bad ratting out Gabriel to Genovese, sending him into a trap, but it had to be done. Maintain the peace, trust in the money, in the fact that as long as everyone was making dollars, war was in no one's interest. Wasn't that the beauty of capitalism?

47

Louis stood alone outside the stage door, waiting to be let into the concert hall. There was snow in the air, falling to earth, in the black puddles at his feet, sailing across the reflections of the lights up above.

The door opened to reveal a fresh-faced young white kid in a cardigan. Recognition flashed across the kid's face, then a smile.

'Sorry to keep you waiting, sir,' said the kid. 'This way, please.'

He held up a hand and Louis smiled and followed him through the entrance, down a long, cement corridor lined with pipes. They turned a corner and the kid opened a door onto a function room packed with people and buzzing with backstage chaos. There were tables of canapés laid out, trays of champagne flutes, red and white wine.

'Your dressing room's just over there,' said the kid, pointing to a door on the far side of the room.

As they made their way towards it, people stopped Louis to say hello: friends, well-wishers, journalists, musicians. They slipped on through the crowd and came face-to-face with two men standing next to each other, wine glasses in their hands, who paused their conversation on seeing Louis. The first was 'Big' Sid Catlett, who'd be playing the drums that night, the second was a younger man in horn-rimmed glasses and a goatee beard; Dizzie Gillespie – one of Louis' most vocal critics, who'd called Louis out for pandering to whites, for playing the Tom, for being everything the younger musicians were reacting against. Although they'd met earlier in the year and had made up with each other, there was still a frostiness between them, a distance.

'Louis,' said Catlett.

'Sid,' said Louis, stopping even though he didn't want to, even as he was wondering what Gillespie was doing there.

'Diz said he wanted to come along,' Catlett said, gesturing to the man standing next to him. 'So I comped him.'

Louis nodded. Gillespie nodded. Catlett had played with Gillespie on a number of bebop recordings, was one of the few older drummers who could easily transition between the old styles and the new. Louis noted Gillespie had gone to Catlett, rather than Louis, for the free tickets.

'Cool,' said Louis. 'How's tricks, Diz?'

'Yeah, good,' Gillespie shrugged. 'Looking forward to hearing you play.'

'Well, that's grand,' Louis said. 'I'll catch up with you after the show.'

'Sure thing,' said Gillespie. 'Break a leg.'

Louis nodded, turned to the kid, wanting to get away from the awkward, icy exchange as quickly as possible. As he and the kid moved on through the crowd, thoughts of his luckless streak filled Louis' mind, all the signs telling him his time in the sun was up. What better sign could he have been sent than crossing paths with the ambassador of the young guard so close to going on stage?

Eventually, they got to the dressing room, and Louis slipped inside, closed the door. It was a long room, with sofas against one wall, and mirrors and dressing tables opposite them. There was a clothes rail at the far end, and Louis saw his suit hanging up, freshly cleaned and pressed, still wrapped up in the laundry's cellophane. Glaser's meticulous planning. His manager would be at the concert that night, box seats. It was unusual for him to show up to gigs, but then it was an unusual gig.

On one of the dressing tables Louis saw a card with his name on it. He walked over, put his trumpet case down, sat. He noticed a sheet of paper left next to the card. The set list for the night. Louis picked it up and scanned it quickly.

There was a knock at the door.

'Come in.'

The door opened and Ernie Anderson appeared. The young promoter glowed with boyish excitement, animated by that same jitteriness he'd displayed in Glaser's office the previous week. Louis wondered if it was on account of him, or if he was always like this.

'How is everything, Mr Armstrong?' he asked.

'Everything's great,' said Louis. 'Thanks for arranging all the music. All the fine people. It's really something.'

Anderson beamed. 'You're happy with the playlist, how it's all going to go?'

'Sure, pops. Sure.'

'Good. I thought you'd like to know, it's standing room only now. There's just one thing.'

'And what's that?'

'Sidney Bechet's called in sick. Said he can't make it.' Anderson's brightness dimmed a touch on giving Louis the news.

Bechet. He'd been asked to sit in with the band, join in on a few numbers. Louis wondered if it was fate again, or just the usual ego tricks from his old colleague. The man had been pulling the same stunts back in New Orleans twenty-five years ago.

'That's cool,' said Louis. 'We'll manage without him.'

'I think we will,' said Anderson.

He grinned and left the room, taking with him his nervous energy, making the place seem suddenly empty, lonely. Louis had planned to put on his suit then go straight back out into the reception room, mingle, joke, but as he sat there alone, with his coat still on, staring at his reflection in the halo of lightbulbs that ringed the mirror, he hesitated.

Bechet had cancelled last minute, Gillespie had told him to

break a leg. The nervousness Louis had experienced on the ride over returned. He hadn't been nervous before a gig in years. Because for years he'd known he was the best musician on the stage, that no one in the audience was expecting much. The last show he'd played before this was in a tumble-down old hall in Altoona, Pennsylvania, where the hotel owner had warned them not to walk the streets at night. But here he was about to perform with some of the greatest musicians on the planet, in front of one of the most discerning crowds there was. Top billing in the last-chance saloon. Right in the middle of a spell of ill-fate that made him feel like he was about to fight history single-handed.

He paused. Maybe that was the trick. To fight it. To ignore the black cats, the spilled salt, the pennies found tail up, all the other signs that said you didn't control your own fate, and try and forge your own future regardless.

The door opened and two people stepped in. Jack Teagarden and Bobby Hackett, the band's trombonist and its second trumpet player. They were laughing at something and were brought up abruptly when they saw Louis.

'Oh, shit, Louis,' said Teagarden. 'Didn't know you were in here.'

'That's cool,' said Louis.

The two men grinned, recommenced chatting. On their heels came the rest of the band – Cary, Catlett, Haggart, Hucko. They came in buzzing with noise, warmed the place up with their chatter and laughs, and Louis felt relieved to have people around him. Fellow musicians. He thought back to his Chicago days, to his old buddies from New Orleans, to his mentors, long gone now.

He rose and walked over to the clothes rail, grabbed his suit, brought it back to the dressing table. He took the cellophane wrapper off and its dull, synthetic smell wafted through the air. He dressed, checked himself in the mirror.

Behind him the others were putting their suits on, chatting, sharing cigarettes whose smoke was forming a fug under the room's low ceiling. Louis opened his trumpet case, assembled the instrument, checked it, ran through his exercises. His fingers slipped on the valves. Sweat. He looked around the people collected in the dressing room – no one else was sweating, and there was a rumble coming from the air conditioners over the door. He grabbed one of his handkerchiefs, wiped down his fingers and the trumpet valves. He ran through his exercises once more.

The stage manager came in and gave them a five-minute call, and no time seemed to pass at all before he was back again telling them they were on.

Everyone rose, grabbed their instruments, checked their shirts and ties in the mirrors.

Louis rose last of all.

'You all good, Louis?' asked Teagarden.

'Yeah,' said Louis. 'All set.'

And his voice didn't even sound convincing to himself.

They filed out. The crowd in the function room outside had already thinned. They walked down the corridor to the wings. Waited.

Fred Robinson was onstage, compering. He tossed off a few jokes in the patter that had made him one of the most popular jazz DJs on the radio, he got a few laughs. Then he introduced the band to a wall of applause. They stepped out onto the stage. Robinson passed them on his way to the wings, smiled at Louis.

It was a quarter past eleven. The house was full. The people looked excited. It felt like a homecoming in a way, even though Louis had never gone anywhere. Had people just forgotten? Like old King Oliver with his vegetable stand back in Georgia, Bunk Johnson and his sugar wagon? Was perpetual re-invention the only way to stay constant?

Everything went silent.

In the glare of the stage lights, specks of dust floated, shined.

The first track on the playlist was 'Cornet Chop Suey', a song full of knotty, clarinet-like figures Louis had written back in the twenties to show off his virtuosity. He looked at Catlett, who had settled himself behind the drums. At Teagarden, at Hackett, at the others. All of them waiting for him. He felt the silence swirling about the stage. For the first time in his life, Louis had everything on the line.

Fight it, he thought.

And raised his trumpet to his lips.

48

Ida didn't want to be there. Driving with Gabriel through the snow, out of the city to the airport, to a possible meeting with Faron and whomever else Genovese was sending. But Michael had been right, Gabriel was on a revenge mission, and it was better someone was there to make sure he didn't ruin everything for them. So Ida had gone, and Michael had stayed behind at Gabriel's apartment to look after his niece, because Michael had said he was too old to go out and be involved in the ambush. Too frail, too unsteady. That he'd only slow them down. He'd suggested he stay back and look after the girl, because they might be double-crossed after all.

So it was Ida heading out into the darkness with Gabriel, against her better judgment, weighed down by a heavy sense of foreboding. If Gabriel picked up on her trepidation, her discomfort and doubt, he didn't show it, but instead kept his eyes fixed on the road in front, the shadowy fields, the bleak, murky backwoods.

The Cadillac's radio was on, tuned to a late-night dance music show. At some point the announcer introduced a broadcast from the Copa Lounge. She turned to look at Gabriel. He smiled and shrugged his shoulders.

'Why just the two of us?' Ida asked.

He shrugged again.

'Because I don't trust any of my men for this one.'

'They could be bringing an army.'

'Faron's an army. It'll be him and a few other guys. One car-load. Tops.'

She nodded, not wanting to contradict him. Even a single car-load was plenty.

They continued on. The macadam unreeled in front of them, the cones of the headlights cut a path through the blackness, countless snowflakes careened in the glare.

'Tell me about Faron,' she said.

'Why?'

'I want to know what kind of man he is. Michael said you spent years looking for him.'

Gabriel paused. Then he told her a long tale about his search for the man, how he'd trawled through Faron's crimes, unearth-ing a trail of murder victims through the wastelands of America, through the years of the Depression, all the way back to the mountains of Appalachia, in whose mists the trail vanished. He told her how Faron tortured and killed the women, how all of them were drawn from the country's endless, faceless underclass.

'If there's broke people out there,' said Gabriel, 'vulnerable people, that's where he is. In amongst them. Killing.'

Ida nodded and an uncomfortable silence descended on them, needled them. They each stared out at the darkness in front, and thought their own dark thoughts.

At some point Ida saw lights in the distance, a whole field of them – the airport, glittering in the black. It had been her idea to pick the airport at that hour for the ambush. It was an easy buy to think Cleveland might be leaving town, in the dead of night. She also guessed the place would be quiet. But she hadn't figured on just how isolated and desolate it was.

Gabriel pulled into the lot in front of the airport building. It was empty save for five or six cars, a short line of cabs, a couple of limousines. They parked as close as possible to the airport's entrance, front of the car pointed out. Ida checked the clock on the dash – they were a couple of hours early.

They got out. Ida looked up at the building. It was a small, oval-shaped, two-story affair. Its facade was made of bulging glass, through which bright, white light spilled out onto the asphalt of the parking lot. Behind the building was the runway and the hangars.

They walked inside. Made a circuit. Didn't see Faron, didn't see anyone they pegged as a mobster. They went to the cafeteria upstairs. They ordered coffees. They sat by the windows that looked onto the parking lot in front. They waited.

Every half an hour or so a plane flew overhead, disappeared behind the roof of the building. Just as often buses arrived from the city, dropping off and picking up tired-looking travelers. Other than that the only movement outside was the wind heaving great sheets of snow and ice across the fields and the parking lot.

They carried on smoking and waiting. The radio played a selection of Brazilian songs. Ida tried to put the danger they were in out of her mind, tried to think of California, the Pacific, golden beaches.

About an hour later, a passenger bus came into the parking lot, stopped near the entrance to the airport and started unloading half-asleep travelers. Ida guessed most of them were booked in on the same flight they'd bought Cleveland a ticket for.

Porters moved luggage from the bowels of the bus onto trolleys. Ida peered at the bus passengers, checking for gun bulges, other signs they might be in Faron's group. One of them, a tall man in a camel-hair coat, wasn't looking at the airport building, or at the luggage being unloaded, but was instead staring at the cars parked in the lot, scanning them.

A few moments later, a car appeared on the approach road to the airport. Ida turned her attention to it, watched as it entered the lot, slow-rolling. It crept past countless empty spaces. The man in the camel-hair coat nodded at the driver of the car.

The slow-roller came past, its headlights sweeping as it turned. 'This is it,' said Gabriel. 'They followed the bus.'

'Or they're using it as cover.'

The car stopped and idled. The man in the camel-hair coat turned and walked into the airport building, no suitcase.

'That wasn't Faron, was it?' Ida asked.

Gabriel shook his head.

Two men got out of the car, waited around in the snow.

'What about those two?' she asked.

Again Gabriel shook his head. 'He's not driving the car either.'

She followed Gabriel's gaze to the car below them, through the windshield to the two front seats, where a burly driver sat behind the wheel.

The car started up again, commencing another lap of the lot.

'They're not checking the bus passengers,' said Gabriel. 'They're checking the parking lot.'

'They know we're here,' said Ida.

She turned to look at Gabriel.

'Let's grab the one who came inside,' he said. 'Before his buddies catch up with him.'

He rose and turned, rushed off. Ida dashed after him. They clattered down the stairs, came out onto the first floor by a long row of unmanned check-in desks. Behind the stairs was a waiting area. They looked in it for the man, but he wasn't there.

They checked the concourse adjoining it; people from the bus were milling about, filing in through the entrance. Beyond them was a concession selling travel goods, an information booth, and a diner counter, where a grill cook and a waiter were serving food to a clutch of customers.

Then they spotted him, the man in the camel-hair coat, walking over to the concession. They headed over, falling in behind him. He walked into the concession, peered around one of the aisles. Gabriel moved his gun into his coat pocket, lifted it, pressed it against the man's back.

'Where's Faron?' Gabriel asked.

The man paused. Gabriel shoved the gun further into the man's back, causing him to stumble forwards a half-step.

'He's not here,' said the man. 'It's just us.'

Now Gabriel paused, thought.

'We're gonna walk to the restrooms,' he said. 'Move.'

The man deliberated for a few seconds, then did as Gabriel commanded. They walked down the aisle, out of the concession and back onto the main concourse, through its people-filled expanse to the restrooms on the other side.

When they were about halfway across, the two men from the car entered from the parking lot.

Gabriel and Ida both saw them, Gabriel pushed the first man, trying to get him to move faster. The man turned, saw his colleagues. He spun, side-stepped Gabriel, screamed at his friends.

The two men from the car saw what was happening. Everything slowed. The two men pulled guns from their coats, lifted them towards Ida and Gabriel. The airport came alive in an eruption of gunfire. The shelves of the concession crumpled, glass exploded. A hellish chorus of screams rose up.

Ida ran for cover, rushing to the waiting room behind the stairs. She made it. Dropped to the floor, spread flat. Got her gun from her holster. She raised it and looked along the floor to the concourse in front of her, where the gunfire still filled the air, the bullets still roared into the concession, into the walls either side of it, all down the diner counter and the information booth.

She saw a puddle of blood in the middle of the concourse, streaks disappearing behind the opposite side of the stairs. Someone had been hit, had been dragged away.

And then the gunfire stopped. And all was quiet.

Ida looked back across the hall. There were people cowering behind seats, terrified, pressing themselves into corners. The concession was half-destroyed, in the racks, the newspapers and magazines had been turned to pulp by the bullets. The diner counter was empty. The sound of meat and eggs sizzling on the un-manned grill, the howl of the wind outside, people sobbing, filled the air. Somewhere near the entrance, broken glass clinked to the floor.

Ida spotted the sleeve of a camel-hair coat poking out from behind the check-in booths further inside the building, the first man. Then she saw Gabriel, crouched behind the till of the concession.

Where were the two gunmen?

She turned in the direction she'd heard the glass smash. There they were, standing by the entrance. If the man in the camel-hair coat wanted to get back to his friends, he'd have to run right through Gabriel's and Ida's line of fire.

A stand-off.

Ida shared a look with Gabriel, a nod indicating they were both OK. Neither of them knew what to do. She glanced at the man in the camel-hair coat, saw him lean forward, make eye-contact with the two gunmen. A look passed between them. Then the man was up and running, not towards Ida and Gabriel and his friends at the entrance, but the other way, into the depths of the airport.

Gabriel jumped up and ran after him. The two gunmen saw him and sent bullets after him and the hall filled once more with the sound of gunfire. People screamed again. Gabriel and the man disappeared down a corridor. The gunmen by the entrance stopped firing. Ida turned to look at them. One of them ran outside, another ran off after Gabriel.

She heard the sound of a car peeling out of the parking lot. Then a gunshot, from the direction Gabriel had run off in. She got up and ran down the side of the check-in desks, down the corridor. She saw the gunman running through a staff-only door at the far end of the corridor, and before it, a retirement-age security guard lying on the floor, clutching a bloody shoulder.

She reached the security guard, stopped. He was lucid, wincing with pain, his fingers clamped tight over the gunshot wound on the top of his opposite shoulder. Ida leaned down, assessed his injury. He'd live. She rose.

'You're going after them?' he said to her, incredulous.

She ran.

'Ma'am!' he shouted after her. 'Ma'am!'

She pushed through the door at the end of the corridor into howling wind and snow. In front of her was the great asphalt airfield. She scanned the space, fanned it with her gun, the dark, gaping entrances to the hangars, the row of planes, the refueling trucks, the mobile stairways.

Gunshots. To her left. In the distance, where a high-wire fence ran the length of the airport's perimeter, two figures moved. An orange bloom of muzzle-fire in the blackness and then the sound of gunshots again.

She ran over there, her eyes fixed on the figures and the fence beyond them, on whose far side were empty, frozen fields.

'Here,' she heard Gabriel shout.

She saw him a few yards ahead. He'd taken up a position behind a luggage truck.

She ran over to him.

'They're over by the fence,' he said, gesturing to where she'd seen the figures.

'They've got an escape plan,' she said. 'I heard their car driving off just when you ran after him.'

In the darkness beyond the fence they saw headlights moving at speed. The gunmen's driver going to meet his accomplices, to pick them up, get them to safety. The two men seemed to have reached the fence separating the airport from the fields, were climbing over it.

'They're gonna get away,' Gabriel said.

The look on his face was unsettling, ugly emotions contorted his features.

He rose and ran towards the fence. Ida followed.

The two men were already in the field on the other side, disappearing into its shadows.

Ida and Gabriel reached the fence, pulled themselves over it, headed off into the darkness, running, slipping and falling on the icy, uneven ground. In the blackness, Ida could barely make out the horizon line, let alone the figures getting away somewhere in the distance.

Then there was a noise over the howl of the wind – an airplane. Coming in to land. Ida looked up at it through the clouds and snow. It was in front of them, and it was coming in low, its lights shining through the snowfall, beaming onto the fields. It would be passing over them in just a few seconds.

'Gabriel,' she shouted, reaching out a hand, grabbing him.

He turned to look at her, frowning, confused.

'The plane,' she said. 'Get down.'

It took him a moment, but he realized what she had in mind.

They both dropped to the freezing ground, aimed their guns on the blackness in front of them. The roaring light of the plane approached, swept over the ground, illuminating it, yard by yard, like a prison spotlight. Eventually, it picked out the silhouettes of the two men in front, making them emerge, materialize, out of the darkness. They were almost at the end of the field, where the tree-line started, where the car was waiting for them. Ida and Gabriel both fired. One of the men went down.

Then the plane had passed over the men and they were subsumed by blackness. Then the plane reached Ida and Gabriel, burning their eyes. Then it was over the runway and its light was gone and they were plunged into darkness once more.

A few seconds later they saw the car lights moving off, disappearing up the road.

'Fuck,' Gabriel shouted.

They stood. The wind roared around them. Ida tried to steady her breathing, calm herself, think.

'When we fired off,' she said, 'did you see one of the men drop?'

She wanted to be certain. Gabriel nodded.

'You see him get back up?' she asked.

'No. The light hit my eyes.'

'Maybe his body's still down there,' she said, nodding to the corner of the field where they'd shot the man.

'Or more likely his buddies helped him into the car and he got away,' said Gabriel.

'Not if he was dead,' said Ida. 'Not if they were panicking and it was dark and they wanted to get the hell away. They might have left him there. With evidence on him.'

He stared at her, then looked at the blackness where they'd shot the man.

'We can't go looking for him now,' he said. 'In the dark, with the police on their way.'

He gestured behind her. She turned to look at the airport in the distance. On the road leading up to it a line of red-and-blue flashing lights was approaching through the gloom. More red-and-blues were heading towards the airport from the road the men had escaped down.

'We need to get out of here,' he said. 'We can come back and look for the body when it's light.'

'We can't go back to the parking lot,' she said. 'We'd never make it in time.'

'Come on. There's a commuter town a couple of miles from here.'

'You know which direction?' she asked.

He turned around, got his bearings, and they stalked off across the field. As they walked, Ida looked at the tree-line where the car had driven off; beyond it, far above, the lights of Manhattan were reflected in the sky, making the clouds shine eerily, like some spectral presence was hanging over the city.

They reached the end of the field and turned onto a narrow road that led up a hill.

'They knew we'd be there,' she said, turning to him. 'They didn't come looking for Cleveland. They came looking for *us*.'

'I know,' said Gabriel.

'So who set us up?'

'I only told two people,' Gabriel said. 'My cop friend who passed on the info. And Costello.'

'Which of them d'you trust the most?'

'The cop.'

'So now we've got Genovese and Costello after us?'

He nodded.

'You need to get back to New York,' Ida said. 'Get Sarah and make sure she's safe. Hide somewhere or run away.'

He nodded again. Too easily, Ida thought. Like he already knew a life on the run was a possibility, something he'd reconciled himself to long ago.

'Sure,' he said. 'But what about the body?'

'I'll go back. You get the train,' said Ida.

He paused, thought, made an anguished calculation.

'No,' he said. 'You get on the train. You go back to the apartment, grab Sarah and take her somewhere safe. You can get her to safety better than me; you don't have a contract out on you. I'll go back and look for the body. I know the roads around here. I can get rid of a body more easily.'

She stared at him. She didn't buy his logic. She could see there was some other reason he wanted to go back to the field alone, but she nodded. She wanted to get back to New York, to see Michael.

'OK,' she said. 'How about we meet back at Michael's?'

'Sure. I'll boost a car. I can be back in New York an hour after sun-up.'

She nodded. They trudged on up the hill through the snow. She didn't voice the question that was on her mind, the ominous question that had been bugging her since she'd realized Faron wasn't one of the men who'd attacked them – if Faron wasn't at the airport, where was he?

49

Wednesday 12th, 11.31 p.m.

Michael sat on the sofa in Gabriel's lounge and took in the luxury around him. It looked like the nightclub business paid. The apartment was overloaded with expensive furniture, the Scotch collection was country-club sized, there was artwork all over the place, including a bizarre, abstract painting propped up against the wall. He wondered if it was something the girl had painted. The more he looked at it, the more the paint seemed to be dancing across the canvas, left to right, up and down, conga lines of blots. He lost himself in it and realized how groggy he felt.

He went to the drinks stand and poured himself a single malt. Saw the radio scanner next to it, kneeled down and switched it on. Wasn't surprised to hear it was tuned to a police frequency.

Body found on bus. West 40th Street Bus Depot. Request attendance of Homicide Bureau Detectives—

He turned the volume down low so as not to wake Gabriel's niece, who was asleep in her bedroom. He listened to the police reports, the grotesque tapestry of night-time New York that they weaved. Despite the weather, there seemed to be no letup in crime.

He heard a noise and turned to see Sarah padding into the lounge from the hallway, wearing a fluffy pink dressing gown so large its hem trailed along the floor behind her.

'Did I wake you?' Michael asked.

'No,' she said. 'I couldn't sleep.'

She slumped onto the sofa and the dressing gown settled

around her into a giant pink ball of fluff. She picked up a comic book, leafed through it listlessly. Michael wondered if he should switch off the scanner, spare her the gore, but she didn't seem to mind.

When he and Ida had arrived at the apartment earlier that evening, Gabriel had explained to Sarah that they were going out to work, and Michael would be staying to keep her company, the housekeeper having been given the night off. Sarah had nodded, had stifled her anxiety well, had taken it all in her stride. Her response made Michael realize she knew exactly what her uncle's work entailed.

'How long are they gonna be?' she asked without looking up.

He wondered how Ida and Gabriel were getting along at the airport. Even though he knew staying behind and looking after the girl was the best help he could offer it still rankled, the fact it was happening out there, and he couldn't influence the course of events in any way whatsoever.

'I'm not sure, kid,' he said. 'They could be a while still.'

Reports of a domestic disturbance. 2082 Lexington between 125th and 126th. Officers in the vicinity, make yourselves known—

He moved to the window, stared down onto 64th Street and 4th Avenue. The snow was starting to settle, a white sheen of it lying across the sidewalks and cars. He saw a black Ford parked up on the opposite side of the road, could tell from the make and model and the antenna on its rear that it was an unmarked cop car. He couldn't see if there was anyone inside it.

He turned away from the window, glanced at the bizarre painting, perched himself on the window ledge.

Sarah looked up at him from the comic book, a quizzical look on her face, mischievous almost.

'You don't look like the normal people my uncle works with,' she said.

'No?' Michael said, although he knew full well what she meant – Michael looked like a cop, not like a gangster.

She shook her head. 'How comes you're working together?' she asked.

Good question.

'We're both looking for the same man,' he said. 'So we thought we'd team up.'

'Who?'

He wasn't sure how to reply. She looked concerned, and he wanted to alleviate that, but he couldn't tell her the truth, that they were chasing the man who killed her mother.

'A murderer,' he said. 'He killed some people up in Harlem, and my son was accused of the crime. We're trying to free him.'

'By catching the real killer?'

'Exactly.'

'So your son's in prison?'

'Jail.'

'I'm sorry,' she said. 'You'll get him out.'

'I hope so.'

'Why's my uncle looking for him?'

Michael paused. 'I'd like to tell you, kid,' he said. 'But that's for your uncle to explain. He might not appreciate me revealing his business.'

She nodded, accepting the situation, but a darkness passed over her features, a shadow of sadness.

'He does this a lot,' she said.

'He's doing it to protect you. Because he loves you.'

She didn't look convinced.

'I know he loves me,' she said. 'It's just a funny way to show it, is all. Keeping everything secret.'

'Sometimes you have to keep things secret,' said Michael. 'So the people you love don't get hurt.'

She mulled this over, her fingers picking at the corner of the comic book. She looked at Michael and he got a sense that she was appraising him, then her expression softened, as if she sensed some pain behind his scars.

'Is that what it's like with you and your son?' she asked.

Michael paused. He thought of Tom in Rikers, refusing to let Michael visit. Tom hiding out in New York ever since he'd been blue-slipped, refusing to tell Michael the truth, even when he was facing the electric chair, keeping secrets so people didn't get hurt. He suddenly felt foolish. Stupid and old for not seeing it before, not putting himself in Tom's position.

'Sure,' he said. 'That's what it's like with me and my son.'

And he turned to look out of the window so she wouldn't see his face.

Probable break-in on East 67th and 3rd. 201 East 67th. Ongoing. All cars in the area, please respond.

He wiped the tears from his eyes, peered down into the street, waited for the Ford to start up, speed away in response to the call, just a few blocks away. It didn't. It stayed where it was. Engine off, lights off. He took another sip of whisky, watched, waited.

Repeat. Probable break-in on 201 East 67th. Ongoing. All cars in the vicinity, please respond.

Nothing moved except the snow. Then a telegram messenger appeared around the corner, approached the building. He looked in the direction of the car. Did he nod at it? Did a shadow in the car move in response? Michael cursed the snow that was obscuring the view, the shadows, but most of all his age, his deteriorating eyesight.

And then the phone rang, making him jump. He turned, saw the girl was leaning over the arm of the sofa to grab the receiver.

'No,' he said.

He must have said it louder than he wanted to because she turned to look at him with a worried expression.

'I got it,' he said.

He crossed the room, picked up the phone.

'Hello?' he said.

'It's David, Mr Leveson,' said a nasal voice.

'Mr Leveson's out,' said Michael. 'I'm a friend of his.'

433

'Oh. This is David, I'm the concierge downstairs. There's a telegram messenger here for Mr Leveson. Shall I send him up?'

Michael froze. He hadn't imagined the nod. Scenarios, game plans, permutations, escape routes paraded through his mind.

'Shall I send him up, sir?' said the concierge.

Michael thought. 'No,' he said. 'I'll come down. Tell him I'll be two minutes.'

'I can take it on your behalf, sir,' the concierge said.

'No,' said Michael. 'I'll come down. I need some fresh air.'

'Sure thing, sir.'

Michael hung up.

'We have to go,' he said. 'Now.'

Sarah looked at him. 'What?' she said.

'There are men here. We have to go. Is there a service elevator in the building?'

She shook her head. 'I need to get changed,' she said.

'Throw some pants on over your pajamas. Where're your coat and shoes?'

'In the closet by the front door.'

'I'll get them. You change.'

Michael ran to the window. The car was still there. He went and got Sarah's shoes and coat, brought them into the bedroom. Saw she'd pulled some slacks on. He tossed her the shoes and coat. She put them on. He led her to the kitchen, where he'd seen the fire escape. He opened up the window, looked around.

The phone started ringing again. Scaring them both.

He peered into the street below, 4th Avenue, around the corner from where the car was parked up. Surely they'd have a man guarding the rear. He couldn't see anyone in the street, but again he didn't trust his eyesight.

He turned to Sarah. 'Can you see anyone in the street?' he asked her.

She looked, shook her head.

They stepped onto the fire escape, crept down it as quickly as they could, making as little noise as possible. When they got to the second floor, Michael took his gun from his pocket, checked it.

'I'm going to let the end down. If anyone comes around that corner,' he said, pointing to the intersection with 64th, 'you run the other way, no matter what. Got it?'

The girl looked at him fearfully, then nodded.

He pulled the latch on the fire escape's ladder, let it drop to the ground slowly, as noiselessly as he could, then they made their way down it. Then they ran.

And just like when he'd run at the docks, each step rattled his joints and bones. The shockwaves pulsed through him with so much pain, he wondered if they would break him, cause him to topple and crash to the ground. By the time they turned the corner onto 63rd, Sarah was already yards ahead of him, and he was out of breath, lungs burning.

She turned and slowed, waiting for him.

'Don't stop,' he shouted at her.

She nodded, turned and ran. And Michael followed as best he could. They made it onto 3rd Avenue, ran underneath the El tracks. As they reached the intersection with 62nd, Michael saw there were maintenance works up ahead, a wire-frame fence in the middle of the road, behind it scaffolding leading all the way up to the crumbling underside of the El. Further down there were lights, a station three blocks away on 59th, where there was a cab stand, people milling about. That was where Sarah was headed. Smart.

Then a car roared. He turned to see the Ford swerving onto the Avenue behind them. He turned back around. Carried on running. They made it to the maintenance works. They ran past the wire-frame fence which surrounded the scaffolding. Michael turned to check on the Ford again, lost his footing, slipped, went sprawling, landed with a thud on the road between the fence and the cars parked up on the curb.

Sarah turned, saw him. Doubled back.

'Keep going,' he shouted at her.

She paused, not wanting to leave him, but the fear was writ large all over her face.

'Keep going,' he shouted.

She nodded, turned and ran.

Michael pulled himself up, felt a pain in his knee, knew he couldn't run anymore. But the Ford would be there soon enough. All he could do now was buy time for the girl. Sacrifice himself. He prayed he had it in him.

He rose, stumbled over to the parked cars, took up a position behind one. Got his gun out, aimed it. Waited.

The Ford screeched to a stop just yards away, its path blocked by the fence. The front passenger door opened. A giant got out. Faron. It had to be. Tall and upright and strong-looking, but not the stocky, wide-framed figure Michael was expecting; he looked like an athlete. Faron pulled his gun from his pocket, swung it into the air, aimed it through the wire fence to Sarah, running towards the station.

Michael aimed at Faron, fired off three rounds. Faron dropped behind the Ford and Michael wasn't sure if he'd hit him or not.

He looked up the street in the opposite direction. Sarah was past the next intersection, gaining on the light and people below the station. He turned back to the Ford, to see Faron, unharmed, with his gun trained on him. The muzzle on Faron's gun flashed, emitted a black smudge.

It hit Michael in the chest, knocked him onto the sidewalk behind the car he was using as cover. He landed on his back. The breath was knocked out of him, his head spun. He tried to sit up, couldn't. He was finding it hard to inhale. A drowning sensation took hold of him. He looked up and through the row of cars, saw Faron run past the scaffolding, heading off after Sarah. Michael tried to focus. As long as he delayed Faron she was safe. He put all his being into sitting up.

He managed it. He grabbed his gun with both hands, raised it,

arms shaking, aimed at Faron's back, the spot between his shoulder blades. Fired. Missed. Caught him in the thigh. Faron stumbled, fell to the ground. For a second. Then he got back up and
hobbled down the street. Then he collapsed once more.

Michael exhaled, lowered himself back onto his elbows, then
onto the asphalt. He felt the coldness of the snow on the back of
his head. He lifted his fingers to the wound in his chest.

This was how it would end.

Not in a hospital, not at home, but in the streets, under the
night sky. It wasn't so bad. He'd died saving a girl's life, saving
his son's life, too. What better way to die, doing what he'd always
done – helping others, out on the street.

He stared at the darkness above, watched the snowflakes
whirling to earth, catching the light as they turned, the flicker, saw
in that moment how the gleam of eternity shone through fleeting
things.

PART NINETEEN

DAILY NEWS

NEW YORK'S PICTURE NEWSPAPER

City Edition Final   Wednesday, November 12th 1947

NATIONAL NEWS

MOTION PICTURE INDUSTRY ISSUES ANTI-COMMUNIST STATEMENT

FATE OF 'THE HOLLYWOOD TEN' DECIDED

Charles Judson

Manhattan, Nov 11th. – After a multi-day meeting at the Waldorf-Astoria, the head of the Association of Motion Picture Producers announced the effective blacklisting of those movie-men who were cited for contempt by the House of Representatives earlier this month. AMPP president Eric Johnston declared that no studios would employ 'the Hollywood Ten' until they had been acquitted or declared under oath that they were not communists. The ten studio employees brought about the contempt charges by failing to testify at the House Committee on Un-American Activities, or by testifying and not renouncing any previous or current support for communism.

The statement (printed in full below) comes after the heads of all the studios met at the Manhattan hotel in an emergency meeting to decide what to do about this latest twist in the ongoing saga of the anti-communism investigation that has shaken Hollywood to its core. Forty-eight studio representatives were present at the meeting, and although there seems to have been much discord among them, the statement released was approved by all the studio heads.

The AMPP statement:

'Members of the Association of Motion Picture Producers deplore the action of the ten Hollywood men who have been cited for contempt by the House of Representatives. We do not desire to prejudge their legal rights, but their actions have been a disservice to their employers and have impaired their usefulness to the industry.

We will forthwith discharge or suspend without compensation those . . .'

50

It was still dark when Ida's train roared into the station. They said their goodbyes and Gabriel trudged back into the tiny commuter town, through the snow and the icy, freezing wind. Outside the town's general store he found a car. The store was still closed. The sun still hadn't risen. He walked around, found a rock, smashed one of the car's windows, slid in, pulled the cover off the bottom of the steering column and sparked the wires there to bypass the ignition. After a few attempts, the engine started, and Gabriel was surprised he'd managed to do it after all these years. He drove. He turned the heating on full whack to counteract the draft coming in from the smashed window, felt warm for the first time in what felt like years.

He was back near the airport in less than a quarter of an hour. He parked up on a side road by the tree-line where the car had picked up the two men the previous night. He waited, watched the sky fill with light, watched the darkness dissolve from the land.

He got out of the car and the cold wind nipped at his skin, burned the inside of his nose. He stepped into the field where he and Ida had chased the men. The snow had frosted into ice, made him slip, but at least it saved his feet from sinking into the black butter of the field.

After a while he could see the airport in the distance, the spindly metal towers poking up into the white sky, the blur of the fences, the lights scattered on the frosty ground like fallen fruits. He could see the parking lot and the entrance. There were still

443

police vehicles there, tiny figures milling about. As far as he could tell, they hadn't extended their search beyond the limits of the airport. There'd been a good amount of snowfall to cover their tracks, but still he felt exposed, the murderer returning to the scene of the crime.

When he was just a few yards into the field the peace was shattered by a rumble overhead, and a few seconds later, a plane was roaring through the air above him, so close it wasn't quite believable. He looked up at its great smooth belly, white and encrusted with ice, leaving behind it a jet-fuel haze that shimmered in the sky. The image of a whale sprang to mind, leaping out of the sea. He watched the plane as it dipped towards the airport, landed and nestled itself amongst the twinkling lights of the runway.

He carried on walking and came to a stretch of ground that was covered by a murder of crows, strutting about, pecking the frost. And there amongst them he found the body. It lay face down, covered in as much frost as the rest of the field, so easy to miss, even from just a few yards away. He kneeled and pulled it free from the frost and there was a great cracking sound, and the body tumbled over onto its back. The crows rose off the soil, spiraled into the air, squawking pell-mell, then after a few seconds, resettled on the ground like a crashing wave.

Gabriel stared at the man. His face was white from the cold and fixed into a grimace. He had a ruddy complexion beneath the white film, a nose broken many times, short, wiry yellow hair. A blocky figure. The exit wound was like a great black cave where the man's heart should have been. A wedding ring on his finger. Gabriel guessed he was in his early forties. He didn't recognize him.

Who had killed the man? Had Gabriel fired the fatal bullet or had Ida? A rush of guilt ran through him. For all his years as a gangster, cleaning up other men's crimes, he was not a killer.

He rose, grabbed the body by the ankles and dragged it behind him, like he was pulling a wheel barrow. The ground was too hard to dig a grave. The body itself was too stiff and frozen to disfigure here, to remove the teeth and hands and make a mess of the face so that it couldn't be identified. He knew all this from his days as a night undertaker. Here he was after all these years, having to dispose of a body, back to square one.

When he was at the edge of the field another plane roared past, another soft white belly of a whale. He wondered what the passengers staring out of the windows must have thought, seeing a man dragging a body across a field, leaving a trail in the frost. Welcome to New York.

Soon he could see the car, peeking out from behind a hedge. He left the body a few yards from the car, checked no one was around, then moved it to the road and hauled it into the trunk. He got inside, sparked the ignition and prayed to God he could start the car a second time.

It started. He reversed around and headed off away from the airport, thinking of what to do with the body. When he'd gone a couple of miles, he pulled over, went to the trunk and opened it up. Now he had the time, he searched the man's belongings. There was nothing on him but a pack of cigarettes, some matches, and a wallet. The wallet contained a few small bills, a studio shot of a woman, and a membership card to a boxing gym. It had the man's name on it. Gabriel knew the gym. It was a Mob place, run by John Bova. The rat in Costello's organization, the pimp at Costello's the morning he'd been given the job of finding the money. He thought of the girl from Bova's stable who'd been cut up by Faron. And now one of Bova's goons had been sent to kill Gabriel.

Bova and Faron and Genovese.

And maybe now Costello too.

Gabriel wiped the wallet down, slipped it back into the man's pocket, closed the trunk, got back in the car. He'd hoped to find some clue on the body that would lead him to Faron and the money. With the money he could get Costello back on side, and maybe leave town without the whole Mob after him. But it wasn't to be.

He'd messed it all up. Costello and Genovese would be coming after him, and on top of that the auditors would deliver the racetrack accounts later that day, and Gabriel would have Anastasia to deal with, too. There'd be no clean break now. The escape plan he'd spent all those years devising lay in tatters. What life would they have now, forever on the run? He'd always tried to do right by Sarah, get her to Mexico where they could enjoy a semblance of normality. All he'd ended up doing was ripping the last shreds of normality away from her.

He struggled against the despair that was rising up in him, threatening to engulf him. He couldn't let his failure – complete and irreversible – sink him. He still had to dispose of the body, find Sarah and get her out of town. He lit a cigarette and tried to place himself on a map in his mind, looked around. A memory surfaced. A farmhouse a few miles from where he thought he was. Just off the road on the way back to New York. He started up the car and headed off.

When he arrived he wasn't sure if it was the same farm or not. It had been so many years, and most of the times he'd visited he'd done so in the dead of night. But when he drove past the front fence, he saw that the name on the sign above the gates was the same.

He drove in, pulled up in front of a sprawling wooden farm-house flanked on either side by barns. Two men came out of the left-hand barn and stared. When he asked after the farmer he used to know, he was told that the man was dead, but one of the men there was the man's son, and he remembered Gabriel and the old family business. They moved the body out of the trunk and the man's son said he would take care of it. Gabriel paid him, and the man's son took the money without saying thanks.

Then Gabriel reversed out of the farmyard and got back on the road. He needed to get back to New York to pick up Sarah then get out of there again as fast as he could, before one of the men who'd been sent after him killed them both.

He pulled up to the intersection with the highway, and was about to merge onto it when a truck rattled past, shattering the peace. He braked. Let it pass. It was a juggernaut with Florida plates. On its side was the logo of a distribution company, a cartoon flamingo painted an intensely artificial pink. Gabriel watched the giant pink flamingo fly past, watched it disappear, garish against the wintery, crystalline colors of the landscape.

He thought of Benny, of flamingos following him around. He almost started laughing. It was only then he noticed the sun had cracked the ice in the sky and dampness lay across the fields. He stared at the empty road in front of him, checked his watch, put the car into gear, and floored it back to the city.

51

Ida sat in the waiting room feeling like an ocean of black water was pressing down on her. She looked up and saw the policeman in the seat opposite her had fallen asleep. And here she was, alone, with a .38 that was half out of rounds.

She wondered how long the surgery would take, how long till she found out if he was going to live. A bullet to the chest. The doctors had taken him into surgery. If it had hit his heart or lungs, it'd take a miracle for him to survive. She dry heaved, and the policeman woke up and looked at her.

'You OK?' he asked.

Ida nodded, wooziness sloshing about her head.

'You want me to get you a bucket or something?'

She frowned at the mention of a bucket, then realized why he'd said it and shook her head.

'I'm gonna get a water.'

She rose and swooned. The policeman caught her. He helped her upright.

'You sure you're OK?'

She nodded.

'Don't go too far,' he said.

Ida teetered off towards the water cooler. She kept going, turned a corner, found the restrooms. They were filled with a harsh electric light that burned her eyes and an acrid smell of lemon bleach. She splashed cold water on her face and its chillness soothed her skin. She looked at herself in the mirror and the person who stared back might well have been a stranger.

She'd returned to Gabriel's around seven. There had been no answer at the apartment. She'd spoken to the concierge. The man had palmed her off. She'd persisted. He told her there'd been a shooting out on 3rd Avenue. She raced round the corner, into the middle of a crime scene. She spoke to the passers-by who were gathered on the corner watching, the storekeepers, the newspaper boys. An old man had been shot in the early hours, had been taken to hospital.

She ran over to the police, asked if the victim had been identified as Michael Talbot. She told them she was a colleague. After twenty minutes of fruitless questions and answers from both sides, she was in a cop car being driven over to the hospital. All she'd learned was that Michael was still alive, and that he was the only casualty – there was no mention of Gabriel's niece, or Faron, or anyone else.

When she got to the hospital, the doctors had told her Michael was in surgery. *A delicate operation*, they'd said. She asked if anyone had contacted the next-of-kin and was told Michael's wife had been notified early that morning in Chicago and that she'd told them she'd catch the next train to New York.

They took Ida to the waiting room and when she checked the corridor leading to the operating theatres she was shocked to see there was no one guarding him, just a single policeman there to keep an eye on things. Hospitals weren't safe. Even if Michael pulled through, they might come back. She'd sat down opposite the cop and waited, leaving only to go to the payphone a few times to call Carrasco. But he was nowhere to be found. She left messages. It would be her and the sleeping cop against whoever came to finish off the job.

She couldn't help but imagine the worst – the doctor coming in to tell her that Michael was dead, that he'd lost too much blood, that there was an infection, a clot, that the bullet had punctured his lung, ripped through his heart, that she'd have to identify the body. She imagined how Annette would feel. She remembered the pit of despair she'd fallen into when her own husband had died. Anger filled her. She had to find Faron and bring him to justice. For Michael. For everything her friend had done for her, for everything he had taught her. She owed him.

She left the bathroom and walked back to the waiting room, turned a corner and saw two men heading towards the corridor that led to the operating theatres. There was something in the two men's stride, in the look on their faces. They had cop written all over them, but what type of cop?

They reached the start of the corridor. Ida followed them, watched as they approached the swing doors that led to wherever it was the doctors were trying to save Michael's life. She fumbled for her gun, pulled it from its holster. Pointed it at the backs of the two men.

'Freeze,' she shouted.

The two men spun about to look at her. They reached for their guns on instinct, then saw the .38 in her hands and stopped, confused by the sight of a woman holding a gun in a hospital waiting room. She heard gasps from the people behind her. She heard footsteps. The sleeping cop had woken up, was by her side. He looked from her to the two men.

One of the men addressed the beat cop.

'We're here from the DA's,' he said. 'You want to tell us what the hell's going on?'

The beat cop looked at Ida.

'Ma'am, put down the gun,' he said.

'I want to see ID,' she said.

The men gave the beat cop *are you serious* looks. The beat cop shrugged.

The men reached into their pockets, slowly, and pulled out their wallets, held up their badges.

'What are you doing here?' she asked them.

'They're with me,' said a familiar voice behind her.

Ida turned to see Carrasco walking up the corridor.

'Put down the gun, Ida,' he said. 'We're here to guard Michael.'

She almost burst into tears. She dropped her arms to her sides, shook her head.

'I'm sorry,' she said. She put the gun back in its holster. Carrasco hugged her and she felt the weight of black water shifting.

Carrasco said something to the two men and they strode off down the corridor, then Carrasco and Ida turned and went to sit in the waiting room. She looked around her and saw all the other people staring.

'I thought they were here to kill him,' she said.

'He's still in surgery, Ida,' Carrasco said. 'They'll wait to see if he lives before they try again.'

She nodded. 'Of course,' she said. 'I'm not thinking straight.'

'You know what his status is?'

'Bullet to the chest. That's all they said. They've been operating for hours. It doesn't look good.'

He took this in, nodded.

'We've got this, Ida,' he said. 'You can go home if you want. Get some rest.'

At the mention of home she thought of Chicago and wanted to cry. She thought of her hotel room, and it seemed to her about as welcoming as the morgue.

'I'll stay,' she said.

'What happened?' he asked.

She told him about Gabriel and the airport and Michael staying back to look after Gabriel's niece. When she'd finished he gave her a funny look.

'What is it?' she asked.

'There's something else. It wasn't just you and Michael they attacked last night. Tom too. Up in Rikers. He would've been killed if a guard hadn't walked past. That's where I've been this morning, the Rikers Island infirmary.'

Ida nodded, took this in. They'd planned the attacks all at the same time – Gabriel and Ida at the airport, Michael at the apartment, Tom in the jail.

'How was he?' Ida asked.

Carrasco shook his head. 'Had a face like a balloon. But he'll be fine. Thing is . . .' He gave her a sorry look. 'Thing is he's going to change his plea. He figures if he pleads guilty they won't try to attack him again, he might actually survive prison. Soon as his lawyer gets there they'll make it official. I tried to talk him out of it, but he wouldn't listen.'

Ida's heart sank. A guilty plea would mean a plea hearing in front of the judge, admission of guilt, confession. It would be all but impossible to reverse. Once the plea hearing happened, Tom would be looking at forty years, best-case scenario.

Carrasco took some papers from his pocket.

'The phone records from O'Connell's old boarding house,' he said. 'Where he received the call from Cleveland last month.'

Ida glared at the papers.

'What's the point?' she said. 'It's over. We've failed.'

52

Gabriel drove the stolen car all the way back to Manhattan, through snowfall that was getting heavier, was settling, even in the city. He reached the Upper East Side and drove around his block a few times to make sure no one was waiting for him. He'd get the passports, pick up Sarah, buy a new car and get the hell out of New York as quickly as possible, before the weight of all the five families came crashing down on him. If it hadn't already.

He parked up a block from his building, checked his gun, got out, ran through the snow and up the steps. As soon as he was in the lobby he could tell something was wrong. The concierge looked at him with scared-rabbit eyes.

'What?' Gabriel asked.

'There's been a shooting.'

The concierge told him about a diversion with a telegram messenger in the middle of the night and a few minutes later the sound of gunfire and the messenger bolting, and an old guy in the street round the corner gunned down.

'What about Sarah?' Gabriel asked, heart racing.

'I went up and checked the apartment,' the concierge said. 'No one answered.'

Gabriel tried to think, tried to run the angles. Michael was shot in the street, meaning he might have gotten Sarah out of trouble.

'Did a woman come here looking for me?' Gabriel asked.

He described Ida to the concierge. The concierge nodded.

'She came here and then she left,' he said.

'She leave a message?'

'Sorry, Mr Leveson, no.'

'OK,' said Gabriel. 'You don't tell anyone you saw me here today. You got it?'

The concierge nodded. Gabriel ran over to the elevators, smashed the call button.

When he got to his floor, he took out his gun, pressed his ear to the door, listened. Silence. He unlocked the door and stepped inside, padded down the hallway, could sense something was off even before he reached its end. He paused again, listened. He could hear the traffic on the avenue below, meaning the windows had been left open.

He raised his gun. He spun round into the room. It was in disarray. Everything had been tossed. The paintings had been thrown onto the floor, the chairs and sofas had all been upended. Every piece of fabric and upholstery had been slashed through with knives. He stepped through the carnage, checked the kitchen, then the bedrooms, then the bathrooms, then the fire escapes.

Sarah was nowhere to be seen. Had she managed to get away? Or had Faron caught up with her? If she had escaped, he prayed she remembered everything he'd taught her – what to do in these situations, where to go, who to contact, how – God forbid – to shoot a gun. He needed to call Michael's apartment to check if she was there, but he couldn't do it from the apartment phone.

He stared at the destruction around him, thought of the staged break-in he had imagined as part of his plan to get out of town. Here it was, for real. But there would be no more clean break now. A life on the run, and it started today.

He checked the stash spots. They'd found two of the more obvious ones, the money and guns were gone. The other three were still intact. He took bills totaling twenty thousand dollars and an extra box of bullets. He prayed the intruders hadn't got to the roof. He walked back down the corridor, said goodbye to the apartment. As he was stepping out, he noticed his mail among the debris on the floor by the front door. He paused. Sarah must have picked it up the previous day. He spotted an envelope, recognized the Doc's handwriting. He picked it up, took a letter out and read it.

He who wishes to revenge injuries by reciprocal hatred will live in misery. But he who endeavors to drive away hatred by means of love, fights with pleasure and confidence; he resists equally one or many men, and scarcely needs at all the help of fortune.
—Spinoza

The meeting with the Doc, where Gabriel had asked what the philosopher's thoughts on revenge were. The Doc had said he'd look into it and he'd come through. Gabriel stared at the last four words – *the help of fortune* – and almost laughed. He slipped the letter into his pocket, left the apartment for the last ever time and walked up the stairs onto the roof to get the passports.

He readied his gun, opened the door, looked about. There was no one there, there were no footprints in the snow, and thankfully, the pigeon coop was still intact. He walked towards it, the snow groaning and creaking under his feet. As he reached the coop he saw the door was open, the padlock on the ledge was broken, the strongbox tossed on the floor.

'Drop the gun,' said a familiar voice behind him. 'Or I'll shoot.'

Gabriel laid the gun down in the snow.

'Now turn around.'

Gabriel turned to see Havemeyer standing behind him, the passports in one hand, a gun pointed at Gabriel in the other.

'Looking for these?' said Havemeyer, waving the passports about.

Gabriel's heart sank. Old man Havemeyer from the back room of the Copa. Of course. Havemeyer was in charge of club security, the bouncers he employed trained at Bova's gym.

Genovese didn't just have Bova as a rat in Costello's organization. Now, it seemed, he had Havemeyer, too.

'What do you want?' Gabriel asked.

Havemeyer paused, a look of regret, apology even, playing across his features. 'I'm too old to be working nights, Gabby,' he said. 'The contract they've put on you, it's enough for me to retire on. The others figured they'd toss your apartment. I knew you'd come back here though. Froze my ass off. I'm sorry, pal. It was too good a chance to pass up.'

Gabriel nodded. 'OK,' he said. 'You do me a favor before you shoot?'

'What?'

'You tell me where Sarah is?'

Havemeyer shrugged. 'She's still out there somewhere.'

Gabriel nodded again.

'I want you to walk to the edge of the roof,' said Havemeyer.

The old man wanted it to look like Gabriel had jumped.

'Two sets of footprints on the roof,' said Gabriel. 'They'll never buy it.'

'It's snowing. By the time they get here they'll all be covered up. Walk.'

Gabriel walked, reached the edge of the roof, stopped. Here he was again, a gargoyle looking down on the city.

'I'll let you do it yourself,' said Havemeyer.

He said it like he was being generous, and maybe he was. Gabriel looked over the edge, to the street far below him, he saw the roof of Havemeyer's car parked up. He should have spotted it when he'd cased the place before he'd come in.

He watched the snow fall past his feet, delineating the space through which he was about to plunge. He'd always imagined himself falling to his death, had visions of it ever since his sister had died, and now, here he was. He'd die from the wings he never had, a gargoyle smashed to rubble on the sidewalk.

The snow continued to dance through the void. Gabriel turned around and stared at Havemeyer.

'I'm not jumping,' he said. 'You want to kill me, be a man and kill me.'

Havemeyer stared back at him with those red, rheumy eyes. Gabriel saw him wavering. Gabriel leaped forwards. Havemeyer fired. The bullet whizzed past Gabriel's shoulder. Then they were both on the snow, fighting, tumbling for the gun. Gabriel got his hands on it and a shot rang out, and Havemeyer went slack. An odd sound wheezed out of him, like a groan, like a ball deflating. He twitched. He lay on his back, a red puddle forming, oozing. Snowflakes fell on it, sailed a moment, turned pink, capsized.

Gabriel stared at the body of his friend and felt like he couldn't breathe, like his lungs were filled with boiling ice. Then he realized blood might get on the passports. He jumped up, scrabbled around Havemeyer's pockets, grabbed the passports. He stared some more at Havemeyer's body. He let out a sob. Then he remembered the last time he was on the roof, stashing the passports, the old woman looking down on him.

He spun about. No one was at any of the windows.

He got up, dragged Havemeyer's body, hid it behind the coop. He needed to think. He couldn't leave Havemeyer on his roof. He couldn't have the police after him on top of everything.

Think.

He rose. He pulled Havemeyer's car keys from his pocket. He ran across the roof, picked up his own gun. He went down to the apartment. He found a pair of gloves and a luggage trunk. He put on the gloves, wiped down the trunk, hauled it up to the roof. He hauled Havemeyer into it, locked it shut, prayed the blood wouldn't seep out of it. He closed up the pigeon coop. He dragged the trunk down the stairs and into the elevator.

When he reached the lobby, he had the concierge look after the trunk. He ran out and drove Havemeyer's car around, had the concierge help him load it into the car's trunk.

'You going away?' the concierge asked.

'Yeah,' said Gabriel.

He wiped down the trunk where the concierge had handled it. They stood on the street and stared at each other. Gabriel took his apartment keys from his pocket, tossed them at the concierge.

'Like I said. I was never here today. Got it?'

The concierge got it.

'Go up to my apartment and take anything you want. There's a painting that looks like someone puked up on it that's worth a few bucks. If the police call, if *anyone* calls, you never saw me today.'

'Sure thing, Mr Leveson.'

Gabriel got in Havemeyer's car. Drove. The first payphone he saw he jumped out and called Michael's apartment. No answer. He got back in the car and drove it to the Copa. He parked up on the alleyway next to its side entrance. He left the alleyway. The cops would find Havemeyer's body in a luggage trunk locked into the trunk of his own car, outside his place of work. Gabriel didn't have a clue what they'd think, but hopefully it would confuse them enough not to go looking on Gabriel's roof.

He walked around the corner, paused to stare up at the facade of the Copa. The maroon awning. The logo of the Brazilian woman with the head wrap. Havemeyer had helped him all those years to conjure up the fantasia of Rio in that Manhattan basement, now he was dead. Gabriel thought of his sister, of their childhood spent on the streets of New York, running through the dust all those years ago. He'd miss the Big Apple, but he was right to turn his back on it.

Now he had to find Sarah and get the hell out of New York before he bumped into anyone else looking to collect on his contract.

He walked to 5th and caught a cab back to where he'd parked the stolen car, drove it over to a breaker's yard he knew, swapped it for a '42 De Soto that was on its last legs.

'You want me to top up the anti-freeze,' said the kid at the yard, 'put some skid-chains on?'

Gabriel looked up at the sky, at the snow falling ever more heavily. If it was this bad in Manhattan, how much worse would it be on the country roads they might have to navigate on their dash from the city?

Gabriel nodded and the kid got to work. He ended up paying way over the odds. He jumped in and started making the rounds.

He was at it hours and there was no trace of her. He tried all the stash spots, the meeting places. He went to the buildings of three of her school friends whose addresses he knew. They looked down their noses at him and told him they hadn't seen Sarah since the day before.

He went back to the stash spots and the meeting places once more. He thought of other places she might have gone. The Copa? Mrs Hirsch's sister in Queens? Havemeyer's? Maybe she'd been picked up by the cops. He called Salzman but couldn't get through to him. He called Ida's hotel. He drove to Michael's apartment.

Nothing.

He wanted to keep at it. As long as he stayed out, as long as he prowled the streets, as long as he kept moving, Sarah was still alive.

When he returned to Grand Central to look for her once more, it was the middle of the evening commute. The place was somehow busier than it usually was, people swamping the information booth, in rows in front of the departure boards. Gabriel stumbled through them, spinning left and right, trying to catch a glimpse of her through the crowds.

And there she was, bundled up in her coat. Relief coursed through him, joy and gratitude, so strong it made him catch his breath. He rushed over to her, bumping past people, sending up shouts. But before he was halfway there, he realized it wasn't her.

Just some other little girl, alone in the heart of the city. He stopped. His elation soured, his anxiety returned, all the more powerful now after the temporary letup. He cursed his mind for playing tricks on him.

He stared at the girl. She looked lost, alone. Another newly arrived runaway. He thought of the noticeboards of missing persons in Times Square. Wondering if she'd end up one of the names, one of the *GIRLS, GIRLS, GIRLS*. He wondered if Sarah might end up one of them, too.

It was only then that he honed in on the words coming over the tannoy . . . *Disruption* . . . *Cancellations* . . . *Blizzard* . . . He looked again across the concourse and realized that not only was it busier than usual, but the crowds weren't rushing here and there like they normally did. They were standing about waiting for announcements, frozen. Except at the information booth, where a horde of people were swamping the desks.

Gabriel headed over there, shouldered his way into the crowd, managed to get within earshot of the employees manning the booth.

'No trains coming in or out,' shouted one of the men behind the desk, looking as irate at the passengers surrounding him.

'What about putting us on buses?' shouted one of the people in the crowd.

'Bud, there's a blizzard coming in,' he said. 'From Maryland to Maine. What buses are we gonna put you on? The highways are closed. There's no roads, no buses, no trains, no subway, no planes, no boats. Everything's shut. Take my advice, go to tourist information and find a hotel for the night before all the rooms have gone, too.'

A roar of disapproval rose up from the crowd, passengers shouting back at the man, the man rolling his eyes and folding his arms over his chest. Gabriel slunk back through the crowd, mind reeling. He was trapped in New York. The very night he and

Sarah were supposed to be escaping and there was no way out of the city.

A wave of nausea overtook him. He hyperventilated, from panic and stress and sleeplessness and drugs. He needed to get out of the press of people. He needed to sit down before he fell. He stumbled back out of the crowd, the nausea making him lurch like a spinning top. He saw some benches lined up against a wall. He reached one, sat, leaned his head all the way back, closed his eyes, breathed. Against the darkness, a carnival of horrors careened through his mind, visions of slaughter. How completely he'd failed to protect his family. All his planning had come to nothing.

He opened his eyes and found himself staring up at the Milky Way moving across the ceiling of the station; the gold-trimmed constellations fixed in a deep-blue wilderness. He looked at the figures in their flowing robes, floating over the people's heads like the billboards floating over Manhattan, making their way happily on invisible orbits through a world which was denied most men.

He cradled his head in his hands. Breathed. Tried to think. Lit a Luckie. Tried to think.

He'd lost Sarah and he was trapped in New York. She wasn't at Grand Central. She wasn't at any of their predetermined safe spots. What to do? Check all the meeting points again?

The image of Havemeyer flashed into his mind, standing on the rooftop in the snow, gun raised. What if Havemeyer had lied to Gabriel when he said they didn't have her? Maybe Faron *did* have her. A steely fear ran through him. He had to check, and he knew how.

He rose and rushed out of the station, onto 42nd. Into the darkness and gloom. He saw the snow falling now like feathers from the sky. Manhattan was always a few degrees warmer than the countryside around it, a little more sheltered, a bubble. The road closures and blockages wouldn't hit the island till after everywhere else. He still had maybe a few hours before Manhattan's streets shut down, too, maybe a few hours to find Sarah.

53

Time passed. Michael's surgery finished and they moved him to a room. No one was allowed in, but there was a window in the door, which Ida made the mistake of peering through. He was lying on the bed, hooked up to a machine that looked like a pump, that looked like it was breathing for him, rising and falling, emitting a whine, then a hiss, then a whine. The tubes that came out of it went into Michael's nose, or maybe his mouth. It was hard to tell. All around his face was surgical tape, pasted on like plaster, beyond it blue bruises, unnaturally lumpen. She'd heard about noses being broken to get breathing tubes inside, teeth accidentally knocked out. What little she could see of his face looked old; lined and worn and papery. The image of him lying there like that, so close to the image of a man in a coffin, knifed into her. The dread and panic of losing him ran through her veins once more, causing her heart to jump, her muscles to tense. Images rioted through her mind.

She stared at the garland of tubes around his face, watched the machine pump and decompress, then Michael's chest rise and fall. She stepped back from the window, sat in the corridor with Carrasco and his two men and let out a sob. Carrasco put an arm around her.

'He'll pull through,' he said. 'He's the toughest bastard I ever met.'

Ida nodded, noted how it was in times of stress that people

spoke in clichés. She took a handkerchief from her purse and wiped her eyes.

'Thank you,' she said. 'For coming here, and for everything else you've done.'

Carrasco shrugged. 'I wouldn't be here today, if it wasn't for him. Me or my family.'

He told her the story, of a day years ago back in Chicago, when it all could have ended for him were it not for Michael putting himself on the line.

'There's not many people as good as him,' said Carrasco. 'And if there's any justice in this world, he'll come out of it alive.'

And she knew he was right. Michael *was* a good man. And it wasn't because he was simple or naive, nor because he expected to receive anything in return. He'd told her more than once that he always tried to act with integrity because of his belief that in a crushingly corrupt world the only compass that could be trusted was a man's own morality, the decency that came from within, that had to be cultivated through honesty and action. That was what he'd passed on to Ida, had explained to her, had made her see. And in that moment, she realized the weight of it, and that it was her duty to pass that on to someone else, whomever that might be.

She put her head on Carrasco's shoulder and closed her eyes, felt the smoothness of his cotton jacket against her cheek. Then a nurse was standing in front of her suggesting she could go to an empty room and rest a little. The room was just a few doors down. She decided against lying on the bed and instead sat in the chair next to it. She looked out of the window to the yellow bricks of the building opposite, and the space over the road, which was filled with snowflakes pirouetting their way to earth. The same snow that fell on Chicago nearly thirty years ago, when she'd gotten off the train from New Orleans and walked to the Pinkerton offices and met Michael for the first time. From a scared, young girl to a widowed mother, all in the time it took for a snow-flake to flutter past a window.

She closed her eyes and drifted in and out of an uneasy, flickering sleep.

There was a knock at the door and it woke her and hope quivered in her chest that it was a doctor telling her everything was going to be all right. Instead, it was one of the cops who'd come with Carrasco.

'There's a girl here,' he said.

Ida rose and looked through the doorway to see Gabriel's niece standing in the corridor. Her eyes looked raw, her shoulders were hunched, her coat askew, her hair a mess. She had a bulging backpack slung over one shoulder.

Ida nodded for her to come in. Sarah stepped into the room and turned to face Ida, her hands clasped in front of her.

'Is Michael OK?' Sarah asked. Her eyes filled with tears and guilt.

'We don't know yet,' said Ida.

Sarah nodded, took this in. 'He saved me,' she said.

'I figured. Your uncle know where you are?'

Sarah shook her head.

'He must be out scouring New York for you,' said Ida.

Sarah shrugged.

Ida thought. 'It's not safe here,' Ida said.

'But the police are outside.'

'Even so.'

There was a moment of stillness, then Sarah burst into tears.

'I'm sorry,' she said. 'I'm so sorry.'

Ida hugged her.

'I need to get you somewhere safe,' Ida said. 'Your uncle'll want to know you're safe.'

Sarah nodded. 'Where?' she asked.

Ida thought. She told Sarah to wait in the room, then she went back to see Carrasco. Told him where she was going in case

Gabriel called. Then she went back down the corridor, back down the stairs, outside. The snow was coming down, thicker than ever, suffusing the air with a crispness she could almost smell.

She did a sweep of the parking lot. She saw a cab and called it over, told it to wait. Then she went back in and got Sarah, took her by the hand. When they reached the hospital entrance, Ida did another sweep then hurried Sarah into the cab, gave the driver Michael's address and they were off, crawling through the afternoon traffic and sunset gloom, Ida checking over her shoulder the whole way.

54

Gabriel parked the De Soto on a road leading up to Columbus Circle. It was completely dark now and the street lights were on. In the center of the circle the statue of Columbus on his plinth was already foamed in snow.

He lit a cigarette and waited, staring at the apartment block a few doors down the street, the entrance to Bova's main parlor. All the brothels in New York worked similar shifts, the young, expensive girls worked five to midnight, then from midnight the older women came on the clock, the ones more likely to take a beating in their stride from the drunks who were abroad at that time of night.

Bova did the rounds at shift change. Gabriel hoped he hadn't arrived too late. He looked again at the snowman Columbus on his plinth in the gloom, fixed into position at the apex of the circular roadway which surrounded him, at the red-and-white lights of the cars spinning endlessly about. On the other side of the circle, behind Columbus, was a building with a giant electric Coca-Cola billboard affixed to its roof, thousands more red-and-white lights, blinking into the night sky. *Thirst knows no station.* In the gaudy illumination that spilled out from it, two whores walked up and down the street, braving the snow, clutching fake furs tightly to their necks.

Just as Gabriel was stubbing out his cigarette, the door to the parlor opened and Bova stepped out. Perfect timing. Gabriel got out and trotted over. Bova was approaching a parked Cadillac when Gabriel reached him.

Bova turned and saw Gabriel standing behind him, pointing a .38 at him. There was no one on the street except the two of them; the cars rushing past paid them no heed.

'Good evening to you, too,' said Bova.

'Unlock both the doors,' said Gabriel, waving the gun at the doors on their side of the car. 'And get in the front.'

Bova took in the situation, did as he was commanded. Gabriel got into the rear passenger seat.

'Hands on the dash,' said Gabriel.

'Are you serious?' said Bova, catching Gabriel's eye in the rearview.

Gabriel said nothing. Bova exhaled and shook his head, exasperated. He put his hands on the dash.

'Can I at least start up the engine so we both don't freeze to death?' he asked.

'No.'

'Jesus.'

'I want an address for Faron,' said Gabriel.

'You're crazy.'

'You know where he is, Bova.'

'Like fuck I do.'

'You and him are both working for Genovese. You lent him men from your gym for the airport sting. You fed him one of your girls that was causing trouble. You know where he's operating from. I want an address or I kill you.'

'You're no killer.'

'My niece's missing,' Gabriel said. 'And thanks to you and your pals I've got a contract out on me. I've got the commission coming after me from now till I die. I've got nothing to lose, Bova.'

Bova eyed him through the rearview. Gabriel caught a sliver of uncertainty.

'Well, if you kill me, how are you going to find him?' Bova said.

'I'll settle for shooting you in your stomach and watching you die slow. Tell me and you live.'

The lights of the cars spun about the circle as the game of who folds first played out. Gabriel had the gun, and the element of surprise, and the air of a man with nothing to lose, eventually his advantages would make themselves plain.

'Can I at least turn on the fucking heating?' said Bova, admitting defeat.

'No,' said Gabriel, pressing home his victory.

The lights at the south end of the circle turned red and the road next to them began to fill with cars pulling up at the junction. They sat there in the gloom, both of them bathed in the crimson glow of tail-lights. Bova exhaled dramatically once more.

'He's in an apartment over a garment factory in Hell's Kitchen. Across the street from Pier Eighty-five.'

'I'm gonna get you to drive over there,' said Gabriel. 'And if you're lying, you're dead. Now you sticking with that story?'

'I'm telling you the truth,' said Bova. 'He's got the whole floor above the factory to himself. He's been there months. But there ain't no point going there tonight. He's out on a job.'

'Yeah, sure he is.'

'He's out on a job for Genovese and then he's skipping town. Like he always does. You missed your chance, Gabby.'

Bova looked at Gabriel through the rearview and grinned.

'Who tipped Genovese off about the airport?' Gabriel asked.

Bova laughed. 'You really want to know?'

'Sure.'

'Costello.' Bova grinned at him again, his gold teeth glinting in the gloom, the scar on his face a trench of deep shadow.

The traffic signals changed, the cars started moving, their lights sweeping through the Cadillac once more.

'You worried you got played by Costello over the airport?' said Bova. 'You've been played the last thirteen years. Costello's always known who you are, why you joined. He's always known Faron was over in Naples. And here you were running around like a sucker trying to find him and everyone's known. You're a joke, Gabby.'

Before he knew it, the butt of Gabriel's gun was swinging across the back of Bova's head. There was a cracking sound, a gasp, a spurt of blood. Bova leaned forward, his hands over his head, convulsing with pain. He checked his hands and saw they were slick with blood.

'You fuck,' Bova muttered. 'You fuck.'

He tried to turn and face Gabriel, but it cost him too much in pain to twist the muscles in his neck so he only quarter-turned and looked all the weaker for it.

'Eyes front,' said Gabriel, pointing the gun at him. 'Hands on the dash.'

Bova turned forward once more. Blood seeped down his neck.

'We're gonna drive over to Faron's,' said Gabriel. 'And then you're going to give Genovese a message from me. I get any kick-back from him I let the commission know he was in on Benny Siegel's scam with the Flamingo money.'

'You're way off the mark,' said Bova. 'Benny and Vito hated each other.'

'Bullshit,' said Gabriel. 'Vito was the only one in New York who didn't invest in the Flamingo, because Benny let him know it was a scam to steal all the money.'

Bova frowned, puzzled.

'Vito didn't put any money into the pot because they got sore at each other.'

'They met while Benny was in town,' said Gabriel.

'To talk about the dope routes,' Bova said. 'Vito started getting his dope from Asia again, and had dumped the Mexicans Benny had hooked him up with. It meant Benny wouldn't get a cut no more, right when he needed money for the casino. They hated each other. You got nothing.'

Gabriel glared at Bova. He tried to think, tried to shift the arrangement of the cards, to make sense of what Bova had just told him. Benny and Genovese had fallen out. Then he realized – Benny hadn't been going around New York looking for Cleveland *with* Genovese, but *against* him. Somehow Benny had found out about Cleveland and tried to use him as leverage in their dope route dispute.

Just as Gabriel was getting his head around it, the car filled with movement. Bova's hands flew away from his neck. He jolted for the glove-box, flipped it open. Gabriel saw gun-metal gleaming in the shadows. Gabriel raised his gun, Bova turned with a .38. The inside of the car was lit up with two flashes, Bova's head exploding in a mist of blood and gunpowder.

The gunshots deafened Gabriel.

All went black. A shrill ringing in his ears. The smell of smoke in his nose. He felt warmth on his face, on his neck. He realized he had his eyes closed. He opened them. The car had been transformed, doused red by Bova's blood. The warmth he'd felt on his skin must have been blood. Then he noticed it in his mouth too. Gabriel must have had his mouth open when the bullet splattered Bova across the car.

He vomited. A gush of acrid liquid splashed into the footwell, onto his shoes. He dropped the gun and wiped what he could from his teeth and his tongue. He prayed he hadn't swallowed any. And even as he was furiously wiping his mouth, he knew no amount of cleaning would ever clean him of this.

He'd never killed a man in his life, and now he'd killed two in just a few hours. He needed to think. He needed to get away. He picked up his gun, slipped it into his pocket. He got out of the car. Wiped down the door handle, the edge of the door. He pulled up the collar of his trench coat, flipped his hat down low; he headed for the De Soto, trying his hardest not to break into a run, not to vomit once more, as the car lights spun about him, and Columbus looked on.

55

Thursday 13th, 5.03 p.m.

Ida stood in the kitchen, waiting for the kettle to boil. Through the window all was clouds and falling snow. Central Park was turning white. People were coming and going up the street. There it was, picture-postcard Manhattan. Snow-globe Manhattan.

The kettle came to a boil. Ida finished making the tea and returned to the living room. Sarah was where she'd left her on the sofa. Ida handed her the tea and they both sat and looked out of the windows a while.

'You mind if I put the radio on?' Sarah asked.

'Sure,' said Ida.

Sarah rose, turned it on, tuned it to *Boston Blackie* just as the show's presenter boomed out its tag line: *Enemy to those who make him an enemy. Friend to those who have no friend.*

On that evening's episode, Boston Blackie travelled to Honolulu to help a woman whose husband was trying to kill her. Ida thought of the sound-effects artists making it seem like the jewel-thief-come-detective was on a tropical island. Hawaiian guitars twanged, reed skirts rustled, ice-cubes dropped into cocktail glasses, a volcano erupted.

Sarah listened, huddled up on the sofa, knees to her chest.

'Are you and Michael cops?' she asked.

Ida shook her head. 'We're private detectives.'

'For real? Like Boston Blackie?'

'I suppose.'

'I didn't think girls did that.'

'Sure they do,' said Ida. 'Although I'm not really a girl any-more. One of the first ever real-life detectives was a woman. Kate Warne. She worked for the Pinkertons.'

Sarah smiled. 'I'd like to be a detective, too,' she said.

'Maybe some day you will.'

'I don't think I'm brave enough.'

'Bravery's not a trait,' said Ida. 'It's a skill. You practice, you get better at it. Like I did.'

Sarah thought about this and her face brightened, and she smiled again.

'Where are you from?' she asked. 'I like your accent.'

'New Orleans. But these days I live in Chicago.'

Sarah nodded. Ida awaited a comment about jazz or voodoo or hurricanes or swamps, but it didn't come.

'You married?' the girl asked.

Ida shook her head. 'I was. I've got a son. Jacob. He's a little bit older than you. He used to like radio detectives, too.'

Outside the wind changed direction and a flurry of snow blew against the windows. In Hawaii, Boston Blackie was safely back at his luxury hotel, the killer in custody, explaining to Inspector Fara-day how he'd gotten to the bottom of the mystery. The theme song was played and the sponsor's announcement came on.

'I know you don't want to talk about it,' said Ida, 'but I need to know what happened last night.'

Sarah nodded. Told her the story of the firefight, how after-wards she had run off, dazed by what had happened, had hopped on a subway train, had gone up and down the line till she'd got her head straight.

'I knew not to go to the police,' she said. 'My uncle told me that. I went back to the apartment. I knew I shouldn't. Someone had broken in. I picked up some things and I left. Then I went to some places – meeting places, the stash spots Uncle Gabby had told me about, but he wasn't at any of them. Then I saw in the papers about Michael going to the hospital and I wanted to see if he was OK.'

She was trying to stop herself from sobbing. Ida took her hand, held it, squeezed it. Not only was Sarah battered by the trauma of what had happened, but also by guilt, for following Michael's commands and leaving him behind.

Sarah wiped away tears and continued in a trembling voice. 'Was the man who attacked us Faron?' she asked. 'The big man?'

Ida paused, surprised she knew the name. 'Maybe,' she said. 'What did he look like?'

Sarah gave her a description that matched Faron's.

Ida nodded. Sarah took it in, then a look of dismay spread across her features.

'He shot at me,' she said. 'Faron. He looked at me. I think he realized who I was. Then he shot at me.'

Something about the way she said it tugged at Ida's thoughts, like there was something she was missing, something Sarah assumed she knew.

'You'd never seen him before?'

Sarah shook her head, again that look of dismay, now with added confusion, as if Sarah was wondering why Ida wasn't reacting more. What was Ida missing?

Tears came down Sarah's face in a torrent now and Sarah wiped her eyes, and that's when Ida realized, and felt foolish for not figuring it out before.

The girl's blue eyes.

So different to Gabriel's brown eyes, but matching the description Gabriel had given her of Faron. Gabriel had told Ida his sister was attacked and raped by Faron and months later threw herself from a hospital window. That the attack had happened thirteen, fourteen years ago.

Ida continued staring at the girl, studying her, making sure.

'Faron's your father?' Ida whispered.

Sarah nodded. Burst into tears. Ida reached out and cradled

her, felt her body convulse, and it was as if the sobs and wails were the only things keeping her upright. The convulsions came in waves, stronger, then more slowly, then they stopped altogether. Ida continued to hold her, imagined what it must be like for the girl, to have been attacked by her own father.

'You're safe now,' Ida said. 'I'm here. Your uncle'll be back soon, and you'll leave New York and you'll be fine. He won't get you.'

Sarah nodded, sniffed back the last of the tears.

'I'm not supposed to know,' she said.

'That he's your father?'

Sarah nodded again.

'Uncle Gabby never told me. Just said that Faron killed my mom after I was born. But I knew he was lying.'

'How?'

'About a year ago, we went to the library on a school trip, the big one on Forty-second Street, and they showed us the periodicals room and how to use it. I went back the next weekend. I looked up what happened in the newspapers. Faron had raped her, and after I was born, she killed herself. She waited till I was born then jumped out of the hospital window. The same night. She was just waiting for me.'

Sarah stared at Ida forlornly and Ida hugged her again. Then Ida suggested she lie down. Sarah nodded. Ida went to Michael's bedroom and changed the sheets. Sarah went in there and was asleep as soon as her head hit the pillow. Ida stopped in the doorway and stared at her, saddened by the girl's plight but also impressed by her youthful resilience.

Ida went back into the living room. The radio was broadcasting a news report about a meeting in the Waldorf, how the movie industry was hanging the Hollywood Ten out to dry. Proof that people elected their villains as surely as they elected their leaders.

She took a sip of her tea and found it had grown tepid. She

checked her gun. Looked around to see if Michael had hidden any other weapons anywhere. She checked the lines of sight from the windows once more, the fire escapes. She saw the bag Sarah had brought with her. She'd mentioned stash spots. Maybe Sarah had picked up a weapon.

Ida went through the bag. Ten thousand dollars in cash, a few clothes, a sketch pad, colored pencils. Ida opened the sketch pad, saw odd drawings mixed in with superheroes; day-of-the-dead stuff, Mexican skeletons, in musical bands, as gangsters. They reminded Ida of the Voodoo Barons from back home in New Orleans. She thought about the violence the girl had just been through, the violence of her birth, the knowledge of who her father was. Ida looked again at the gun-toting gangsters and they took on new meaning.

She returned everything to the bag. Went into the kitchen to make more tea. Saw the snow piling up on the window ledge. When Jacob was little, she'd scoop snow up into bowls, pour raspberry syrup on to it, and they'd eat it in front of the radio. It never tasted that great, but the feeling of turning weather into dessert felt magical for them both.

She walked back into the lounge. The radio was still on. A weather report about the snowstorm sweeping across the north-east. She only half listened. Her mind wasn't in the room, it was in the hospital. She stared out of the windows at the snow flurries falling ever thicker. She could see the lights of the skyscrapers opposite gleaming.

She rose, walked over to the phone, dialed the hospital.

The operator connected the call and it went through to the ward, to the nurse on duty.

'He's woken up,' said the nurse brightly. 'It looks like he's got through the worst of it.'

Ida burst into tears. Heaving, sobbing tears. She must have cried for a while, because when she looked up she saw Sarah standing next to her.

'Is he OK?' Sarah asked.

Ida couldn't speak. She nodded. Sarah smiled. She kneeled and hugged her. And in that moment, Ida imagined it was Jacob she was hugging, all those miles away in California, on the other side of the great night that lay glittering across the land.

56

Gabriel sped away from Columbus Circle as quickly as he could, away from Bova and the blood-splattered horror of it, trying to outrun the nightmare. Bova's words shook his thoughts – Faron had a job planned that night. Was the job anything to do with Sarah? Was that why he couldn't find her? And then he thought about what Bova had said about Benny and Genovese falling out, and how Costello had known all along where Faron was. If it was true, everything Gabriel thought he knew was wrong.

On the corner of 38th he saw a liquor store. He yanked the De Soto to the curb, took off his blood-stained coat and rushed out into the snow to get a bottle of vodka from the store.

He returned to the car and poured some into his mouth, rinsed, spat the vodka out of the car window. He did it again and again, till the bottle was empty, but still his mouth didn't feel clean. He wondered if he'd ever be able to eat or drink anything again without, somewhere in the back of his mind, thinking of Bova and the blood-splattered nightmare.

When the bottle was empty he threw it out of the window. He started up the engine, but as he was about to drive off, something caught his eye on the sidewalk – a news-stand, its owner battling against the snow and the wind to board it up before the blizzard really hit. On the hoarding that ran along the roof of the stand were posters displaying the headlines from the evening papers, headlines which formed a ticker-tape of the previous day's events – *Movie Producers Issue Statement, India and Pakistan*

477

go to War, Jackie Robinson wins Rookie of The Year. And there in the local news section, given top billing – *Shooting Shocks Upper East Side – Victim Taken to Hospital*.

Victim Taken to Hospital. Gabriel jumped out of the car, ran over to the man and grabbed a copy of the paper. Michael had been found alive. Gabriel had assumed he was dead.

'Where's the nearest phone?' Gabriel asked the man.

He pointed to a cigar store halfway up the block.

Gabriel ran over to it, went in and rang the hospital. Asked if there were any people there with the victim of the shooting, was told the hospital couldn't give out that kind of information.

He drove there. Double-parked. Ran through the entrance. He found the corridor, saw the two cops outside the room. They eyed him, pegged him for a mobster as soon as they saw him. He walked past them. Waited. Unsure what to do. He turned around and approached them.

'I'm a friend of the victim's,' he said. 'And his friend, Ida.'

'Sure you are, pal,' said one of the cops.

They rose.

'Mind if we frisk you?'

He froze. The gun he'd used to kill Bova was still in his pocket. In his rush he'd forgotten to leave it in the car. It could see him sent to the electric chair.

'I've got a .38 in my coat pocket,' he said.

The cops eyed him, pulled guns.

'Raise your hands.'

'No,' he said. 'All I want to know is if Ida was here.'

'I'm not going to ask you again,' said one of the cops.

Just then another cop turned the corner of the corridor, saw what was going on and approached with nothing more than a mild look of curiosity on his face. He frowned at Gabriel, as if trying to place him.

'You're Gabriel Leveson,' said this new cop.

Gabriel nodded.

The new cop gestured to the other two to drop their weapons.

'Lieutenant Detective David Carrasco,' said the new cop, introducing himself. 'You've got a contract out on your head.'

Gabriel paused. Even the cops knew. He was as good as dead.

'I'm just looking for Ida,' he said.

'She's not here,' Carrasco replied. 'Your niece came by this afternoon and Ida took her back to Michael's apartment. They're waiting for you there.'

'She's OK?' Gabriel asked. Hope rose so quickly inside him it made him dizzy, light-headed.

Carrasco nodded. 'She was fine. They're waiting for you.'

Gabriel grinned. Relief coursed through him, warmed him, made his eyes water.

'Thank you,' he said.

'Pick her up and get the hell out of town,' Carrasco said. 'We won't tell anyone we saw you.'

Gabriel frowned, wondered why the cop was being nice to him.

'Thanks,' he said. 'How's Michael?'

'A bullet to the chest,' Carrasco said. 'He got it saving your niece.'

That was why Carrasco wanted him to get away, to make sure Michael's sacrifice was worth it.

'Is he gonna be OK?' Gabriel asked.

'He's through the worst of it.'

Gabriel took this in. 'Tell him I said thank you,' he said.

Carrasco nodded.

Gabriel turned and strode down the corridor.

The first payphone he found was in the hospital's lobby. He put a call in to Michael's apartment.

Ida picked up.

'She's safe,' said Ida. 'She's with me. You need to get around here as soon as you can.'

'Sure,' said Gabriel, tears of relief streaming down his face.

There was silence a moment, then Ida spoke.

'They attacked Michael's son in Rikers,' she said. 'He's going to plead guilty. It's all over. We've failed.'

'No,' Gabriel said. '*They* failed. They tried to kill us all at the same time and they didn't manage to get even one of us.'

She paused a long while before answering.

'Maybe,' she said, unconvinced.

Gabriel stopped, realizing something. If Sarah was safe, then what was the job Faron had on that night? Suddenly he knew.

'Listen,' he said. 'I spoke to someone who worked with Faron. He said Faron was on a job tonight for Genovese and he was leaving town right after. At first, I thought he was talking about Sarah, but now I'm thinking it's Cleveland. Cleveland's the only job that's still outstanding.'

There was silence on the line.

'Makes sense,' said Ida. 'He's only been sticking around in New York to finish the job. If they kill Cleveland tonight and he leaves, it really is all over.'

'Maybe for Michael's son, and for me,' said Gabriel. 'But I think there's a way out of this for Sarah. I know where Faron's holed up.'

It was only now that he knew Sarah was safe he realized it. Bova had said Gabriel was too late, but maybe Bova was lying, or just plain wrong. Gabriel had Faron's address and if Faron had stashed the two million there, maybe Gabriel could turn that to his advantage. He'd been dealt a bum hand, a useless hand, but maybe he could bluff his way to some kind of victory, like Costello and his endless games of solitaire, maybe he could rearrange the structure to turn fate to advantage. Maybe he could ride the chain from Bova to Faron to the missing money to safety for Sarah. He was as good as dead himself, but maybe he could save his niece.

'If you can hold tight at Michael's for a couple of hours, I might be able to fix things.'

Static rustled down the line.

'Gabriel,' said Ida, 'you've got a contract out on you. You've got at least two Mafia families after you, maybe the police too. You need to get here and get the hell out of New York as fast as possible.'

'I can't,' he said. 'Haven't you heard the weather reports? Everything's shutting down for the blizzard. The roads are closed. No buses, no trains. No way out.'

And then he realized something else; the blizzard wouldn't just have an effect on his own escape plans.

'No way out for me,' he said. 'No way out for Faron.'

'Then you need to lay low.'

'No. I need to use this time to try and put things right. I can't just hole up in a hotel room while there's still a chance. I need to put things right, Ida. Two hours.'

'And what if you . . .' Ida trailed off, resumed in a whisper. 'What if you don't make it back here?'

'Then tell Sarah I love her. She knows where all the money is. Tell her to take it and go and see Mrs Hirsch.'

Again there was silence. 'You better come back here, Gabriel.'

'I will.'

He stepped out of the hospital, back into the snow. He saw a Rexall's over the road. Ran over, bought three Benzedrine inhalers and returned to the De Soto.

He sat in the car and checked his watch. He ripped open two of the inhalers with the help of his car keys, took out the paper strips in the center, the strips soaked with the drug. He rolled them into balls, swallowed them dry.

He hit the accelerator, headed across town to Faron's hideout.

57

Thursday 13th, 7.04 p.m.

Ida put down the phone and walked over to Sarah, who was sitting on the sofa, looking up at her.

'That was Gabriel,' she said. 'He's fine. He's got some business to take care of and he'll be here soon.'

Sarah smiled, laid her head down.

Ida went over to the kitchenette and poured herself a whiskey, thought about what Gabriel had told her. Faron was killing Cleveland that night, probably dumping his body somewhere it would never be found. Their witness would be dead, and their alternate suspect would flee the city as soon as the weather cleared and never be caught. Tom would either fry or spend the rest of his life behind bars.

She thought about him in his cell in Rikers, Michael in his hospital bed. She thought of Annette, rushing from Chicago to New York and how her train had probably been stranded en route somewhere by the storm. Ida added her to the list of people hurt by all that had happened. She thought about how she'd failed so completely. She wondered if Boston Blackie or Dick Tracy would have fared any better.

She sat on the windowsill, saw that the snow was accumulating in banks on the sidewalks, that an Arctic whiteness was descending on the city.

'I hope you don't mind,' she said to Sarah, 'but while you were asleep, I was checking the place for guns, stashes, to see what we had. I looked in your bag. You said you'd gone to a stash spot, so

I thought maybe you'd picked up a gun. Anyway, I just wanted to say sorry for looking in your bag, but I had to.'

Sarah looked alarmed, then nodded. 'That's fine,' she said.

'I saw your sketch pad,' Ida said. 'You're talented.'

'Thanks.'

'We've got skeletons in New Orleans like those ones you drew,' Ida said. 'I liked them.'

Sarah smiled and that dismayed look came over her again.

'They were for a school project,' she said. 'The skeletons. Mexican Day of the Dead.'

She spoke abruptly and Ida could tell she was lying. She frowned and wondered why. She thought about the clothes and money in the girl's bag. Was the sketchbook the reason she had gone back to Gabriel's apartment? Was she really so attached to it she'd risk going back there?

They fell silent. Ida looked out of the window, watching the snow, drinking Michael's rye. Sarah lay on the sofa, listening to the radio. At some point she drifted off into a sleep and Ida covered her with a blanket.

She went over to the radio and lowered the volume, then turned the dial, flicking through the frequencies. She stopped on a station playing modern jazz, the same kind she'd heard in the club on 52nd Street. She paused, thinking it strange to hear that kind of music on the radio. She left the dial where it was, rose, poured herself another drink and sat on the windowsill again.

The song came to an end and the disc jockey came on, a deep, white voice speaking in an affected *cool* patter. 'This is "Symphony" Sid Torin, your all-night, all-frantic one. Broadcasting live on WMCA. Playing all the latest and greatest bop, like this fresh-pressed number from the Charlie Parker Quintet. Out on the ever brilliant Savoy Records label. Let's give this a go . . .'

Ida heard the scratchy static of a vinyl record, then a song came on the air, all dissonance and knotty chords, solos plunging from high registers to low and back again with breakneck agility.

She smiled. She thought back to the jazz club, the band, the conversation with Shelton. She thought about the song she had heard, 'Relaxin' at Camarillo'.

'Camarillo,' she whispered to herself, unsure why. She thought about the tale of Charlie Parker going mad in LA, being confined to the mental hospital. She thought about Billie Holiday, all the down-and-outs she'd encountered during her time in New York. A whole generation gone mad, dragged down by the undertow of addiction. She thought about mental hospitals, rehab centers for jazz musicians. The place Louis mentioned Holiday might go to when she got out from behind bars. What Shelton had said about having no choice in what notes came out, but having instead the choice of how to play them. Rather than fearing the void, these musicians, this mad generation, were sculpting it.

'Camarillo,' she said again, and in the roll of the syllables, she heard the shush of the blue Pacific. A tremor of a memory. Camarillo. And in that moment, it flashed through her mind.

She knew where Cleveland was.

Thoughts streaked, exploding like fireworks. An energy built up in her heart, both heavy and light.

She knew where Cleveland was.

And Faron was hitting him tonight.

Maybe there was still hope.

58

The snow was coming down in sheets by the time Gabriel got to Faron's address. He saw the garment factory looming over the corner, all its lights off. He saw a thin row of windows at the top, unlit too.

He looked around. Across the road from the factory were the piers, dark and silent, stretching out over the black river like fingers of snow. To the side of the piers was a giant gas silo with the words *Welcome Home, Boys* painted across it in huge letters. Presumably for the soldiers returning from the war via the piers.

Gabriel sat and waited to see if there'd be any movement on the top floor of the factory. After five minutes nothing had happened. He got the last of the Benzedrine inhalers from his pocket, broke into it, swallowed the strip.

He stepped out into the snow, crossed the street, walked around the building, casing it. He was leaving footprints all over the place, but the snow was coming in so thick it didn't matter. Round the back he found the fire escapes, and a corrugated iron lean-to in the alley adjoining, in which a couple of cars were parked up.

It looked like the apartments above the factory had their own entrance via a stairway bolted onto the side of the building, that rose up all the way to the top story. Gabriel checked the door to the stairway, figured he could shoulder it. It took six attempts. By the time he was done his shoulder was bruised to high hell, and he was wondering if he hadn't broken something.

If anyone was in, they'd know he was coming.

He checked his gun, stepped through into a cramped entry space. Above him the staircase towered. He ascended five or six stories to the top floor. Came out onto a doorway which was covered by a metal roll shutter, padlocked into an iron bar which was bolted to the floor.

He went back down the stairs, searched the De Soto's repair box. Found a wheel jack. Took it back up the stairs. He spent fifteen minutes bashing the corner of the jack into the padlock, heaving it down with all his might, over and over, powered by the dizzying rush of the Benzedrine. By the time the padlock broke he was dripping in sweat, breathless, woozy.

He took a moment to regain his breath, rolled up the shutter, stepped into an open space that took up the building's entire floor plan. Long rows of windows on all sides showed nothing but night sky and falling snow. Through what little light shone into the space he could make out rows of cement columns, a dusty, bare cement floor. Empty. Except for one corner, where partition walls enclosed a rectangular space.

Gabriel raised his gun to the partitions, stepped towards them. There were two doorways in the partitions. He reached the first, fanned his gun towards it, stepped inside.

A make-shift bedroom. A mattress on the floor, a blanket, a sheet, a pillow. All rolled up, neat and tidy. Military style. Next to the bed was an electric lamp, a chair, a chest. And that was it.

Gabriel kneeled, opened up the chest.

Empty.

He left the room, stepped into the next one, a bathroom of sorts. Tiles on the floor, a toilet and a sink, and a tap high up in the wall that someone had been using as a shower. Then Gabriel noticed something else – iron rings. Cemented into the wall above his head, cemented into the floor. Four of them forming a square. He kneeled, studied the tiles. They'd been wiped clean, unlike the dusty cement floor everywhere else. But in the spaces between the tiles, dried blood.

He rose. He stepped out into the main section. Looked again across the floor. This time he noticed brown stains streaking across the cement. From the bathroom to the entrance. Gabriel thought of Pearl, the girl Bova had sent to Faron, her body sliced up and dumped in a breaker's yard.

He stood in the silent gloom, felt the Benzedrine kicking through his system. He'd come there to toss the place, to search for stash spots, to rip up floorboards, slash furniture, pull down wall panels. Check all the places where a man might hide two million dollars.

But there was nothing to toss. Faron lived in a cement box. With a square for sleeping and a square for chaining people up and that was it. No clues, no personal effects, no hints as to where Faron might be, might have come from, might be going to.

No money. No humanity.

Faron had come and would be leaving, and he hadn't left a trace.

This was it. This was defeat. Final and irrevocable.

He tried as hard as he could not to start sobbing. He let out a wail. Then he shook his head, turned and left, knowing the longer he spent there, the less likely he was to get out of New York alive.

He walked down the stairs, stepped out into the street.

As he was heading towards his car, he thought of something, paused.

The lean-to.

He turned around and went back over to the mouth of the alley where he'd seen the cars. Over the entrance was a chain-link fence with a swing-gate set into it, padlocked shut. The two cars were parked behind it. The second car. A brown Chrysler sedan. The same sedan that had been there when he'd found the money in East Harlem. The sedan Faron had gotten out of when he went to speak to the two cops whose car had ended up in the river.

Gabriel scrambled over the fence, dropped down onto the other side. Peered into the car. Nothing.

He popped the trunk. It was packed. Four holdalls stuffed in tight, all ready for Faron to make his getaway. Gabriel opened them one by one: in the first were clothes, in the second guns and a machete, in the third and fourth were two million dollars cash.

Gabriel thought about waiting there for Faron, in the shadows of the alleyway, killing him when he returned from killing Cleveland. But then he thought about Sarah, he thought about the Doc's note. *He who wishes revenge will live in misery.*

He pulled the two bags out of the trunk, closed it, walked over to the fence. With first one bag and then the other, he scrambled up and managed to toss the bags onto the snow on the other side.

He ran over to the De Soto, threw the bags in. Hauled north.

Twenty minutes later he was on Central Park West, pulling up outside the Majestic. He ran in, told the concierge to call Costello's apartment.

'Mr Costello's out,' the concierge said.

'It's Mrs Costello I want. Tell her it's Gabriel. Tell her I'm waiting for her in the lobby. She has to come down.'

The concierge frowned, then put the call through. Gabriel went to the car and lugged the two holdalls in, dumped them on the floor.

A couple of minutes later the elevator opened and Bobbie walked out, dressed in slacks and a sweater. She looked him up and down. He still had Bova smeared across him, dust from Faron's hideout.

'Gabby,' she said, doing a good job of suppressing her shock, 'what are you doing here? Frank's out.'

'I know.'

'What happened to you?'

Gabriel shrugged.

'I heard they're gonna come after you,' she said.

'They've already started. There's something I need you to do for me.'

He gestured to the holdalls at his feet. 'There's two million dollars in those. Frank's money. He asked me to find it for him. Get the concierge to take them up in the elevator for you. Give 'em to Frank.'

She looked at the holdalls uncertainly, nodded.

'What do you want in return?' she asked.

'Sarah stays out of it,' Gabriel said. 'I'm leaving New York. Sarah's going to stay, with our housekeeper. I want your word, that no one ever bothers her, no one ever uses her to come after me. She gets to live in safety.'

He looked at her, saw her expression soften, going from apprehensive to pitying. Childless Bobbie, who was always asking after Sarah.

'I trust you, Bobbie,' he said. 'I know if you give me your word, it'll happen. You'll get Frank to promise. And if you get Frank to promise, it'll happen.'

She nodded, tears in her eyes.

'Sure, Gabby. I give you my word. Sarah'll be safe.'

59

Thursday 13th, 9.00 p.m.

Thursday 13th. Nine p.m. The hour Gabriel's life had been geared to for the last six years. The point when his escape plan was supposed to kick into action, the faked break-in and disappearance. So many years of planning and where was he? Driving through a blizzard to pick up Sarah with half the underworld after him. Costello's job had been his undoing. If it wasn't for the job, he wouldn't have learned Faron was back in town, wouldn't have tried the stupid trick at the airport, wouldn't have frittered all his plans away with bad judgment.

When he got to 59th, he parked up and ran across the street, rang Michael's apartment, spoke to Ida on the intercom and she buzzed him in. When he got to the apartment, he saw the door was slightly ajar, Ida standing behind it, a gun in her hand.

She let him in, and he entered a cramped living room, saw Sarah curled up on the sofa, asleep.

'Did you fix it?' she asked.

Gabriel nodded, turned to look at her.

'I fixed it,' he said. 'I fixed it with Costello so it's safe for Sarah to stay in New York. She'll stay with our housekeeper. I go on the run, Sarah gets to carry on with her life. Once Costello puts the word out, she'll be safe.'

He felt Ida studying him, wondering what he'd done to secure Sarah's safety. He prayed she wouldn't ask him what it was, and she didn't.

'So what happens until Costello gets the word out?' she asked.

'She has to lay low.'

Ida nodded, and Gabriel noticed a restlessness in Ida, energy itching to get out.

'What is it?' he asked.

'I know where Cleveland is,' she said.

And it took a while for the words to register in Gabriel's head.

'You told me Benny Siegel was looking for Cleveland too, right?' she said.

Gabriel nodded.

'Well, what if he found him?' she said. 'What if Siegel found Cleveland but he never told anyone?'

Gabriel paused, realization spreading through him like a warm glow.

'Where'd he put him?' Ida continued. 'A junkie he wanted to keep safe.'

He grinned. 'A drying-out clinic,' he said.

'We never thought to check the high-end hospitals, the private clinics, 'cos how could Cleveland afford them?'

'He couldn't,' said Gabriel. 'But Benny Siegel could.'

Flashes of Benny's apartment in East Harlem. The roaches in the ashtray, the needle and dope in the sideboard. Benny had found Cleveland and had hidden him in the apartment, then, when Benny was going back to LA, he'd moved Cleveland out to the clinic. That's why Cleveland had left his dope stash in the apartment. Where else would a junkie be going where he didn't need his dope but a drying-out clinic?

'I got a musician friend,' said Ida. 'His manager knows a place. Expensive, secretive, one that takes colored people. I called him, I'm just waiting on the address.'

A memory surfaced – Benny's driver saying he visited Joe Glaser. Glaser had a drying-out place he used for his clients. Benny had gone there for a recommendation. Then Gabriel remembered something else.

'I know where the place is,' he said. 'Benny's driver told me he visited a clinic uptown. I figured Benny must have caught something, but it must have been to put Cleveland in there.'

'You know the address?' Ida asked.

'Riverside Drive,' he said. 'Just near the George Washington Bridge.'

'You said Faron had a job on tonight?' Ida said. 'Maybe the snow has slowed them down. Maybe they've called it off till tomorrow. Maybe we've still got a chance. I'm going to head up there.'

'On your own?' Gabriel asked.

'If I have to. I called Michael's friend at the hospital, the cop, left a message for him to come get me.'

Gabriel saw the despair on her face, the sense that her last chance to save Michael's son was slipping away. How long ago did she figure out where Cleveland was? And she couldn't leave the apartment because she was waiting for him to get back and take Sarah, and all the while the snow was piling up on the streets.

'Ida, that clinic's all the way uptown. Getting Michael's friend from the hospital? He won't be able to make it in this weather. I barely got here myself and I've got snow tires on the car. Plus if he comes to get you, he'll be leaving Michael unprotected.'

'Then I'll go there on my own.'

'How? There're no cabs, no buses, the subways aren't working. The El sure as hell won't be.'

'Then I'll walk.'

Gabriel stared at her, suppressed a sigh. Tried to think. Tried to come up with a plan and surprised himself by doing so.

'I've got friends on the PD,' he said. 'People I trust. They're based uptown. Not far from the clinic. I can tell them to go and pick up Cleveland, put him in protective custody.'

'I have to be there, Gabriel,' she said. 'I can't trust this to strangers.'

Despair suffused her features once more, was in her voice too, making her words quiver, her natural poise now stretched to its limit.

'I'll call my friends,' said Gabriel. 'And then I'll drive you up there. Drop you off.'

'No,' said Ida. 'You need to lay low till the weather clears up.'

'I'll drop you off there and then I'll lay low.'

'And what about Sarah?'

'I'll take her with me.'

'No.'

'It's safer than leaving her alone,' said Gabriel. 'I take you there, the cops arrive, then Sarah and me leave. We go find a hotel to hide out in.'

'And what if Faron decides to attack Cleveland while we're there?'

'What are the chances? You said it yourself, Ida, the snow's probably slowed them down. They've probably put the hit off till tomorrow.'

He paused to let the logic of what he was saying sink in.

'Michael nearly died saving Sarah's life,' he added. 'You have to let me help his son in return.'

They stared at each other, Ida desperate to accept his help, Gabriel desperate to give it.

'Uncle Gabby,' a voice said.

They both turned to see Sarah had awoken, was sitting up on the sofa staring up at them. Gabriel smiled at her. She jumped off the sofa and over to Gabriel and clasped him in a hug. Tears streamed down her face and Gabriel felt her warmth against him.

'What's going on?' she asked.

Ten minutes later, all three of them were in the De Soto, ploughing through the storm, its fog lamps making golden tunnels through the snowfall. They had to navigate accidents, rubberneckers, cars abandoned in the middle of the road. They were barely making five miles an hour. Further uptown the conditions were even worse – the snow had settled more thickly, had buried the city, enveloped it in an eerie stillness that made it feel like they were driving through the necropolis of Gabriel's nightmares.

Eventually, they made it all the way to Riverside Drive. They drove along it, gradually climbing the high ridge on which it was built. They passed under the bridge and the incline increased sharply. They passed a row of red-brick apartment blocks. And there, just beyond them, was the clinic. It was the only low-rise building Gabriel could see, maybe the only townhouse on that stretch of Washington Heights which hadn't been replaced by a modern block. It was set in its own garden, a railing marking its perimeter. A peaceful, luxurious place to kick a narcotics addiction, high up on the cliffs overlooking the river.

'That's it,' Gabriel said.

He drove past it and parked the car a half-block further down the narrow street, in the middle of a row of cars that had been turned into a lumpen bank by the snow. He killed the engine, looked behind him, through the rear window. On one side of the road was the clinic, on the other an embankment that dropped steeply to the Henry Hudson Parkway, and towering over the road in the distance was the giant shadow of the bridge, arching over Manhattan all the way to New Jersey.

They waited. After a while an unmarked police cruiser approached up the street. It stopped a few cars away. Ida and Gabriel both got their guns ready. Gabriel checked the rearview mirror and caught Sarah's eye, saw how hard she was trying not to look scared. He gave her an *it's OK* look and then he flashed the lights. Two men got out of the cruiser, walked over, got in the backseat next to Sarah, both of them wiping snow from their hair.

Salzman looked at Gabriel and nodded.

'Ida Young,' said Gabriel, 'this is Lieutenant Detective Salzman, from the NYPD's Narcotics Squad.'

Salzman nodded at Ida. 'This is Lieutenant Gallo,' said Salzman, introducing his colleague, a tall, young detective in a tan raincoat.

'Thanks for coming,' Ida said.

Salzman shrugged off her thanks. 'Gabriel explained on the phone,' he said. 'The witness is inside?'

'We think so,' said Ida. 'He's got a history as a pusher, too, so I guess you could bring him in under that.'

'All right,' said Salzman. 'We've got some beat cops coming, but what with the weather, they've been delayed. We'll go in there now and get the witness into custody, then the beat cops'll guard the place in case anyone tries to attack it. Sound good?'

Ida nodded.

Salzman turned to look at Gabriel. 'I heard about what went down,' he said.

Gabriel figured he meant the contract, his imminent life on the run. 'It happens,' he said.

'Good luck,' Salzman said.

'Thanks, buddy.'

Salzman nodded, then turned to look at Ida and Gallo. 'All right,' he said. 'Let's get this over with.'

Salzman and Gallo got out of the car.

Ida turned to look at Gabriel, then at Sarah.

'Thank you, both,' she said.

'Go get him,' Gabriel said.

Ida nodded, stepped out into the yowling blizzard, and within a few seconds, she was lost from sight.

Gabriel stared at the snow spinning about through the orange gloom of the street lights. He wondered if Ida would be safe if Faron attacked the clinic, just her and Salzman and Gallo. He debated waiting for the beat cops to arrive.

'How much did you hear in the apartment?' Gabriel asked.

Sarah frowned. 'I heard you talking about coming up here,' she said.

'Did you hear me talking about leaving town?'

She shook her head.

He paused. 'I'm gonna be leaving town, Sarah. And you're gonna be staying.'

'What do you mean?'

'You can stay here in New York, with Mrs Hirsch,' said Gabriel. 'I fixed it so they won't come after you to get to me. You'll be safe here in New York. I'll leave. You can carry on your life here.'

Tears welled up in her eyes, and Gabriel felt his own eyes beginning to water.

'I'm sorry I tried to control everything,' he said. 'It's all my fault. Always has been.'

She shook her head. 'No, I want to come with you,' she said.

'It's not going to be like how I planned. It's not a clean break anymore. I'll always be looking over my shoulder. But you don't have to live like that. I've messed up your life too much already, Sarah. I'm sorry.'

She shook her head again. 'I'm coming with you,' she said. 'You can't just dump me here like this. You're all the family I've got.'

His heart wrenched. He leaned over the seat and they hugged, and they stayed like that a while.

'Let's go find a hotel to stay in till the weather dies down,' he said.

Sarah smiled.

Gabriel started the car and inched out into the narrow street. Just as they were about to turn the corner, Gabriel happened to look in the rearview mirror, saw headlights glimmering on the road behind him.

60

Ida trudged towards the clinic through the whirling wind and the clumps of snow hurtling through the air. She hadn't realized how bad it was while she was in the cocoon of Gabriel's car. The two cops eyed her, then they pushed open the gate set into the railings and went through a front garden that was nothing more than an undulating sea of snow.

They went up the front steps to the porch and rang the bell. Waited.

The door was opened by a tall, middle-aged woman, thin-faced, her hair in a severe, shoulder-length bob.

Salzman held up his police badge.

'NYPD, ma'am.'

'Yes?' she said, a slight frown knitting her brow.

'We have reasons to believe one of your residents is wanted in connection with a series of murders. We also have reason to believe some men are coming here to attack him.'

'Good lord.'

'Yes, ma'am. I believe he is.'

The woman stared at them, confused and perturbed.

'Please, come in out of the cold,' she said eventually, in a surprisingly warm voice. 'I'll get the director for you. He's not been able to leave on account of the snow.'

They stepped into a broad, high-ceilinged hallway. There were white tiles on the floor, and whitewashed walls and the space was filled with antique furniture. Ida got the impression of a clinic trying very hard not to look like a clinic.

The woman led them through the hall and down a corridor. At its far end she stopped and knocked on a door.

'Wait here, please,' she said, and stepped inside. A few seconds passed and the door opened. The woman exited with a rotund man in his fifties, sporting thick glasses and a scruffy mop of brown hair.

'I'm Dr Howard,' he said. 'What's going on?'

Salzman flashed his badge again and repeated what he'd told the woman at the door.

'What's this resident's name?' the doctor asked.

'Gene Cleveland,' said Salzman. 'But he probably checked in under an alias. His treatment was paid for by Benjamin Siegel.'

Recognition flashed across the man's face. Then his expression hardened.

'I see,' he said. 'Do you have a warrant?'

'No,' said Salzman. 'We wouldn't be able to get one until tomorrow morning, but since we have reason to believe men are coming here tonight, I think it's in everyone's interest if you let us speak to the man, see if he won't come into custody voluntarily, for his own safety. Some beat cops from our precinct are on their way here to protect you in any case.'

The doctor looked at Salzman, considered.

'Very well,' he said eventually. 'Wait in the lounge. I'll go and speak to him.'

The doctor led them back down the corridor and up two flights of stairs to a large room littered with high-ticket sofas and armchairs, bookcases, games tables, all in front of a bank of windows which looked out onto the snowstorm beyond.

The doctor left, and they waited.

Gallo collapsed into an armchair, lit a cigarette, looked at the ornate ceiling above him.

'Nicest damn clinic I ever saw,' he said.

Ida thought about Michael in his room downtown, the mask attached to his face.

She walked over to the windows, looked through them at the bridge arcing through the sky, disappearing into the blizzard, the steep, tree-lined drop to the river far below. A couple of minutes later the doctor returned in the company of a skinny, gaunt-looking colored man, dressed in slacks and a thick, woolen sweater. Ida looked him up and down and felt a sense of disappointment. He was completely unremarkable in all respects.

'I'll leave you to talk,' said the doctor, stepping out of the room.

Cleveland stayed where he was, standing next to the door, fidgety, nervous.

Salzman flashed his badge.

'Genovese and his men have found out where you are,' he said. 'They're coming here tonight, to kill you. Come with us and we'll protect you.'

'Bullshit,' said Cleveland.

Salzman grunted, turned to look at Ida.

'Mr Cleveland,' she said, walking over. 'My name's Ida Young, I'm a private investigator. I was hired by your old neighbor's family to investigate his case.'

'What neighbor?'

'After you fled the Palmer Hotel your upstairs neighbor was arrested for the murders. I'm trying to secure his release.'

Cleveland frowned, trying to take in the information.

Ida wondered if he knew what had happened in the aftermath of the murders, if he'd seen the newspapers between the time he ran away to the time he entered the clinic.

'Shit,' Cleveland said. 'I don't know nothing about no one getting arrested.'

'He's been coerced into pleading guilty,' said Ida. 'I need a statement from you. Something. Anything. To help free the boy.'

Cleveland shook his head.

'We don't have much time,' said Ida. 'Faron's on his way. You've seen what he can do.'

'I ain't going to jail,' said Cleveland.

'Why would you?' Ida said. 'No one's going to pursue you for the blackmail. Or the dope they found in the apartment, the cops have got that down as Bucek's. All we want is for you to make a statement and help get your neighbor released.'

'You want me to testify against Genovese?' said Cleveland, laughing. 'He was up on that murder charge last year. Remember what happened to that? The witnesses all got bumped off.'

'We don't want you to testify against Genovese,' said Ida. 'Just tell the truth about what happened that night at the hotel. That Faron was there. Just enough to get your neighbor off the hook. Please, we don't have much time.'

Cleveland stared at her. Clearly he harbored a deep suspicion of the authorities, too much suspicion to entrust himself to their care.

'You've got no reason to trust us,' she said. 'But an innocent boy's life is at stake. And on top of that, we're the best option you've got. You make a statement and don't implicate any of the higher-ups, and maybe they'll let you be. And if not, they'll relocate you. One way or the other you're going to be running for the rest of your life. We can give you a better escape than you could ever manage on your own. You think you can outrun Faron without our help? Forever?'

She paused to let the words sink in.

'But we can talk about this later,' she said. 'Please. We need to get you into the precinct before they kill you.'

Cleveland thought about it, stared at her, something softened in him.

'If I go with you,' he said, 'what happens?'

Ida turned to look at Salzman.

'We'll take you to the precinct,' Salzman said. 'Get a statement. We'll take that to the DA and the judge first thing tomorrow.

You'll be put in protective custody, till the time of the trial. You'll be in an apartment, with cops guarding you. You'll be safe. Then after the trial we'll help you to move somewhere far away, where they'll never catch you.'

Cleveland squirmed.

'If I'm cooped up in an apartment all on my own for weeks, I'll start using again,' he said. 'I know I will.'

'There'll be police there,' Ida said. 'They'll keep you from it.'

He thought. Outside, the snow continued to fall through the darkness.

He looked around at the plush surroundings, smiled sadly. 'I guess all good things come to an end.'

61

They stepped outside into the storm and somehow it had gotten even worse while they were inside. Ida could barely see her hand in front of her face.

They made it down the steps, across the garden, out onto the street. She looked up and down, could hardly make out the police car.

'We can't drive,' Salzman shouted over the roar of the storm. She nodded.

'How far's the precinct?' she shouted.

'Six blocks along,' he said. 'One north. We could go back in and wait.'

Ida shook her head. 'We don't want to be here if they come.'

Salzman nodded.

They turned and headed north. They'd made it half a block when Gallo fell to the ground. Ida thought he'd tripped. It was only seconds later she heard the shot, a dull thud softened by the falling snow.

She grabbed Cleveland and pulled him to the ground, behind the snowbank of parked cars. They hit the sidewalk and she looked up to see a bullet rip through Salzman's neck, another hit his skull. The power of the shots pushed him backwards, smacked him into the railings of the building behind them, dislodging settled snow. Again the noise of the gunshots came after it should have. More bullets fizzed around them. Into the cars, into the brickwork of the building, pinging off the railings. There was more than one shooter, more than one machine-gun. And they had Ida and Cleveland trapped on the narrow stretch of road, between buildings on one side and the embankment dropping down the cliff-side on the other.

Ida scurried to the edge of the car. Thought about the bullets that had ripped through Salzman's neck and head, left to right, on a flat trajectory, used that to figure out the location of the shooters. She rose into a crouch and looked over the snow bank, saw a car further down, stopped diagonally across the road. Man-shaped shadows moving closer, hosing the street with orange spurts of machine-gun fire; bullets flying at right-angles to the falling snow.

She lowered herself down again, behind the car.

'We need to run,' she said.

Cleveland nodded, gestured to the embankment on the other side of the road; there was an opening, steps, a staircase leading down the cliff-side to the Henry Hudson Parkway.

They made a dash for it, across the road, to the stairs, which were so covered in snow, it was impossible to see where any of the steps were. They made it down the first few by luck, and then they tripped, fell, stumbled, managed to right themselves. Kept on going.

Eventually, the highway below them came into view. Not a car on it, pristine snow, and on its far side, a steep, tree-covered drop leading sharply downwards to the river.

They raced across it, their legs dropping into snow to their knees. They were easy targets for the men above them until they reached the tree-cover on the other side.

When they were halfway across, bullet-sized holes pocked the snow blanket around them. The sound of gunfire rang out once more. They were almost at the tree-line when a bullet caught Cleveland and he fell. Panic spiked through Ida.

She grabbed him, hauled him up, prayed he was still alive. He stumbled to his feet and Ida felt a pang of relief. There was blood all over his arm and shoulder. She pushed him on. They made it into the trees, down the slope a few feet, then they collapsed into the snow.

'You OK?' she asked.

He winced. His right hand was clasping his left shoulder. He moved it and Ida saw blood. They'd been shooting from behind. An exit wound.

'Turn around,' she said.

He did so, wincing again, and she found the entry point, an inch or so higher up, just above the top of his shoulder blade. No organs hit, but blood was pumping out of him. They needed to get him patched up or he'd bleed to death.

'Can you walk?' she asked.

'Sure, I can walk,' he said. 'But where the hell are we going?'

She turned to look back the way they had come. Above them the highway ran along the ridge. In front of them, the bank descended ever so steeply through the trees, all the way to the river. The tree cover wasn't dense, but the snowstorm made it feel so.

'We try and lose them in the trees,' she said.

'What kind of plan is that?'

'They'll be down those steps in a few seconds and they'll follow our tracks in the snow. It's the only chance we've got. C'mon.'

He grimaced at her. Then he nodded, rose and they picked their way down the bank, then headed parallel to the river, blood dripping off Cleveland's shoulder, leaving a trail in the white for the men to follow.

Ida kept checking all around for signs of the gunmen and didn't find any. She was starting to think that maybe they'd lost them when she heard a noise behind her, turned to see a shape coming at them. They started to run, stumbling through the drifts. But Cleveland tripped, fell down the bank, towards the river.

Ida lost sight of him, turned and ran down the bank. Behind her she could hear the men shouting and getting closer. As she ran, she picked up speed, too much to control on the downward slope. She looked ahead and saw the trees petering out, and after them, open sky. The last few yards of the bank was an escarpment of ice-covered stone, and Cleveland was tumbling down it, all the way to the river below. She grabbed onto a tree to stop herself from falling and it took all her strength to hold on and get her footing.

She watched in horror as Cleveland bounced and tumbled towards the great white sheet of the river. He was going to fall into the freezing water and die. But then something strange happened – when he hit the surface of the river, he rolled across it. It took her a moment to realize. The river had frozen over.

Ida turned to look behind her, the shapes approaching. She prayed and let go of the tree, slid down the stone escarpment and, as she landed on the river, she heard the ice crack – fissures appeared all around her. Cleveland was already hobble-running along the edge of the frozen river, disappearing into the blizzard. Ida got up carefully, not knowing how thick the ice was.

She heard a noise and turned to look up the bank behind her, three men with guns standing at the tree-line where she had held on before sliding down. One of them towered over the others. Faron. She jumped over the cracks in the ice and ran. They spotted her. Shots rang out. She turned and saw them scrambling down the escarpment. Then there was a scream – one of the men had fallen on the same spot Ida had, breaking the cracks that she and Cleveland had opened up, falling in.

She looked ahead of her and carried on running, but she couldn't see Cleveland anymore. She kept on, unsure where she was going, out into the nothingness.

A great gust of wind smacked against her, knocked her off her feet. She fell onto the ice and hit her head. Everything went black. She felt the world spin beneath her. Tilt. Rebalance itself.

She opened her eyes groggily, and looked around. She couldn't see the riverbank to her side anymore. She couldn't see any landmarks anywhere. With a sense of panic she realized that in every direction there was nothing but the white sheet of ice, sparkling blackness above, the falling snow. There were no gun-shots anymore either. There was nothing but the howling wind.

Then that, too, faded.

The snowflakes above her slowed their descent.

Everything was still.

Timelessness stretched all around. Maybe this was the unknown to come. The nothingness. All her fear and panic evap-orated. Was replaced by a grain of something powerful, something that could only be forged in loneliness.

The moment yawned into eternity.

And then she could hear something, faintly at first, but getting louder; her own heartbeat. The sound of her breath. Filling the void. The noise of the storm.

Snow fell through the emptiness once more.

She got to her feet, regained a sense of ground and sky, grav-ity, time, fear. She heard something in front of her. The gunmen. How could they be in front of her?

Of course. She'd spun around when she'd fallen. She'd lost her bearings. She turned and ran in the opposite direction to the one that her internal compass was telling her to take.

After a few seconds, she saw Cleveland in front of her, hob-bling along, and beyond him, further in the distance, a hulking shadow lying across the river – a pier. She looked behind and saw gunfire blooming. Two sets of guns. Firing rapidly. Wildly. They didn't know where she or Cleveland were. All of them were stranded and lost out on that ice sheet. But Cleveland was still leaving that trail of blood.

She ran, made up the ground between them.

'You OK?' she asked when she caught up with him.

'Sure.'

She looked at his shoulder, his other hand clasped over it, drenched in red, the dried blood sparkling like ice.

He nodded at the shadow in the distance.

'It's a pier,' he said. 'Boats, cabins, bandages, places to hide. Maybe radios too.'

Ida stared at the pier all that distance away across the ice, studied Cleveland, saw how weak he was. She put her arm under his good shoulder, and taking some of his weight, they ran as best they could across the ice. Every few moments she turned behind her, tense and fearful, to see the shapes emerging from the wall of falling snow.

They kept on. Slowly, painfully, the shadow of the pier grew larger, began to take on details, substance. Eventually, she could see the boats moored along it – tugs, pleasure craft, yachts – all of them rising up with the ice, frozen into off-kilter positions, like a wave had washed across them and stopped halfway through.

Just as they reached the first of the boats, the shots started once more, hissing into the ice behind them. They stumbled around the side of the boat, hiding between it and the pier.

'You hit?' Ida asked.

'No. You?'

She shook her head. She turned and peered round the side of the boat, saw their two pursuers approaching, just yards away now, and for the first time, she got a close view of Faron. Tall and powerful-looking, despite the fact that he was walking with a slight limp. Both he and the other man had automatics in their gloved hands. Ida's fingers by contrast were so frozen that she doubted she could even hold her gun.

She turned back around.

'We need to get out of here,' she said.

Cleveland shook his head. 'I can't move,' he said. 'I can't do no more running. Not now. I need a few minutes.'

Ida looked at him and knew it was the truth. But she only had seconds before the men caught up with them.

'OK,' she said. 'Let's just move you a little.'

She walked behind Cleveland, helped him up, settled him down again just a few steps from where he was, propped him up against one of the pier supports. She checked she'd left a blood trail in the snow. She had. Then she ran underneath the pier, hid behind one of the supports on its far side, a sniping position for when the gunmen came around the corner and followed the blood trail to Cleveland. She scrabbled her gun from its holster, and it was as she'd thought, her fingers were so frozen she could barely grip it in her fist.

She looked at the section of snow where she expected the gunmen to appear, trained her gun on it, waited, her heart pounding, racing with dizzying force.

Faron arrived, following the blood trail, looking between the boats and the pier. He saw Cleveland slumped by the support, turned, raised his gun.

Ida tried her hardest to squeeze her finger over the trigger. She fired off two shots that went hugely wide, thudded into one of the supports. Faron turned towards her. Their eyes met and she felt Faron's stare boring into her, his eyes as blue as battery acid.

She wondered why he wasn't shooting back at her, then realized she had her gun pointed at him, and he had his gun pointed away, at Cleveland. Maybe he'd mistaken her missed shots for a warning.

'Drop the gun,' she shouted over the roar of the storm.

He continued staring at her, shook his head.

Out of the corner of her eye, she could see Cleveland, scrabbling to his feet, loping away down the underside of the pier.

Just then the second gunman walked into view, machine-gun pointed at Ida.

She dashed behind the support and both men's guns spat fire, and the ice around her started cracking and she felt the world shake. She crouched down and made herself small as the bullets rained down around her. The fear of death pumped through her; hyperventilating, she tried to gather herself. Tried to think.

She couldn't run. They'd mow her down. And she couldn't stay where she was, because the ice would break and she'd fall into the water and freeze. She had three bullets left, and Cleveland had run away. She flexed the muscles in her fingers. Trying to warm them. She waited. The gunfire ceased.

She took a breath and spun about, and it happened all at once. The two men trained their guns on her, and the world slanted from the tilting ice. The second gunman's face became a red smudge and he fell forwards, and Faron fell too, and all this without Ida firing a shot.

She ran from the cracking ice, to the next pier support along, turned once more to see the body of Faron's partner, blood pouring out of his head, daubing itself across the whiteness in wind-blown streaks. And there was Faron, crouching behind the keel of the boat near where Cleveland had been hiding.

And there was Gabriel, approaching from the same direction Faron had come, gun raised, scanning the space. But Faron was hiding where Gabriel couldn't see him.

Ida screamed at Gabriel. Too late. Faron rose and shot Gabriel, and Gabriel went down, landed on a stretch of ice that was breaking off, rapidly becoming an island. He'd been hit on his flank. He rolled, and as he tried to stand, the island slanted. He was going to fall off, slide into the endless, freezing darkness.

Ida watched Faron as he limped towards Gabriel. Then Sarah appeared behind Gabriel, running towards him. She picked up his gun and swung it towards Faron. He halted. He frowned. Ida stopped. Felt a revulsion as she looked on. The girl kneeling next to Gabriel, holding the gun up at Faron. Faron just yards away, on the other side of the cracks.

Faron grinned at Sarah.

He said something to the girl that Ida couldn't hear over the howling wind. Sarah screamed and fired off two shots. The second hit Faron on his torso. He staggered backwards. Ida fired, emptied her gun. One bullet caught him side on. He went down. His gun skittered across the ice and disappeared into the black water below.

Ida walked towards them, keeping her empty gun aimed at Faron, who was thrashing about on his back, trying to get up, slipping, making a blood angel on the pristine white.

Sarah urged Gabriel to get up, tried to pull him up.

When Ida reached them, she saw how bad it was – Sarah and Gabriel were standing on a stretch of ice that was now surrounded completely by the jagged black water of the river.

Ida screamed at them to move back, but they couldn't hear.

Another gust of wind hit Ida. She fell onto the ice once more, cracking her elbow. A flurry of snow battered her, stung her eyes. She got to her knees, wiped the snow from her face and looked up at Gabriel and Sarah.

But they were gone.

Where the island had been there was now just dark water. The void had consumed them.

Ida stared at the blackness where they had been just a few moments before, felt herself pierced by a razor-sharp hopelessness. Her muscles went slack, her heart pounded. She screamed along with the wind, till everything was a scream.

Then she felt something tugging on her, pulling her back.

Cleveland. She rose, put her arm under his shoulder again and they stumbled down the ice, found a spot where they could climb onto a tug. As they did so, Ida turned to her side and saw an empty red smear where Faron had been, then a trail of blood running parallel to the river's edge, disappearing into the storm.

'Did you see him?' she asked Cleveland, gesturing to the blood trail.

He shook his head. He was frozen, swaying, could barely speak.

They made it onto the deck of the tug, into its murky cabin. Ida found a first aid kit and bandaged up Cleveland's shoulder as best she could, buying them time. She looked around for a radio, found one, stared at it, unsure how it worked.

'I know how to use it,' Cleveland said.

She turned to see him slumped in the corner, peering up at her through the shadows.

'They taught us in the army,' he said. 'Lift me up.'

She helped him to his feet. He hobbled over to the radio, studied it, turned some switches and it came to life in a hiss of knotty static. He grabbed the microphone from its holder and slumped back down onto the floorboards, lifted the microphone to his mouth and mumbled a distress call into it.

Ida sat down next to him, prayed someone would hear them, would be able to locate them. She closed her eyes and prayed and wept. For her son. For Michael. For Tom. For Gabriel and Sarah.

Next to her, Cleveland continued his mumbling, chant-like incantation. Outside, the storm howled on through the blackness.

PART TWENTY

DAILY NEWS

NEW YORK'S PICTURE NEWSPAPER

City Edition Final   Monday, November 17th 1947

LOCAL NEWS

BLIZZARD DECLARED WORST IN RECORDED HISTORY

CLEANUP EFFORTS HAMPERED

Manhattan, Nov 16th. – The United States Weather Bureau confirmed that last week's blizzard was the worst in the city's history, with the level of snowfall exceeding even that of the blizzard of 1888. Although the damage from the storm is still being assessed, so far it is estimated over fifty people have perished. City officials involved in the relief efforts have stressed that this number is likely to rise as further bodies are discovered as the snow thaws out and more missing people are reported.

Trains and buses are up and running again in the city, but most suburbs and outlying regions are still isolated – with thousands of cars abandoned and marooned on highways and side streets exacerbating the travel problems.

Although the effects of the blizzard were felt from Northern Maine to Washington, it was New York City that bore the brunt of the storm's unceasing snowfall. There is still so much snow to clear no one is sure where to put it. Snow piles from plowing are exceeding twelve feet in height on some streets, and authorities in Manhattan are requesting the Department of Sanitation allows them to shift the snow directly into sewers. Private contractors have been seen dumping snow directly into the Hudson and East Rivers.

IN THE GENERAL SESSIONS COURT, MANHATTAN

STATE OF NEW YORK

STATE OF NEW YORK)   Indictment no.: 47GSC-21883
)
      VS   )
)
TALBOT   )
(Defendant)

MOTION TO DISMISS

COMES NOW the State of New York and moves that
a motion to dismiss be entered in the above
captioned case as follows: New evidence has come
into the possession of the prosecutor to suggest
the defendant's innocence in the crimes listed in
the indictment. Summary of evidence is attached
hereto as EXHIBIT A. Based upon the foregoing,
the State has determined that a dismissal be
entered in this case.

This 20th day of November, 1947.

                        Frank S. Hogan
                        District Attorney
                        New York County

DAILY NEWS

NEW YORK'S PICTURE NEWSPAPER

City Edition Final   Thursday, November 20th 1947

POLITICAL NEWS

LOCAL REPRESENTATIVE ADDED TO THE HOUSE COMMITTEE ON UN-AMERICAN ACTIVITIES

Washington DC, Nov 19th. – Congressman Paul J. Helms has agreed to replace departing House Committee on Un-American Activities member Herbert C. Bonner (Dem, NC) after he stepped down last week. Committee chairman Edward J. Hart (Dem, NJ) announced the appointment today, saying the Congressman from New York would be an excellent addition to the committee, which is tasked with combating subversion and propaganda that threatens the state.

The move comes as something of a surprise as it was thought the Congressman was edging towards a seat on the committee congressman Estes Kefauver (Dem, TN) is attempting to form to investigate alleged nationwide organized crime. Congressman Helms said, 'The real threat to this country is not from any so-called organized crime syndicate, for which there is no evidence, certainly not on a nationwide scale, but from Communists and agitators, the presence of whom the committee has so clearly demonstrated with its ongoing investigations of

Hollywood. For these reasons I am happy and proud to do what I can in my new role in the house committee. I wish Congressman Bonner all the best.'

The Committee's investigation led to 'the Hollywood Ten' being cited for contempt by the House of Representatives and their being blacklisted by the Association of Motion Picture Producers in what has become known as 'The Waldorf Statement', issued from the Waldorf-Astoria earlier this month.

62

The hospital had something it called a garden, but it was nothing more than a courtyard at the center of the building with some shrubs and benches in it, and dreary cement walls on all four sides. So when Michael wanted to get some fresh air, or to smoke, he went to the sidewalk in front of the hospital. The doctors had told him it was too cold for him to be on the street, that he was risking infection, but he had no interest in heeding their warnings, so even when there was a bitter wind sweeping in off the East River, he'd ask a nurse to push his wheelchair outside.

Michael had been there fifteen minutes already that morning, eyes glued to the direction from which he guessed Tom would be arriving. He hoped again that he and Tom could patch up their differences, go back to how they were before the case, be honest with one another. Michael checked the time on the clock of the bank on the corner. He smoked another cigarette. He watched the pigeons huddling together on the wrought-iron lampposts. Traffic glided up the street, passing the great blackened lumps of snow dumped either side of the road by the ploughs. New Yorkers hurried down the sidewalk next to him, ignoring his presence, making him wonder how close to a beggar he looked.

He'd wanted to be there at Rikers Island when Tom was released. He'd wanted to be there on the ferry, too, when he landed in Manhattan. He'd imagined it all, a reunion on the waves. But it wasn't to be. The bullet to the chest and pints of lost blood and streams of morphine had seen to that.

So Tom had been released and it was Annette who'd been there instead. So Michael imagined that. His wife waiting for Tom on the glowing marshes of Rikers Island, the two of them traveling back on the ferry, going to the apartment, then Tom coming to the hospital to see his old man.

He checked the time once more, watched the men in the deli opposite, as they hung up a poster about their Thanksgiving promotion in the window. It felt like only yesterday it was Halloween. He finished his cigarette and tossed it into the gutter.

Then he saw Tom walking down the street, dressed in the navy-blue suit he'd worn for his court appearances. His face was marred by cuts and bruises, was swollen still from the beating he'd taken. He was walking with a slight limp that Michael hoped wasn't permanent.

He saw Michael and smiled as much as the bruises allowed.

'Pop,' he said when he'd reached him.

'Tom.'

Tom reached down and they hugged each other. Pain rippled through Michael's chest, but he didn't care. People walking past stared at them – the scarred old white man in a wheelchair hugging a beaten-up colored man.

They let go and looked at each other, at the injuries yet to heal.

'Aren't we a pair?' Tom said.

Michael smiled. 'But we both got through it.'

'Sure we did. You wanna go inside?' Tom asked.

'That place?' said Michael, gesturing to the hospital behind him. 'It's full of crepe-hangers.'

Tom laughed, then he looked up at the building.

'I did some of my training here,' he said wistfully, as if remembering a lost world.

There was a bench a little way off. He wheeled Michael over to it and sat. They watched the traffic, the people, the Thanksgiving display going up opposite.

'Thank you,' said Tom, turning to look at Michael.

'Don't be stupid.'

'If it wasn't for you and Ida I'd still be locked up. Dead maybe.'

'If it wasn't for me and Ida,' said Michael, 'you wouldn't be looking like that.'

Tom smiled again in that pained way.

'Sure,' he said.

'What do you want to do now you're out?' Michael asked.

'Honestly? Have a hot shower. I feel like I've been cold the last three months. Have a shower then get into bed and sleep. Sleep for days and days.'

'I know the feeling,' Michael said.

'Then I was thinking,' Tom continued. 'I might move back to Chicago. See if I can get work.'

A warm feeling filled Michael, that perfect joy that was both uplifting and calming all at once.

He smiled, and Tom smiled back, and Michael got the impression that Tom felt it too; the sense that just at that moment, just at that place, all was right with the world.

'Good,' Michael said.

They watched the street a little more. A wintry wind gusted down it, rattling awnings, making the shop-signs swing. Michael had debated over the last few days, whether he should say anything. At first he'd thought he should keep his mouth shut, but slowly he'd realized that that had been the problem all along, and he needed to end it, or rather, start afresh.

'I know why you moved to the flophouse,' he said. 'The prosecution got hold of your discharge papers, spoke to your old landlady.'

Tom froze. Then his gaze darted to the paving stones of the sidewalk. Michael wondered if he'd made a mistake bringing it up.

'You could have told me, son,' said Michael.

Tom shook his head. He looked up and Michael saw his face

was wet, the bruises glistening with tears. He put his arm over his son's shoulder and for all it was costing him in pain, pulled him close. Tom turned, accepting the embrace.

'I didn't want anyone to hate me,' Tom said through the tears.

'How could I hate you?' Michael replied. 'Look at what me and your mother had to face.'

Tom absorbed the words, nodded, stifled a sob. Tears formed in Michael's eyes, too. They cried at their mutual pain, but also at the strength of the embrace. Stronger than any bullet, stronger than the wind blasting down the street, the oncoming winter.

They stayed like that, locked in their embrace, as the people rushed past, two stones in the river.

IDA YOUNG INVESTIGATIONS LTD.

CHICAGO, ILLINOIS

CONFIDENTIAL

HIGHLY SENSITIVE. USE RESTRICTED.

Transcript
Date: Monday, November 17th, 1947
Time: 10.35
Location: Room #403, Manhattan Criminal
Courts Building, Manhattan, NYC
Participants: Ida Young, Gene Cleveland,
Lieut. Det. David Carrasco, NYPD

    IY: Thank you, Lieutenant.
    DC: All set.
    IY: This is Ida Young. State your name,
please?
    GC: Gene Cleveland.
    IY: Thank you. Also here is Lieutenant
Detective David Carrasco of the NYPD. Mr
Cleveland. This is purely a voluntary
statement. None of this will be released
publicly. You understand that?
    GC: Yeah, I already told you that. How
many times?
    IY: It's for the purposes of the
recording.
    GC: Yeah, all right.
    IY: You're set ...

GC: I'm all set. Let's go.

IY: Start at the beginning?

GC: With Helms?

IY: Wherever you think the beginning is.

GC: I guess it's Helms. I dunno. I
thought it'd be an easy squeeze. I didn't
realize he still had Mob backing. I didn't
mean for all this killing.

IY: But you knew he was involved with
Genovese during the war?

GC: Yeah, during the war. I didn't
realize they were still buddies back in New
York. None of us did. Plus, we were supposed
to keep things hidden, you know.

[PAUSE]

IY: How about you start with the war?
That's where you met Arno Bucek and John
Marino, right?

GC: Right. Met them in Naples. 1944.
Operation Husky.

IY: Can you tell me about that? About
Naples?

GC: Sure. Naples was something. I ain't
never seen a hell like Naples in 1944. I
mean that, hell. The Nazis took everything
they could before they ran away. The Allies
bombed the shit out of it before we invaded.
We turned up and the place was like the
world had ended. No water, no electricity,
half the buildings demolished. People looked
like skeletons, eating rats.

We set up on the docks and all the ships
start coming in. All the supplies for the
invasion of Italy, all coming through

Naples. Our battalion was part of the Quartermasters Corps. We were a colored battalion, so weren't allowed to fight. All that back-of-the-bus shit. They put us in charge of looking after cargoes, running distribution out to towns and villages. Shit work. Fine by me.

IY: And it was in the docks you met Arno Bucek and John Marino?

GC: Yeah. We'd heard rumors, you know. About how the local mobs were paying servicemen to help 'em steal shipments, drive the trucks out of the base and into the countryside, where the local mobsters picked 'em up. I'd heard about it. Then Bucek approached me. Told me he had someone on the outside that wanted the food packages, the clothing parcels, medicine, anything we could get our hands on. Offered a kickback if we'd help them. All we had to do was load up the trucks and sign the dockets.

You gotta understand, we had warehouses full of the shit. Every day there were ships coming in. All the supplies for the troops. All the reconstruction packages. All the sweeteners for the locals. Me and a bunch of the boys in the platoon agreed. Every week we loaded up trucks and got paid in cash. No one got caught 'cos everyone was on the take. The white boys, the black boys. Even the top brass was in on it. You know who the Allies put in charge of Occupied Italy?

IY: No.

GC: Charles Poletti. Former New York
Governor. Associate of Lucky Luciano. We put
a New York mobster in charge of Occupied
Italy. And one of the first things he did was
hire Genovese as his main advisor. It was
like they were telling every single GI out
there it was OK to go steal what you wanted.
One third of everything Uncle Sam brought
into that port ended up on the black market.
Courtesy of Genovese and Vizzini, the local
Camorra boss. They were making millions
while people all around 'em were starving,
dying of infections 'cos the penicillin had
been stolen.

IY: Did you know the black marketeer you
were passing the goods off to was Vito
Genovese?

GC: Hell, no. Not back then. I thought we
were passing the things over to Vizzini. I
didn't know he was Genovese's partner till
later. Genovese used his job in the
administration to pay off the big-wigs, so
everyone was looking the other way while he
looted the military cargoes. And what did
the administration care? Most of the
Americans there hated the Italians, looked
down on them like they were rats. These
people had been our enemies a few weeks
earlier. The only ones losing out were the
tax-payers, all those suckers back home
buying war bonds. And if they were too pussy
to come out and fight with us, who cared if
they lost some money?

IY: And how did you meet Congressman
Helms? Was he part of the black-market
operation, too?

GC: [LAUGHS] I never met Helms. I saw
Helms. Difference.

IY: Was he part of the black-market
operation?

GC: Maybe. Like I said, everyone was
involved in the black-market operation. It
was like the gold rush over there.

IY: Then what were you blackmailing him
over?

GC: Shit. You sure you wanna know?
[PAUSE]

GC: One day out on the docks, Bucek and
Marino come to see me all het up. They're
supposed to be driving two trucks out to the
hills, to the drop-off point for Vizzini,
but their buddy who's supposed to be driving
the other truck has gone missing, and they
don't know what to do. I tell 'em I can
drive the truck and they look at each other
like it never entered their heads before
that a colored man could drive. Once they
get over the shock, they agree. Marino
drives the first truck and Bucek and me
follow him in the second.

We drive out of Naples, into the hills,
up looking for this village that Vizzini's
got on lock. We pass the A.M.G. check-points
and we're out in the middle of nowhere. Keep
on driving up, and up, and up. Eventually,
we reach this cliff, and I see there's
burnt-out U.S. Army trucks all dumped in a

ravine underneath. We get to a village right
on top of the cliff. We hop out. Marino goes
to find Vizzini's guys 'cos he's the only one
of us who speaks Italian.

We see a little bar there. Bucek wants to
go in while we wait for Marino to come back.
I'm nervous about going in. The Italians
liked us Negroes, 'cos we got kicked about
by the Americans and the Germans, just like
they did. But they hated us, too. I ain't
sure on the reception I'll get. But Bucek
tells me it's cool. He's been to this place
before. Says there's Americans that drink
there. There's a whorehouse out back. He
says he's desperate for a drink, but I'm
wondering if he just wants to get laid. So
we go in.

There's a few other GIs in there.
None of 'em would talk to us 'cos I was
there. We order drinks, sit in the corner.
Bucek's in a good mood. I'm sitting there
hoping I don't get thrown down that
ravine.

Then there's a ruckus outside, shouts,
women screaming. We all run out into the
street. There's an old Italian man out
there shouting, banging on the doors of
some house down the road. He's got a
shotgun. Some locals come out, heavies,
drag him away. He's screaming something in
Italian. 'Il demone.' 'Demonio.' Something
like that.

There's a crowd gathered. We all go over
to the house, step in. Looked like a

brothel. There's old women wailing. The
locals are having some kind of conference.
All the buzz is happening at a room at the
back. Corridor stinks of puke. We manage to
squeeze through, look in the room. It's a
bloodbath. There's a couple of dead girls.
There's Helms, naked, blood all over him.
There's another man in there, too. Helms is
looking all dazed. Like he's strung out on
something, or maybe the locals got a few
punches in. These dead girls are young.
Teenagers. Maybe not even.

Marino comes back and talks to the locals
and we figure out what happened. The old man
was selling his granddaughters. Happened a
lot. Italians used to come up to us in the
streets, offering us their wives, daughters,
nieces. They even used to offer them to us
Negroes, that's how hungry they were. Like I
said, I ain't never seen a hell like Naples
in '44.

The other man with Helms, he's big.
Man mountain big. Hayseed-looking. Brown
hair. He's arguing in Italian with the
locals.

IY: This other man was Faron?

GC: Maybe. I didn't know who Faron was at
the time. Plus it was dark, they were
bloody. It was hard to tell.

IY: OK, go on.

GC: Turns out the locals want to lynch
Helms and this other man, but some of the
other locals know this other man is in
tight with Vizzini. That's what they're

arguing about. We don't stick around. We
head back to the base. Weeks go by. And I
keep seeing Helms around Naples, smiling,
joking, getting on with things like he
don't have a care in the world. I press
Bucek and Marino for information 'cos
they're going up to that village every
week. Turns out Helms and the other man
got set free 'cos Vizzini stepped in. The
old man, the dead girls' granddad, doesn't
give in, he's gone crazy with guilt. He
goes and files a statement with the local
police, with the judges down in Naples. A
few days later he ends up in the bottom of
the ravine.

A few days after that Marino sees a
notice outside one of the courthouses,
an appeal for witnesses. I'm all for
making a statement. Marino says it'll get
us killed. Bucek had the deciding vote and
he decided to do the right thing. We go
and speak to the officers running the A.M.G.
make statements. Days go by. Nothing
happens.

Marino takes us to the courthouse, sits
there while we make statements and
translates them into Italian. Nothing
happens. The police issue a warrant for
Helms and nothing happens. Months go by and
nothing happens. I'm still seeing Helms
around town. It was like that arrest warrant
didn't mean nothing. We figured he had pull.
We figured something had got lost in the
bureaucracy. It was like that over there.

Chaos. That's what we were fighting.
Not fascism, not Italians, not the Mafia.
Chaos.

IY: What happened to Helms?

GC: Nothing, that's what I'm telling
you. The A.M.G. moved him north and I never
saw him again. Till years later I'm back
in New York.

IY: Tell me about that.

GC: What happened after the war? I came
back halfway through '46. I thought that was
it. Back to the grind. Back to the race
hate. I went back to playing horn, shooting
some horse. I had some Midtown customers.
Entertainment industry types. It was at one
of their parties I saw him. Lieutenant Paul
Helms. 'Cept now he's called Congressman
Paul Helms and he's getting slaps on the
back from everyone for being such a swell
guy and I'm thinking maybe I'm the only
person in the world knows there's an arrest
warrant for multiple homicide with his name
on it back in Italy. And here I am, living
like a bum, slinging dope to my friends to
get by.

I figured I'd put the squeeze on. 'Cept I
know someone like me ain't got no pull. I'm
gonna need some white boys to help. So I go
and look up Bucek and Marino. And what do I
see when I meet them? They're just as down-
and-out and broke as me. Bucek's back living
with his folks, and Marino's getting screwed
over by the Mob like every other sucker
working on the docks. I go and tell them

what I've seen and how we can put a quick
squeeze on Helms and we figure out on doing
it together. Bucek and Marino went to talk
to him. He said he'd get the money together
and pay it over, but it'd take him some time
to do it, you know. We believed him. Shit.

[PAUSE]

IY: Gene?

GC: What?

IY: What happened next?

[PAUSE]

GC: A few days go past. A couple of
weeks, I dunno. I don't hear nothing. I get
to thinking maybe Bucek and Marino collected
the money and decided to cut me out of the
deal. I start to get mad. But then Bucek's
knocking on my door, going crazy. Says
Marino's been murdered down at the docks and
earlier that day some men were hanging about
outside his house. He pegs them for
mobsters, they spot him, they chase him, but
he gets away. He reckons they're going to be
coming back. I say it's cool and he can stay
with me till things calm down or we can
figure out what the hell to do. He stays with
me, I pay the hotel manager to keep his
mouth shut. Looked weird, you know - a white
boy staying there, so he had to stay in the
room most of the time and he was going stir-
crazy. Talking about the demon from Naples
was after him.

IY: Bucek knew the man you'd seen in the
village that day was Faron?

GC: I guess. The men who were waiting

outside Bucek's house, the ones he'd run
away from, one of them was big, like Faron.
Bucek said he thought he was the one from
the village. I didn't believe him. Not at
first. But he was saying how he'd asked
around. Heard all these stories about Faron
being some wild-man killer. Bucek was
tearing himself up about it. He was going so
crazy I had to give him some dope to keep
him quiet. He stays with me for a month
while I put the feelers out. I know people.
I find out Helms is backed by Genovese and a
lot of this shit Bucek was saying about
Faron was true. And that's when I put it all
together — Genovese and Faron and Helms,
maybe they all met somewhere in Italy during
the war. And after we'd put the squeeze on
Helms, Helms had gone to Genovese to get him
out of the hole and now we got a whole Mafia
family after us. So we figure we need to get
the hell out of town. We start to put a plan
together then one night the door crashes in.
They kick in the door and they're just
standing right there, knives in their hands,
both of 'em.

    IY: Who?

    GC: Faron and some other Genovese
button.

    IY: How'd you know it was Faron? You
recognize him from the village?

    GC: Nah. I didn't know it was him. I
don't know if it was the same man from the
village, but he was big like Faron's
supposed to be, so I figured it must be him.

IY: OK, go on.

GC: Bucek was closest to the door so he gets it first. I just dived for the window and, you know, got the hell out of there. I keep on running and the other one tries to chase me down.

IY: The intruder who wasn't Faron?

GC: Yeah. He runs after me on the street. But I lose him. I go and stay the night with a friend of mine.

IY: O'Connell?

[PAUSE]

GC: Yeah, you know about that? Then I go see a friend of mine owns a bar downtown. I hide out in a cat-flat around the corner. Then my friend from the bar, he comes and sees me. Says there's this other gangster who hates Genovese who'll help me, and that's how I meet Benny Siegel. He comes by the cat-flat, and he's a real smooth-talker, expensive suit, jewelry. Charm, you know. He gives me some dope right there. Money, too.

IY: When was this?

GC: When?

IY: Can you put a date on it? Your first meeting with Siegel.

[INAUDIBLE]

GC: Siegel says he'll keep me safe and find me a place to hide out and when he's back in town, we'll put the squeeze on properly. He even says he knows a dry-out clinic he can take me to. The best one money can buy. Don't mind colored folks. I buy it.

Like I said, smooth-talker. He takes me up to an apartment in Italian Harlem, keeps me there a few days while he fixes everything up. Then he puts me in a cab to the clinic. Says he'll be back. Says he has to go to LA for a week or two, but he'll be back.

IY: This was when you checked into the clinic?

GC: Yeah. You want a date on that, too? I dunno. Check with them.

IY: OK.

GC: I nearly go out of my goddamn mind. I'm strung out on Dolophine and I don't know where I am. It's weeks before I can focus on anything. Then I hear on the radio about police still investigating Benjamin Siegel's death, and that's when I find out Siegel's been dead for weeks. I ask the doctors about who's paying for my treatment, 'cos I'm worried I'll get landed with a bill and they tell me he paid for a full course upfront, that's six months, and I start to thinking how, come December, I'm gonna get thrown out of here. Back on the street. And just as I'm planning my next move, you turn up.

IY: OK.

GC: I swear I didn't know nothing about Talbot getting arrested. I didn't know the hotel owner died. I didn't mean for any of this to happen.

[INAUDIBLE]

DC: Your stupid plan got how many people killed.

IY: Lieutenant, please—

GC: Fuck you.

DC: Watch your language. [SPEECH
UNCLEAR]

GC: You ever been in a war, Lieutenant?
[INAUDIBLE]

GC: I went over there to fight fascism,
'cept there weren't no good versus evil when
I got there. Our own troops were getting
drunk and shooting at each other. Our top
brass was more interested in turning a
profit. People getting killed and raped.
Ain't no right or wrong no more. Just
madness. Following us around like a shadow.

I came back from that war and I was flat
broke and there weren't no jobs, no nothing.
I got blue-slipped so none of that GI Bill
shit was open for me. Everything they
promised us would change after the war —
race hate, jobs, ghettos. It's all still
there. They lied to us. You got a hundred
thousand colored men come back from that
war, fought for a country that betrayed 'em.
What's going to happen? All those highly
trained veterans that got thrown on the
shit-heap once they'd done defending
America?

DC: You don't like society, you try and
improve it. Instead of coming up with some
hare-brained scheme—

IY: Lieutenant —

GC: What's society done for us? All that
civilization shit? Where's it got us?
Atomic bombs and death-camps. If that's

what civilization's got to offer, I'm gonna
try something different.

   [INAUDIBLE]

   IY: OK, let's all take ten to calm down.
Gene, you want me to get you a drink?

   [PAUSE]

63

Costello flipped another set of cards from the pack. Nothing. He flipped again. He added a six of hearts to one of the lines on his desktop. Just a couple more good turns and he'd have completed the game. He flipped again. A five of diamonds. He placed it down, shifted lines about, change cascaded through the structure, sets broke and merged, the world rearranged itself, he took a moment to soak it in.

There was a knock at the door and Bobbie popped her head in. 'She's here,' she said.

'Show her in.'

Bobbie disappeared behind the door.

Costello scooped up the cards, turned to look out of the window while he waited. Snow was lying thick on the park, weighing down its trees and bushes. The whiteness covering the grass had been scratched and gouged by the movement of people and things, revealing the green underneath in haphazard streaks, a reminder that spring was waiting, buried thinly under the dark season.

The door opened and a slight woman stepped in. Middle-aged, dark-haired, attractive.

Costello rose. 'Mrs Young,' he said. 'Happy Thanksgiving.'

'And to you, too.'

'Please, take a seat.'

She nodded, crossed the room, and sat at the desk opposite

him. She met his eye, and he got the feeling he was ever so subtly being appraised.

'Thank you for coming during the holiday,' he said. 'I hope I didn't disturb any of your plans?'

'No,' she replied. 'I'm meeting some friends, but not till later.'

A lilting accent – Louisiana, maybe – to go along with a prim and proper manner. Costello thought about Dr Hoffman, about consorting with better types.

'Where's that accent from?' he said. 'If you don't mind me asking.'

'New Orleans.'

'I know it well.'

'Until last year you controlled all the city's slot machines.'

She didn't say it in the sneering way a cop might, and she didn't say it with a smirk, the way a gangster might, to show you how clued up he was. She said it innocently, as if she were simply making a statement. Costello wondered what she hoped to gain by saying it like that. It threw him off his stride. Maybe that was the point.

'I couldn't possibly comment,' he replied. 'Would you like some food or drink?'

'I'm fine, but thanks for the offer.'

He nodded, looked her over again. Prim and proper.

'So, how's your time in New York been?' he asked.

'I did what I came here to do.'

'Get the boy out of Rikers? That's a good thing you did.'

'Thank you.'

'I think one of my friends helped you out.'

'Gabriel?' she said. 'Yes, he did.'

'Such a shame what happened,' he said.

He'd heard from his friends in the Homicide Bureau that this woman had been there when Gabriel had died. He needed to ask her if Gabriel was definitely dead. He needed an eyewitness to placate Anastasia, who'd been in a more murderous mood than usual since he'd found out Gabriel had been stiffing him on the racetrack profits.

'But, Albert, now you get to keep the whole racetrack for yourself,' Costello had told him. But the man seemed unable to absorb the logic. Instead, he ranted about Gabriel having faked his own death. Hardly likely. If Gabriel was intending to fake his death he wouldn't have done it on the ice of the Hudson, just a few hours after he'd dropped off two million dollars at Costello's apartment in exchange for protection for his niece.

The whole episode puzzled Costello. The return of the money, but, even more, Gabriel's embezzlement from the race-track. Costello had always thought of Gabriel as scrupulously honest. A man with a code of honor. It was out of character for him to have ripped off Anastasia, and suspiciously sloppy for him to have done it in a way an auditor could spot. Did Gabriel want out of the Mob as much as Costello did?

'You were there when he died?' Costello asked.

She frowned at him, a delicate rumpling of the skin between her eyebrows. The question had surprised her. She must have assumed she'd been asked here for another reason. Costello wondered what.

'I was there,' she said. 'During the storm.'

'Would you tell me what happened?' he asked. 'Gabriel was one of my closest friends.'

She tried to suppress it, but for an instant Costello saw under-standing on her face. She'd realized why she'd been asked there, because Costello wanted to know for sure that Gabriel was dead.

She told him how she and Gabriel had ended up on the river, how there was a stand-off with Faron, how the ice had broken beneath Gabriel and Sarah.

He stared into her eyes, evaluating, looking to see if she was telling the truth. Deep brown eyes to go with the black hair and dark complexion. He wondered if she had some Negro in her. She was from New Orleans after all.

'There was a gust of wind,' she said. 'The ice they were on overturned.'

Costello nodded solemnly. In the days since the blizzard, bodies had been popping up in rivers and docks every few days, some miles down the coast. But none of them had yet been identified as Gabriel's or Sarah's.

'And Faron?' he asked.

She shook her head. 'I don't know. I lost track of him.'

He noticed her manner had changed. She'd become subdued. Was her failure to catch Faron causing her grief?

'A bad character,' Costello said.

'Quite.'

'You're heading back to Chicago now that your work is done?' Costello asked.

She nodded.

'I know many fine people in your city,' Costello said.

'I know them, too.'

Again she said it flatly, without emotion, like she wasn't playing the game at all. She would have made an excellent mobster if she hadn't been a woman. He realized again she'd caused his mind to wander.

'If you would ever like any introductions,' he said, 'please let me know.'

He passed her a business card. She took it and smiled. She slipped it into her purse, and wished him good day. He watched her slender figure cross the room and leave, and when she was gone he stared at the door she'd left through.

When Anastasia came later that day, he'd tell him the woman had confirmed Gabriel was dead. 'A detective,' Costello would say. 'An out-of-towner with no reason to lie.' He'd push again the angle about Anastasia being in full control of the racetrack and hope this time it might calm him down.

Then he wondered why he was still staring at the door.

He checked his watch. He had another fifty minutes before his meeting with Dr Hoffman. He was already dreading it. He lit a cigarette and as he inhaled, he felt something in his throat, and wondered if a new cold wasn't coming on. He turned and stared out of the window at the park and the skyscrapers on its far side. Faron was out there somewhere.

When Costello had spoken to Genovese, Genovese had said he was cutting the man loose. Costello wasn't sure if he believed him, but tipping him off about the airport had bought them more time. Costello had got the movie producers to vote the way he wanted them to. But Genovese had got his man free from the blackmailers and onto HUAC. Costello called it a draw. War had been averted. The golden days would continue. For a little longer, at least.

There was a knock on the door.

'Yeah?' he said.

He turned to see Adonis stepping into the room.

'These just got couriered in from Vegas.'

He had an oversized envelope in his hand. He passed it over to Costello, who took a few sheets of paper out of the envelope, saw they were the latest accounts from the Flamingo. He leaned back in his seat. He ran his eye over them, absorbing the numbers. He flicked to the profit-and-loss statement. He did some sums, he read between the lines.

He looked up and saw Adonis had sat where the private detective had been earlier.

'Well?' Adonis asked.

'The Flamingo.'

'Everything all right?'

'Sure,' said Costello. 'It turned a profit last month. Three hundred grand. They're projecting more for this month.'

'No shit,' said Adonis, surprised. He took the papers off Costello, started going through them. 'Who'd have thought?' he muttered. 'A casino in Vegas.'

Costello paused, thought about mad Benny Siegel, the missing two million. He still didn't know which family Benny had conspired with to steal it, but at least he'd gotten it back, and now the Flamingo was turning a profit.

'Who'd have thought,' Costello repeated with a smile.

Adonis flicked a look at him, then got back to the papers.

Costello contemplated the new information, envisioned how it would cascade through the status quo, alter it, how the changes would fold into the future.

Maybe the golden days would last a lot longer.

He picked up the deck. He shuffled it, ordering the cards into chaos, into the unknowable void with which he'd do battle. He took a drag on his English Oval, felt a tickle in his throat. He was definitely coming down with a cold.

64

Friday 28th, 9.55 a.m.

Check-out was at eleven, but Louis was arriving to pick her up at ten – had insisted on giving her a ride – so she'd gotten ready early and caught the elevator down to the reception. She paid the bill. The concierge passed over her receipt.

'Oh, I almost forgot,' he said, 'this arrived for you.'

He handed her over a letter. It was surprisingly stiff. A postcard inside the envelope. A goodbye card from Carrasco maybe. She went over to the windows that looked out onto 7th Avenue and waited for Louis.

In the days following the blizzard she and Carrasco had worked closely together. Arranging the interview, helping with the statement, going down to the court to see the case against Tom thrown out, visiting Michael to give him updates. Carrasco had been there when they'd had their Thanksgiving meal around Michael's bedside, eating from paper plates on their laps, food Annette had prepared at the apartment and brought to the hospital in a hamper.

Annette had insisted Ida stay in New York at least until Thanksgiving. If she'd travelled back to Chicago, she would have just spent the day in her apartment, alone, so she didn't need much persuading. Tom was there, his face still bruised and swollen but looking a whole lot better in himself, and that barrier between him and Michael she'd noticed in the visiting room at Rikers seemed to have dissolved, and that was as heart-warming for her to see as anything.

In her statements to the police Ida had made no mention of the Congressman or of Genovese. Neither had Cleveland. They kept it all tied to the murders at the hotel. To Faron alone. Hopefully, that had gotten back to Genovese, and Cleveland might live to see the new year. He'd given his evidence and had disappeared and she would always wonder where they'd taken him.

She'd kept an eye on the papers, and Helms's and Genovese's names had appeared nowhere in connection with the murders. All she'd seen was that Helms had made it onto the House Un-American Activities Committee, and she wondered if that wasn't related to Genovese and Costello somehow. When she'd received the call from Costello asking to meet she'd assumed he wanted to put pressure on her to assist in the cover-up, but instead he just wanted to confirm that Gabriel had died. She had wanted to ask him about Faron, but it seemed Costello knew as little about his whereabouts as she did.

Perhaps she'd never find out what happened to him. The most savage killer she'd ever come across and she'd let him slip away. She thought back to the ice, to the stand-off, to Faron's willingness to kill his own daughter. In the days since, she'd conjured up the various fates that could have befallen Faron. She'd imagined him crawling to some corner and dying of the cold, of blood loss. She'd imagined him making it to some apartment and fixing himself up, boarding a train out of New York. She'd imagined him living decades, murdering and raping ceaselessly till he, too, died, and some new form arose from the void to take his place. She imagined him immortal, a constant presence, the god of poverty, of injustice, always with us. She killed her thoughts, knowing the darkness to which they led.

A car horn blared and she peered through the windows to see Louis' car double-parked outside. She nodded at the concierge, slipped the envelope into her pocket and exited.

She threw her suitcase onto the backseat, next to Louis' attaché case, and got into the front. Louis pulled off into traffic.

'Thanks for the ride,' she said.

'No problem.'

She smiled, lit a cigarette, opened the window a crack and a blast of cold air arrowed in. They headed downtown, talked and joked and Ida saw Louis had that energy back, the liveliness that had been absent when she'd seen him last. She'd followed the response in the press to Louis' show. The ecstatic notices and reviews. In a single concert he'd reminded everyone why he was one of the greatest virtuosos in the business, had maybe got his career back on track.

'Any more news on the band?' she asked.

'Oh, sure,' he said. 'A tour in California, to launch it.'

'That's great,' she said, smiling.

'There're offers on the table from all over the country,' he said. 'But we're going to start out west, so we can do some TV shows, too. We've come up with a name for the band – *Louis Armstrong and The All Stars*. You like it?'

'Sure,' she said. 'The world needs stars.'

He grinned at her.

'So I might be seeing you in LA when I'm over there?' he asked, raising his eyebrows.

Ida stared at him blankly, then realized he was talking about her job offer.

'You might,' she said. 'But I'm not taking the job.'

Louis looked at her and frowned.

She'd come to New York partly to see if she could make it in a strange, new city. But that wasn't what the trip had shown her, the important lesson she'd learned was that her office in Chicago could take care of itself. So she'd fly to LA, but not to work for the government.

'I'm gonna let the office in Chicago run itself,' she said. 'And move on out to LA and start a second office. The Ida Young Detective Agency's moving west.'

She grinned at Louis and he burst out laughing.

'I knew you were going to laugh,' she said. 'What's so funny?'

But he wouldn't say; he just shook his head. She stared out of the window and watched the city slip past. Soon she'd be back in Chicago. She'd go home and make the arrangements and pack up the apartment, and as she did so, she'd finally read the letter left there for her by Nathan's friend from the army, detailing how he'd died. And when she'd read it, she'd put everything in storage and move on out to LA, because even though she wouldn't really stop fearing the future, she could at least sculpt her part in it.

They turned right at 112th Street, roared down Central Park West, through Columbus Circle, all the way to 42nd. Louis pulled up in the taxi rank outside Grand Central, causing a chorus of horns to rise up from the cabs.

'You better hurry,' said Louis. 'Before they lynch us.'

She laughed. They hugged. She grabbed her suitcase and got out, and watched Louis' car as it disappeared into the haze of Manhattan traffic and smog. Then she walked into Grand Central, down one of its great marble staircases. As she crossed the concourse she noticed once more how the movement of people around her mirrored that of the constellations painted on the ceiling above, of the gods gliding through the blue universe as one. This time it reassured her somehow, the thought of all that synchronized progress.

She reached the departure boards, scanned them for her train, found the platform from which it was leaving, then checked she had her ticket. She put her suitcase down, dipped her hand into her coat pocket and felt something strange. She took it out. Alongside the ticket was the envelope the concierge had given her earlier. She frowned. She ripped it open.

It wasn't a goodbye card from Carrasco, but a postcard, with a hand-drawn sketch of a Mexican skeleton on it, smoking a cigar, playing guitar, wearing a sombrero hat, a garland of flowers around its neck. Ida turned the postcard over, and saw the writing scrawled on the back — *To Ida Young, Enemy to those who make her one. Friend to those who have no friends.*

She checked the postmark on the envelope.

Mexico.

She grinned. A glow spread through her, a mix of relief and joyful realization. She shook her head, and still grinning, slipped the postcard back into her pocket.

Then she headed for the platform where her train was waiting, and as she weaved her way through the gray crowds, she was warmed by the thought of California, the sparkling Pacific, the hopeful gleam of new horizons.

AFTERWORD

As with my previous novels, I've tried to make this book as factually accurate as possible, and failed. Mainly this failure consists of moving the dates of certain events from different months in 1947 into November, when the book is set. In a few other instances, I interpreted conflicting histories to suit the needs of the story, and at some points, I invented situations and scenes, but always within the realms of possibility, and always to fit the book's themes. Below are some notes on the recognized history and where I've deviated from it; anything not mentioned here was either too minor to include, or is an oversight on my part, for which I apologize.

In many ways 1947 can be seen as the start of the post-war era, as it was in this year that much of what would come to define the second half of the twentieth century came into being. The CIA was set up, the Marshall Plan was drafted, the Cold War got under way, India gained its independence, and the newly formed United Nations first debated a plan to create Arab and Jewish states in Palestine. It was also the year in which Jackie Robinson broke the baseball colour line, and a mysterious flying object crashed to earth in Roswell, New Mexico.

In the cultural sphere, too, 1947 was a year of watersheds and landmarks; W. H. Auden wrote *The Age of Anxiety*, which gave the era a name; film noir reached its zenith; Jackson Pollock (a Louis Armstrong fan) started his first drip painting in January, and elsewhere in New York other abstract expressionists were helping make the city the centre of Western contemporary art.

That so much influential work happened in such a short space of time in one city is understandable given, first, the influx of refugees to New York over the preceding decade, and second, the state of the world's other great cities after the war, and yet, it is still remarkable. While Pollock, de Kooning, Rothko and Kline were in the city helping to found the first truly American art movement, Dizzie Gillespie and Charlie Parker were codifying bebop on 52nd Street, Elia Kazan was founding the Actors Studio in Hell's Kitchen, Allen Ginsberg, William Burroughs, et al. were forming the Beat Generation in dives uptown, the seed of the post-war counter-culture was germinating as dropouts and misfits gathered in Greenwich Village, and a half-forgotten jazz musician with his career on the wane played a concert that would turn his fortunes around.

This is the first of the events whose date I moved – Louis Armstrong's famed concert at Town Hall happened on 17 May, some five and a half months before the start of the book. The sources are somewhat at odds about exactly how big of a turning point the actual concert was, though they all agree that the switch from a big band to the much smaller ensemble that became known as *Louis Armstrong and The All Stars* was a sea change for Armstrong's career. In this book I've perhaps overstated the importance of the concert, but it's a milestone nonetheless, and the switch the concert ushered in helped pave the way for Armstrong to become the pop-culture icon he is remembered as today.

Also moved from earlier in the year was Al Capone's death – Armstrong's old boss died in January. Another Mob death, that of Benjamin Siegel, is slightly off too. He was gunned down in June, but in the timeline of the book this happens a couple of months later in August. The Flamingo first turned a profit in May (not October, as in the book's timeline). This was *before* Siegel was killed, making the reasons for his murder a little less straightforward – why kill him just when his casino was finally starting to take off? His murderers were never caught.

Despite Siegel's death and the floundering start the Mob had in Las Vegas, the late forties and early fifties were the golden age of the American mafia, which at the time was headquartered in New York, its heyday intersecting with the city's cultural flowering. The Mob's level of influence at the time is best summed up in this quote from the book *American Mafia* by the historian Thomas A. Reppetto;

> In the 1940s Costello would name the mayor of New York, Moretti would make the career of America's most popular entertainer, Lansky would come to control a small nation, Siegel would found modern Las Vegas, and Lansky and Dalitz would help make it a fabulous success.

Much of this rise was down to Frank Costello. An excellent manager, negotiator and organizer, he led the Mob to its zenith, all while not actually wanting the job, and without feeling the need to employ bodyguards, cars or guns. Another large factor in this rise was the FBI, and its director, J. Edgar Hoover, who had gone on record as saying he didn't believe there was such a thing as nationwide organized crime. Exactly why he held this view is a matter of debate. The end result, however, was that the one agency with the scope and resources to tackle the Mob turned its attention to fighting communism instead, and the Mob was allowed to flourish. In a modern parallel, after decades in a downward spiral, the Mob has experienced something of a resurgence since the 9/11 attacks of 2001, mainly due to the FBI turning its resources away from organized crime once more, this time to focus on terrorism.

Although Costello had wide-ranging influence, there is no evidence he directly interfered with the outcome of the meeting of movie producers in the Waldorf-Astoria; however, this behaviour is entirely in character – Costello really did employ a telephony expert called Cheesebox to bug people, and he had a long history of influencing votes (most notably, he influenced the election of Roosevelt as the nominee for President at the Democratic National Convention in 1932). Costello had also stated he supported the fight against communism and the work of Senator McCarthy (the two men had met), and given his interests in the Mob-infiltrated unions in California, this is the most likely stance for him to have taken.

Likewise, the idea that Genovese tried to influence the meeting in the other direction is also my own invention, but again, it fits in with the years-long campaign Genovese waged to try and wrestle back control of the Mob from his former underling. Genovese did end up taking control of the Mob, and just as Costello and Luciano feared, his leadership saw the Mob lurch from disaster to disaster, and its power wane. The details of Genovese's time in Italy under, first, Mussolini, and then the Allies, are all true, as are the details of his extradition and trial.

Costello really did visit a psychiatrist called Dr Hoffman, decades before Tony Soprano sought therapy, and, rather bizarrely, Dr Hoffman revealed both the identity of his famous client and the details of his psychological condition to the press. Whether it was through Dr Hoffman's advice or not, Costello spent time socializing with New York's artistic avant-garde.

The information about Ronald Reagan offering himself up as an informant to the FBI, and offering to turn over evidence about his friends, is based on FBI case files. (Case files which only became public after the *San Francisco Chronicle* fought a seventeen-year legal battle for their release.) Reagan's links to the Mob-backed MCA is a matter of public record. When Robert Kennedy convened a Federal Grand Jury to investigate allegations of corruption and anti-trust at MCA in 1962 (one of many official investigations into the company), Reagan gave testimony to the jury, and lied, thereby committing a federal crime.

Joe Glaser, the manager of Louis Armstrong and Billie Holiday, had extensive connections to MCA and the Mob, and he typifies how the criminal underworld and the entertainment industry (jazz, in particular) were intertwined during the period. Whether or not he colluded in Billie Holiday's imprisonment is a matter of debate.

The doctor whom Michael visits at the Harlem Hospital is based on the pioneering African-American surgeon Louis Tompkins Wright.

The New York City blizzard of 1947 actually happened on Christmas Day, a few weeks after it does in the book.

Lastly, a young Stanley Kubrick did go backstage at the Copa to do a photoshoot for *Look* magazine, though this was a year later, in 1948. The photographs he took are available to view online at the website of the Museum of the City of New York. A link is also available via my own website: www.raycelestin.com, as are galleries of other photos from the period, maps, a bibliography, and more information on the quartet of books of which this forms the third part.

*

The fourth, and final, part will be set in Los Angeles in 1967 and will feature characters from the previous three books. The details are a little hazy at present, as I've not started writing it yet. Updates will be available on the website.

RAY CELESTIN
London, August 2018

Acknowledgements

Huge thanks to Mariam Pourshoushtari, Shemuel Bulgin, Julia Pye, Chris Branson, Sam Armour, Jane Finigan, Juliet Mahony, Susannah Godman, Josie Humber, Maria Rejt, Natalie Young. Everyone at L&R, Mantle and Macmillan. Special thanks to Ben Maguire and Nana Wilson, who offered no help whatsoever. Extra special thanks to Cedric Sekweyama, who is solely responsible for the existence of my writing career.